T0161914

Without a glimmer of remorse...

by
Pino Cacucci

Translated by
Paul Sharkey

Illustrations by
Flavio Costantini

First published in Great Britain in 2006
by Read and Noir Books
an imprint of ChristieBooks, PO Box 35
Hastings, East Sussex, TN34 2UX

Distributed in the UK by Central Books Ltd
99 Wallis Road, London E9 5LN
orders@centralbooks.com

ISBN 1-873976-28-3

British Library Cataloguing in Publication Data.
A catalogue record for this book is available from the British Library

CHOISY-LE-ROI, OUTSKIRTS OF PARIS, SUNDAY 28 APRIL 1912

The cart creaked and groaned as, with exasperating sluggishness, it crossed the sixty metres of waste ground. Across the road, among the trees, hundreds of rifles were trained on the house. Since that last gunshot, the scene had been set in the stone of utter silence; the men lying on the platform or taking cover behind the tree trunks monitored the retreat of the cart, so close to the prey that it blocked their line of sight. At which point the horse reared, wearying of hauling its load of hay backwards: it pawed the dirt and let out a whinny that rang through the stillness, leading fingers to tighten on triggers. From behind the seat, the officer gestured to an underling who lowered the whip then, after a few light flicks on its flanks, managed to get the animal to resume the unusual manoeuvre, and the cart covered the last few metres. The walls of the old house bore the scars of gunfire and there wasn't a single pane of glass left intact in the window-frames. The officer leaned over the arch of the wheel and glanced towards the wooden staircase. Then he made up his mind: he snatched up the bag full of dynamite, lay down in the cover of the cart and crawled over to the wall. Once there, he was more afraid of a resumption of the attack than of any reaction from inside the house. He reached the charge that had been laid during the earlier attempt, noted that the fuse had burned to within just centimetres of the detonator, and cursed through clenched teeth. He readied a second charge and signalled to his assistant who promptly handed him the Bickford cable. The officer wiped the sweat from his brow with the back of his hand. The sun was high in the sky now and the bright spring morning promised to turn out hotter than anticipated. For a moment, his thoughts froze in the silence. How unreal! The swallows had vanished from the heavens, the dogs had ceased their barking and even the insect life seemed to have stopped in its tracks, waiting for this hell to finish. With unsteady hands he inserted the fuse into the detonator. Using his teeth, he re-closed the aluminium opening in order to forestall a second failure and slipped the little tube into the clustered sticks of dynamite. Then he began to feed out the Bickford cable with the utmost caution, taking care to leave the fuse as long as possible, and not tug on it. Taking cover again, he threw a glance at his assistant who urged the horse forward with small, cramped steps. The trip back seemed even longer because of the sixty metres of fuse to be fed out before they could take cover.

When the cart reached the middle of the road, a touch too far for a gunshot from the house to be able to hit him, the officer knelt, took a deep breath and lit it. A chorus of voices rose from among the trees, suddenly breaking the tension, and relief that things had begun erupted into shouting, cries of encouragement and applause, the intensity of it growing as the little flame of liberation edged forwards and the snake of smoke and sparks rocketed towards the old house at the far end of the field. There followed a few interminable minutes that seemed to last an eternity, and, once the fuse burned out, silence descended again. A few moments passed, but even now disappointment was bringing a lump to the throats of the policemen, soldiers and thousands of rubber-neckers who had travelled out from Paris. But that was very short-lived.

The rumble ripped through the motionless countryside, shaking the suburban town to the very rooftops; the shock wave bent the branches of the trees and the ladies' white umbrellas, sending up a swirl of dead leaves, silk ribbons, sweat-dampened handkerchiefs and cotton gloves carelessly abandoned on the seats of horse-drawn cabs or the bonnets of automobiles. An immense grey cloud of dust, dirt, plaster and smoke rose, masking the cottage and twisting as far as the road, its dense eddies swamping the shrubby field. A slight breeze dispersed the cloud, turning it into a mist and the old house reappeared like some insolent, pale ghost. It had not been demolished. It had withstood the blast. And from the rifles positioned among the trees came a furious salvo adding kilos of useless lead to the blow that the dynamite had inflicted to the ghostly housefront.

The man seated on the tiles looked at the rubble surrounding him. A fragment of ceiling had cut his face. He stared at his two pistols with a curious expression, almost as if he was seeing them for the very first time. He shook his head and grinned. Slowly, he unclenched his fingers and the pistols knocked together, still dangling from his index finger. He carried on watching them rock to and fro, the muzzles pointed towards his face. At the far end of the snub-nosed black barrels, there sat the glistening points of two bullets ready to hurl themselves at his temples. Perhaps the time had come to give them their head and offer them a sure target. "The heart", he mused, hypnotised by the undulations of the burnished steel. "Better aim them at the heart". And finally stop the accursed heart which had for years been pumping blood frothed with feelings of pain, flooding his arteries with resentment of humiliations, the very same humiliations that so many others just bore uncomplainingly and which had triggered an insatiable thirst for vengeance in him.

He wondered by what obscure quirk of fate it was that some men are born different from the rest, different from those who bend their backs right up to their very last day in a mute resignation that renders their days monotonous and their nights non-existent. He wondered why it was the lot of some people that sundown brought them no greater ease, damned as they were to wait for the dawn that always arrived too soon, ready to prove that each day was going to be worse than the day before. "I'll aim one gun directly at the heart", he thought, "and the other towards the belly." Because his viscera were even more to blame with that inner fire of theirs that had been burning since childhood, fed by hunger and blows and the pointlessness of even the slightest effort to escape the brand of wretchedness. Not that the fire had been set by privations. He knew that. There was no point trying to side-step reality. Millions of human beings are born poor, but few are gnawed by the fires of a noxious sensibility that rattles and clouds the reason and turns into a murderous urge every time one feels slighted.

"And another two slugs for the eyes", he thought, "these eyes which are the bane of my existence, which have dwelt on every instance of suffering the way one would upon a strange spectacle." Eyes that had probed the vulgarity of unbearable faces that just oozed arrogance, the faces of supercilious winners persuaded of their own invulnerability. Eyes that had thought they might be entitled to make comparisons ad infinitum; for every obscene mug sighted, they had substituted a sad, emaciated alternative. Like Justin's, with that sickly pallor, which time had turned ghostly, a memory frozen in his fifteenth birthday snapshot...

His brother Justin. Even as he had walked behind the coffin

4

drawn by a skeletal nag, he couldn't manage to cry. His great eyes, wide open to the horrors of everyday life, had been dry since childhood, from the day when they had refused to release a single tear as he was tossing a fistful of soil on to Justin's poor coffin. He wondered what had been going through his brother's head when he had let himself fall into the river. A suicide at fifteen. His mind had been unable to come up with any reasonable response but his heart and his guts had brought in their verdict and, walking behind the black cart that bore Justin away, he had been assailed for the first time by the instinct for revenge. The first of many, countless times multiplied ad infinitum by every single instant of existence. Justin had taken his own life and somebody had to pay for that too. Reason had failed to come up with any explanation. What his eyes saw as they stared at that coffin and the gnawing in his guts were enough to justify his need to draw tears from other people, the ones who had always been used to laughter.

He closed his eyes tight. The darkness that he craved would not come. Eyes shut, he could still see what the morning light had managed to hold at bay. He recognised Platano with that scornful little smirk of his and that sham lightheartedness tainted with resentment; again he could hear the echoes of his eternally provocative voice and the sarcasm in his every word.

"Clear off, Platano. Leave me in peace now that everything is nearing its end. Leave me be. You have always stalked me, inflicting your insidious madness upon me and the hotchpotch of your lousy ideas; you've persecuted me through all those nights spent listening for noises from the road and made hopeless days interminable... You've won. You were spot on. You alone knew how to drag me too into the swamp of your lunacy. Killing you was a mercy. A mercy to you who got what you wanted; to see me destroyed at the hands of others. But I wish you were here to

share these hours which are as long as our two lives, yours and mine. You were never my friend but you were my only real accomplice. And now, between these walls, crumbling bit by bit, it would be good to see your face. And forget the way you looked when a bullet wiped the hatred from your eyes. Now at last I can accept the notion that that was no unfortunate freak, no cruel twist of fate; the gun went off because we both wanted it to. Begone, Platano. Begone. My final thought will not be of you. It's her I'm thinking about now. Judith, whom you banished from my life when I dreamt that we too might find some bright, quiet corner of this rotten dung heap that makes my head spin with its hubbub. You couldn't stand that. You couldn't accept my leaving you alone to stew in your own juices. And you managed to drag me along. And to get yourself killed on the road that carried me away from her.

She's the one for whom I will write my testament, Platano. I can let you go, saying that I missed you during the irreversible downward spiral of these last few months, that I missed your warped, irrational belligerence. Because you were no madman, Platano, I know that. You were only an inspired and irreplaceable bastard. Can you see how things are going to turn

Jules Bonnot

out? Rest easy. And clear off once and for all. Not a single word of what I mean to write can I spare for you. It's the only pleasure I have left, Platano, damn you..."

He reopened his eyes. And it was only then that he spotted the splinters of wood spinning through the room. More rifle shots. The wooden partitions soaked up the lead without any ricochet. In the corner where he sat, there was no way that they could get a direct shot at him. He picked up a sheet of paper, dusted it off, fumbled for a pencil that he found underneath a scrap of torn curtain and started to write: " I, Jules Bonnot..." He stopped. Holding the paper in both hands he tore off the strip bearing his name. They knew very well what his name was, so there was no need to make himself a laughing stock with a formal opening like that. He began writing again, oblivious of the rubble raining down on to his back.

"... I never asked much. I used to stroll with her through Lyons cemetery by moonlight, kidding myself that that was all we needed in life. That was the happiness I had searched for my whole life long, powerless even to imagine it. I had found it and I had discovered what it was. The happiness I had always been denied. I had a right to live out that happiness. But you denied it me. So much the worse for me, so much the worse for you, for all of you... Should I have regrets for what I did? Maybe. But I feel no remorse. Regrets yes, but not a glimmer of remorse..."

MONTBÉLIARD, 1891

He stopped to watch the river of molten metal falling in a torrent of blinding light. Stooped under the weight of the basket of filings, he gazed in fascination at this glimpse of hell; two naked bodies gleaming with sweat mirroring the fiery red of the river, faces resembling death heads because of those hollow eyes and teeth bared in exertion, and the deafening crescendo of noise, and the heat, the stifling air that filled the lungs but left the craving for oxygen unassuaged... Swivelling his hips, Jules hoisted the basket back on to his shoulder and walked briskly on, dodging obstacles, swerving and skirting the sharp corners of the stacks of steel plate. In one movement he tipped the basket into the sleigh and awarded himself the three second respite to which he reckoned he was entitled at the end of every trip. He was about to turn back when an elderly workman tapped him on the shoulder. Jules turned around to be greeted by the man's mocking grin.

"Hey, lad... You know, it's just as tiring when you rush."

Jules's mouth contorted arrogantly. At the age of fifteen, he was already convinced that advice from grown-ups would not improve life any. Not his at any rate, for he seemed to have been predestined to relive his father's life; his days at the foundry and his nights on a cot waiting for the siren to herald another day at the foundry. The workman ruffled his hair vigorously and added:

"You walk quickly but the basket still weighs the same. And you're killing yourself quicker. That's a fact."

Then he spotted a bruise on the boy's face near the temple. He was about to trace it with his thumb but Jules stepped backwards and wrenched his face aside. The workman looked at him gravely.

"You've had a fall here, or..."

Jules sighed and lowered his eyes. The man took the hint and scratched the long whiskers on his sweat and smoke-begrimed cheeks.

"I get the feeling you've made your father angry again, Jules, what?"

The boy replied between clenched teeth:

"My father doesn't need any help from me to fly off the handle. He has only too many reasons to do so."

"Of course", the workman sighed, "but you're the one he takes it out on, right?"

"I'm an easy target. Cowards always take it out on whoever is closest to hand."

The man ran a finger lightly down his chest in a fond reproach.

"Come on, Jules... I don't like to hear you talk like that. Especially not about your father. He's a sound man. I know him well. But this damned life... In the end, Jules, in time you'll come to understand for yourself what it means to make sacrifices to feed one's children..."

Jules smiled grimly as he hoisted the empty basket on to his shoulder. At which point a blow to the back of the head sent him sprawling for two metres, his face ending up in the iron filings and cinders covering the floor. He jumped to his feet to see the foreman, hands on hips, staring at him and waiting for him to react. Jules felt the blood course through the veins at his temples as a red mist fell over his eyes. He fumbled angrily through the dust, found an iron bar, grabbed hold of it and raised it. The workman, dumbfounded at the sight of the foreman looming behind the stacked sheet metal, rushed at Jules and barred his path.

"No, lad, none of this nonsense... you'll come off worst."

"Leave him be", snapped the foreman. "Let's see if he's any good... Come on, you wee bastard, up you get. I'm going to sort you out..."

Again Jules made to rush forwards but the muscular arms of the workman clamped over him; he might as well have been in a vice.

"Calm down", he mumbled into Jules's ear. "Don't you understand that's just what he wants? Not now, you idiot, not now!"

For a moment Jules remained coiled and primed, like a spring ready to snap. Then he slowly let himself go limp and finally dropped the club back into the dust. The foreman wore a slightly disappointed smirk, shook his head and said:

"I know how to handle your sort, Bonnot. Next time I catch you wasting your time on idle chatter, you won't get away with just a slap. Bank on it."

"It was my fault", the workman piped up, standing in front of the boy. "I asked him to give me a hand on account of this lever jamming all the time and he only paused to help me out. He wasn't chattering..."

"That will do, Garmont", the foreman cut him off. "You'll be getting a mention in my weekly report too. Try to play it straight over the coming days if you want to convince me that you're still of any use in this foundry. Got that?"

Garmont gulped down some sooty saliva together with he words that were on the tip of his tongue, words that would have cost him his job, had he voiced them. Jules picked up his basket and, head down, made for the heap of iron filings. Twelve hours per day he plunged that basket into the heap of scrap metal which, come sunset, had been reduced to quite a small stack only to grow to ceiling height against by daybreak the next day. It was pointless to hope for an end of it. For countless generations of Bonnots, hope had been a meaningless word. "Poverty", Jules thought, his back still bent, "is a red brand mark that one carries for life." At fifteen, he wasn't quite clear yet how it might be removed, but he sensed that there had to be some way. Later, he was to determine that the mark could only be banished by burning it out with another firebrand.

On pay day, Jules queued up outside the window to collect his apprentice's wage. If he could stick the foundry for another two years, three at the most, he would be earning as much as his father was bringing home. With two wages coming in, they might even be able to wipe out their endless debt at the general store in the workers' district. The queue were moving slowly and he had all the time in the world to wonder what the point was of hanging on for another few years if his only prospect was scooping up that mountain of iron filings for the rest of his life.

The guy at the window stepped back and looked him up and down, tilting his head to one side.

"Jules Bonnot, eh? You've wasted your time, for there's nothing down on the register under your name."

He looked the clerk straight in the eye to see if he was joking but the latter made to address the worker standing next in line as if the discussion was over and done with. Jules tried to run his eye over the register.

"Are you deaf, lad?" the fellow added aggressively. "I said there was nothing for you, so take yourself off. You're preventing everybody else from getting paid."

"But how... I haven't missed a single day..."

Jules was still speaking when a hand grabbed him by the collar, trailing his backwards. It was one of the foundry watchmen and he was pushing him towards the stairs and saying:

"The management wants to see you. Behave yourself and

you'll get there in one piece. The choice is yours."

Jules struggled free, but a second guard brought a club down on him and now he had no choice but to climb the stairs, urged on by their kicks.

The manager was behind his mahogany desk, poring over some piece of paper. On hearing him enter, he lifted his head and looked at him through expressionless eyes before turning to the two gendarmes waiting in one corner of the room:

"Ah here he is. Do your duty."

The policemen came over; one of them placed a hand on Jules's neck to hold him still while the other one pulled his hands behind him. Jules leant forward in an attempt to reach the desk, reaching instinctively for the papers that might well be at the root of this nightmare. But the second officer twisted his wrist, forcing him to step back. The manager adjusted his spectacles and absent-mindedly perused the papers in front of him.

"Jules Bonnot... Insubordination, disrespecting his superiors... attempting to incite the section's apprentices to revolt...."

The manager looked up, his icy little eyes boring intro Jules's face.

"Up to now, you've been excused for all that. But your lack of gratitude towards the hand that feeds you has gone too far. And now we've just found out that you're a thief as well."

His head spinning, Jules searched in vain for words, managing only to shake his head in disagreement, without uttering a sound. The manager got to his feet and ambled over to the window. The workers were queuing down below and he spoke again in a loud voice for all to hear:

"You stole from the copper shavings in order to sell it off to some fellow good-for-nothing. You're a disgrace to the firm, Jules Bonnot. And it's your colleagues that you've been stealing from. Because stealing from the firm means putting everybody's job in jeopardy and the more thieves there are in a factory the greater the risk of bankruptcy and the danger of so many heads of households being turned out on to the streets, all because of a few delinquents!"

The manager's sermon echoed through the shed where the workers had suddenly fallen silent. Jules opened his mouth to proclaim his innocence but at that very moment he spotted the foreman leaning against the handrail on the stairs: he had stepped outside just before Jules arrived but had not wanted to miss out on the show. Jules closed his mouth again. "I'm wasting my time trying to defend myself."

The manager turned to the gendarmes and one gesture brought the incident to its conclusion. Jules's wrist was twisted again and he was shoved outside. He kept his head bowed as he passed the queue of workers. Some of them reckoned that he couldn't look at them because of his guilt. At that precise moment, he wasn't thinking anything at all.

At the gendarmerie barracks, he took a few slaps, a sergeant pulled his hair until a tuft of it came away in his hand, but by the time he was taken before the officer in charge of the relief the handcuffs had been removed and they had not taken his laces and belt off him. The officer gazed at him closely for some seconds. He was a man in his fifties, solidly built, grey, blank eyes glinting from a broad face. He wore his hair short and had fair moustaches of which he must have been proud, judging by the way he was forever stroking them between thumb and forefinger. Jules stared back at the policeman who seemed convinced that he was dealing with a hard case.

"You don't seem to feel any repentance about what you did."

"I did nothing to be repentant about", Jules replied quietly.

But this time he averted his gaze, without quite knowing why. The policeman bared his teeth in a chilling grin. He stood up, walked around the table as if to stroll around the room and, once behind the boy, gave him a clip on the ear. Jules fell to the floor, holding both hands up to his temples. He had a hard time regaining his balance and once he was back on his feet, the policeman informed him in neutral tones:

"Your manager is too kind-hearted. He declined to bring a complaint. But you and I will meet again. And next time, Bonnot junior, we shall have a more searching little conversation..."

By the time his father arrived home, he knew the whole story. He had stopped off for a glass of wine at the tavern and a few foundry workers had briefed him on the whole story. For an hour he said nothing, but Jules realized immediately that he knew. He ate his potato soup, carefully wiping the crumbs from around the tin plate and folded up the paper wrapper of the leftover bread. Then, all at home, he took his head in his hands and started sobbing. Jules had never seen his father cry. Except maybe the once when his mother had died, but Jules was only five years old at the time and the memory of that day had been dulled by the need to bottle up suffering. The only thing that he could remember about his mother was her face but that too vanished sometimes; so he would go and open the kitchen cabinet and stare at the faded photograph of his parents on their wedding day.

"The shame of it, my God, the shame..."

His father's guttural voice made him wince. He was well use to his shouting and blaspheming and seeing his face turn red every time he beat him; but this pained note, broken by despair was new to him. He did not stir, waiting for the acid-blackened hand with its deforming calluses to lash out suddenly at his head. But his father sat motionless, looking at him through the fingers splayed over his face.

"They poked fun at me, do you understand? They pretended to console me but in the meantime they were laughing. One of them said: Maybe he'll get further with his thievery than we do by spitting up blood... And they had a great laugh."

Jules made to speak and uttered some inarticulate grunt but once again the words to express what he was feeling would not come. He was beginning to learn to suffer in silence. To accept the futility of offering any defence at all. Talking was a pointless waste of time.

He found another job in a factory in Bourguignon. He held it down for a few months, keeping his own counsel and shunning company. Then there was an accident, two workers lost their lives and he made the mistake of breaking his silence: he stated that it hadn't been an accident, that they had died because of the murderous work-rate and the ban on rest breaks between loading wagons, and that the pipe rack had given way because the bosses at the factory forced them to use gear until it was clapped out. He also said something uncomplimentary about the foremen, referring to them as "guard dogs" and "despicable flunkies". All of this he said to a small group of workers, well away from the office, but the management had ears everywhere. And so, a few weeks later, Jules proved the ideal culprit on whom to pin a petty theft carried out in the changing-rooms. This time they managed to make the thing all the more sickening by accusing him of having filched from his colleagues' pockets the few sous the had been holding back to pay for an after-work drink. Besides this being a pretext upon which to show him the door, they also made him an object of contempt in the eyes of the other workers. Since the firm had suffered no loss, the gendarmerie were not brought into it. He left without saying a word in his own defence.

At the beginning of 1893, Jules left for Besançon. His father had found a slightly better paid job there, enough for him to be able to maintain a wife: he remarried and had more children, but Jules couldn't get along with his new family.

During the May Day demonstrations that year, the army's 145th Battalion opened fire on workers in Fourmies in northern France. Twelve demonstrators were killed and thirty eight seriously injured. Jules, who had just started work in a Besançon factory, was promptly sacked for having backed the protest strike. It was impossible for him to find work anywhere in the area after that. Every manager had a file on Jules Bonnot, "subversive", distributor of anarchist pamphlets, agitator and "an individual person with dangerous anti-social tendencies". He vented his anger in his own way: at a dance at which a brawl erupted, Jules spotted a foreman from the factory, but instead of turning tail as he was going to do, he jumped on him and beat him to a bloody pulp, even though the police had just burst in, lashing out blindly with their batons. He was placed under arrest — and found himself facing the same gendarme as two years earlier, who had been promoted in the meantime and been transferred to Besançon.

"Strange, I'd have sworn it wasn't all that long ago", the officer said with a sneer. "You're craftier than I thought. Even so, here you are again, as you can see..."

He felt the weight of the box holding his file and added:

"You've come on. Not content with thievery any more, eh, Bonnot? Involved in politics and high ideals now, are we?..."

He bared his teeth in a chill grin. At a signal from the officer, the two gendarmes holding his arms tore off his shirt. Jules watched the buttons roll across the floor just as the first stroke of the birch broke the skin on his shoulder blades. He received twenty strokes, without flinching or saying a word. Since no complaint had been brought against him on this occasion either, he got off with a few days in the barracks. When they handed him back his shoelaces and belt, Jules lifted his eyes to look at the officer watching him from a few metres away. There was such a glint of hatred in his eyes that the gendarme chose not to react. The man said nothing, but as he watched him leave, he reckoned that if a bullet was to stop this lad in his tracks soon, society might be spared a lot of troubles.

Back home, frictions were growing along with the number of mouths to be fed and his father's second wife was starting to look upon Jules as a parasite, good only for whiling away his days reading books and "little subversive newspapers". His father decided to move the family to Neuves-Maison near Nancy, where he had found more regular work, adding to the weight of his pay-packet. Jules managed to get himself taken on at the Pont-Saint-Vincent steelworks, trying to hold his tongue and hide his anarchist propaganda from prying eyes. Not that it did him any good. His wits might well save him from any indiscretions at the plant, but sooner or later his heart and his guts were bound to let him down. In one tavern somebody said that the anarchists were the dregs of the nation, traitors to the homeland. Somebody else added that the army had made only one mistake, not having fired more shots in Fourmies and deplored the paucity of lives taken. Jules did not walk into the provocateurs' trap, but a brawl erupted all the same. He did his best to keep out of it, but when one of his pals was almost stabbed, he smashed a bottle over a chair and threw himself into the melee. The following day, a corpse was fished out of the Moselle. Jules Bonnot was not formally charged, but he was among the suspects. Knowing how futile it was to try to defend himself with words, he plumped for a change of air.

Barely three months later, in March 1897, there was a clash in Nancy between anarchists and patriots; the police were quick to intervene, but Jules stood his ground stubbornly and responded to the gendarmes' baton blows with a knuckle-duster. What blows he managed to land earned him days and nights of painstaking, scientific beatings meted out at regular intervals and ceasing only a short time before he was due to appear in court, lest the marks be too obvious. He was sentenced to three months for insulting behaviour, assault and battery and obstructing the authorities.

NANCY, 1897

The July sunshine bathed the bread on the wooden display counters. He was drawn irresistibly by the golden glow. He stepped up to the window, scanned the baskets and the salvers and glass jars filled with biscuits and the faces of the ladies gesturing indifferently at this or that item. The smell of the oven reached him through the open door: it was like an insult to his stomach, beset by cramps and rumbling noises. He had made a mistake venturing into these fine districts in the mistaken belief that he might find some way there of filling his belly by gazing upon the plenty, as if the sight of wealth could have helped him come up with some brainwave. But the only idea that had come up was a conviction that he had a right to steal what others were wasting.

He caught sight of his face reflected in the glass: shirt undone, face gaunt, hair disheveled and moustaches bristling. he had spent his last few sous three days earlier on some milky coffee and buttered black bread. Just then, even the memory of ghastly prison *bouillon* brought pangs of regret.

Two dark shadows in the sun-bathed street caught his attention: gendarmes who had loomed at the corner of the pavement opposite were strolling along toying with their batons. Jules tucked his bundle under his arm and started to walk with his head down, keeping close to the wall. With his starveling appearance, they would have locked him up for vagrancy. "The right to go hungry", he thought to himself, "is conditional upon its not being visible."

Back in more familiar back alleys with their hovels and slums, where not even the summer sun could quite drive out the unhealthy dampness, he set about looking for a sheltered spot to pass the night. Darkness was beginning to fall and the more shadowy corners were occupied by stooped, ragged shadows, the spectral forms of one-time human beings preparing to fight the rats and the cockroaches for a share of their cubbyholes. Away at the far end of one alley he sighted an abandoned cart missing one wheel and bolstered by a heap of rubbish. It wasn't cold but weakness was beginning to make him shiver right down to the bone. With shaky hands, he opened his bundle and donned a jacket that still reeked of prison, that blend of mildew, sweat and urine that infuses the floors of isolation cells. Then he lay down on his side, his knees drawn up to his belly and the bundle of clothing clutched to his chest. He wasn't sleepy but fatigue would help him still his thoughts and slip into a state of semi-unconsciousness that would shorten the wait for sunrise.

The sound of breaking glass made him turn round. A dark frame was teetering in his direction from a few metres away. Jules stood up, his head spinning from the exertion. The man who had thrown the bottle was now only steps away, his face black with grime, with a growth of whiskers, some scratches on the nose and forehead, a glistening sore at the corner of the mouth from which there issued rasping breath that reeked of cheap plonk. The stranger had his fist clenched, meaning to punch him and gave a muffled, animalistic, inarticulate roar. This was his spot and he was standing up to the intruder who had trespassed against his billet. Jules searched the rubble for a piece of wood, grabbing one, but before he could deploy it, a second piece of human refuse appeared in the alleyway, angrily tackling the first.

"You bastard, you've smashed my bottle, my bottle..." the assailant groaned in whining, desperate tones, raining punches and kicks on the wretch's back and sides.

The latter fell to his knees and continued to absorb the assault without making the slightest attempt at self-defence. Jules stood motionless in his corner, watching the scene in disbelief, unable to make any move. Then the recipient of the blows let out a sort of a screech, the yelp of a dying dog, and the assailant stopped. Mechanically repeating "My bottle, my bottle", he slid to the ground, curling up against the wall and started to cry. The assailant's scream died in a breathless coughing fit to which vomiting brought some ease. Spurred by a sudden attack of nausea, Jules gathered up his clothes and took off at a run, catching a shoulder on the slimy wall, stumbling, shivering from cold, hunger and rage.

He wandered aimlessly for at least an hour. Outside a tavern poorly lit by gas lamps, he was all but bowled over by a drunk tossed into the street by the bar-owner who stuck his boot into his legs before retreating indoors. It was all over in a flash. But his blood curdled and a stabbing pain in his temples blurred his vision. Fists clenched, Jules scurried after the bar-owner who was making his way back to the doorway and punched him on the back. The man arched his back and his face knocked against the wooden shutter. Then he turned his head and looked at Jules: there was more surprise than fear in his ruddy face glistening with sweat.

"What the... What do you want with me, you mad dog?"

The bar-owner slowly drew a knife from the pocket of his apron, unfolded the blade and raised his arm. The blade glistened in the poor light emanating from the bistro.

"Come on, then, chum. I'm going to make you regret that."

With a sudden movement, Jules shrugged the jacket from

his shoulders and wrapped it around his arm. The calm that had just come over him again was enough to clear his head and open his eyes to the absurdity of the predicament in which he had placed himself. But it was too late to back down now. The bar-owner took two steps forwards and Jules bent down to pick up a stone, making sure to keep the rolled up jacket between them.

"Fernand! What the hell are you up to?"

The shouting was coming from the doorway of the bistro: a woman with dishevelled red hair, overly made up, her dress brightly coloured and with a plunging neckline. "A prostitute", Jules reckoned, not taking his eyes off the glistening blade which was still poised in the air. The bar-owner had not turned away and was still staring at the stone in his adversary's hand, ready to side-step it. The woman burst out laughing, a phony laughter that was an attempt to break the tension between the two men. She sashayed over and whispered into the bar-owner's ear:

"Bravo, Fernand. While you're wasting your time on these grown-up games, somebody's rifling the till..."

The man's teeth clenched and he grimaced with anger.

"This bastard... it's all his fault. He attacked me for no reason!"

The woman stepped between them, turning her back to the bar-owner. She looked Jules straight in the face and threw him a knowing wink.

"Hang on, Fernand. I know him. He's a good customer. You wouldn't want to deprive me of a punter in these times we're living in, would you?"

The bar-owner retreated towards the glass door, muttering oaths.

"Then try to cool his ardour, Nicolette. Because if he gets under my feet again, I'll sort him out once and for all."

After spitting on the cobbles, the man retreated into his dive, with one last menacing glower.

The woman grinned and gently stroked Jules's chin.

"Tell me, lad... haven't you had enough of this sort of bother?"

Jules scanned her face. It was a familiar face, but he couldn't recall where he knew it from. Meanwhile, he noted the twinkle in her bright hazel eyes, overpowered by the crude make-up, and the overly red fleshy lips, and the fragile neck encircled by a frayed silk ribbon stained with sweat...

"Hey... what's going through your mind?" she pressed him in a quiet, hoarse voice.

"Why?"

"Because you have the eyes of a dreamer. And dreamers are dangerous. They bring trouble. I don't like the way you're looking at me."

The woman turned and walked a few steps in the direction of the doorway before halting and coming back to scrutinize him, serious this time and with an inscrutable expression on her face.

"Do we know each other?" Jules asked.

She adopted a mocking expression and replied:

"I was there too, at that dance three months back... I was with a punter and then you had the brain-wave of beating up that cop with your knuckle-duster. I never thought I'd see you again so soon. You've got balls, lad. The rest of them melted away but you stood your ground."

Jules walked up to her and when he was close to her he held out an arm for her to link him. She stared at him challengingly, raising her eyebrows and linked her arm with his.

"I'm Nicolette... what do they call you? "

"Anyway, Nicolette... thanks."

It had cost him some effort to speak that word. And she laughed in her false and joyless way.

"But what did you think you were playing at? When I stopped Fernand, I had no idea who you were. And I get the feeling I'd have done better not to stick my nose in. Maybe you need teaching a lesson... so as to teach you how to behave in this world."

"I thanked you but that doesn't mean that I needed your help. I can look after myself, don't you fret", Jules blustered, suddenly aggressive.

"Oh, but that caps it all... The little cockerel's hackles are up! Just tell me this: how much money do you have in your pocket?"

Jules stared at her, not understanding what she was getting at.

"Because of you I've left a punter in the lurch and at this time of night I'll be lucky to find a replacement. I don't charge much and the very least you could do is compensate me. Oh, let's come to some accommodation... In return, you'll be entitled to everything on the menu."

She placed her index finger under his chin, raising his face. Jules tore his eyes away and shrugged his shoulders.

"Had I the money, I wouldn't hand it over to a whore", he stated harshly.

Her lips parted in a little mocking grin and she looked him over from top to toe, pityingly.

"That's the truth, as I can see. Judging by your appearance, you haven't eaten in quite some time, right? And, let me tell you this, lad, you stink. I'll wager you're just out of prison..."

Jules nodded.

"And you've nowhere to stay?"

He gestured evasively and turned on his heels, making for the darkened alley.

"Hey!"

The girl stopped him.

"If you carry on like this, it won't be long before you're back in the dark. Listen..."

Jules's eyes burned into her. She raised her eyes to the

heavens, muttering oaths between clenched teeth and sighed:

"Oh to hell with it. I'm definitely going to regret this, you can bank on it... but the guy you were defending is a friend of mine. And he's long gone. I must be completely off my head, but... well, just for tonight; I have a mattress back home and you can flop there tonight. But tomorrow you make yourself scarce. Understood?"

Jules clamped his lips together and couldn't think of anything to say. He needed a bed, a roof over his head, a few hours' peace. And something to fill his belly. Anything.

"Well, shake a leg", she said, taking him by the arm. "At this time of night, they're all pissed. Might as well turn in for the night."

Jules followed her lead, keeping his head down and breathing in her cheap perfume, mingled with sweat. He found that it made for a warm, pleasant smell, the smell of a friendly body. She, on the other hand, held her nose.

"Dear God..." she exclaimed. "You really stink of downright misery, lad. It's be better if you were to have a good wash first, for I don't want you bringing any fleas into my place."

Then she glared at him severely.

"And let's be clear about something". she added. "I don't give freebies, not even to the parish priest. Don't go getting any funny ideas or that'll queer the pitch."

Outside in the street a carter was shouting something. The open window flooded the little garret with sunlight and the noises of the day sounded so clear that Jules opened his eyes wide and sat up with a start. He looked around, trying to remember where he was. There was an ache in his temples and he remembered the previous evening when, after a wash, he had slept like a log, slipping into hunger-induced oblivion. He took in the bedclothes, wrinkled but clean and off-white. And he saw the small table in the centre of the room, with its bottle of milk and bread. He jumped up and nearly fell on his face on the floor. He grabbed hold of the milk, gulping it until he almost ran out of breath, then cramming bread into his mouth, digging his fingers into the little butter dish and greedily licking them clean.

A few minutes later, he calmed down again. There were odd noises coming from his stomach, very nearly a noisy celebration of the breaking of his fast. He felt the strength flooding back into his legs and arms. The headache was fading and slowly his eyes were clearing. A door had been left ajar. He crept over as discreetly as he could. But the floorboards creaked.

Nicolette had her back to him. She was stripped to the waist and was sitting in front of a dull, streaky mirror, brushing her hair. She wheeled around unaffectedly, unafraid despite the sudden noise. Jules stood and gazed at her breasts which were large and still firm, the pink nipples barely drooping. She might have been in her thirties and in the absence of make-up was a lot prettier that she had seemed out on the street. Nicolette tilted her head and smirked.

"What's up with you? I wouldn't have thought that three months in the clink would have made you forget what they look like..."

And she slipped her hands under her breasts, hoisting them up.

Jules swallowed. She noted his embarrassment. She let out a short, amused laugh and stood up to fetch her bodice from the chair. She pulled it around her chest, waiting for him to do her up.

"Hey!... Are you going to help or not?"

Jules went over and delicately did up the laces. But his fingers were shaking and he didn't even know how to criss-cross the laces. She threw him a serious look.

"Now you smell of milk like a new-born babe, which is a big improvement on yesterday. But you look as if you've grown a bit.

She reviewed his naked torso, her eyes drifting downwards to his wrinkled, grimy underpants.

"Here, tug on these laces and pull tight", she added wearily.

Jules tried again and she leant forwards.

"Tighter, for God's sake! And place a knee against my back. Otherwise you'll never manage it."

He did as he was told and this time tugged tight enough to cut off her breath.

"See? A little milk and butter and you're a new man."

Jules's hands strayed over her back, barely skimming the skin, then stroking her neck. Nicolette stiffened.

"You're beautiful", he mumbled. "Why do you mess up your face with that muck...?"

Nicolette broke free and poked him between the legs.

"Easy now, Jules... Don't forget what I said last night: no freebies, not even if an archangel were to come down the chimney."

He smiled, pleased to hear her speak his name for the first time. Nicolette sighed and added:

"I don't charge a fortune... but it's still beyond your budget. Check your pockets. There's nothing there except dust and fleas and you certainly can't afford that sort of mad expenditure..."

Jules instinctively backed away, on the defensive. She gestured impatience.

"Oh for God's sake, calm yourself: I gave those awful clothes you have on a good soak and I needed to check the pockets first, right?"

Then she quickly daubed some rouge on her lips, made up her eyes, sprinkled powder on her neck and cheeks and finally put on her shoes, raising one leg at a time, hurriedly.

The dress was pulled up over her thighs and Jules could not help seeing the white flesh, a contrast with the pink garters. Her legs were solid, muscular, well put together and nimble. Nicolette gazed at him but he kept staring. So she lifted her skirts a little bit more and giggled:

"I could have been a dancer in a dance cafe with those, don't you think? Instead... I walk the streets..."

She dropped the hem of her skirt and straightened the bodice over her breasts.

"I hope to be bringing somebody a bit better than you back here in a half an hour at the outside. A paying customer. So see to it that you make yourself scarce. Got that?"

She grabbed her little purse and left without a backward glance. From the stairs she called out:

"There's a pair of trousers and a shirt in the wardrobe. Get them on and skedaddle. I'm not running a doss-house here."

He went back that evening. To pick up his clothes. That was his excuse at any rate. All day long he had mulled over what she had said, unable to understand the reason for her abrupt cooling, that need to put some distance between them again. Basically, he wasn't looking for anything. And hadn't asked her for anything. He felt slighted. And for the first time in a long while, anger yielded to sulking. Partly by chance and probably on account of his face looking less aggressive and resentful, he had found some casual work, helping with the unloading of bags of lime at a building site. It paid nothing but it had brought him a solid feed that had put him back on form once and for all. However, his sullenness hadn't quite left him, even with a full stomach. Instead his sluggish digestive system had made it feel thicker and heavier. "She's only a whore", he had been telling himself as he clambered up the scaffolding with bags of lime on his shoulder. "A whore. What can you expect from a whore?"

Yet she had been kind to him, and not from any expectation of reward. Nobody had ever offered him hospitality without knowing him well. And as for those who knew him well... well, they were worse. His father had put him out of the house as a disgrace to his new family, because he was a jailbird. His own father... But a whore, a woman used to selling herself and mingling with the dregs of society, had welcomed him into her home and asked nothing in return. The recollection of her bare shoulder and full breasts which he imagined must be comforting and soft, heightened this strange, unfamiliar sensation, the profoundly oppressive sadness that was gnawing at him, driving out the hate and the lust for revenge. He had stumbled upon the unwholesome pleasure of surrendering to a dream only to come away impotent and disillusioned. He couldn't love a whore, much less one he didn't really know. He realized that. But it was possible to feel regretful, even if he wasn't sure about what or why. Regret and melancholy, he had discovered, offered temporary respite from his worries.

On the stairs he crossed paths with a gent with his head down, hurriedly buttoning up his shirt and trailing a wake of beer fumes. Jules turned for a better look at him. He struck him as like a big, smug, cocksure rat rushing off to further dirty work. Before knocking on the door, Jules slicked down his hair and rubbed a hand across his eyes, before drawing a deep breath to still the sudden pounding in his veins. He heard the sound of rushing water and of a pitcher knocking against a washbowl. Followed by an oath. And footfalls crossing the floor. The door creaked open. Jules was in the half-light and it took her a few seconds to recognize him. The circumspection and severity generated by her guardedness were suddenly transformed into giggles:

"What a ninny you are!"

She seemed relieved, as if she had been expecting a more disagreeable caller. She opened the door wide and when the embarrassed Jules stepped inside, she quickly slipped a hand around the back of his head, riffling his short hair.

"I was about to toss them out, those rags of yours."

"Actually... I'm here to pick up my clothes."

Niciolette sighed and rolled her eyes.

"Oh, of course, I was forgetting. The young gent has great notions about himself... What's eating you? I was expecting you, of course. Otherwise why would I have let you borrow those?" she said, tugging at the front of his trousers.

Jules stood motionless in the centre of the room, feeling out of place and not knowing what to do. He simply stared at her. Nicolette had nothing on but a worn and faded dressing gown that she was now holding closed across her belly with one hand.

"You've been tramping the streets all day, I suppose", she said in a curiously friendly tone. "And you're hungrier than you were yesterday... or am I wrong?"

"No, no... "he stammered, forcing a smile. "I found some work and had a large lunch."

"Work? You?"

"Yes... But... not a penny of pay... Just lunch."

And Jules lowered his eyes. Nicolette came over and stroked his cheek with one hand. It was almost a caress.

"I don't like those long whiskers. And the gendarmes like them even less. There's a razor in the cupboard."

She pointed it out to him, then stepped behind the curtain dividing the bed from the rest of the room. Jules found the razor and even a sliver of shaving soap and a well-used shaving brush. He paused to listen to the rustle of clothing while gazing pensively at his reflection in the mirror. His hair was matted and plastered with lime, his eyes were bloodshot, his cheeks hollow and coated in a growth of beard... Nicolette's face appeared alongside his. Jules raised the razor and tested the blade on his palm.

"Yours?" he asked sarcastically.

Nicolette turned her back to him and strode to the door.

"Doesn't belong to anybody. You can use it and that's that", she said without a glance in his direction. "There's some bread and a little cheese in the food safe. If you're going out, don't forget this."

She tossed a key on to the table.

"And... what if I'm not going out? I mean to say..."

She waved a hand.

"Do as you see fit. I never bring them back here at night. Doorways do just fine... they finish more quickly and don't hang around to tell me their troubles."

She said this last remark maliciously, as if to challenge or wound him. When the door closed, Jules stood for a bit, contemplating the emptiness Nicolette left behind.

By the time she returned, he had been asleep for hours. The sun would be coming up soon. Nicolette did not light the lamp. She moved cautiously through the room, trying not to make the floorboards creak. But she bumped into the washbowl that he had set on the floor after washing and shaving. Jules's eyes opened but he didn't move. He feigned sleep, watching her in the dim light. Nicolette sat at the foot of the bed and kept her head lowered, drawing the occasional deep breath, as if weariness had drained her of the strength she needed to undress and climb into bed. Jules could feel her legs touching his feet and growing anxiety increasingly stopped him from shifting them. It was as if a wave of heat from there was rising towards his chest, making his heart beat faster and pounding in his ears, leaving his hands sweaty and forcing him to tense his toes underneath the bedclothes. Nicolette fumbled through her purse and drew out something that she raised to her mouth. A flask, from which she sipped for a few seconds.

"Want some?" she asked, reaching it to him.

Jules sat up and took the flat-bottomed flask which was almost empty.

"You've got sparkly eyes. You should have kept them shut if you wanted me to go away immediately", Nicolette mumbled.

Jules took a quick swig of what seemed to be cheap brandy.

"It was because I was afraid you might go away immediately that I feigned sleep", he replied.

She turned to look at him, her head slightly tilted, then laid a hand on one leg and gave it a firm squeeze.

"There are some nights... that seem to be never-ending", she sighed, exhaustion in her voice.

Jules stretched out a hand to stroke her neck and ruffled her hair, his fingers gliding around the back of her neck. Nicolette surrendered to this and slid into his arms, capsizing in a quest for silence and darkness and anything that might bring time to a halt, make her forget about the imminent sunrise and the approach of another day like all the rest.

She liked his hesitancy. He didn't jump on her and he didn't pull her to him roughly nor did he do anything else designed to parade his strength, determination and lack of hesitancy... Quite the opposite. This was all new to Nicolette who was used to punters made boorish and brutal by poverty. New, maybe, or perhaps just a distant memory. She was a good ten years older than him but she could sense a seniority about him, a substitute for hopefulness. Jules kissed her breasts with the delicacy of one afraid of breaking something fragile and his every move bespoke an almost childish timorousness. Nicolette did not feign pleasure and offered only what she had to offer him: a feeling of intimacy and a body heat that banished the chill of loneliness for a few hours.

Back at the site, they only needed labourers one or two days each week when the cartloads of sand, tiles and gravel arrived. It wasn't a real job, but it brought in enough for Jules to be able to buy wine, some potatoes for stew, or even a joint of boiling beef for feast days. Nicolette provided everything else. And Jules didn't feel like a leech, but rather like an invited guest, a friend who — it varied from night to night — could sometimes spoon with her in the same bed, either fending off an early autumn or clinging to the illusion that waiting for the dawn was easier when there were two of them. They even had a giggle and had fun chatting about everything and nothing, even poking fun at past miseries as if these had happened to somebody else. She used to joke about his obsession with burning paraffin and candles, poring for hours over his obscure books and newspapers with their peppering of threats and exhortations to social vengeance, but she had noticed that Jules, even though he was prepared to laugh at one and all, did not like it when she teased him about "politics". On the rare occasions when she had agreed to have a serious conversation, she argued that such ideas were good for nothing except keeping the guillotine sharpened and that the only hope for a better life lay in stumbling across a punter with a well-filled wallet, relieving him of it and making a fresh start. Overseas, perhaps, where she told herself that it would be child's play setting up a business as long as you arrived with substantial savings.

"I'm not going to stagnate here", Nicolette always concluded. "And as for the lot of the oppressed... I'm only too familiar with it and they disgust me as much as the oppressors do. They're all the same when it comes down to lifting your skirts and slamming you against the wall..."

Jules let it drop, looking dubiously at her and shaking his head. He too knew how hard it was to talk about equality and solidarity when they were faced with the spectacle of contemptible behaviour on the part of wretches eager for redemption, he having been flogged by poorly paid policemen, clubbed by equally poorly paid gaolers, and degraded by jumped-up bosses paid scarcely any better than their subordinates and subjected to insult and cruelty by most of the poor bastards he had met along the way. But he felt that there had to be something, some means, some method whereby the abstract notions in his books might be turned into consciousness, into a spirit of brotherhood, something that might turn misery into revolt and go further than brute violence between society's outcasts. The damned of this world had one great strength: the devastating power derived from their having nothing to lose, but they did not appreciate this. With the right propaganda, the right newspapers and books, maybe...

"You're a dreamer, Jules", Nicolette mumbled, massaging the tense, knotted muscles at the nape of his neck. "And in these streets awash with bastards and traitors, dreams are just a guarantee of an early death."

The days passed in a climate of seeming serenity. Jules had needed some respite and Nicolette someone who would not treat her like a whore. As long as it lasted, neither of them needed anything else. Her earnings were more than enough to cover their food bills and rent and his sense of guilt about this was without foundation: Jules never accepted money from Nicolette, but his odd-jobbing enabled him to make an occasional contribution to the table or buy himself a second-hand shirt for the winter. True, he still felt a certain dissatisfaction and from time to time thought that he ought to have gone looking for something else, a real job, but, when all was said and done, the anaesthetising, monotonous passage of time, which neither aroused enthusiasm nor inflicted any suffering, carried him along.

One evening he came home from the site after a particularly tough day, his back aching, his hands pitted by the lime burning into the skin at the finger joints. For the twelve hours he had spent hoisting buckets up scaffolding that hung in the air, they had given him enough to pay for a little gift for Nicolette. He had been thinking it over for a long time — and knew that she would have loved some curtains for the attic window so that she wouldn't have to shut the rickety shutters every morning, when she got up to make coffee. Nicolette slept in the nude and the window directly faced a building where at least two old buggers would be punctually waiting at that hour for her to rise. Once she had even discovered a squad of urchins huddled at the window opposite, jostling for the best vantage point. She laughed at the thought. Jules, on the other hand, had not been at all happy with her attitude.

"You're right", she had told him sarcastically, "no freebies, not even for street urchins. All the same, it pays to advertise..."

Jules was definitely not jealous of the punters drooling over her every day, but he was angry with her, angry that she could giggle like that and be so brazen about her profession.

"While I'm around you're no prostitute", he had once told her in all seriousness.

And Nicolette, in order to punish him for his presumption of ownership, had stayed out all night long and much of the following morning.

Anyway, Jules was going to buy her the curtains the next day with the pennies he had in the pocket of his overalls.

The first blow of the cosh struck him right in the chest, winding him. Instinctively, he raised his hands to protect his teeth as he slumped towards the banister. He rolled down the stairs. The second blow from the cosh hit him in the back. He stumbled blindly down the passageway connecting the carriage entrance to the courtyard, trying to straighten up. A kick in the ribs sent him hurtling towards the wall opposite. He finished up face down in the dirt. He coughed and spluttered, the dust he had swallowed burning his chest like a white hot iron.

"That'll do, Pierrot. Let me just say a couple of things to him..."

Jules turned towards the voice, his hands over his head to ward off another blow. He made out a silhouette through the fog and blinked his eyes in an effort to fend off the nausea. He had to avoid throwing up. If he couldn't stop retching, just one more blow and he'd drown in his own vomit. He could pick out the larger fellow, the one who had to be Pierrot: he was holding a cudgel in the air, ready to bash his brains out. The other guy was skinny, tall, hair brilliantined and slicked back, pretty dapper, with a scar around his neck that made him look like a pimp with aspirations. Pierrot lifted Jules up, grabbing him by the collar with one hand and flattening him against the wall. The slick-haired guy stepped up, opened a flick knife and grinned, pressing the tip of the blade under Jules's left eye.

"I don't like having to resort to such methods", he mumbled venomously. "I mind my own business and I don't like trouble. Everybody hereabouts respects me, because I don't tread on anybody's toes and I'm always ready to work something out whenever a problem crops up in the district..."

He pressed the flat part of the blade against Jules's cheek and brought his face closer. He caught the scent of a sweet after shave and Jules's stomach churned again. If he were to vomit over him, this guy would kill him. Of that much he was certain.

"You see, chum... among my business interests... there's

Nicolette. Maybe you weren't aware of that and I can understand that: you thought it was an awful waste that there was no man around to look after that blessing she carries between her legs..."

He sighed and slowly shook his head:

"I know her only too well, Nicolette. The fault lies with her. In fact, I've no quarrel with you. So, I'm letting you clear off out of here to somewhere where you won't have the misfortune of running into me a second time."

He stepped back and gestured to the hard case holding Jules by the throat. Pierrot was burly, with the face of a throwback: there was no clue in his appearance to the speed of his fists. He dealt Jules a combination of punches worthy of a well-trained boxer. In the short space of time it took Jules to slump to the ground he never even knew how many blows he had taken. Pierrot followed this up by grinding his heel into the middle of Jule's back and Jules saw a flash of red lightning. like a firework, followed immediately by utter silence. At which point he vomited. Luckily he was face down on the ground, so he did not smother when he promptly passed out.

The money in his overall pocket would no longer be used to buy Nicolette her curtains. He was back on his feet, a little stooped maybe, but the mist had left his eyes again. He had held his head under the fountain for several minutes, the gushing water drenching his shirt and much of his jacket. But it had cleared his head and put paid to his stomach cramps. He walked through the district unable to get his breath back, staring straight ahead, his hands clenched at his collar for protection against the cold and when he stepped inside the narrow shop, several kilometres from where Nicolette lived, the knife-grinder looked him over suspiciously.

Jules was soaked and his teeth were chattering so badly

that his speech was incomprehensible. He took a look around him. He picked out a horn-handled knife with a broad, ridged blade, like the ones used for slaughtering sheep. He pointed it out to the knife-grinder. The man hesitated for a moment then told him the price. Jules put his hand into his pocket, drawing out a wad of folded notes, tossing them on to the counter and added a few coins, counting it all frantically. He was a few centimes short. The knife-grinder reached across the counter and swept the money into the drawer with an open hand, shrugging his shoulders. Jules nodded slightly by way of thanks for the slight discount. Then he turned briskly on his heels and left.

That night he did not go home. Keeping his head down, his face buried in his upturned collar, he tramped through the streets and alleys of Nicolette's usual 'beat'. At around midnight, he spotted her outside Fernand's tavern. She was with another prostitute. They seemed to be waiting for one last punter before turning in for the night. Jules leaned against a tree in the darkness, scanning the glass-paneled door of the bistro. About a half an hour after that, a man came teetering past; he was so drunk that he didn't even see Jules and headed straight for the two women. After some brief haggling, the man picked Nicolette and showed her the cash. She tucked it away deftly, bade her girlfriend goodnight and headed towards a carriage entrance with the punter. Jules followed at some distance. No more than ten minutes went by, although it seemed like an eternity to Jules, and when the man slipped away, tucking his shirt back into his trousers, he was suddenly assailed by a bitter taste on the lips that he had started to chew the moment the couple had vanished into the shadows.

Nicolette walked back slowly, occasionally kicking a stone in front of her. When she arrived outside the tavern, the other girl had gone. She stepped inside the bar, spending about a quarter of an hour there. When she emerged, she headed for home, at a rather brisker pace this time, rubbing her arms against the chill.

Jules hung around for at least an hour, counting a dozen prostitutes coming and going and spending no more than five minutes inside. His teeth were chattering and he was shivering uncontrollably. But the moment he saw him turn into the street, he became calm and clear-headed again. The fellow had finished making his collection and was preparing to make his way home after one last round of drinks. He was in no great hurry, his heavy overcoat protection against the icy blasts sweeping the street. He had two noisy companions in tow who were sniggering and stopping from time to time to punctuate the tale of some recent feat with sweeping gestures. They split up at the corner of the little square. And the man was now on his own.

He lived quite close by. And in a narrow, poorly-lit street at that. Jules covered the ground with great loping strides, taking care to run as noiselessly as possible. The time it took for the man to fumble for his key and put it in the lock of the coach entrance was enough. Jules already had the knife opened and was holding it alongside his body. In a fraction of a second, he slipped an arm around the man's neck, using it to silence him while simultaneously plunging the blade into one of his buttocks. The man let out a protracted caterwauling, a cry of pain that was stopped by the rough, thick material of a sleeve. To stop him from crying out, Jules continued to saw away, muttering into his ear:

"How does it feel, a blade entering your hide? Hot? Cold? Or maybe I haven't driven it deep enough for you to be able to tell..."

He twisted the sleeve again, pressing with increased force before working the blade up and down. It was as if the man had suffered an electric shock. He bucked and banged his head against the door frame several times. Jules released his hold and grabbed him by the hair at the back of his head. The screaming stopped the moment the teeth crashed into the bronze door knocker and after a series of bashes against the door, the man collapse with a gurgling noise. The blood was gushing from his shattered mouth. Jules pulled the blade from his buttock before stabbing it three times into the right thigh and thrice into the left one, pressing the fellow's head into the step.

"Do you understand me? Do you understand what I'm saying to you?"

Jules held the bloodied blade against the carotid artery. The man hastily nodded agreement.

"Good. Now listen, and don't miss a word of this because I haven't the time to repeat myself. You carry on looking after business, but I get wind of you laying as much as a finger on Nicolette, I'll be back to cut off your head and hang it from that street lamp over there."

He drew the blade down the man's cheek, breaking the skin.

"And if you reckon you can get yourself of this hole by dispatching some low-life orang-utan from your retinue against me... very well. Remember, I've got friends of my own who are ready to go to war. Think that over before you do anything silly again."

From his pocket he drew a handbill that some anarchists had given him a few days before. The first two lines read: "The night harvest will soon be upon us and like ripe ears of corn we'll be bringing in a harvest of the heads of the proletariat's exploiters." He reckoned that message was tailor-made for the situation. He stuffed it into the fellow's mouth, right to the back of his throat, and added with a chilling grin:

"Read it, once you've spat out your teeth. It's educational."

They never spoke of it, Nicolette and he. She must have known about it, but she never brought up the subject. She merely went quiet for a time and must have reckoned that what it boiled down to was business, one pimp farming things out to another. So, when she came home in the evenings, she got into the habit of leaving her earnings in Jules's drawer. He took umbrage at this but once again said nothing, merely transferring the money regularly to the next drawer every morning. He heard no more about the man, whose name he didn't even know. But he had noticed a strange attitude on the part of the neighbours he bumped into in the streets and local shops. They used to acknowledge him with unspoken and vaguely unsettling nods. He didn't crave the respect due a feared pimp quick to use a knife, but from from now on that was his status and there was nothing for it but to "mind his business". Anyway, what mattered most to him was his relationship with Nicolette which had survived in spite of everything. From time to time, perhaps, he would catch her looking pensive, as if wondering what he wanted from her, but Jules steered clear of any situation that might have forced him to broach the issue. In the end, as he was saving all her money for her, Nicolette might some day be in a position to abandon the local alleyways and set off for the New World she was dreaming about with greater and greater frequency.

Nothing of any note happened over the ensuing weeks. Time slipped by without leaving any particular marks behind and Jules, who had a lot of free time on his hands, would spend it stuck in the house reading books threatening vengeance and, more recently, occasionally switching to the literary classics, picked up for a few pence from the second-hand booksellers along the Seine. Up until 15 November 1897.

Nicolette was still fast asleep and Jules was lying beside her, waiting, as he did every morning, for her to open her eyes and smile at him after a few seconds once she realized that he was the man lying alongside her. The pounding on the door was so violent that he jumped up, looking around for a weapon to defend himself with. When Nicolette woke up frightened, Jules signalled to her to keep quiet while he grabbed a large knife from the sink.

"Police! Open up or we'll break down the door."

Jules seemed to melt. He set the knife down on the table and looked at Nicolette. There was a sort of sad farewell in her suddenly saddened and tender eyes. Whatever they were after, this could not but signal the end of their peaceful times. He went to open up.

There were two uniformed officers who looked him up and down and sneered. The senior one pointed at him sarcastically and the other made a face, wrinkling up his nose. Maybe the allusion was to the smell of cabbage from last night's dinner.

"Jules Bonnot?"

He acknowledged the name, without lowering his eyes. The pair stepped inside. The first one paused to leer at the bare back of Nicolette was hurriedly getting dressed. Then he went over to her and made her turn around, forced a grin as if to emphasize that they were old acquaintances and reached into the neckline of her dressing gown.

"Congratulations, Monsieur Bonnot", he exclaimed with sham gaiety, slipping two fingers under Nicolette's throat. She shied away from him, seething. "A very cosy set-up..."

The gendarme moved around the room, rifling through scattered articles and books, one hand clutching his baton behind his back. Then he stared pointedly at Jules.

"Pimping certainly brings in more than breaking your back at the foundry, doesn't it, Bonnot?"

Jules stared back at him without flickering. He had thought that they were there in connection with the stabbing incident. All pimps were police informers and the likelihood was that this pair were here on the basis of information received.

"You used to go the foundry to thieve", the other officer stated, "not to break your back."

And he taunted him with his eyes, expecting a reaction.

Jules remained impassive. Nicolette, who had finished dressing, recovered her composure and stood in front of the senior one, hands on hips and quivering with anger.

"Might I know what you want?"

"From you, my beauty, not a thing... At least, not right now", the gendarme replied.

From the inside pocket of his tunic he extracted a piece of paper which he unfolded and waved under Jules's nose.

"Duty calls, Bonnot", he said with a snigger. "I doubt if the country will get much out of a gallows bird like you, but in the end... the army might set you on the straight and narrow. Who knows?" he added, handing Jules his call-up card.

Jules read it through, his eyes all dull surrender. He had been drafted into the 133rd Infantry Regiment stationed in Belley in the Ain department.

"Lucky for you that I know this lady", the senior man resumed, throwing a questionable look at Nicolette, "and that I knew I'd find you here. Otherwise, you'd have been posted as a deserter."

"Come on, get yourself dressed. We've wasted enough time", the other one piped up, tossing the trousers he had snatched from the chair into Jules's face.

Jules pulled them on, his eyes fixed on the floor in order to avoid meeting those of Nicolette who came over, kissed him on the lips and murmured, smiling through the tears fogging up her eyes:

"So long. Promise me you won't give them any excuse. They'd break you if you were to show any stubbornness towards them. Don't give them the satisfaction..."

Jules kissed her and hugged her tightly, squeezing the breath out of her. When he released her, she mumbled into his ear:

"Come and visit me. I'd love to see you how you suit a uniform."

The senior gendarme shoved Jules outside, grumbling:

"Come, come, I've to have my breakfast yet. You disgust me. A pimp and his whore. You'd think they were newly weds!"

Jules stiffened. He was about to elbow him right in the face when Nicolette stayed his arm, wrapping one of her scarves around his neck by way of a souvenir and kissing him on the cheek. A goodbye kiss. They both sensed that they would not be seeing each other again and that this spelled the end of a dreamy time together.

The senior officer looked at Nicolette and, unheard by Jules, out on the staircase, brazenly told her:

"Tomorrow morning, have a deep bath, perfume yourself and powder yourself and all that. I'll drop by in the afternoon. And if I don't find you home on the first visit, I'm not going to lift a finger on your behalf."

He winked at her and closed the door.

Nicolette spat on the floor, then rubbed her eyes to wipe away the tears.

MAJOR MANOEUVRES

At the start, he felt ridiculous in uniform, embarrassed and silly, on account of the standing to attention, the perfectly marshalled ranks, the badgering about the shine on his boots or the angle of his cap. But as the days slipped by, he discovered that, oddly enough, there was one crude advantage to this artificial, unpalatable situation: in the army, Jules Bonnot's past didn't matter any more. Nobody cared that he had done time in prison, that he sprang from the bleakest poverty or that his father had thrown him out of the house. He was a regimental number and nothing more. The only thing that mattered was how he performed: the alacrity with which he jumped out of bed at the first blast of the trumpet, the extent to which he could ignore the provocations from his superiors, holding his tongue and remaining impassive in the face of the sergeant's tantrums. Barrack life held no terrors for Jules who was well used to all manner of humiliations and forbearance. Whereas some of his comrades were at the end of their tether and spent the evenings on their bunks crying, missing their loved ones and their homes. Having neither loved ones nor home, Jules could look to a new form of indifference and confined himself to taking a distant, detached and unemotional approach to everything. Besides, he had very quickly discovered a fresh interest in the army, one that he could explore on his own to some advantage: an attraction to automobile engines, a fascination with the miracle that kept dozens of steel components operating in harmony, an irresistible curiosity about every single mechanism and for mechanics, which, to him, looked like something very close to religion with all its rules and rituals which could be brought to a standstill by the slightest imperfection. And he had felt the same sort of attraction to the new Lebel rifle with which the 133rd Infantry had been issued. The harnessing of the blind force of an exploding cartridge, and finally the bullet spinning along the rifled barrel and whizzing through the air to hurtle into a wooden silhouette sixty metres away with maximum force. On his first day's training on the shooting range, the real meaning of everything that he was doing never even occurred to him; he was being trained to kill. Jules was fascinated by the flawless operation of the assemblage of steel and wood that he was holding, by the muffled noise produced by the breach as a bullet was loaded into the barrel and by the bang that pierced the ear drum like a needle when the slightest pressure was applied to the trigger. It was important that the trigger mechanism should not be too sensitive; the index finger had to reach the crucial point only once the heart rate had returned to normal; otherwise, the throbbing in the muscles would have knocked the little lead shot in the sights off target. Like engines, guns are not controlled by brute force, but by the delicate touch and intuition required by fragile creatures. And the fact that they were anything but fragile constituted a mysterious contradiction intriguing enough for a more searching investigation.

From the very outset, he developed a passionate love for engines and firearms.

The scoreboard stuck up above the embankment. Ten. Jules made do with an imperceptible twitch of the lip. Another perfect bullseye. He was just about to reload when he felt a slight tap on his thigh from the toe of a boot. He turned. The sergeant showed no sign of being pleased with his performance and was looking at the target. Five bullseyes in a row. But his bald head scarcely moved. Not that he was the sort to sing his men's praises; his deadpan response and calm voice meant that things were going well. He was one of those career soldiers ignorant of life beyond the barrack walls, but who instinctively knew, deep down, how to make the most of the slightest variation in the character of his own men's peformance. An NCO who was priceless on the field of battle, the sort that every captain wanted by his side when the time came to attack. Highly skilled in handling conscripts, he stripped them of any aspiration or need unnecessary to fighting machines.

"That'll do, Trooper Bonnot."

Jules got to his feet, dusting off his uniform with a few swipes of his left hand, his right standing the Lebel on the ground. Then he decided to stand to attention at last. The NCO frowned and his eye all but disappeared under his bushy red eyebrows. He was irked by the time that it had taken Bonnot to snap to it.

"Where'd you learn to shoot, Trooper?" he hissed between his teeth.

It was worse when he spoke in a quiet voice; if his subordinate failed to get the message, there was a danger that he might fly off the handle.

"Here."

"What do you mean?"

"I mean to say... that I never fired a gun before. I learnt it here, with the regiment."

The sergeant looked him up and down slowly. A deadly silence had descended upon them.

"I still didn't quite get your answer, Trooper. What language is that you're speaking to me in?"

"French," Jules replied instinctively, regretting it as soon as the words were out of his mouth.

The sergeant slowly shook his head.

"Oh... I get it. French. Which means that you can spend the three days you'll be spending under close arrest on learning some other language. The one we speak here in the army. The French army, to be more precise. And in the French army we cite the rank of the questioner, preceded immediately by 'yes' or 'no', depending on whether the answer is positive or negative. Is that clear, Trooper Bonnot?"

"Very clear, Sergeant."

"Bravo. Those three days under arrest have now become four, thanks to the redundant words in your answer. Seek out the corporal of the guard, surrender your rifle, laces and belt to him and have the platoon escort you to the punishment cells."

"Yes, Sergeant."

Jules clicked his heels and marched off in search of the corporal. In his head he was wondering how he might fake an accident and shoot the sergeant in the back during some exercise. But there was nothing in his attitude to betray what he was thinking.

The lieutenant strode up to the NCO and, watching Jules march away, said:

"Best marksman in the company. Pity he's so headstrong."

"He's not, Lieutenant. At least not in his actions... Bonnot might even make a good soldier, but he reeks of hostility and rebellion ."

"Reeks... Sergeant?" the officer queried, dubiously.

"Yes. I have a sixth sense for when I'm in the presence of a skiver. I like Bonnot because he never speaks and gets on with his business and turns in a good day's work every time he's on fatigues. But there's something in his eyes that's different from the rest. He's a lone wolf and, if he could, he'd tear me and my uniform to shreds. I can sense it and I'm not wrong. I'm going to have to work on his body so as to drive the rottenness out of him and bring out any fighting qualities he possesses."

"Are you referring to his marksmanship skills, Sergeant?"

"No. I'm referring to the fact that Bonnot is a potential killer. Which is why I have put his name forward for the engineers, Lieutenant."

"Agreed," the officer replied with a puzzled, vaguely uneasy expression.

Jules would never have acted on his schemes for revenge. Killing a sergeant just because he had imposed an unfair punishment was like trying to scoop out the sea with a teaspoon. The army was full of bastards like that. And Jules, guaranteed his rations every day and afforded the opportunity to study engines and have a bit of fun with his rifle, would definitely not have placed his own life in jeopardy just to finish off one cur among the thousands. Then again, he found himself much better off among the sappers than in the ranks of the infantry. He became champion marksman of the company and was put up for promotion to corporal. The uniform, complete with its stripes and elite marksman's badge, would finally allow him to exact a little revenge: the gendarmes he came across while on furlough greeted him respectfully and frequently finished up offering him a drink to get him to speak his mind. He enjoyed poking fun at the thicker ones who didn't even notice that he was spinning them a line of bull, chuckling to himself at the sight of all these tipsy faces and their nods of thoughtless agreement. Learning to keep his laughter and suffering inside and not letting them show on his face had become a sort of a secret, personal endeavour of Jules's, a demanding practice that kept him continually on his toes.

His superiors had him down as a disciplined, efficient soldier. He looked upon them as wastrels given a place in society only by the uniform. And these imbeciles puffed up with hubris and fanaticism must never suspect what he really thought of them. It cost him a lot of effort, but he pulled it off.

In 1899, Jules took part in major manoeuvres and in his capacity as sapper corporal and marksman he was accorded special accommodation and was not required to share the blue bivouacs or trudge through the muddy encampment every morning. Out by Vouvray, there was a farmstead occupied by a widow with a long pedigree, a Madame Burdet. She made Jules welcome and treated him like a son. The bunk in the loft was more comfortable than his bunk in the barracks and the widow's coffee every morning and steaming soup every evening, made him think wistfully about things that he had never had, missing the warmth of a hearth that he had never known and rousing feelings that, to begin with, he registered with an instinctive annoyance. But among the widow's daughters there was Sophie. And on the evening when he was left alone with her, after everyone else had turned in for the night, looking into those stunning, utterly innocent eyes, those lips so oblivious of their own sensuality, and eighteen year old Sophie's open features... on that evening, Jules realized that a real effort would be required from him if he genuinely wanted to remain the lone and angry wolf, the cold-hearted loner that he had always been.

But fate determined that Sophie should develop a crush on the weary, mud-spattered, glum and brooding corporal who sat at their table every evening. Sophie was like a small animal prompted only by instinct and never querying the reason why. And behind the lugubrious, cold-hearted outer shell of a soldier absorbed by a mysterious grudge, she sensed a sensitivity, little details and barely perceived tensions that would have escaped the notice of others. It became her practice to sit up late around the table with him. Besides, her mother never made the slightest attempt to dissuade her. In the eyes of the widow, worn out by thousands of everyday chores, an army corporal was definitely a better prospect than some local farmer.

It was nice talking with Sophie. She could melt the ice through which Jules viewed the world with the very sweetness of her presence, the warmth of her tone and that way she had of looking him straight in the eye. So before the major manoeuvres were over, sapper corporal Jules Bonnot had surrendered unconditionally to his heart, once and for all banishing the cold reason that sought to keep him lonely and angry with the whole world. By his reckoning, the oppressed could very well do without thoughts of revenge and the oppressors escape that vengeance, and at the age of twenty four, having witnessed and endured all manner of cruelty, he made up his mind to marry and have children and find himself a more satisfying job than target-shooting and to live in peace, far removed from strikes, brawling, prison and hunger. He told Sophie this, but confined himself to a declaration of his love for her. Unsolicited, she came up with an endless series of schemes, dreams, promises and everything that might make for the happiness of them both. She would wait for him to be demobbed, while spending her time building up her trousseau. Within a few months, Jules was promoted to sergeant. Just in time to leave the barracks with a brand new uniform and some fancy stripes on his sleeve.

They were married on 14 August 1901. Jules had no misgivings: even if a man has never known peace of mind he recognises it when it comes. And he had peace of mind. Life was finally offering him some respite.

Corporal Jules Bonnot

Brussels, 1903

The boy might have been twelve or thirteen; he was frail and nervous and his hollow eyes didn't miss a single detail but there was a restless and sombre glint to them that made him look older than his years. These were adult eyes which had travelled through childhood but never known what it was to be carefree and innocent. He wore a Russian-style purple and white checked smock, a common sight among the little ragamuffins of his age in the Ixelles suburb, an impoverished district south of the Belgian capital. He scuttled briskly along the steep back streets, an enormous red cabbage in his arms.

The middle of the month had inexorably come around again, and the boy came from a family that ate its fill during the first ten days of the month but where there was no point even pulling a chair up to the table for the last ten. That red cabbage would make a soup to tide them over the middle of the month, a sort of a transitional period between memories of quiet digestion and the gnawing hunger that would shortly make for interminable evenings in the little furnished room.

The adolescent was profoundly irked by the jealous looks from passers-by and moved briskly along, looking forward with relief to the moment when he might set the cabbage down on the table, safe from the envious eyes of those who, even at the start of the month, were in no position to light the fire under a saucepan.

He crossed the busy Rue Blaes and slipped down an alleyway into the shade where the sun, even had it made up its mind to light the nooks and crannies of those wretched hovels, would have had a hard time getting a single ray to punch through the forest of rags stretching between one window and the next. He emerged into the small street where he lived and, slowing down, used a sleeve to mop the sweat from his face. He was within metres of the coach entrance when he became aware of a presence on the pavement opposite: a squat fellow, more or less the same age as himself, was staring at him and sniggering. He was wearing the thick glasses of a myopia sufferer, linked by copper wire, and behind the lenses twinkled eyes fired by mischief. And here they were, presented with a purple and white checked target with a red cabbage stain in the middle. The youngster started to laugh and folded his arms. The boy felt the heat of anger surging through him: despite that normally pensive expression of his, he was inclined to respond to teasing with a brawler's enthusiasm. He set the cabbage down on the doorstep after wiping away the dust with one hand, and then strode, head slightly lowered, hands hanging by his side and fists clenched, in the direction of the other boy.

"What are you laughing at, Four Eyes?" he hissed once there were only centimetres between them.

Not that the smaller boy was in any way intimidated by this. He looked down his nose and then replied:

"For one thing, I was laughing at that shoot-on-sight smock of yours: ten points if you can hit a white square, twenty for one of the purple ones. But now that you're nearer, I'm laughing at the idiotic head sticking out of your collar. Want to make something of it?"

The boy in the checked smock raised his right hand and punched him on the shoulder. Whereupon the other boy turned serious and retaliated. At which point the first lad was about to throw a punch but his adversary took a step backwards and whipped off his glasses, stuffing them into the pocket of his patched trousers. This brief interval had the effect of easing the tension , especially as the smaller boy, instead of putting up his fists, erupted into laughter and pointed across the street. The taller boy turned to see a skeletal, mangy, scabby dog sniffing around the cabbage left on the doorstep. He darted across as if he was spring-loaded and chased the animal off before it could piss all over his dinner.

"That's where you're going wrong," the other boy called out, putting his glasses back on. "A good squirt of dog piss would lend your dinner some flavour. "

The boy in the checked smock threw him a dirty look, wondering if he should cross back over and teach him a lesson. Then he shrugged his shoulders, picked up the red cabbage and stepped inside.

He saw the same boy the following morning, hunkered on the steps opposite as if waiting for him. He ignored him but the boy began to tail him. When he wheeled around abruptly, ready to pick up their quarrel where it had left off, the little boy in the spectacles grinned and offered him his hand.

"Raymond Callemin," he said.

Caught on the hop, he shook his hand brusquely and mumbled:

"Victor... Victor Kibalchich."

"What... ? ...Are you Turkish?" asked Raymond, laughing.

Victor threw him a sidelong look and replied:

"No, you ignoramus, it's a Russian name. But I was born right here in Brussels."

Raymond expressed a phony admiration, opening his arms to take in the wretched hovels surrounding them, as if to underline what a stroke of luck it was to have been born right there in these famished surroundings. Victor shook his head and finally allowed himself a smile of amusement. After which they wandered aimlessly through the back streets, Raymond a few steps ahead of Victor, as if to stress that he was the leader of the expedition.

Initially, theirs was a very strange relationship. It looked as if teasing each other was the main reason they met up every morning. Then, gradually, they came to be an inseparable duo, wrestling with the day to day adversity of a life lived for the most part on the streets, in a sort of mutual alliance against the town, against a milieu every manifestation of which, they sensed, was hostile.

They were bound by a singular sort of friendship made up of instinctive respect on the part of Raymond, who sensed that Victor had the edge on him, being better educated, more experienced and willing to face a challenge. Victor felt a deep affection for Raymond, even though he resisted his frequent excesses and never went along with his exaggerations and self-destructive notions. And much later on, when he came to sign his books as Victor Serge Kibalchich, he would remember him as a lad brimming with innocent anger and so attached to absolute truths that they nick-named him Raymond-la-Science.

Raymond's father was a cobbler who drowned any hopes he had nourished in his socialist youth in cheap booze, so his son virtually lived on the streets in order to keep away from the squalid room at the back of the shop, the living quarters for the entire family. Victor was often left to his own devices in the furnished room in Ixelles because of the frequent travels undertaken by his parents in connection with work or their frequent legal wrangles. Raymond found that room a priceless haven and Victor shared his reading matter with him, especially Louis Blanc's *History of the French Revolution*; their imaginations running riot over the illustrations depicting armed men and women flooding streets like the ones in which they had been raised.

The first time Raymond ever set foot in the little room with its poor-quality worn-out furniture, which was nevertheless more attractive than where he used to sleep, he had been taken aback by gloomy photographs hanging on the walls: they showed hanging victims. Victor had grinned with a shrug of his shoulders.

"Relations and friends of the family. The only ones to avoid the noose are exiles for life."

Whereupon he had recounted the tale of the underground group in which his father had been active, and the attempt on the life of Tsar Alexander II. And he told him about the first Kibalchich, a distant relative, hanged along with a band of conspirators successfully captured by the St Petersburg police. Victor had been born in Brussels quite by accident, at the end of a roundabout journey through Austria, Switzerland, England, France and Belgium. And his childhood memories were populated by endless heated arguments about egalitarian ideals to be implemented in Russia on the day she would be free of the bloodthirsty yoke of the tsarist dynasty. Meanwhile, every time they moved lodgings, the photographs of the hanged to be hung from the walls of their new accommodation were growing.

"My father has discovered the solution," Raymond commented sourly. "Any time his thoughts turn to socialism, he drains his glass quicker. A half-bottle later, he's forgotten all about it."

In between their reading, they roamed the streets, ranging as far away as they could from the wretchedness of the neighbourhood. Once they got as far as the Cambre woods where they got carried away reliving the misadventure of the hapless Salvat, a creation of Zola's, tracked through the Bois de Boulogne; they paid tribute to him under a cloudburst that left their clothes drenched.

One day Raymond suggested that they might explore the courthouse, a rather familiar setting to the local denizens, a goodly number of whom finished up in the dock there sooner or later. Victor welcomed the suggestion without the usual long discusion. They had no problem slipping in among the bustle at the main entrance and had merely to follow the signs in order to reach the roof; every time they read "No Entry", they headed up the grand staircases and corridors, slipping through rooms that were not in use, where their shoes kicked up storms of dust where it had gathered over the years.

It was a sunny afternoon and the fresh air gave them an uninterrupted view of the town stretched out at their feet. Raymond walked over and sat on the parapet, his legs dangling over the edge. Victor opted instead to squat down beside him, not showing the same contempt for their sheer height. They stayed there for a moment, silently staring at the neighbourhood rooftops and the shapeless movement of the plebs below in their inescapable drudgery. From below, the boys looked like a weird blotch, highlighted starkly against the upper part of the wealthy, opulent city; so majestic and indifferent to that sink of anger and despair beneath them. There was the grey stain of the women's prison, with its courtyards and the prisoners circling relentlessly. The clatter of their clogs was a constant sound reaching the courthouse rooftop, albeit a muffled, distant sound occasionally drowned out by the chirping of the swallows darting back and forth in the sky.

All of a sudden, Raymond jumped to his feet, his eyes trained on something in the middle of the square down below; a black horse-cab, scarcely any larger than a toy dragged along by an invisible string. Raymond quickly unbuttoned his flies and started to piss over the edge. Victor burst out laughing at the sight of the jet falling earthwards.

The cab pulled up at the courthouse entrance and a little man in dark clothing stepped from it, a satchel under his arm and a top hat on his head. A lawyer, for sure. Or some judge on his way to meting out years of hard labour, swaggering his way towards his everyday employment, immune to pity and to the piss falling from the skies.

"One good stone... ", Raymond said, not taking his eyes off the cab. "There might even be a decent brick that we can pry loose up here."

And he checked behind him, scanning the crenellations.

"And what good would it do you?" Victor asked, his eyes turning in the direction of the white clouds scudding along the horizon. "Reformatory and a good hiding, in return for one dented skull."

Raymond shrugged his shoulders and spat forcefully into space.

"I'm not afraid of a beating."

"Nor am I," added Victor, "though I'd rather give than receive."

Raymond gave him a sarcastic, mischievous look. And behind those thick spectacles, Victor caught an unwholesome gleam. He was too young then, but in time he would come to appreciate the meaning of that glint in his friend's eyes.

JULES AND SOPHIE MEET THE 20TH CENTURY

They were in love; that was the only certainty of those years of grey skies leading up to the breaking storm; a dark grey, bordering on black, the same indefinable hue as gunpowder.

The widow Burdet had moved across the nearby Swiss border to Geneva, leaving the house in Vouvray to the newly weds. Like something out of a serialised novel, Sophie was a seamstress. The soldier and the seamstress. Jules quickly put barrack life behind him and took to his new life as a young husband enthusiastically like a duck to water. And Sophie had no shortage of work. Jules set about hunting frantically for a steady job. Everything had changed now that he was able to introduce himself as a sapper-sergeant, free of the baggage of the past.

He was taken on at the railway depot in Bellegarde, near the border. At first, Jules reckoned he could make do with a regular wage, the love of his wife, quiet evenings spent reading in an easy chair while Sophie stitched dresses and smocks. But within a few months, his eyes betrayed him by lingering more and more often on his bosses' abuses of their power and the arrogance of the management. The discipline that he had suffered and blithely endured in the service, boiled over once Jules returned to civilian life. While a soldier could resign himself to getting accustomed to the irritations of barracks regulations, such humiliations could not be borne by a workman who, even if he broke his back, had no guaranteed board nor any of the authority that a uniform carried and merely ran the risk of being manhandled on the street if he dared talk back.

Jules did try to remain deaf and blind. But he couldn't quite stay mute. And when his reaction came, he found himself immediately summoned before the management. In no uncertain manner it was hammered home that the slate was not completely clean as far as past brushes with the law were concerned; these had merely been 'temporarily forgotten' on account of his splendid service record. If he was going to revert to being the criminal he once had been, he had better get it into his head that he was not going to be able to find another job. His name would be blacklisted after that.

"I said as much right from the outset, that your sort only changes the day the coffin lid is screwed down", the manager hissed, contemptuously. "If the army was ready to keep you on, you were an idiot to return to civilian life."

There were two other men in the office. Jules glanced at the hunting rifles leaning against the walls. He had only to stretch out a hand and he could point them at him before he could move a muscle. He looked them over, one after the other, with a sinister smirk. Then turned and walked out.

Back home, Sophie said nothing. Jules sensed that her silence was a refusal to award him her endorsement. He had lost his job and that was the only fact that his wife could plainly grasp. Everything else — the meandering prattle about the future of humanity, equality between human beings, the idyllic anarchist society wherein everyone would contribute according to ability and take according to needs... Fine words, that had always fascinated her. But even as he was speaking them, Jules had had a steady wage coming in. Now the ideals from his books certainly weren't about to feed the children that would come along sooner or later. Sophie had no wish to make things worse, but nor did she have the strength to lie to him any more. It was hard enough for the two of them to get by on what she earned as a seamstress, let alone feed three mouths.

Inquiries made locally got him nowhere. The blacklist was spreading like an oil slick and there was no-one ready to take on the ex-sergeant. Jules decided to move with Sophie to Geneva to be near his wife's mother. This solution hurt his sense of pride as if he had been burnt alive, but he had no option. The damned blacklist of the French held no sway in Switzerland. And Geneva was a wealthy city, where lots of the bourgeois owned automobiles. He had high hopes of being taken on immediately as a mechanic. Engines were Jules's passion, but he lacked experience However, it did not take him very long to learn the secrets of connecting rods, pistons, gear box mechanisms and suspension. Within a few months, his energy and determination had come flooding back and he enjoyed plunging his greasy hands into the mysterious heart of these new, gleaming, expensive monsters as delicate as the fragile, complicated make-up of any thoroughbred. Their owners watched inquisitively as this French fellow with the pencil moustache stooped over the bonnet, working out how to remove the scorched valve, a glint in his eye as he checked one spark plug, rather more blackened than the rest, working out whether the problem lay with the carburettor, his hands operating with the elegance of a goldsmith as he inserted a pin or adjusted the platinum screws. As for the garage-owner, he regarded the conduct of the apprentice Bonnot as above reproach and the lack of experience which, of necessity, slowed his work-rate, was made up for by his profound interest in the job. He often forgotten about stopping for lunch and even about knocking off after sunset, and carried on tinkering away with monkey wrenches and screwdrivers by the light of a paraffin lamp.

Sophie loved him the way she had that first day and forgave him for not arriving home until practically dinnertime, even though she was starting to miss him under the bedclothes when he sat up late at night studying maintenance and technical handbooks. In any case, she reckoned that this reading material was undoubtedly a lot more beneficial than the subversive writings he had been devouring up until the year before.

Jules had discovered that in Switzerland the first single-engined motor car had been the handiwork of one Fritz Henriod, who had constructed it in 1893. Automobile technology had made great strides in the space of a few years. In France they were building the magnificent Panhards and Levassors, powered by Daimler engines imported from Germany, where Benz was the most serious competition. From Italy came the put-put of the first Fiats that seemed to be enjoying a certain success in Switzerland. True, these were still cars that were more like horseless carriages, but Jules was very soon confronted with the thrill of one that suddenly surpassed its rivals tenfold; that was on the day that an eccentric Genevan millionaire stopped his 60 horse-power Mercedes in front of the garage, leaving Jules stunned and petrified. White, with a fiery red chassis and two black leather seats, eight thousand seven hundred cubic centimetres of capacity, the Mercedes ticked over gently, this growing to a mighty roar once Jules activated the carburettor and brought his head out from under the great, gaping bonnet.

"Fantastic", he mumbled reflectively, looking the same way as one would at a sensual, beautiful and unattainable woman. The lucky owner was only after an oil-change, which Jules dragged out for as long as possible, so as to be able to admire every detail of the vehicle, and taking a dressing down from the garage-owner for it. Not that he even heard, drawn as he was by the throb of its sixty horse-power raring to be gone in a cloud of dust...

His passion for engines in fact concealed a fire that still burned beneath ashes which, though thick and compact, could not quite extinguish it. The less that cars held any secrets from Jules, the more alive he became to the need to get back into politics. At the same time as books filled with complicated technical descriptions and thermo-dynamic notions, he had started reading the press again. And every time a strike ended in the death of a worker or in the sacking of an entire site crew, it left him with a burning sensation in his gut as a shudder rose from his innards to set his mind alight. During his time in the army, the news of the Dreyfus Affair, the officer charged with treason simply on the basis of his being Jewish had left him feeling the same way. But those were special times, a time of curious indifference to the world, and even a reading of Emile Zola's *J'accuse!* had left him cold except for a fleeting identification with the feelings of outrage. Now, on the other hand, anger was gaining ground and Jules strove daily to keep out of it. He started to leave work at closing time and began to frequent Genevan anarchist circles. He felt that he no longer had any faith in notions of popular insurrection or emancipation of the exploited masses; relentlessly growing inside of him there was a tendency to believe that the individual, alive to his own position and alert to injustice, was entitled to rise in revolt without waiting for the whole of the proletariat to stir itself.

Sophie smelled danger right away. And this time she tried to ward it off. Jules, who loved her sincerely and unreservedly, ignored her broken-hearted pleas not to get involved or do anything that might lead to his being classified as a subversive by Switzerland too. They talked a lot about this and squabbled over it only to make up again and neither of them was prepared to silence their opinion on the matter, so in the end they spents hours on end in interminable hectoring. Every so often, their love for each other prevailed over their misgivings and ideals and Jules would hug and kiss Sophie, and she was always happy to cling to him with that first-blush tenderness, hoping in her heart of hearts that in love-making he might rediscover the true worth of that relationship and family, the only realities likely to redeem him. Until one day, with eyes twinkling with emotion and grinning triumphantly Sophie announced that she was pregnant. Jules's reaction was exactly as she had hoped: he skipped for joy, washed his hands of his anarchist friends and began to shower her with attention and tenderness again.

When Émilie was born, Jules even managed to shrug off a weight that had been torturing him for some time: he wrote a long letter to his father, informing him that he was grandfather to a bouncing baby girl and pleading for forgiveness for past offences, looking forward to seeing him again soon and showing him his beautiful granddaughter...

The letter took four days to reach its destination. Even as Bonnot senior was turning his face into his collar with emotion, clutching the letter from his son Jules with a trembling hand, little Émilie was dying, laid low by a congenital disease.

Jules walked all night through the rain, fell on to his knees in a puddle of mud, and bellowed at the black and empty heavens, raging against the life that was carrying on unperturbably all around him, and screamed like a wounded animal, like a stray dog with a broken back, spitting blasphemies and curses into the empty air, spewing up bile from a knotted stomach, plunging hands and face into the slime, and only the icy chill of dawn, a purplish, sunless sunrise, was able to calm him and turn his feet homewards again.

It took only a few weeks. The Swiss police had already placed him under surveillance. At the first sign of "anti-social" behaviour, an order was issued for the expulsion of Jules Bonnot and of Sophie Bonnot *née* Burdet. His father offered to take them in and the pair moved to Neuves-Maisons.

Not that that lasted long. Full of venom directed at the whole of society, Jules resurrected his old differences with his father. It had been utopian to believe that they might live alongside each other, especially given the blatant hostility from the second wife, whom Jules regarded as the wickedest of step-mothers. They had to move on, and as soon as practicable. In her last letter, Sophie's mother had assured them that she had arranged a fresh residence permit for them. They tried to settle in Geneva again, but were expelled a second time. They resolved to move to Lyons; several years had passed since Jules's difficulties with the law and perhaps they could make a fresh start.

To begin with, it looked feasible. With the financial assistance of her mother and her meagre savings, Sophie bought a dairy, while Jules started work as a skilled tradesman in an automobile plant. By 1903 there were over thirty thousand automobiles on the roads of France and his skill in the installation of cylinder heads secured him a steady job and a wage good enough to revive hopes of a "normal" life. But precisely because of this security, Jules very soon got caught up in trade union activity at the plant. The management took note, but for the moment merely turned a blind eye to the dangerous ideas he peddled and focused instead on his ability as a car-assembly worker.

On 23 February 1904, Sophie gave birth to a boy, a healthy, sturdy child this time and she managed to exploit the occasion to extract a promise from Jules: no more trade unionism and subversive friends. He readily gave in to her, happy as he was with the idea of becoming a father and being able to support his family through his unaided efforts. At which point, he realised that humiliation and poverty had left him profoundly exhausted.

By the time the siren sounded, Jules had already arrived at the gates. That morning he blinked happily at the guards, but they saw this as provocative and nervously gripped their batons. He burst out laughing and that really caught them on the hop: it was the first time that this ball-breaker Bonnot had looked relaxed, instead of parading his usual sour expression.

In the workshop, Jules took out the bottle of wine and displayed it to his workmates.

"For a toast", he announced, "come lunch-time. We're going to call him Justin-Louis and he weighed in at... oh, I've forgotten his weight, but it's a delight to hear him wail!"

The others huddled around grinning and the odd one slapped him on the back, but the news that he had become a father was received rather coolly. Jules was taken aback at this and looked at them, one by one.

"What the hell's the matter with you all? Has somebody died?", he asked, teasingly.

"Pretty much", answered the dour Vignon, a workman in his fifties who was highly respected on account of his commitment to the union.

"Callot was damned nearly killed", volunteered Berry, one of most hot-headed youngsters. "The rolling mill took his arm off. And now he's a useless cripple and they'll throw him out on the streets as soon as he's discharged from hospital."

"Assuming that he survives any infection", somebody else added.

Jules was suddenly deflated. The bottle in his hand was as

heavy as a block of iron. He tucked it back inside his lunchbox and looked at Vignon. Vignon said:

"Time and time again we've complained that safety standards here are non-existent. Sooner or later, it was bound to happen. Tomorrow we strike."

"Why not right now, damn it?" erupted Berry.

"Save it", Vignon retorted. "We've already discussed that. A strike needs to be properly organised, word fed out to all the workshops and we need to get together this evening to coordinate support in other plants. Going off half-cocked would serve no purpose. We have to make maximum impact and secure the total backing of the unions."

"They're a fine lot, they are", grumbled Berry. "On the pretext that the left are now the majority in the government, all they do is dampen things down."

"Save your voice for the strike tomorrow", Vignon silenced him. Then, turning to Jules, he said: "Now, we meet at the clubhouse this evening. Make sure you're there."

Jules shook his head, his face drawn in a pleading expression.

"Damn it, Vignon... my son's just been born... "

"I appreciate that, Jules, and I'm sorry that this tragedy is spoiling the party for everybody. But I certainly don't need to tell you... "

"It's not that", Jules stated quietly, dodging his colleagues' eyes. "You have to understand me... I have an extra mouth to feed now and I can't help thinking about his future. If I was a free agent, well, you know me, right. But I have a record already, and... "

"What on earth are you talking about?" Berry interrupted. "That poor wretch Callot is on his death bed, and if he pulls through, nobody will have any work for him any more... they've burned away the shreds of his right arm with a torch just half an hour before we got here!"

Jules clamped his jaws closed. Then set about twisting his moustache but made no reply. Vignon threw his arm over his shoulder and drew him to one side.

"Listen, Jules... I understand. You mustn't feel like a coward should you decide to report for work in the morning. Give my best to your wife and tell her to concentrate on shoving milk into your little... what did you say his name is?"

"Justin-Louis", Jules answered, staring at the floor. Then, as Vignon made to leave, he grabbed him by the belt of his overalls and asked him: "How many kids have you got yourself?"

"I've three, all boys."

"And how will they manage if you lose your job?"

Vignon shrugged his shoulders and sighed.

"God only knows. All I know is that some day they'll be factory workers and they won't be treated like pieces of meat but as men, with dignity and respect. But that will depend on what we're prepared to do today."

Jules nodded. On returning to his station he noticed Berry glaring at him. Later the youngster found some pretext to come over to him and taunt him.

"You! When I think of all the speechifying I've heard from you at meetings! Then... " He stopped short, biting his lip lest he say anything more. But a second later he hissed something between his teeth and it hit Jules like a whip: "So it was just talk, eh? Even you are a scab!"

Jules rushed forwards and lifted Berry by the scruff of the neck, shoving him back on to the workbench.

"Never dare hang that label on me. Never. Got that?"

Berry stared right back at him but said nothing. He neither showed fear of the threatening tone nor regret for having tagged him as a scab. Jules released his grip and Berry straightened his overalls angrily. Before he moved away all he said was: "Don't let us down, Jules."

That evening, Jules tried to clear his head by playing with the new-born, watching him as he suckled greedily at Sophie's breast and he grinned at the watching Sophie who was at peace and contented, thinking that this new life appeared to be trouble-free now.

The following day, Jules stopped a couple of steps outside the gates. The strikers were out in strength, joined by activists from the anarchist clubs and rank-and-file socialists. A chorus of whistling and jeering went up as a first batch of white collar staff and workmen who had not supported the strike made to leave. In front of his colleagues, Vignon rolled back his sleeves and bellowed at them not to take the bait, that their strike was a success and that being drawn into confrontation might ruin everything. But the guards intervened even before the two factions had come into contact and, on the pretext of offering protection to the strike-breaking workers, they surged forwards, brandishing clubs. Which was all the cue that the police, lined up to one side, had been waiting for. Blows started to rain down on the strikers' backs as they scarpered in all directions, routed. A few, though, held their ground. Jules, for one. Stationary and crouching with muscles tensed and fists clenched, he kept his eyes on the man in black uniform who was heading straight for him with his club raised. Once he was within reach and once the club started to descend towards his skull, Jules flexed his knees and head-butted him right in the chest. The guard's mouth opened and he dropped his club before he collapsed and was left lying on the road, gasping for breath.

Had this been a gendarme, the game would have been up that day as far as Jules was concerned. As it was, the guy he had butted was a factory guard and the Bonnot name was one of the first of the list of those to be sacked. But the management was not content with just that. It forwarded a detailed report to the prefect of police for further action: Sophie's trading licence was withdrawn and her slender hopes of living off the income from the dairy evaporated a few days later. Now they were both out of work and doomed to go hungry once their savings had been used up and that looked like it might be just a fortnight away.

Jules and Sophie decided to leave the child with his maternal grandmother who travelled to the border to collect him and take him back to Geneva. The couple then moved to Saint-Etienne where Automoto had its works. Jules was taken on exclusively because of his skills as an expert mechanic. Obviously the file on him was a rather sluggish traveller and for a number of months he was able to bring home a decent wage, so much so that he wrote Grandma Burdet that they would soon be collecting little Justin-Louis again. Sophie was hit hard by the absence of her child and her relations with Jules were profoundly affected by this. Only the hope that the three of them might be reunited in a sparsely furnished but adequately heated apartment could have salvaged a marriage that was sinking into resentment.

"You've no sense of responsibility, Jules. You've brought a son into the world only to doom him to becoming an outcast like yourself... "

Jules made no reply. He retreated into a silent, frightful, prickly and profound hatred that became the only thing that could keep him going. At work he spoke to none, and his colleagues thought him a sort of a misfit. From time to time one of them would try to show him a little human warmth, some glimmer of solidarity, until, as time went on, Jules let himself be talked into attending the union meetings, where he bumped into Besson, the organising secretary, who made no bones about being an activist, a rabble-rouser, someone who enjoyed a magnetic hold over the workers. Jules heard him out carefully, rolling cigarette after cigarette which he then smoked while he coughed with a ticklish, suffocating and increasingly persistent cough that was beginning to get on Sophie's nerves. As if she didn't have enough to complain about.

Little Justin-Louis was returned to his parents and Sophie called a truce. Having her son around injected fresh energy into her and helped her rediscover her innately optimistic outlook on life which was made up primarily of naivety and an urge to see the world; after all, she was only twenty four years old and her adolescent years had been spent in rural isolation, sustained only by dreams and schemes that were unilkely to become reality. With Jules, she had briefly deluded herself that she might achieve everything she had dreamt about on the farm back in Vouvray. Now that her husband was a skilled hand at the Automoto plant and that Justin-Louis was learning to walk in the parks of Saint-Étienne, Sophie was beginning to regain her belief in a peaceable life, one that —who knows? — might be happy for a while.

She went with Jules to the union local and listened to fiery speeches from Besson, a man who certainly had a gift for enthralling the workmen as well as their wives and sweethearts. However, she continued to clash with her husband over political matters. She urged him to spare a thought for his family and urgently advised him to look after what seemed by then to have developed into chronic bronchitis, but at the same time she was drawn to the friendly, fraternal atmosphere she had found at the union and struck up friendships with women like herself who were bound to men who were fighting for recognition of their own rights. She found Besson not just interesting on account of his impassioned rants against man's exploitation of his fellow man, but also sparkling and charming during evening spent over a bottle of wine or on the excursions that the club would occasionally organise in the local area.

Naturally suspicious, Jules on the other hand looked upon Besson as a slick "popular spokesman" as he termed it, investing the term with a lot of contempt, especially when he could sense Sophie's instinctive sympathy growing the sourer his remarks became, and he even went so far as to refer to him as one who "peddled smoke in a quest for personal power".

Then there was an unusually violent strike and the Automoto management received a report from the gendarmerie stating: "Jules Bonnot is a person of violent character, whose aggressive temperament is inclined to lead him into confrontation; intelligence gathered about him — unfavourable in every respect — suggests that he is utterly incorrigible." So once again Jules Bonnot found himself joining the millions of unemployed that a turn-of-the-century Europe grappling with colonial conquest and Belle Époque frenzy had difficulty coping with, falling back upon relentless deployment of anti-riot squadrons and gangs of gunmen in the hire of the big industrialists.

Not that Jules had the time to spare a thought for how he was going to find some new means of supporting himself, for his lungs were so afflicted that within days of his being sacked he was racked by violent coughing fits. He spat blood and could scarcely get his breath back. What little cash he had went on the hospital bill, where he made a rather quick recovery, thanks in part to his sturdy constitution and partly thanks to the hate that left chunks of undiluted energy coursing through his veins.

IT WASN'T YOUR HOUSE

Barely out of hospital and you were having problems fighting against the dizzy spells that came over you at the slightest exertion, or hauling yourself up those stairs, clinging to the bannister and taking a breather at each step. It wasn't your house. You'd never really had a home of your own and that one was less yours than any of the others. You were thinking about Sophie again and about how she had said there's no money left for rent. What money we had we used for your hospital bill. Your hospital bill, she had sighed. It felt like betrayal, hearing her talk about your illness as if it were some new whim, just another way of making her life a misery, adding yet another problem to the ones you created for her on a daily basis. So Sophie moved in with the bold Besson, that big-hearted trade unionist who gave generously of himself for those less fortunate. She, who had lately stopped bombarding you with whingeing and advice and seemed almost to have accepted you as you were, to having to live with a man who was regularly shown the door without anything ever coming of it.

In her eyes, in the eyes of us all, you were just a maverick. Which you knew as you climbed that staircase, ready for the humiliation of begging Besson for hospitality, after you'd traduced him to Sophie, tried to destroy her admiration for the great trade unionist. The more scornfully you spoke of him, the more she defended him. Strange that it should have taken Besson to open her eyes to the heroic side of the trade union struggle. Then, two steps from his door, you asked yourself how sure you were that he was acting in bad faith and where, as you could now admit, naked jealousy began. Because, for some time now, Sophie, in addition to seeming more relaxed and at peace, had also been spacing out her hospital visits, and when she did come, had stayed for shorter and shorter periods, as if eager to get back to the new world she had so recently discovered. There was a worrying look in her eyes which darted everywhere except in your direction. Sophie.

All through the journey from the hospital to this place, you had been rehearsing a speech full of carefully considered words, a speech that would have set the seal on your ultimate surrender: We have a child, Sophie, and only now have my eyes been opened to all the damage I've done to you both. The quiet of the hospital and the loneliness have helped me think things through and appreciate the value of what I was losing. We can start afresh, Sophie, I swear to you that we can do it. If not here then we can go far away, somewhere unreached by police files, a place where there are so many cars in need of the services of a good mechanic. We can bring it off, you'll see.

Who knows how long you stood there, your hand poised above the door, undecided as to whether to knock. What if Besson should open up? It was his home, after all. You had been hoping to hear her voice whispering softly to the child, or playing on the bed. The noise you heard was a creaking, the unmistakable creaking of bedsprings, but there was no playful talk, no happy gurgling from Justin-Louis. You knocked. Two gentle knocks, barely brushing the recently revarnished wood. Nothing. Utter silence. The creaking had stopped abruptly. So you stopped thinking, seeing, listening. You slapped the door with the flat of your hand, a dull thud. You were reluctant to think any more and you just sensed something unwholesome and dirty that made you blush with shame. You refused to harbour the evil thoughts knotting in your heart, which you would rather have crushed like a serpent.

Then there came a rustling and finally Sophie's voice. At first you couldn't comprehend what she was saying to you, because your head had starting spinning and a dizzy spell had made you teeter backwards and it was only by clinging to the banister that you avoided falling down the stairs. You leaned towards the door again and knocked harder.

"Go away, Jules, and leave me be. It's over, Jules. Can you possibly not understand that?"

And you leant your forehead against the wood, your thoughts nonsensically concentrated on the smell of varnish rather than on Sophie's shouted words.

"Let us have a life, Jules. I can't take any more. Go away. Let us have a life."

The boy and her. Her... she and Besson.

Who knows how you dredged up the strength to throw yourself against the door so hard you knocked it off its hinges. Sophie's bodice was open. Backing away, she struggled to hide her breast as she recoiled in fear. She never looked at you and had eyes only for the laces of her bodice as she tied them them. She wasn't even aware that she was wasn't wearing another stitch and when she stumbled against the chair behind her, she ended up sitting in it, her legs parting momentarily.

He had time to pull on his trousers, but his feet were bare. He walked towards you, open-armed, as if prepared to stop you from falling rather than to ward off any attack. You grabbed him by the neck, but you had used up all your energy on the door: your legs could take no more and you had a hard time keeping your hands up and holding him.

Meanwhile, Besson punched you in the stomach, not all that viciously, the sort of thing one does to a drowning man to stop him dragging somebody else down with him. You dropped to your knees. Sophie had started screeching again, and you turned your eyes to her. She had managed to close her bodice and had a hand clamped between her legs to hide a body that you knew better than you did your own, every single centimetre of white flesh, every centimetre of warm, soft flesh. You could even have let her in on a few things she didn't know about herself, like the little beauty spot on her ankle, the tiny scar in the crease of her arm, where you would stroke her back to see her arch it or kiss her to listen to her moan.

She was screeching at you to get out, to leave her with her new life and to stay away, for the love of heaven. Besson had bent over to help you to your feet, shoving your inert weight in the direction of the door. Like a man possessed, you turned Sophie's last words over and over in your head. For the love of heaven. Who knows if there really was love in heaven, because here on earth, and you knew it, there was room for nothing but hatred. How much hatred can a heart hold, Jules? A few seconds before, you thought you'd reached saturation point. Only to find that there is always room, no limit to the room for hatred, as immeasurable as the universe. Hatred was infinite. Only love... you thought as Besson was dragging you towards the stairs... only love had boundaries.

Before he could close the door, you let slip the two words for which you could never forgive yourself afterwards. In a voice you did not recognise, you said: my son. And you stared at Sophie as you said them, as she lowered her eyes. But at that point you weren't worried about your son at all. Later on, yes, but not just at that point. Your thoughts were on her, not on your son, yet you used the boy in a clumsy effort to soften her heart and invoke the only thing you two still had in common.

On the street that night, your thoughts dwelt on those last two words and you felt like you were a louse for having uttered them, when really all you meant to say was Sophie, and say it loud, angrily, as if asserting your rights rather than seeking a concession. Instead, you mumbled them in a voice distorted by that blow to the guts, but which sounded gruff with annoyance and despair. It may not have been the first time in your life but it would certainly be the last. Never again, in any event, would you ask for anybody's pity. Pity would be the only thing that the human race would never feel for you. Hatred, contempt, fear, terror... But not compassion. Never again."

The First Step

Besson reckoned that he had the measure of Jules. He thought of him as one of the many debauched types bereft of political consciousness who hung around in labour circles for the sole purpose of finding some excuse for a punch-up. And this Bonnot also had a a personal grudge now that made him dangerous. He was a potential killer, an outcast capable of any crime. So thought Besson; so much so that he retreated to Switzerland with Sophie and young Justin-Louis, so firmly convinced was he that he had to ensure that they were beyond the reach of this criminal lunatic's vengeance. She let herself be talked into it, even though she instinctively knew that Jules would never do her any harm. She knew him; Besson did not. But a little time away from France would do them all a power of good. The trade union secretary was "sound", a determined character, respected for his standing in society and even the employers held him in regard on account of his moderate, realistic views. Besson was a man who could offer her the assurances she had always dreamt about, the ones she had thought initially that she might get out of Jules. And as for love...

Sophie had grown up too quickly of late. She knew the difference between passion soured by deprivation and honest feelings sustained in financial security. Besson was not a rich man but he appeared capable, influential, not some impulsive, naive boy likely to squander everything because he did not know when to quit. And she had had her fill of fascination with the sort of "artistic temperament" which, harnessed to poverty, led only to destruction. Weariness overpowered love and a motherly sense of responsibility did the rest.

Jules appeared again shortly after that. He stood across the street, waiting for her to catch sight of him. He hadn't dared knock on the door. He hadn't wanted to scare her much less invite a scuffle with Besson. Maybe he didn't hate Besson enough. He disliked him. For Jules, hatred played such a big part and counted for so much that he was reluctant to squander it on someone he regarded as a "cowardly, boot-licking worm". Besson was a contemptible creature who played the workers for fools and exploited their despair. Now he did the same to Jules's wife, mother of his child, and is what most saddened him.

It was his mother-in-law who first sighted him.

"Shall I call the police?" she asked her daughter.

Sophie signalled no and came out without saying a word.

Besson had had to return to France to settle some dispute but he had arranged to to come and fetch her shortly. All she had to do was go and face Jules and try to talk some sense into him. She could not carry on living in the nightmare of seeing him pop up in front of her every time she stood at the window. She walked up to him determined, certain that it was over beteween them.

"Bonjour, Jules. Were you wanting to talk to me?" She asked so icily that he instinctively shrugged his shoulders by way of reassurance.

"I wanted... It's just Justin-Louis... I'd like to see him."

"I'm sorry, Jules. It's better this way for us all, believe me. Don't force me into doing what we, none of us, want.

I've already instructed a lawyer to sort everything out. There isn't a court that would force me to grant you access, you know."

Jules nodded. He knew. He knew it only too well. Given his record, there was no court that would side with the law-breaker Bonnot, an anti-social, incorrigible individual.

"Sophie," he mumbled, "are you really sure... that this is what you want?"

"It's the only solution," she said, dropping her eyes for a moment. "If I were to let you inside, it would complicate things more... and you would just be hurting yourself. The quicker he forgets about you, the better his prospects for the future are going to be. You have to face up to this, Jules."

His mouth contorted and his pained expression took on the look of a sombre smile. He was smiling at fate, which he was beginning to accept, forgetting any illusions.

"Have you really fallen in love with this pig, Sophie?"

Her initial toughness flooded back.

"And who are you to sit in judgment of him? It doesn't much matter whether I love him. He can offer my son a future, and... "

"Our son, Sophie."

"No. He's all mine. It's not enough that you slept with me for you to stake your claim to fatherhood. When were you ever a father to him?"

Jules opened his mouth. But not to speak. He was simply trying to fill his lungs with air, but to no avail. He was learning to live with this tightness in his chest cutting off his breath for endless seconds. He swept a hand across his face, nodded and smiled to cover up his embarrassment at having come all this way for further humiliation.

"I don't know if I can handle that, Sophie..." he said somewhat lamely before proceding on his way.

"Sure you can," she insisted in a cold voice which he had never heard from her before. "You'll forget about me, just as I'll forget about you."

He turned and shook his head in disagreement before striding briskly away in case somebody, especially Besson, caught sight of him with the veins sitting out on his forehead, his eyes misting over, and notice how his lips quivered while he gnawed edgily on his moustache.

The sight of terror in other people's eyes. A strange, truly strange sensation, it was. But not an exhilarating one, at least not as far as Jules was concerned. It was like taking on a great burden of responsibility: the responsibility for determining whether the terror-stricken person facing him would be killed or spared. Plainly, there was no reason to kill a vintner, even if the fellow was a crook who served short measures, as Jules had patiently watched him do. He had ordered a small one and then waited while two customers made up their minds to buy the four bottles of champagne at which they were staring in amazement, jabbering unbearably. There was more cash in the pockets of this pair than in the till, and no mistake. But Jules had stepped in just to see if he had the guts and determination to carry out a robbery. Mugging two idiots on the street would not have been the same thing. True, a drinking den was no bank, but even so it was a public establishment. And when he eventually pressed the point of his knife to the throat of the vintner, he had suddenly realised what terror was and what it did to people. The man raised his eyes, as if by not looking at the face of his assailant he might ward off his death. Jules emptied the drawer in a few seconds, noting that the raid would net him under a hundred francs.

"Is that all of it?" he hissed, pressing rather more heavily on the knife, but without breaking the skin.

The man tried to nod but one false move and he he might get his throat cut, so he mumbled something that Jules could not make out.

"Where's the cash? Come on. If we waste time, somebody could come in, and then... "

"No, no, I beg you, I swear, the takings today have been poor, I beg you... "

He hadn't tried to talk down to Jules, had been quite obsequious in his mode of address. So there was one unfailing way of commanding other people's respect: you just had to strike terror into them, that's all.

Jules was about to give him a slap, convinced that the businessman had some money hidden in a hole behind the shop, when he caught sight of the butt of a gun poking out from behind a dishcloth. He slowly slid a hand over it, taken aback by the respectable weight of this burnished, well-oiled weapon. He was almost as familiar with guns as he was with engines and he recognised this one almost before he read the markings on the grip: it was a semi-automatic, broad-chambered Steyr-Mannlicher, like the regulation Mausers issued to Prussian officers and just about as bulky and cumbersome.

"What the devil are you doing with that?" he asked, genuinely intrigued.

The man had begun to sweat large drops and one now hovered on the tip of his nose, ready to drop on to Jules's hand as he withdrew the knife and tickled his face with the barrel of the handgun.

"Well?"

" It's... I've been held up twice, and... "

"And did you use this the other two times?"

"No, no... I mean, I've only just bought it... didn't have it before... "

Jules gave him a couple of flicks on the cheek and his hand glided through the sweat...

"Well, old chum, as you can see... You've wasted your money... "

And out he went, without giving him a hiding or tying him up, because he reckoned that the shopkeeper was so stunned that it would take him at least half an hour to come round. In fact he came to immediately and ran onto the street screaming for help. Jules muttered under his breath, and, taking off at a run, wheeled round to threaten him with the pistol, but the vintner's terror had given way to a sort of suicidal recklessness; he was standing in the middle of the street, letting out long piercing screams and flapping his arms. The gun aimed over the businessman's head, Jules squeezed the trigger in the hope that the report might shut him up. But the safety catch was on. So he decided to waste no more time and took off as fast as his legs would carry him, zigzagging through the stunned passersby. There were no gendarmes around. By a stroke of great good fortune, his first armed hold-up ended well, thanks to the fact that the folk drawn by the screeching had no notion what was happening.

He would have given anything to know what had induced that nincompoop to buy himself the silliest, most useless and most cumbersome gun on the market. He could come up with only one explanation for it: the vintner was stupid enough to have bought the biggest handgun he could find, imagining that size might be a deterrent. The difficulty was that the Steyr-Mannlicher used ammunition that was simply unobtainable, especially in France, where no military unit had been issued with it. Unable to resist the temptation to put it to the test, Jules took himself out into the open countryside and walked for kilometres until he came to a small wood, where he fired three of the seven shells in the magazine. No doubt about it; the Steyr-Mannlicher was accurate and powerful and made for long-range ammunition. But who on earth would be able to get him a box of 7.63 shells? Delving into the underworld, Jules had finally tracked down a guy who had about twenty 7.73 calibre Mauser shells, but scarcely had he returned to his shabby lodgings than he spotted the difference, however slight, between the two types of ammunition. And the cash he had forked out for these twenty splendid-looking capsules of gleaming brass was money down the plug-hole. The shells just about fitted the magazine but once up the spout they would definitely stick there and jam.

"Shitty bloody Krauts!" he snapped between gritted teeth for much of that evening. "But then what would you expect from them? It's just typical of them... Any nincompoop who sets up a factory is free to make his own cartridges!"

When he realised that he was talking to himself now, he started to curse himself for an idiot for not having asked the vintner for other ammunition. He must certainly have had some somewhere in his shop. It would nearly be worth Jules's while holding him up for a fourth time, he thought to himself, as he laid back on the soiled mattress with its stink of stale sweat.

A finger poking into a pat of butter, unable to make much inroad but slowly making headway while the surrounding matter curled and splayed. Not all that different from the image of an oxy-acetylene torch cutting through the solid metal of a safe. It required a steady hand, concentration and lots of patience to keep the jet pointing in the same direction at all times, without shifts in position that might risk letting the metal cool and delay the buckling. He had laid out a pretty penny for his safe-crackers' equipment. The proceeds of every one of the robberies carried out over recent months had more or less gone into it. But it was worth it, Jules reckoned as he watched, enthralled, as the blue flame sliced through the belly of the strongbox. This was definitely more profitable than holding up shopkeepers or passers-by. Besides, the safes always belonged to well-to-do folk, wealthy folk, representatives of the bourgeoisie against which Jules had declared a silent, unspoken war, preferably conducted on rainy, moonless nights, so that the noise of the storms might drown out the roar of the torch and any metallic clatter, a war in which battles won boiled down to the look of stupefaction on the face of some rich idiot arriving home to his warm, desirable household at daybreak, half drunk with champagne, only for his gaiety to evaporate in an instant at the sight of his gaping safe. He didn't do it just for the money; there was also the satisfaction in robbing those who grew fat and were so profligate, exploiting their fellow men. On this particular night, Jules had slipped into the home of an engineer by the name of Guenod, having monitored his habits for a long time, researching them the way one monitors a bird of prey so as to steal its eggs the moment it leaves the nest.

In the end, the lock suddenly gave way in a little shower of sparks. Jules used the back of a glove to wipe away the sweat and stopped for a few seconds with his ear cocked: there was no noise outside, just the monotonous pitter-patter of rain against the windows. He pulled the door towards him, bracing his legs; there was a creaking sound followed by a click that led to his falling backwards. The torch knocked against the cylinder with a dull clink that echoed through the room for a long while. Jules fought back an oath and cocked an ear again for noises from outside. He reckoned that he could hear a rumbling, and then nothing. Distant thunder, perhaps. Or a car engine backfiring as it reached the turn in the road three hundred metres from engineer Guenod's home.

He set to work, his hands delving into the strongbox. With some difficulty he pulled out a heap of papers and documents, then a case that might have held some precious gem but which was frustratingly empty, a brass box inlaid with mother-of-pearl with a certificate of authenticity for something which was missing and... an expanding wallet, swollen and bulging and held shut by a pretty snakeskin rope that he used his teeth to tear away. Holding it between two fingers, he lifted it up and it gaped open, disclosing nothing but a lousy one hundred and fifty francs in the last compartment. Had he not been preoccupied with that unidentified noise Jules would probably have set fire to the place. Several days and nights of work, the risk of taking a bullet in the back, the exertions of cracking a brand new, most uncooperative strongbox and all he had to show for it was a hundred and fifty francs. He had laid out twice that sum for the torch.

And the bloody torch was a dead weight, although the cylinder of oxygen was nearly empty. The weight was all the deader on account of his frustration and tiredness and the strain on the nerves that drained a lot of energy from him. He loaded up the kit-bag on his shoulder: the Steyr-Mannlicher that he had brought along with his last four remaining slugs slipped to the side, the sights rubbing against his belly. How was he supposed to crack the safe of the sonofabitch with a thirty centimetre-long pistol in his waistband, Jules wondered, cursing himself for an idiot once again. One hundred and fifty francs, he was repeating like a litany, gnawing at his moustache under a downpour that had turned torrential. He hadn't the time to retrace his steps and exit via the patio window, so he made up his mind to exit as quickly as he could via the front door.

It was sheer animal instinct that made him protect his throat. He heard the panting just in time and threw himself aside. He slipped and fell into the muddy garden, the dog leaping over him and sinking its fangs into thin air. Like a thing possessed, Jules lashed out with his feet, fending it off for a few seconds, until he had managed to swing the kit-bag between him and the huge black dog that was still pawing at him, tearing at his clothes and shredding his jerkin and shirt. Like all dogs bred to kill, the beast uttered only low growls and did not bark. It was now in front of him, up on its hind legs and struggling ferociously against the length of chain by which it was tethered. How come he hadn't spotted the damed dog before now? Where had the bloody thing come from?

Jules knelt down, panting and untangled the Steyr-Mannlicher which had snagged on his trousers and torn them. Finally, clutching it in both hands, he aimed the firearm at the dog's skull. The animal somehow knew what the gleaming steel thing was for. It knew that it was a firearm. There was no other possible explanation, for it suddenly backed off and stood motionless and staring. Looking Jules right in the eyes and not looking at the gun. There was no fear but it was as if he was waiting for the report. Whoever had trained it had certainly taken care to accustom it to the sound of gunfire. Jules aimed between the two glowing embers and squeezed the trigger. His trembling ceased and there followed a moment of unreal calm: the incessant rainfall, the dog staring at him, motionless, its jaws clamped shut. The outstretched arms and the hands only centimetres from the target. There was no way that he could miss. The dog had it coming. Watchdogs, he thought, are like certain of the exploited masses put in uniform, given a rank and the power to misuse it; they become faithful servants of those who keep them in chains and often prove to be fiercer than those who have long since become accustomed to the exercise of power. "

He lowered his arms, slung the heavy kit-bag over his shoulder and retreated a few steps, holding the gun in his outstretched hand. The dog carried on staring at him but made no move.

When he reached the garden gate he heard a growl. It struck Jules as a signal of frustration like the one that was eating at him. He made for the street to retrieve the old bicycle that he had left under a bush a hundred metres away.

STREETS

Victor was leafing through a book by Elisée Reclus that he had found under a stack of old books in the bookshop-cum-drugstore in the Rue de Ruysbroek. In fact he had read it already, then lent it to a comrade who had been in prison in Brussels for the past few days. It occurred to him that he should buy another copy for his journey but his entire fortune was the wretched ten franks in his pocket

"Hey, Kibalchich!"

Even before he turned to look, he recognised the booming voice of Carouy, the giant of a lathe-operator standing on the threshold with his arms flung wide. Victor smiled and shook his head as the bookseller-drugstore owner frowned and looked each of them up and down. A second after that and the skinny figure of the Russian exile was swallowed up by Carouy's arms and muscular chest; Carouy then looked at him with sadness in his eyes.

Edouard Carouy

"The word is that you're leaving. Tell me it's not true, Kibalchich."

Straightening his shirt in embarrassment, Victor nodded.

"It is, Édouard. I've had my fill of Brussels and of Belgium."

"But... why?" his friend muttered in cavernous, melencholy that made him seem fragile and defenceless. "And what are the comrades going to do... what are we going to do without you?"

"Nobody is indispensable. And since when have anarchists needed guides and leaders?"

"No, no, that's not what I meant," Carouy stammered, his eyes downcast. "It's just that... we were beginning to make some headway and putting a spanner in these sons-of-bitches' works."

Victor shook his head.

"Brussels isn't worth the bother, believe me. The trade unions, the cooperatives, the Social Democrats... There's no room for ideas hereabouts. They all still know how to close ranks. There's no chance to make changes in this town. We might as well be on a different planet. And we're rushing headlong towards self-destruction. Listen, Édouard, you should clear out too, before they do you to death on the street and forget about you the very next day."

Carouy displayed his big fists, his little, shy eyes expressing astonishment.

"Oh no, Kibalchich. My hide will cost them dear. If I have to die, I'd rather go out the way Sokolov did."

Victor reached out and held his shoulders.

"And what good did it do Sokolov? Remember? He poked fun at our demonstrations. And perhaps he was right. But all he could do was barricade himself into a hotel room and keep shooting at the cops until they got him. Now, as far as people are concerned, he was just another criminal. Even he couldn't change anything. Unless it was for the worst."

Carouy nodded while glancing round to suggest greater discretion. Victor looked at the shopkeeper who was watching them. Rumour had it that he was a police nark and Carouy had actually come to this silly little shop with its store of spices and stationery looking for some pretext, some piece of evidence on which he might strangle the fellow with his bare hands. Victor grinned.

"What difference does it make now? Could be just tittle-tattle. We're all going off our heads. Anyway, I'm off tomorrow and he can say whatever he pleases."

Carouy suddenly embraced him in a bear hug that squeezed the breath out of him. Once he had broken free, Victor spotted a glint in the eye of the giant who tore his eyes away and feigned interest in the book he was holding. Victor went up to pay for it and handed it to his friend.

"Kibalchich... " Carouy mumbled, stroking the cover of the elderly, broken-backed, dog-eared volume. Before I got to know you and the rest of the group, I was a brute. But for those books of yours, I wouldn't have had any understanding."

"Books aren't everything, Édouard. You should reach out as well and talk to other folk and familiarise yourself with other realities. That's the reason I'm going away. Don't hold it against me. I have to do it."

Carouy nodded vigorously, as if to assure him that he didn't see him as a traitor.

"And... where will you go?"

"Who knows? This direction, that direction. Paris, for sure. But first I want to earn a living en route."

Raymond Callemin was handing out advertising leaflets on behalf of an outfitter. Yet again he had lost a job on account of his brazen anarchist activism and distributing leaflets was only the latest career for a young man who had no sense of proportion. Victor saw him approaching from a long way away at the junction of two housing blocks and he slowed down and went up with a sarcastic smile.

"Salut, free man. Is this what you meant by political work on the streets?"

Raymond pretended not to have heard and, turning to Victor, handed him an advertisement while making a theatrical show of reverence.

"There you go, good fellow, you'll be needing a new outfit for your journey to a new life. Tell them I sent you and they'll cut you a good deal, you'll see. Tell them you were sent by the only surviving free man in this shitty town."

Victor (Serge) Kibalchich

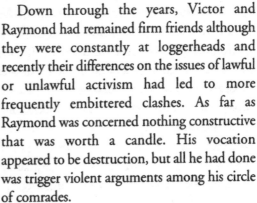

Raymond Callemin
aka Raymond-la-Science

Down through the years, Victor and Raymond had remained firm friends although they were constantly at loggerheads and recently their differences on the issues of lawful or unlawful activism had led to more frequently embittered clashes. As far as Raymond was concerned nothing constructive that was worth a candle. His vocation appeared to be destruction, but all he had done was trigger violent arguments among his circle of comrades.

He still had a package of leaflets left to distribute. He looked at them with an expression of distaste and tossed them into the gutter.

"Day's work done?" asked Victor.

Callemin shrugged his shoulders and started to walk away. They meandered aimlessly through the city centre streets. From the Rue de la Régence, they wandered into the Place du Petit Sablon then cut through the Egmond Gardens.

"Don't think I'm going to stay here, Victor," Raymond suddenly announced, stopping in his tracks. "Another two weeks of this leafleting shit and I'll have enough put by to buy myself a good pair of boots. And then... To hell with Brussels, Belgium and all these zombies stinking up my nostrils."

He had uttered this last phrase looking straight at a couple who happened to be passing. At first the man looked at him inquisitively, before lowering his head when he caught sight of Raymond's glowering expression, quickened his step and dragged his wife along by the sleeve.

"Come with me then," Victor suggested.

"Where to?"

"Paris, sooner or later."

"And why Paris exactly?"

Victor brushed that off as if an answer would have been redundant.

"Because it's the city where the Commune was born," he said, "the home of Anatole France and Jehan Rictus and the CGT and a host of self-managed newspapers, neighbourhood gatherings, immigrants' associations... The city where Lenin wrote Iskra, among other things."

Raymond agreed, with a sarcastic pout.

"And what does that mean, Iskra?"

"Spark."

Raymond looked sideways at his friend.

"Well, if you really want to know, this Lenin of yours is not at all to my liking. If you've decided to throw in your lot with the authoritarians, then piss off to Paris. When a spark is mentioned, I think of a fuse attached to a good dose of dynamite, rather than Lenin and all these hifalutin' talkers who think of nothing else but carving themselves out a slice of power. Scratch the surface a bit and you'll find they're still nationalists rather than revolutionaries."

They ambled along the great Avenue Louise where a few rare automobiles sounded their horns as they overtook all the horse-cabs trotting along in disciplined ranks. At the passage of these strange noisy creatures, some of the startled horses were spooked and the cabbies would tug sharply on the reins, muttering curses at a world changing to fast.

"Who knows, Raymond. You might well be right. But you'll never be able to resist any swing towards authoritarianism if you stay in these parts."

"And who's talking about staying here? I'm off too, but

definitely not to Paris, because, as I see it, that's the city that drowned the Commune in blood rather than the city that created it. It's all a matter of opinion, Victor dear."

"So where will you be going?"

Raymond dropped his arms.

"Doesn't matter where, but to to a city. Tramping the road anywhere. For a breath of fresh air and to be rid of all these pig- and sheep-headed folk that surround us."

They started walking again and an hour later they parted in the Ixelles neighbourhood where the first streetlamps were lighting up. It was plain that all further argument between them was now pointless. They shook hands and embraced each other. Then Raymond relented and threw his arms around Victor who returned his hug, trembling, overwhelmed by a range of indefinable, mixed and muddled emotions: anger, impotence, sadness... which he overcame afterwards, once he was left on his own, with an awful, searing melancholy.

Raymond headed for the Ardennes, then on to Switzerland, trying his hand at all sorts of casual work, from harvester to hod-carrier and even forestry worker. He had the look of a defenceless child about him, with those little glasses of his that made him seem like a frail, bewildered high-school student, a soft fedora pulled down over his eyes and a book of Verhaeren's poetry in his pocket: "Intoxicated with the world and with ourselves, we carry our new men's hearts through the ancient universe... ." His favourite poem from that collection was the one that went: "Open up, or dash your fists against the door!" A better option might be to break it down, he thought, rather than remain mouldering behind it.

Slinging over his shoulder a bag holding a change of shirt, a note-book, a few photos that never left his side, and ten francs, Victor caught the train for Lille. He found lodgings in the attic of a miners' barracks, then tried his luck asking for a job at the mine, but they laughed in his face;

"You'd be dead in two hours, lad!"

By the fourth day he had only four francs left. He switched to a rationing system: twenty five centimes for a loaf of bread and a kilo of green pears. By the end of the first week, he was suffering dizzy fits and could no longer stand upright. Thanks to a new friend, a pipe-layer, he was introduced to a photographer from Armentières and taken on at his development lab for four francs a day. He carried on living in the miners' barracks and every morning he set off with the silent, dour labourers through the fog that shrouded everything.

In the evenings, after ten hours spent in a dark-room, Victor strained his eyes to read Jaurès's paper, L'Humanité, and it was hard going for, in addition to tiredness, there was a couple on the other side of the wooden partition wall, the man of the house almost always coming home drunk and beating his wife. Between sobs, he could hear her pleading:

"Beat me then, beat me."

Then they would make love. And the more he beat her, the more passionate and satisfied the woman seemed, as if the beatings were an actual token of his affections.

This crude contact with the mine-workers, this dive into the reality of misery and resignation banished all illusions about solidarity among the oppressed. It just added to Victor's misgivings and worries. What sort of revolution would be feasible without emancipation of the individual? And if an unassuming, broken woman took blows as the only antidote to her partner's indifference, what would be the point of talking to her about wage exploitation or overthrowing the balance of power between labour and capital?

By candlelight, Victor jotted down in his notebook: "Is it going to take centuries before this world and these creatures are transformed? Yet each of us has only one life to live. What are we to do?"

He thought of an answer, but it was personal to him: so he set off on his travels again and made it to Paris.

LYONS, 1907

"Mankind makes sacrifices for certain core ideas, among them truth, justice, duty... that it regards as ideals. These obsessions must be destroyed. My cause is not universal, although it is unique, just as every individual in unique... We ought to cling to the truth of the unique and reject as false anything that is not properly mine; both society and the State, which you invest with your strength and which exploit you, are false."

Jules underlined this paragraph in pencil and closed the book: *The Ego and Its Own*, by Max Stirner, the Bavarian philosopher and theorist of individualist anarchism. The broken-backed cover was smeared with stains and spotted; the grease and sweat off his hands which were back working with engine oil again. The candle flame flickered, soaring and then falling sharply, a sign that the wax and tallow mix was giving up the ghost. He had perhaps another ten minutes of light left before the wick would burn out. He reopened the book and searched for the chapter he had just read at least ten times over, scribbling an exclamation mark in the margin.

"Revolution and rebellion should not be regarded as synonymous. The former consists of the overthrow of the status quo, the established order and is therefore a political and social phenomenon. The latter, even though an inescapable consequence of it is a transformation of the current state of affairs, arises, not from that state of affairs but rather from men's individual discontentment. It is not an armed uprising but an outpouring by individuals, an incitement to rise up heedless of any consequences that this might entail. Revolution has its sights set on a new organisation; rebellion on the other hand prompts us to reject being organised any longer but rather to look to self-organisation and places no great hopes in institutions... The revolution commands us to create new institutions; rebellion to rise up and raise ourselves up."

"Rebellion", Jules mumbled, propping himself up. Rebellion, not revolution. Any attempt to replace a reactionary government with a revolutionary government, he reckoned, would assuredly leave in place, if not the exploiters per se, then at least the methodology of exploitation as a function. The State might change its aims, but not its means. Stirner had grasped that. And Nietzsche had defined Stirner as "the most fertile mind of his day"... Jules smiled and nodded and his lips pinched in a sour grimace. The most fertile mind, to be sure, but one that died in poverty and loneliness, ignored by the bourgeois, scorned and ridiculed by the socialists and left to the hunger that had been his boon companion for much of his life... What good was having such a big brain if it had not managed to change anything? Society, the State, the world at large were ready to acknowledge him as a philosopher, now that Stirner was a small heap of bones lying forgotten in some graveyard in the world's most socialist country. These German Social Democrats, Jules thought, scratching his head vigorously. The notion that there might have been lice in this greasy garret left him bemused... But no, it was only dirt. He hadn't had a bath in a long time and the iron dust at the plant was worse than lice. He found his train of thought again. So the Social Democrats were the cream of revolutionaries who, on entering parliament, had announced loud and clear: "From now on the German worker is a citizen with Reichstag representation and henceforth has obligations to Germany which take precedence over any towards his own class... "Jules sighed and was immediately assailed by a coughing fit. Damned dust. Whether it was inhaled on behalf of Bismarck or Social Democracy, what did it matter if the sole aim was the manufacture of cannon for enslaving the peoples of Africa or Asia, or for a show of strength to impress the neighbours in Europe? And that senile old fool Engels, Jules remembered, who had finished up disowning the *Communist Manifesto* and declaring that the German Social Democrats had a duty to pass the military budget in order to fend off an attack from tsarist Russia... Same old story, all the time. As for Russia... Jules glanced at the heap of old newspapers and the anarchist journals strewn all over the cramped attic. Two years previously, there was the mutiny on board the battleship Potemkin. A good thing too, no doubt. If only it had had long-range guns that could be trained on Lyons... But Lyons was too far inland. Maybe it could have fired at the Côte D'Azur. Just to clean it up a little... This time he started to chuckle but stopped just before his coughing fit could return to torment him. The battleship Potemkin, the officers and men who had taken up arms... But what sort of revolution was it when it was miliary men who started it off? He was familiar with the enclosed lives and blinkered outlook of the military. No matter what the intention and no matter the reason behind their mutiny, they still suffered from the typical shortcomings of the barracks mentality. No, there were no grounds for hope there. Not in revolution at any rate. Now, rebellion, that was another matter. True, Stirner hadn't changed anything. Any more than that Parisian cobbler, one Léon Léauthier, another anarchist, had changed a thing by walking into a luxury restaurant in the Avenue de l'Opéra and sticking his awl into the belly of the first symbol he came across, the most cadaverous death-mask

Monza, 24 July 1900: anarchist Gaetano Bresci assassinates King Umberto 1 (Flavio Costantini)

his eyes had lighted upon, and who just turned out to the Serbian minister, a Monsieur Georgewich. The sort of thing that diplomatic incidents are made of. And what good had it done him? Goodnight to the cobbler. The Minister's place was taken by someone just as bad. "I'd have done better to have used dynamite", the cobbler had announced before he was hauled away for a beating. Yes, dynamite, and how!...

The last flicker died away and the candle burned out. Jules struck a match, searching for his cigarettes. He had one left. The first lungful set off his cough, but after the second, he felt a pleasant lightheadedness.

Paris, 12 February 1894: Emile Henry
(Flavio Costantini)

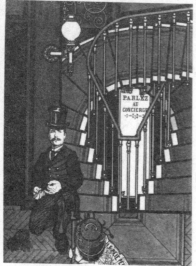

Paris, 11 March 1892: Ravachol (Flavio Costantini)

Gaetano Bresci came to mind and he wondered what could have driven a man to offer up his own life for the sake of setting an example. Three bullets fired into a king's chest, a king who was such a decent fellow that he had awarded the military medal to General Bava Beccaris for turning his artillery on demonstrators... At the time that Bresci was emptying his pistol into Umberto I, Jules had been receiving his sergeant's stripes. He had read the details in the press, locked in the latrines lest his superiors or any informer discover him. Less than a year after that Bresci had been beaten to death in solitary confinement. Suicide, so the official verdict ran. But what else could anyone have expected? In essence, his had been a suicide mission right from the start. As for kings, they always have children to pass the sceptre on to and control of the artillery to be trained on the crowd. There hadn't really been a single change in Italy, Jules concluded. But, when you got right down to it, was there actually any way of changing things? And had the murderous bombs of an Emile Henry or a Ravachol achieved anything? While Jules regarded the latter as a semi-lunatic, Henry had been an intellectual and a fine writer whose parents had fought on the side of the Paris Commune and he had been driven to the extremity of procuring three kilos of potassium chlorate, a flask of sodium and twenty sticks of dynamite after he had woken up to the fact that the spoken and written word availed nothing against the repression of the State. But the slaughter of bourgeois and of policemen had furnished the powers that be with a pretext on which to excite public opinion into acquiescing in the implementation of laws of which the worst of tyrannies would have been proud, laws equipping the police and the courts with unlimited powers in the persecution of "subversives". Ravachol, Henry and so many other anarchists had paid the price for their "exemplary" acts on the guillotine. So that they might be walked to the scaffold without giving any trouble, their testicles had been

Errico Malatesta, 1896
(Flavio Costantini)

bound with a leather strap attached to their wrists, a guarantee of absolute compliance. Reading those details, Jules had also felt the urge to excuse any act of slaughter. But the anarchist movement had emerged from all those bomb explosions broken. Errico Malatesta, who enjoyed implicit respect from Europe's anarchists, had been obliged to condemn these indiscriminate and bloodthirsty methods in public. Jules read and relished Malatesta's writings, but his sort of theories required two, three, ten generations of patient endeavour. Some day, who could say?, the world might take on a new consciousness, an egalitarian outlook, a so far unknown spirit of fraternity.

Meanwhile, life moved on and Jules had used up a lot of it to no particular purpose. He had never bowed his head, but what had he done that he could feel proud of? He had been a starveling, a failed hold-up man, a skilled workman waiting every time he started a new job, for the arrival of the inevitable dossier complied by some eager-beaver inspector... Even now that he had started work in the Berliet plant, could he hope to enjoy his meagre wages in peace? How long was it likely to last? And, yet again, the price to be paid was for him to hold his tongue and keep his nose out, lest his name end up on the desk of the nearest gendarmerie post.

So who would ever see the advent of the just society advocated by Malatesta? Maybe not even their children's children's children. And Jules Bonnot had even been denied the hope of making the world a better place for the sake of his son. Because he had no son now.

The image of Justin-Louis in Besson's arms tore the heart out of him. He opened his eyes wide in the darkness in order to banish the painful vision.

Action. Action was the only thing left. But action without sacrifice, without claim of responsibility, without offering one's throat to the hounds. Hitting the exploiters with their fondness for the guillotine and for champagne in precisely what they cherished most, their purse. Not for the sake of lining one's pockets, but so as to repay them in kind for a little of the terror they spread, so cocksure that they were unreachable. And not with bombs, but at gunpoint, wresting back a fraction of everything that they were hiding from the millions in despair.

"Or maybe just out of a taste for vengeance", he mused in his half-doze, not looking to impossible revolutions or to the enlightened societies of an all-too-distant future for excuses. In one final flash of insight, Jules, inside his head, cursed the daylight which was about to require him to walk through the gates at the Berliet plant again, facing the prospect of another twelve hours of dust, grease, sweat and degradation.

"You're wanted in the office."

Jules set the monkey-wrench down on the floor and crawled out from below the lorry. The chargehand was just checking his stop-watch, which he used to monitor the rate of the assembly line. One had only to be running ten seconds late and a reprimand would be issued.

"In the office?... How come?"

The foreman threw him a sidelong glance.

"How the hell should I know? Jules Bonnot. That's you, isn't it? Yes or No? Right then, leave your station and make your way to the office. You've ten minutes, starting from now. Now get a move on."

He used a rag to wipe his hands, climbed out of the inspection pit and tapped his feet together to clean his boots of the engine gunk and drained oil. Then he made his way briskly towards the offices. The foreman watched him go, wondering yet again what sort of a character this Bonnot was, how he was to rate him and, above all, what on earth could be going through his head while he held his tongue over a twelve-hour shift.

Jules tapped at the window. A guard opened it and nodded for him to come through. He reported to the office of the works manager, Monsieur Dupré, a corpulent fellow with a jovial manner, the man in charge of assembly of the new long-distance lorries.

"Ah, Bonnot!" he exclaimed, rubbing his hands as if delighted with this encounter. "Good news for you. Have a seat."

And he pointed him to a chair.

Jules went over, his hands slightly shaking, and sat down. A surge of adrenaline swelled the veins in his forehead. He was certain in his mind that this had to do with that inevitable blacklist and thus with his dismissal. But

Monsieur Dupré struck him, all-in-all, as a decent fellow. He wouldn't have greeted him like that just to show him the door. Yet he kept his muscles flexed and his hands clutched his beret.

"So, Bonnot. The company has decided to put some workers through their driving test. You have a thing about engines, which has not gone unnoticed. What do you think of that?"

Jules gestured vaguely, trying to get on top of the confusion in his head.

"A driving licence? " he mumbled. "And... then? I mean, I'm interested of course, but working on cylinder-heads... "

"Oh, we have bigger things in mind for you! Some lessons at driving school, your licence and then the chance of your driving the lorries leaving the works for the dealerships. After that, who knows?... we might even have need of you as an outside driver. Anything's possible. And as a driver, there'd be a small promotion in it for you."

The manager watched him for a few seconds, wearing a satisfied grin. Jules merely accepted.

"I don't see a lot of enthusiasm there, Bonnot."

"No, no... quite the opposite. Learning to drive is something I'd been hoping for for a long time. I'm much obliged to you, monsieur le directeur."

"Very well. You'll receive your training, starting on Monday. You can make the necessary arrangements"

His head buzzing, Jules returned to his place in the pit. The foreman stopped his stop-watch: eight minutes fifty six seconds. He drifted away, doing his best to disguise his obvious disappointment: lateness on Bonnot's part would have provided an ideal excuse for putting him to the test and drawing off some of the poison that he had inside him. Because there was no doubt, there was something fishy about this Bonnot and the way he looked at him was not at all to his liking...

The driving lessons unleashed his passion for mechanical vehicles yet again. He sailed through the test and on 17 September 1907 was awarded a dense bundle of papers peppered with dates and stamps and signatures and featuring his name and forename in capital letters.

He left the workshop and its pits filled with grease and gunk behind and turned his back for good on his heavy work-boots. Now he needed leather-soled shoes affording a delicate appreciation of the precise tension in the accelerator and brake pedals, so that he could make the requisite adjustments in the event of any need to press down or ease up. As far as the accelerator was concerned, he became so adept in its use that he could control it intuitively. True, it took brawn as well to drive the big Berliet trucks and often he was made to sweat while handling the big steering wheel, but Jules was not going to have to wait long before he could realise a little dream that he had been nurturing: getting his hands on the controls of Monsieur Dupré's Panhard or brand new Levassor.

"Forgive me, Jules... but beyond that little clump of plane trees, there's a rather sharp bend, with a ghastly pothole in the middle of the road. It you carry on with your foot to the floor, I'm afraid that my rheumatism might flare up again."

Jules promptly slowed down, blushing slightly in confusion. He had been speeding along on all six cylinders, having forgotten all about Monsieur Dupré.

"I beg your pardon. It's just... I was trying to put the engine through its paces. Testing out the revs., I mean, Monsieur Dupré."

"That's fine, don't worry. I was getting a bit carried away myself because, you know, I've never taken her up to this speed. But... Don't you thing something might give if you keep the engine running at maximum power?"

Jules took care to negotiate the bend with the utmost delicacy, neither tilting the big Panhard on its suspension nor rocking the manager from one side to the other. Then he turned around partly, without lifting his eyes from the road ahead.

"The valves could well overheat. But the crucial thing is that we keep an eye on the temperature and the oil levels. As long as she doesn't run out of oil, I don't reckon the engine will suffer any harm. Provided, of course, that we don't ask too much of her."

"Of course", Monsieur Dupré agreed, pretending to have understood all that.

In point of fact, even though he was a director at Berliet's, his concern was more with the assembly line and boosted throughput and, as far as engines went, his knowledge did not extend beyond the absolute minimum he needed to know. Besides, his assembly shop put together the cylinder heads for trucks which would be running in low gear and certainly not breaking any records.

"I can see that you're in your element here, handling a steering wheel", he added, testing the ground.

"I couldn't ask for anything better, Monsieur Dupré. Driving is more than just a job to me. How could I explain it to you... ?"

"Try, Jules", the manager replied.

"Here goes... The throbbing of an engine is like its language. It has a voice and a means of conveying what it likes and what ails it. The educated ear can pick up on every message, even the merest grinding noise or abnormal knocking..."

Dupré leant forward slightly, captivated.

"Go on, Jules."

"Well, Monsieur Dupré, I wouldn't want you think that I'm a bit touched. But to be honest I do believe that engines have souls."

Dupré's eyes widened and he smiled in amusement.

"Souls? Souls indeed! Ah, Jules, if only my wife could hear that, she'd start off by making the sign of the cross over you, then get out at the next church to ask the Lord for forgiveness..."

There was a momentary silence, then the manager erupted into laughter. Jules grinned as well, just to play along with him.

"You'll have to play it very careful", Dupré began again. "If you want to be my personal chauffeur, you'll have to learn to stay away from drawing comparisons between man's wretched handiwork and God. In my wife's view, dear Jules, modern cars are a sort of affront to the laws of the Creator. She's very God-fearing..."

He let out a noisy sigh that seemed to underline that a wife like that was a cross to bear.

"In Yvonne's view, there was nothing wrong with horses and they served the purpose, not to mention that horses are God's creatures, whereas cars might well prove to have a cloven hoof!"

And he burst into laughter again.

This time, Jules said nothing and merely stared straight ahead. His ears were burning. His hands weren't shaking now, but excitement had spread through his face and made his ears burn. Personal chauffeur... Monsieur Dupré really had said that, hadn't he? Jules had thought that his intention had been simply to spend a Sunday checking out his performance behind the wheel, or perhaps considering him as a stand-in driver when his own was away. In fact, he had just now discovered that the director meant to take him on as his driver... "

"Come now, Jules, let's not overdo it. You can step on the accelerator a little, this time at any rate, since there are just the two of us here. But remember to keep to a steady speed when another member of the family is around. Especially my wife. And keep clear of potholes. Otherwise the saintly lady will force me to revert to the horse cab."

"Monsieur Dupré... "

"I'm listening. Jules."

"Did you mean to say... that you'd take me on as your personal chauffeur?"

The director drew a cigar from his pocket, clipped it with some little silver scissors dangling from a chain and carefully lit it before finally saying:

"Why not? You know your way around a car and you're just what I need for the upkeep of mine. The driver I used to have was a good driver, but he knew nothing about engines. You can change a wheel, check the oil levels, the lights, the fan belt... In short, I need somebody who will not just drive me around but who can carry out basic maintenance so as to avoid a breakdown along the way. In which regard my wife could be close to the truth: a horse only stops when his heart gives out, but cars always have something going wrong with them."

"Which is what makes them even more delicate than horses. More sensitive."

Dupré exhaled a mouthful of dense white smoke. Once the breeze from the open window had dispersed the cloud, he leant forward again.

"Jules, tell me more about this business of a soul. What

did you mean by it?"

He needed no coaxing. During the half hour that it took them to get to the country house, Jules regaled him with his theory of the osmosis between man and car, the synchronised throbbing of heart and pistons, the transmission belts being like tendons, and tempered steel like a nervous system, liable to reach breaking-point due to excessive tension, and how important it was to "sound" the car just the way one would a horse, so as to assess its strengths and weaknesses, and to shower it with love, savouring the harmony of all the parts which, by some magical mystery, brought forth energy, speed and power.

Monsieur Dupré listened enthralled, thinking that maybe this young man was a bit of a queer fish and definitely different from what he had imagined, but that, deep down, there was rather more to him than to the others: an infectious, overpowering, passionate enthusiasm. An enthusiasm that boded well, if directed along the right lines. The very next day he would send him off to his tailor to be measured for a uniform, complete with cap and black boots, as befitted the chauffeur of a Berliet director.

Things went splendidly with the lady Yvonne. She would count her beads as she gazed out on the countryside while mumbling ejaculatory prayers, crossing herself as she passed by churches, graveyards, sanctuaries, the monuments commemorating the soldiers who had perished in action and, in some instances, even the cement blocks measuring out the kilometres along the national highway, and which she mistook for tombstones or who knows what else. Jules drove with extreme caution; the good lady would not deign to look at him, but her haughty silence meant that she greatly appreciated the services of the new chauffeur.

"He avoids the potholes", was the only comment he heard her make to her husband.

And that was something.

With Monsieur Dupré, things were going swimmingly. For a representatve of the ruling class, he was, if anything, too likable. To be honest, Jules was in a bit of a quandary, in the sense that he was retreating from certain absolute certainties, along the lines of "The bosses are all swine", or other catchphrases which he had long since taken to heart. It is true that Dupré wasn't really a boss, but was a director: however, in the light of Jules's past experiences, that sort had always treated him worse than the bosses. In short, he was forced to concede that just being on the opposite side of the barricades didn't automatically make one a swine. All in all, he had a high regard for the man. And he could not understand how he had managed to reconcile his kindness and cordiality with his function in society. Besides, Monsieur Dupré was jovial, light-hearted and ready to share a glass of pastis with his driver, and Jules had learnt to recognise the way he lowered his voice as he pointed out a roadside tavern, as if stopping off for a drink was somehow undignified, something one should take great care to treat gingerly, with a whispered:

"Hey, Jules, what would you say to our pulling in for a while to rinse the dust from our mouths?"

Yes, this curious brand of industrial manager tickled his fancy. And so, one time he had ventured to express an opinion about his plans to stand in the elections. Dupré talked about this in vague terms, about something that might happen sometime in the future, but Jules couldn't help but offer a confidence and had told him:

"If I were you, I'd give politicians a wide berth."

Dupré was startled into silence. But he had not cold-shouldered him as convention required when one's driver said something out of place. A few kilometres further on, he had pressed him:

" And, as you see it, why shouldn't I stand?"

Jules had shrugged his shoulders and said:

"Because, Momsieur Dupré, you don't have fangs sharp enough nor is it your habit to trample over your neighbours."

An embarrassed silence ensued and it lasted until they reached their destination.

Dupré had been at a loss for at least two days. And he never raised the matter again with Jules.

That lasted for some months. Time enough for illusions to grow.

One morning, Monsieur Dupré hailed Jules without the usual lightheartedness and without the usual wisecrack. Taking care to avoid speaking to him, he spent much of the trip poring over the papers in his briefcase. As they reached Montplaisir, he pointed to a little side road.

"Sorry... Do you want me to turn here?" Jules asked.

Dupré agreed with a grunt of irritation. Jules slowed down and was moved to say:

"The surface is very rough here, sir. And, what with the rain this evening, I wouldn't want us to get bogged down .."

"Okay, okay. Pull up wherever you can."

Jules did just that, at a loss as to what on earth they were supposed to be doing out in the fallow fields. He picked out a bank where the earth seemed less saturated and grassy enough not to give way under the car's weight. He locked the hand-brake and turned to look at the director, awaiting further instructions.

"Come on, Jules. Let's stretch our legs a little."

Jules followed him, feeling increasingly uneasy.

They walked on for a few minutes, then Dupré stopped abruptly, removed his hat and pushed a hand nervously through his greying hair.

"Dear God! What do you want me to do now!"

He was thrown. Jules had never heard an oath from him before.

"I don't follow... What do you mean, Monsieur Dupré?"

The director looked him right in the eye for the first time and chewed his lip as he searched for the right words.

"Listen, Jules... Personally, I have no quarrel with you. Try to understand me. I trusted you and I'd have trusted you with anything, even the lives of my children! And it isn't every day that someone in my position lets his children go walking on their own with the chauffeur! Have you any idea how much I trusted you?"

He was speaking in the past tense. Jules felt all the energy drain from him as he resigned himself to what was to follow.

"And last evening... the prefect of police came around for dinner. You appreciate, Jules, that someone in my position... and nothing to do with the elections, for the love of heaven! But the plant would never forgive me. They'll soon be in the know, so I'd rather be the first to tell you and look for the least painful resolution for both our sakes."

Jules nodded. He was no longer wondering where things were leading, so plain did the final outcome look to him.

"You see, the prefect spoke to me in confidence... He said that a few days from now a dossier on you is to be forwarded to the plant."

Jules attempted a melancholy smile.

"Good heavens, I can't leave myself wide open. You understand? Even if I were to refuse to follow their... their advice, the plant would act upon it. And you'd be dismissed in any case. Because it's the plant that pays your wages. They assigned me a driver and I... I... what could I do?"

"Not a thing, Monsieur Dupré", Jules mumbled.

In a sudden fit of anger, the director slammed a fist into his open palm.

"Damn it, Jules! But can you explain to me what on earth your connection with these people is? Eh? You, in cahoots with these criminals, killers tossing bombs into courtrooms, into police stations... ?"

"I throw no bombs anywhere, Monsieur Dupré."

"That's all we'd need! That would put the tin hat on it! But you're on record as an anarchist, and, these days, anarchists cannot be kept on at a big firm of national repute. Let alone at Berliet's!"

Dupré paced nervously up and down, shaking his head:

"I'm not saying that you're some mad assassin... no. But the police consider you dangerous, someone to be kept at arm's length. If it was up to me, if I were your pay-master, I'd have laughed in the prefect's face and told him to concentrate on more serious business!"

"Are you sure about that, Monsieur Dupré?" Jules ventured.

The two men looked each other up and down for a few seconds. Jules could see from the pained expression that the director probably would have given that sort of an answer. And it was he that lowed his eyes first:

"You're not to blame. I know that. It's out of your hands."

Dupré clenched his fists and looked out over the fields.

"There are some laws... overly stringent and maybe wrong-headed laws, perhaps... but, my God, it's a far cry from that to planting bombs. You've unleashed the barbarians! And we've come to a point where one need only be on file as an anarchist in order to wind up crushed... "

His eyes switched back to Jules. Dupré's eyes were twinkling and he seemed to have aged a lot. Powerlessness had wrought a change in him.

"Jules... would you be in a position to explain to me what anarchists expect of this society? Because I just can't fathom that, you see... "

"As for the anarchists, I couldn't say. But as for myself, Monsieur Dupré... I have no expectations."

PARIS, 1908

To Victor, the city of the sumptuous Champs-Elysées — the city of the Grands Boulevards with their shining windows, the city of well-groomed parks where ladies and gentlemen, in couples, would parade their elegant clothing and precious trinkets — was a strange place, enemy territory. His Paris was a grey maze of canals, graveyards, waste ground and crumbling buildings, rising from the working class districts of Charonne to the heights of Belleville and Ménilmontant, districts teeming with a noisy, chaotic humanity, mud-spattered in winter and dust-covered in summer-time, frantically busy earning its daily bread and trying to stay alive. Among these dishevelled, haughty ladies and insolent, often shady menfolk, ready to attempt any crime and capable of the vilest acts, underneath the iron bridges where the breeze reeked of putrefaction, sweat and rotting fruit, Victor found himself on home ground again, mixing with rebels without country, eternal outsiders who claimed to be anarchists because only anarchy could express all the various interpretations of revolt. Even these anarchists' very own Montmartre stamping ground was different from the Montmartre of cabarets, artists, oil-painters and balmy sunny mornings. The only cabaret they frequented — a sort of no man's land between bohemia and penury — was old Frédé's Lapin Agile, where they sang along to the ballads of François Villon, the vagabond, rebel poet who came to a bad end on the gallows. Their Montmartre was laid out at the foot of the dusty, stone-strewn sites where the basilica of Sacré-Coeur was slowly taking shape against the backdrop of walls stained with the blood of the last executed Communards. It was there that Victor made the acquaintance of a fellow of indeterminate age, half-tramp and half-preacher, who hobbled around on crutches but whose upper body was powerful, who had a mane of wavy hair and a bushy beard. Albert Libertad, brawler, inspired orator, indefatigable agitator and unrepentant Don Juan, would mingle with the poor queueing for their meals just a few steps from the construction sites and would sow disorder and incite rebellion, holding off-the-cuff aggressive, violent meetings which, thanks to his irresistible charisma, would end in brawling with the gendarmes. And Libertad certainly was not one to hold back; he would flail those crutches of his, cursing furiously. His anarchist individualism was rooted in one simple doctrine, blindingly clear in its watchwords: "Don't wait for revolution. Those who hold out the promise of revolution are clowns like the rest. Being free men means living like free men. One doesn't build up to anarchy. All we can do is be an anarchist and live like an anarchist."

Libertad had launched a review, *L'Anarchie*, drafted and printed in an old house in Montmartre that served as a sort of a commune, forever prey to a frenzied parade of failures, ringing to the sound of singing, laughter, heated discussion, the clatter of printing and presses. Victor started to drop by this house and very quickly became an ideological reference point and a tireless contributor, whether there was an inflammatory article that needed writing or he had to carry bundled copies on his shoulder for distribution. Shortly after that, in 1908, Libertad was implicated in yet another clash and this time he was jumped by too many policemen

Albert Libertad (Flavio Costantini)

for his crutches to cope with. Given a bloody beating, he was removed to hospital. He died there, but not before he had penned this short will and testament: "My carcass I leave to the students of anatomy, for them to use in the advancement of science." After that, Victor became the leading light behind *L'Anarchie*, making his stand on Elisée Reclus's principles of "permanent revolution", preaching the utter necessity of revolt but distancing himself more and more from the suicidal course chosen by the "illegalists". Purporting to live on the margin of society, Victor argued, is an illusion, for society has no margins. One had no option but to be part of it and picking up a weapon to break free of the cycle of exploitation merely meant becoming a wanted man.

And then, one day, Raymond showed up.

He had grown weary of sunlit roads and fresh air, rain and wind. And Paris had drawn him like an irresistible magnet. The solitary life had soured him, making him even more radical in his options. He professed a deep-seated love of science which he thought of as offering a solution to humanity's ills and he believed a strict vegetarian diet to offer a remedy to the world's violence. But as to the violence of men, Raymond was a true believer in illegalism. And he hadn't come alone. Somehow he had teamed up with Édouard Carouy who had decided to follow him to the capital. They were delighted to see Victor again and for a few hours it was all celebration. But later, their ideological differences and differing life preferences cropped up again in more aggravated political form. There followed an irreconcilable rift at *L'Anarchie*. A fascination with direct action and personal revolt was eventually fleshed out as a dangerous brand of fetishism. Raymond and Édouard were in a morbid love affair with firearms and ammunition. Like them, many anarchists started to go around with guns tucked in their waistbands. Worn out, Victor washed his hands of *L'Anarchie* which passed into those of Raymond and his illegalists.

The Advent of the Slot Machine

Monsieur Dupré had handed him a letter of recommendation in which he was described as an outstanding driver, skilled in engine maintenance, a discreet person who enjoyed his trust, and other statements which might one day return to haunt the director at Berliet's. But the jovial, affable fellow, such a contrast to the superiors Jules had been used to, had written the letter in the rip of a wave of unconditional affection for his chauffeur whom the police and a fair segment of society regarded as an incorrigible thug. Jules thanked him for it.

Monsieur Dupré shook his hand but avoided looking him in the eye — and that was the end of his ninth honest job.

Jules was none too sure what to do with this reference. In France, anybody who hired him would sooner or later be forced to let him go. Car owners who could also afford chauffeurs were persons of influence and often so close to the authorities that they could not make do with a mere letter awash with his praises. They would have been looking for further information and it would have been back to the streets again. Jules thought that Monsieur Dupré had gone out on a limb for him to no avail and that it would be compromising him if he used his name in his search for a new position. Even so, he kept the scrap of paper in one of the pockets in his bag, more as a souvenir of an almost idyllic period than with any hope of ever driving a limousine again with a chauffeur's uniform on his back.

In order to get by, he came up with a rather odd pursuit in a field that looked like expanding rapidly; he distributed slot machines imported from America to cabarets and casinos and looked after their maintenance. He found himself a shabbily dressed associate, one Blumenthal, a Jew of around fifty years of age, swamped by debts but rich in terms of optimism, with whom he dreamt for a time of making some quick, easy money. But already competition in the industry was cut-throat.

One evening Jules was driving the truck loaded with slot machines that they had picked up from a ship docked in Le Havre for immediate delivery to Paris. Blumenthal was snoring alongside him, sleeping off the litres of beer that he had downed, as usual. He never seemed to get drunk but he was eternally adrift in a state of blissful semi-consciousness, lulled by the beer that blurred the sharp edges of his present and future problems. Jules didn't like drunkards, but at least Blumenthal was always up-beat and had the advantage of dropping off to sleep before he could become unbearable. As they rounded a bend, the headlights of a car sitting stationary in the middle of the road flicked on. Jules braked and Blumenthal bumped his head against the windscreen.

"For heaven's sake, Jules... what possessed you?"

They weren't given time to say more. The barrel of a revolver was thrust against Blumenthal's cheek (he having left his window rolled down) while the door on the driver's side was pulled wide open and a heavy-set fellow pointed a sawn-off shotgun at Jules's belly. Jules climbed out without a word, keeping his hands in clear view. When they were both in front of the dazzling headlights, a man emerged from the dense shrubbery and greeted them:

"Evening, gents. We're sorry, but your journey stops here."

Elegantly dressed, a ring sparkling in his ear, and with golden buttons on his sleeve, the man sighed and feigned regret.

"It's a lousy line of work, take it from me. The sooner you get out of it the more likely you'll be to be left to live in peace."

He signalled to the hot-head behind him who strode towards the lorry, wielding a two-headed, long-handled fireman's axe. Another leapt quickly on to the back of the lorry and started pushing out the brand-new slot machines. The great ape hit each machine smack dab in the body, just one blow, but with such force as to wreck the mechanism. The clatter of crushed plate metal and burst springs left poor Blumenthal cowering and every new blow seemed to make him shrink even further. Jules showed no reaction. He was watching the guy holding them at revolver point. The big dandy was definitely armed, judging by the bulge in his jacket, but with a bit of luck he might knock him down and give him a smack before he had a chance to draw his gun. The problem was Blumenthal: he couldn't expect the slightest assistance from him, given his state. Now he was sobbing openly and mumbling:

"How am I going to pay for these... They're going to kill me, I owe them so much money... "

The dandy shook his head and said:

"You should have thought about that earlier. We did warn you."

Jules had no idea what this meant and he felt a sudden hatred for Blumenthal who had kept him in the dark about the risks. The guy with the revolver burst out laughing, his body rocking, and for a fraction of a second he was distracted when Jew collapsed on to his knees. Jules darted forward, elbowing him in the jaw and leaving his arms dangling. The guy spun around but did not drop the gun straight away and by the time Jules managed to wrest it from him, the sawn-off shotgun was pressing against the back of his head.

The gang leader came over, weighing him up with amusement.

"You're quick off the mark, my lad. And you're not short of gumption. There are four of us and you... well, since your deadweight associate has shit his trousers, we might as well say that you're completely on your own. Bravo. You're just the sort of quick-thinking fellow I'm on the look-out for."

The guy who had been elbowed in the face got to his feet, daubing at his bleeding mouth with a handkerchief. He spat out a tooth and threw a glance at his boss, hoping for permission to take his revenge. But the boss stopped him in his tracks with a sharp gesture.

"Easy does it, Gachot. I'm still waiting for the lad's reply."

Jules stared right back at him and mumbled:

"No, thanks. I've had enough. You're right. It is a lousy line of work."

"Are we quite sure about that?" the fellow asked mockingly, as if addressing a child in need of coaxing.

"Quite sure," Jules replied.

The dandy made a disappointed face, then turned to the guy with the split lip and nodded wearily. Which was all the confirmation this guy had been waiting for. He punched Jules three times in the bread-basket, followed up by three underhanded kicks that took his breath away and doubled him over. He collapsed face down and was only spared a back-heel right in the face because the boss snapped peremptorily:

"That'll do, Gachot."

Raising one hand, he gave the order for them to withdraw. The guy with the sawn-off emptied one barrel into the front left tyre and the other into the windscreen;

the big ape with the axe swung it into one headlight and then the other and cleft the radiator in two with a blow of which any professional executioner would have been proud.

The raiders climbed back into their vehicle and vanished into the night. By the time Jules struggled to his feet again, the purring of the engine had already died away in the distance. Meanwhile, Blumenthal had started walking in the opposite direction, grizzling at the moon.

Jules trotted along behind him. The nearest village with a railway halt was at least fifteen kilometres away.

"Time for a change of scenery and to get out of this mess," he thought to himself, dragging his feet and rubbing his belly from which a sinister gurgling came with every step he took.

SIR ARTHUR'S NEW DRIVER

The engine of the Landulet Lanchester purred monotonously and regularly as it powered through the Sussex countryside. The sixteen horse-power lurking beneath the bonnet could have provided some additional speed, but today the owner, Sir Arthur, was in no special hurry to reach his destination. Seated comfortably in the back seat, comfortable enough for him to throw one leg over the other, with the inevitable cigar in his hand, Sir Arthur was chatting with his friend and fellow author, Ashton Wolfe. The driver watched the road and seemed focused on his driving, but in fact he never missed a word of the conversation going on behind him.

Sir Arthur Conan Doyle

"To be honest, my dear Arthur," Ashton was saying, raising his voice, a sure sign that he was feeling excited, "I find the title in the worst possible taste: Arsène Lupin versus Sherlock Holmes. For a start, he had an obligation to seek your leave and... "

"Leave?" Sir Arthur interjected. "But it's only a game with him, indicative of his intention of poking fun at the poor cocaine-fiend."

He stroked his thick moustache, with just the hint of an amused smile. Ashton sighed and tapped the door.

"Yes, yes, I'm familiar with your little digs at Holmes, and even though I may not agree, I'll concede that you're quite within your rights to deal with your creation however you see fit. But you should be on your guard against certain slights!"

Sir Arthur frowned, his drooping moustache drooping even lower.

"Come, come, Ashton... what you term my creation has turned into a veritable ball-and-chain tugging at my ankles, a real curse and I'm not sure any more how to go about freeing myself of him. But we've said enough on that subject already, so let's drop it. As for slights, let's not exaggerate. Maurice Leblanc is perfectly within his rights to poke fun at a character who has acquired greater renown and more reality than his upstart author. I certainly am not about to complain. On the other hand, I think one good way of limiting the damage done by Holmes might in fact be to start to poke fun at him."

Ashton sighed, turned to take a look at the countryside and let the matter drop. But a short time later he couldn't resist saying:

"Unheard of. His own creator is his most implacable detractor. You're wrong, Arthur and I've lost count of the number of times I've told you that."

"Yes, you may even have told me it a little too often," replied Sir Arthur, delicately flicking the ash from his cigar with the nail of his little finger. "And, take it from me, poor Leblanc will also wind up cursing his character, come the day he realises that people are going to remember Arsène Lupin longer than they will his creator. And, like myself, he can write something much more worthy and a lot more profound, but the public, silly and shallow as it is, will continue to be interested only the adventures of his gentleman burglar. I'm just wondering if he's aware of the predicament he has created for himself."

Then, in an attempt to change the subject, he called out to his driver:

"Tell me, Jules, have you ever heard tell of one Arsène Lupin?"

And he winked an eye at Ashton, inviting him to listen for the answer.

Jules pretended not to have been following the conversation and, suddenly attentive, asked:

"Arsène Lupin, did you say, Sir Arthur?"

"I did. Does the name mean anything to you? Countryman of yours in fact," Sir Arthur added, winking again at Ashton who was now leaning forwards lightly.

"Yes, I know," Jules stated blandly.

Ashton wore an expression of exaggerated interest, relishing what was to follow. They had had a chat about the character of the new driver, whom Sir Arthur reckoned was educated far beyond the average and downright exceptional in picking up the English language, in which he had made great strides in just a few weeks. Ashton, sceptical as ever, queried whether a person of intelligence and an educated one at that could settle for that line of work. So, in light of Jules's reply, he pressed him, maliciously:

"And tell me this. Where might you have come across this Monsieur Lupin?"

"In France, Sir Ashton," Jules calmly replied. "Not personally, alas. But I know enough about him to consider him an interesting character. Very interesting."

He bit his lip and his eyes returned to the road. He could sense that he had said too much. But these two Englishmen hadn't even the remotest idea of the character they were talking about, and Ashton Wolfe's sarcastic tone was starting to get on his nerves.

"Forgive me, Jules," Sir Arthur piped up. "There might be some mistake here. Arsène Lupin is the hero of a novel, an invention of your countryman, a certain Maurice Leblanc. "

"No, Sir Arthur," Jules interrupted, with unaccustomed confidence. "Leblanc invented only the name, not the character. And if he were a man of honour, he would pay a portion of his royalties to the rightful inspiration behind his little novels."

A jolt caused by a pot-hole closed Ashton's mouth with a dry clicking sound. He was fortunate not to bite his tongue. As for Sir Arthur, he had dropped some cigar ash on to his belly.

"I seem to discern a degree of sourness with regard to Leblanc in your remarks, dear Jules. May I ask what wrong he ever did you?"

"Me? None. But he is lining his pockets at the expense of a man who is no longer in a position to defend himself. Even though I imagine that Jacob must burst out laughing when he reads his books."

"Just a moment," Sir Arthur asked hurriedly. "Tell me, who was this Jacob?"

Jules took his time, using the pretext of wiping the dust from his goggles with a cloth he kept beside him. Why had he allowed himself to be dragged into this nonsensical discussion? He shouldn't have showed his hand to that extent. The serious-minded driver who kept his opinions to himself, as it appeared to his employer, could not suddenly indulge in a resentful plea on behalf of a man who, in his eyes, was courageous and exceptionally dignified, but who was, in the view of the two English gentlemen seated behind him, primarily a criminal and incorrigible thief.

"Well, Jules?" Ashton pressed him.

"Marius Jacob is the fellow who carried out at least three hundred raids at the expense of the wealthiest individuals in

Paris, 1 October 1901: Alexander Marius Jacob (Flavio Costantini)

France and the police were never able to understand how he did it. He is Arsène Lupin. All Maurice Leblanc did was to read up on his exploits, top him up with champagne and surround him with affected flibberty-gibbets, that's all."

"Damn it!" Jules thought. "If they're writers, let them learn a little something about real life." And if this meant his placing himself at a disadvantage, too bad. Marius Jacob was worth that gamble. It was the least that he could do for him.

Sir Arthur winked triumphantly at his friend Ashton. He had told him after all that his French driver was a surprising fellow. Then, intrigued, he asked Jules:

"And where might one find this gentleman?"

"In French Guyana. Hard labour for life."

Ashton stifled a laugh then pronounced sarcastically:

"Lupin has shown greater skill, up to now at least. If this Jacob of yours finished up in Guyana, he couldn't have been all that uncatchable."

"An accident down to third parties," Jules replied. "He was finally trapped on account of his refusal to abandon his friends in difficulty."

"So it was not his practice to work alone," added Sir Arthur, smoothing his moustache repeatedly, a signal of the deep interest that the conversation had aroused in him.

"Sometimes it was, sometimes it wasn't," Jules explained. "It all depended on the nature of the job. When he did need assistance, he had valiant helpers he could turn to. They were known as the 'Night Shift'. But he was always the brains. Without Marius Jacob, the others couldn't have done anything."

The two Englishmen exchanged a lingering glance. Ashton shook his head. This French fellow was proving to be a really singular individual. For a common driver, he could converse on the most unlikely matters.

"And could you describe one of these stunning criminal enterprises for us?" Sir Arthur ventured.

Jules braked delicately and backed up. A herd of cattle had just trooped across the road and the last one, seemingly fascinated by Sir Arthur Conan Doyle's Landaulet, stood in the middle of the road watching with an attentiveness odd in a a cow. Jules pressed on the horn several times. The cowherd doubled back and brought his stick down on the rump of the cow who, without displaying any particular resentment, decided to take a few steps forwards while continuing to look over its shoulder at the strange creature making the rattling noise and belching the acrid smell of stale smoke. Jules accelerated to normal speed and a few moments later decided to tell the tale:

"Everybody, or nearly everybody in France remembers Marius Jacob's first massive bluff. It was back in 1897, I think. Like his other coups, this one only came to light because he disclosed it at the trial. He was a master of the art of disguise. But on this occasion he made do with posing as the 'secretary' of one of his associates, posing as someone older with more gravitas and donning top hat and wearing a tricolour sash across his chest. They showed up at the pawnbroker's shop and waved a phony warrant under the manager's nose that referred to receiving stolen goods and, after double-locking the door, they set about drawing up an inventory. Given that in the world of the money-lender there is always some sort of usury to be covered up, it definitely didn't occur to the manager to obstruct them. After three hours of painstaking investigation and having drawn up a list of the most valuable items which were to finish up inside their enormous suitcase, Jacob slipped some handcuffs on to the manager and told him that he very much regretted that he was obliged to arrest him pending inquiries.

Sir Arthur carried on smoothing the right side of his moustache, while Ashton, who was showing signs of impatience, exclaimed:

"And they left the poor fellow, cuffed at the wrist, in the pawn-shop?"

Jules shook his head.

"No, because Marius Jacob was not so much interested in robbery as in holding institutions up to ridicule in the most spectacular fashion. The poor broker," he repeated sarcastically, "suffered from a bad conscience on account of certain high-interest loans extended on valuable items on his behalf, and he was too busy thinking up an excuse to offer the judge. Jacob had him climb into a waiting cab, ordered the cabbies to take them straight to the courthouse and escorted the manager straight to the office of the official prosecutor. He had the manager take a seat on a bench in the corridor, stepped inside the office where he made some run-of-the-mill inquiry, and returned to the corridor where he removed the handcuffs from his victim, telling him to wait until the prosecutor called him in for the usual questioning. And before leaving with the suitcase stuffed with gold, he cautioned him that this was regarded as a very serious business. "

Sir Arthur chortled noiselessly. Ashton threw him a stunned look.

"Do you see something funny in that?" he asked.

"Not funny, inspired," replied Sir Arthur.

"You're talking about a criminal convict in Guyana, not about Leblanc's Arsène Lupin."

Sir Arthur shrugged his shoulders before relighting his cigar and saying:

"Intelligence and resourcefulness can be misused and placed in the service of crime, but that does not mean that we should not acknowledge them. Anyway, dear Ashton, fate always has the final say. Look at me: as a young man in Edinburgh I was quarrelsome, I used to mix with street thugs and often came home with a black eye and my clothes in tatters. Oh, of course, I usually did it in defence of the weak but my idea of fairness amounted to out-punching the strong. And had my brawling seriously injured an opponent or, worse, unfortunately ended his life, I'd have ended up in prison. I doubt if I'd be sitting here now, comfortably ensconced in this vehicle and savouring my sumptuous royalty payments."

Ashton sighed dubiously and, in so doing, breathed in part of the dense cloud of smoke spreading through the interior and enveloping the occupants before it could be dispersed by the wind. Sir Arthur raised one hand by way of apology, then turned to Jules.

"And the manager of this pawnbroker's, how long did it take him to catch on that a ferocious trick had been played on him?"

"All day," Jules answered, trying not to betray his delight.

"You mean to say that no one asked him what he was doing there, sitting on a bench in the courthouse?" Ashton queried, coughing in order to clear his throat.

"When closing time came around," Jules explained, "an usher came up and the manager started to shout that he was an innocent man, that he knew nothing about receiving stolen goods and such like, which seemed confused but also suspicious to the examining magistrate who had just stepped into the corridor. So he ordered that the manager be placed in a cell until the matter could be cleared up the following day."

"But," Ashton cried, "how did he have him arrested without so much as knowing the charge against him?"

"You see," said Jules off-handedly, "the fact is that the judge was in a hurry to get home and if he had started to make inquiries, draw up a report and open up a new file he'd have had to stay there all evening. It was better to put if off until the following day, rather than to have to resort to extraordinary procedures."

Sir Arthur began to chuckle quietly, his lips clamped shut without making a sound, and was content to rock while smoothing his moustache.

"I must say," he concluded as the vehicle slowed and pulled up outside the gate to the house, "that this Marius Jacob of yours is unquestionably more interesting than the little frock-coated gent so beloved of readers. And Monsieur Leblanc would have a more or less moral obligation to dedicate all of his famous books to him. "

"And what of yourself?" Ashton asked. "Haven't you anyone to thank for being the model for Holmes?"

"Unfortunately not," replied Sir Arthur, turning serious. "If that were the case I could tell people: This is the real Holmes. Go and harass him and leave me in peace once and for all."

Paris, 1 October 1901: Alexander Marius Jacob (Flavio Costantini)

Tours Cathedral, 28 March 1903: Alexander Marius Jacob (Flavio Costantini)

THE MAN WHO TRIED TO KILL SHERLOCK HOLMES

The bed was softer and more comfortable than any he had ever known in the past, and the room, most likely the smallest room in the house, was every bit as spacious as any of the studios he had shared with Sophie; care had been put into every detail, from the engravings on the walls to the carpet on the floor, from the polished walnut tallboy to the worm-eaten desk with all its drawers and compartments, at which he spent much of his free time poring over the books that Sir Arthur allowed him to borrow from his library. There was a wide selection, but it did not include the writings for which Jules had a soft spot: Mikhail Bakunin and Pierre-Joseph Proudhon were not among the thinkers favoured by Sir Arthur who, to be honest, preferred epic war stories to social issues, or, and Jules found this intriguing, favoured countless treatises on spiritualism and the occult sciences. The main hurdle was still the language. Jules made an effort to read in English, in order to polish his language skills and enhance his vocabulary, but there was a huge difference between sustaining a conversation and grasping the subtleties of literature. In the huge library that occupied much of the ground floor, he had come across several French texts and a few translations of Sir Arthur's novels featuring Sherlock Holmes. It was one of the former that Jules was reading by gaslight when he heard two little taps on the door followed by Sir Arthur's serious voice and polished tones:

"Am I disturbing you, Jules?"

He went over to open up, stuffing his shirt hurriedly into his trousers.

"Relax, please. I've come to disturb you because I've had to change my plans for tomorrow. We have to be in London by early afternoon, so I'll have to leave early if I'm to have time to sort out a few matters with my publisher."

"No problem," said Jules. "I was intending to turn in once I reached the end of the chapter anyway," he added, gesturing towards the night stand.

Sir Arthur nodded and was just about to leave when curiosity drew his eye to the cover of the book set on the bedside table: Victor Hugo's *Les Misérables*.

"An outstanding read," he exclaimed, with a little mischievous smile. "I only hope I'm not harbouring a Bonapartist under my roof."

Jules did not dare explain to him that, having read it before in the French, he was only re-reading it in order to improve his English. Instead, and for no particular reason, he shot back:

"He was no worse that his predecessors and those who defeated him."

"Who, Napoleon?" Sir Arthur pressed him, laughing.

Jules made no answer. He was wondering what it was that impelled him to react every time the writer amused himself by teasing him. He could have said nothing and avoided taking any risks. But he couldn't always help himself and sometimes he simply had to answer, thereby breaking the priceless silence that had long been one of his basic rules in life.

"My dear Jules," Sir Arthur resumed in amused tones, "before you get carried away, I ought to tell you that, on the side of my maternal grandparents, I am descended from the Packs. And that a Sir Denis Pack was in charge of the Scots Brigade at Waterloo, where another great-uncle of mine,

Anthony Pack, lost part of his skull to one of Napoleon's men. So you'd be in danger of mentioning the rope in the home of a hanged man. "

"I never found a bit of an English skull among my family souvenirs. I doubt it was one of my great uncles who cracked your great uncle's skull."

The two men looked at each other for a moment. Then Sir Arthur burst out laughing, but this time the laughter was unalloyed and light-hearted, a quite different laughter from the snigger that he normally allowed himself in public.

Jules smiled too and, lifting the book from the night stand, he said: "I found this one much more entertaining. I hope you have others in my native tongue."

Sir Arthur saw the French edition of one of his Sherlock Holmes books, his brow wrinkling with a sigh as his thick moustache dropped even further and he exclaimed:

"Good heavens! Jules, I'll leave you to get on with it. "

And he was about to go when he turned more conciliatory and added:

"Well, at least you've started with the last in the series. Or what I had hoped was going to be the last at any rate."

"I don't understand, Sir Arthur," Jules mumbled, shaking his head.

"What is there to understand?"

"This irritation of yours with the character to whom you owe your worldwide renown."

The writer let out a groan that rose from his heart rather than his throat. Then he made a rather resigned gesture and said:

"Alright, Jules. Since it's not all that late, if you wish, I'll give you an explanation in the library over the cognac which has just arrived from your beloved homeland."

Jules agreed to the suggestion and swallowed any remark about it not being his plan to comment on how "beloved" his homeland was.

Sir Arthur led Jules downstairs and once in the library he showed his driver to a soft easy chair before pouring two generous measures of cognac into a couple of capacious glasses. He then handed one to Jules who wasn't quite sure how to receive it, and sat on the nearby sofa. After a first mouthful, he began:

"I can't stand Sherlock Holmes any more because he's become a blight on my life. I started out writing these novels for amusement and you've just described the one you're in the process of reading as 'entertaining'. But I didn't realise the sort of nonsense he was going to elicit from the public. It's a rather morbid thing. It triggers the same sort of process as jealousy does in affairs of the heart. The reader becomes infatuated with what someone has written and yearns for the author to carry on feeding that infatuation and woe betide the author if he lets him down. These days I write books of much greater literary merit, on more profound and interesting topics. But to no avail. Now people want just one thing from me: for me to carry on churning out blockbusters filled with Holmes and Watson and a whole menagerie of criminals of all sorts."

He finished his cognac and poured himself another. Jules reached over with his own glass. Then they moved on to the cigars and, after lighting these, amid a dense cloud hovering in the centre of the great library, Sir Arthur resumed, in less aggressive tones but with just a hint of melancholy:

"Do you know, my dear Jules, how this is going to end? One of these days the world will remember the detective's name and his assistant's but not that of their creator. And very few people will bother to read my serious works, my historical novels, my essays, the pages into which I've put the best of myself, as an author and as a researcher ."

He blew smoke slowly into the air, staring at a stack of books on a shelf.

"In the very book you're reading I tried. I said to myself: At last I've summoned up the courage to rid myself of him. I even wrote a letter of condolence to my mother, telling her that Holmes had come to his last adventure and that the mere mention of his name irked me. It sparked a sort of a revolt. There followed an avalanche of mail, of objections. One lady called me a brute, and many of them wrote to Watson to plead for his help. Can you understand that? Would you believe me if I were to tell you that in one factory they even went on strike against me for having put Sherlock Holmes to death?"

Jules nodded and tried to look understanding. He was beginning to feel a little bored with this trivial resentment. He could not help comparing the tragedies in his own life with the dramas of an author obsessed with a character. With increasing anger he thought of the news reports he had read the evening before about the Welsh miners' strike, comparing them with the imbeciles who had downed tools, not in order to put food on the table for their families, but in order to plead for Sherlock Holmes to return.

"I've been obliged to bring him back to life," Sir Arthur said, tapping on the arm of the sofa. "The first and only act of cowardice in my life. And do you know the reason why?"

Jules shrugged and pretended to be intrigued, but inside he was thinking to himself: "What the hell difference does it make to me? I'm beginning to feel sleepy and tomorrow I'm to drive you for hours on end, me exposed to the wind and you sheltered and lounging in the rear of that silly car you've bought yourself. "

"Because, after I buried Holmes at the Reichenbach Falls," Sir Arthur droned on, "I found that my bank account also came to its end, gobbled up and drained in just a few months."

Jules made an effort to look stunned.

"An out-and-out boycott. Nobody was buying a single copy of my books any more. It was Sherlock Holmes or nothing.

And so, having tasted poverty and life on the streets in my childhood, you can take it from me that, once you've achieved a certain comfort, you're very much alive to what it means to be penniless and, in short, you'll do anything rather than risk losing that comfort."

"But what could you possibly know of true poverty?" Jules was thinking, even as he agreed and pretended to feel for the author.

Sir Arthur stretched out and spent a few seconds in silent reflection. Jules carried on drinking and smoking.

"Tell me one thing, Jules," the writer suddenly exclaimed, leaping to his feet. "How come the novels with Sherlock Holmes in them are so successful? You've read one and..."

"It's the fourth I've read, not the first," Jules corrected him.

"Oh, very good! Then you must have some notion. Why do people have such an appetite for this sort of reading?"

"Because you give them exactly what they are after."

Sir Arthur was dumbfounded by the speed and confidence of Jules's response. But what was he getting at?

"Could you expand upon that?"

"You tell the sort of story that folk want to hear. You lull them. You offer them certainties, such as justice will triumph and crime will inexorably face punishment. In a world where things function precisely the other way round, reading

Holmes's adventures are a blessed relief."

The writer gazed at his driver for a long time, without making any reply. Then he poured a further two cognacs.

"Interesting. Yes, that's pretty much what I reckon too. But don't forget the morbid fascination that evil exercises over the simple-minded. That could be a factor as well."

"Certainly. But the simple-minded, as you say, are drawn to evil when it strikes other people. There's no dodging lightning bolts, but when they strike the neighbour's house, we heave a sigh of relief because they've spared our own."

There was a hint of a smile from Sir Arthur before his face became grave again. He was intrigued by this driver who, having read four of his novels, could launch into a sociological dissertation. This little Frenchman was rather too self-assured, maybe even slightly arrogant, but subtle. "

"So, according to you, the secret would be story-telling as a means of drawing a veil over real life. Have I understood you correctly?"

"I didn't mean to sound so categorical. But in a well-to-do society that blunders upon the existence of the poor and the desperation of rejects ready to do anything just to get their hands on a fraction of the comforts they can see on the far side of the glass... in a society that sees itself under threat from street crime, blind violence and inscrutable creatures ready to cut their throats for a few pounds... all of this makes the dream of an infallible punisher of evil like Holmes better than an opium pipe. "

This analogy did not appear to be to Sir Arthur's liking.

"So reading my books is like a drug?"

"Anything that helps us forget life's horrors is a good drug."

An embarrassed silence followed. As was his custom, Jules was asking himself why he had allowed himself to be drawn into this conversation until he said exactly what was on his mind, and Sir Arthur, torn between arguing back and reflection, carried on sucking on his cigar, causing it to overheat and turn sour, before jumping to his feet to walk over and stand in front of the shelves where he began running his fingers over the spines of some books.

"I'd like you to read something else of mine, given the insight you've shown in assessing my books. "

Jules thought he sensed a hint of sarcasm in that last remark. He glanced at the clock and groaned to himself: half past midnight. The sleepiness had left him and in the morning he would have to check the oil and the water levels in the radiator of the outlandish Landaulette. In England they produced the superb Rolls-Royce 'Silver Ghost' and this fellow goes out and buys a wheezing, oil-guzzling jalopy like this, its pistons liable to burst through the bonnet.

Sir Arthur was about to pick out one of his studies of spiritualism, but stopped, reckoning that since Jules had found Holmes a substitute for dope, there was no knowing what he might make of an essay on energies surviving physical death.

"Here, this should interest you," he said, choosing a leather-bound edition of *Sir Nigel.* "It certainly can't compete with *Les Misérables*, but when it comes to writing historical novels, I believe I know my trade."

There was that hint of sarcasm again. Jules set down his now empty glass and reached out, saying:

"I'd rather read your war memoirs, if you wouldn't mind."

Sir Arthur stiffened defensively.

"A damnably serious subject. I took part in the fighting against the Boers and I wrote an account solely for the purpose of speaking out on my country's behalf after she was accused, for anti-British propaganda purposes, of carrying out deliberate atrocities. Are you sure you want to read this?"

Jules thought he should play it safe this time. He had hit a raw nerve in Sir Arthur who, talking without drawing breath, had become so worked up that his cheeks were flushed and his eyes were aglow. He swore to himself that he was not going to saying anything on this matter.

"Fine. Take this," the author said snappily, offering a copy of *Rights and Wrongs of the Boer War*. "I've had it published in a dozen countries with help and assistance from British citizens scattered around the globe."

Jules stepped up to Sir Arthur who offered him an English edition and a French one. He opted for the latter; for the moment he had had enough of studying a different language.

It had been a bad evening for him. He was starting to feel the symptoms of inevitably falling spirits; things were becoming meaningless, the knot of nerves in his stomach was getting tighter and tighter and he was growing increasingly bored with his new employer, and a dull anger at the futility of the life he was leading was beginning to rise within him again.

What purpose would there be in his learning English? Maybe he would be able to display kindness and cultivation to the unbearable ladies and gentlemen who called at the house? Or carry on earning a mediocre living with some ridiculous cap on his head, opening doors for the master.

"Something wrong. Jules?"

It was a few seconds before he came out of his reverie, raised his eyes to Sir Arthur and stared blankly at him, a thousand miles away from this home, as luxurious and welcoming as the most gilded cage could be.

"What? Oh... no. I'm afraid it's getting late."

The writer agreed but gave him an odd look.

"Yes, you're right. Time for rest. See you in the morning."

As he turned, Jules stumbled against a huge shell-case used as a pen-holder at the side of the desk. He stifled a curse and rubbed at his knee.

Sir Arthur displayed the hint of an embarrassed smile and said:

"I am sorry. I'm forever meaning to move it. That naval

shell is a souvenir from the battle of Brandfort. You'll find a description of it in that book you're holding."

Jules nodded, stepped back and finally bade Sir Arthur goodnight, receiving a nod in acknowledgment as the writer watched him leave, wondering yet again who this curious Frenchman with the inscrutable character really was.

WAITING FOR THE INEVITABLE

Because of Sherlock Holmes, Sir Arthur was often called in by the police who sought his help in solving complicated and obscure cases. In spite of himself, the writer often ended up agreeing, deploying the subtle powers of deduction that he had always used in plotting the novels on which he had now turned his back. But it so happened that one unjustly convicted wretch looked to him also.

Recently there had been a number of sensational cases, such as the case of George Edalji, the son of a coloured Anglican vicar married to a white Englishwoman. For years, his family had been harassed by anonymous letters and the neighbours' tittle-tattle. And young George, the product of a union that the small-minded parishioners of Staffordshire regarded

George Edalji

as inappropriate, had, of course, been made the scapegoat in connection with an outbreak of horse-slashing attacks by a maniac whom they had never managed to catch in the act. George Edalji had been sentenced to seven years' hard labour. Briefed on the matter, Sir Arthur had carried out a painstaking investigation of his own, reconstructing what had happened and showing that Edalji had had no part in the affair. Then, in the *Daily Telegraph*, he had published a series of articles in which he attacked the local police over their intolerable racism, and accused the Home Secretary of culpable short-sightedness. Scandal had erupted. The government had appointed a commission of inquiry which had compromised by releasing Edalji from prison but refusing to compensate him for the three years already served. Sir Arthur had refused to give up and through the press had carried on denouncing this lack of courage on the part of the courts which were refusing to acknowledge their own mistake.

For once, among the countless enthusiastic letters from his admirers, the writer had also received page after page of abuse and threats dispatched by those same good Staffordshire folk who had persecuted the vicar's family and his mixed race son.

At which point, Sir Arthur let himself be dragged into another similar case. One Oscar Slater of Glasgow had been convicted of the murder of an elderly lady, even though he was far away from the scene of the crime at the time of the incident and even though neighbours' descriptions had pointed the finger

Oscar Slater

at someone quite different. The charge had been based on a gold pin, the only thing missing from the victim's home, and on the fact that Slater had pledged a similar item at the pawnshop. The court had sentenced him to hang, but this was later commuted to life imprisonment. Convinced of Slater's innocence, Sir Arthur decided to travel up to Scotland for a few days to pursue more detailed inquiries. At the time, Jules was driving for up to ten hours at a stint, using Sir Arthur's stop-offs at the court or at witnesses' homes in order to top off the oil, fill up with petrol, tighten a few nuts and change the fan-belt, his uniform wrinkled and grease stained and himself covered from head to toe in dust, apart from the area protected by his big goggles. Occasionally, he snatched a few minutes of sleep and the moment that Sir Arthur approached, grumbling about stupid experts and policemen, his eyes would suddenly fly open and he would leap from the vehicle to give the crank-handle a few turns before he was fully awake. Tiredness even seemed to have relaxed him and his face showed an inner tranquility. For the first time since he arrived in England he had something to feel enthusiastic about. Notwithstanding the stunning distance that separated him from Sir Arthur and his outlook on life and on the whole world, he whole-heartedly shared the commitment with which he doggedly demolished the police's phony charges against poor Slater. That fight was his fight too.

He who confined himself to driving without saying a word for hours on end could sense that Sir Arthur was fighting for something significant. And he was forced to admit to himself that the writer deserved a certain credit for it.

For some weeks they did nothing else. They criss-crossed Glasgow, venturing into the direst slums, knocking at dozens of doors, and throughout this time, Jules would hump around cans of petrol and oil and respond to Sir Arthur's questions about how tired he felt with unprecedented vigour.

"Don't fret on my account. Just concentrate of getting him out of this hole."

On every occasion, the writer would wonder what Jules could know about prison and prison life but he never dared raise the topic and kept his misgivings to himself.

A great stride forward was the discovery that the gold pin, the prosecution's key exhibit, had belonged to Slater for years and had no connection with the victim's pin. Taking this discovery together with the testimony he had collected, Sir Arthur and then Jules thought that they had achieved their aim at last. But it was too late. Whipped up by the press, public opinion had already damned the prisoner. The machinery of the law refused to back down. The police did a little tinkering with the evidence, came up with an appropriately trained witness and it did Sir Arthur no good to demonstrate that the witness should be discounted, being short-sighted and incapable of telling one person from another. So he wrote a short book about the case and had it published in record time. The impact of this nationwide scandal forced the government into appointing a commission of inquiry. The whole thing turned into a farce: while it was conceded that there had been grave mistakes in the trial, the finding was that Slater was guilty nonetheless.

On the way back to London, Jules was suddenly struck by the weariness of many weeks work. He clung on to the steering wheel just to stay upright, the gear-stick seemed to be getting stiffer and stiffer, the roadway faded momentarily and then reappeared with a obstacle in their path. When he barely missed a farmer's cart, Sir Arthur placed a hand on his shoulder and murmured:

"Let's pull over for a few minutes. We needn't be in a hurry to get anywhere now."

They were the first words spoken on the three hour trip.

Jules pulled up on an embankment under a towering poplar and switched off the engine. He dozed for a while, then started at the sound of an angrily crumpled newspaper.

"The swine! It's a disgrace that the press should have such power."

Jules reached for the newspaper that Sir Arthur had tossed onto the front seat. The front page headlines screamed: "Even if Slater is not guilty, he deserved to be convicted". Not that he read the article through. He was already familiar with this form of lynching by highlighting details of peoples' lives suggesting that anybody who pig-headedly insists upon remaining outside the rules of society should be regarded as guilty. It did not matter much if they had really infringed those rules. It was more than enough that they had failed to embrace them.

"The papers are every bit as responsible as the police — and more," said Sir Arthur, clenching his fists. "They have only to make up their minds to launch a campaign and the facts are misrepresented until it becomes impossible to tell the difference between truth and lies." Jules merely agreed, as the writer railed on:

"Yes, this isn't the first time I've come across this. When I think of what they managed to do during the war... I was down there and I saw what the Boers were capable of. But as far as the press was concerned, the British were the oppressors. And they concocted all sorts of outrages and abuses that never took place. However, some day the world will wake up and see who is now in charge in South Africa. And then it'll be too late."

He started gazing at the horizon where a skein of ducks was winging its way between the green of the countryside and the grey sky.

"They found him guilty because of what he is, not for what he's supposed to have done," he added in exhausted tones, slumping back in his seat.

"Same as always," Jules said, wiping the dust from his goggles.

The writer heaved a deep sigh and shook his head.

"No, not always. This is an extreme case, certainly not the norm. And taking the line that there is nothing that can be done is like agreeing to injustice becoming the norm."

"You did everything you could. And you've seen how much good it did."

Sir Arthur's spirits seemed to revive.

"On this occasion, yes, but on others it worked, and how!"

Jules turned to look at him, wondering whether he should carry on or hold his tongue. He spoke:

"In other cases, you were dealing with folk of a certain

standing. But Slater's friends live in the slums of Glasgow. So much for their status in society. He's a gambler or an immigrant out to make his fortune. Slater's father was no vicar and he may well not even have known him. And his alibi boils down to the word of a female starveling like himself and some junior housemaid, both of them public house whores, according to the papers."

Sir Arthur frowned. For a few seconds his eyes vanished under his bushy brows. This was the first time that he had heard his driver speak rancorously, angrily and scornfully. And his eyes... He tore his own eyes away in order to avoid the hatred radiating from Jules's eyes.

For a long time, neither of them spoke, then Jules adjusted his cap, put his goggles back on and in bland, cold tones said:

"We can set off again, if you like."

The writer lowered his eyelids to signal agreement. The gears groaned painfully and the dust-covered Landaulet Lanchester began again to eat up the kilometers through the hills of the Borders. That evening, they stopped at an inn in Carlisle where they dined at the same table And yet there were a thousand questions that Sir Arthur would have had for Jules. The Frenchman was a mystery to him and his instinctive reserve was beginning to seem suspicious. Over dinner, and with no real pretext, he looked him straight in the eye and asked:

"What brought you to England?"

Jules swallowed some soup without looking up. Then he took a mouthful of beer and shrugged his shoulders.

"Nothing special. Looking for work, I would say."

Sir Arthur nodded approval and resumed:

"But a driver like yourself, an expert mechanic, a man of unquestionable education, how come there's no work in France for a man such as yourself?"

Jules gave a fleeting smile, enhancing Sir Arthur's curiosity:

"I was born poor," he said. "And poverty leaves an indelible mark. Sometimes it's only moving away as far as possible that helps the mark fade a little."

"Good heavens!" the writer exclaimed. "What does poverty matter when one has talent and a will to work? I really don't understand."

Jules carried on smiling gloomily and made up his mind to look him straight in the eye.

"You are right. Poverty alone is not enough. The trouble begins when you try to get on a little and notice that there's a world out there, beyond the mire of your home territory. And then one ends up swallowing a heap of things, probably false, all of them. "

Jules returned to eating his meal and Sir Arthur to wondering what he had been getting at. After ordering two more beers, the writer made a toast. And so their eyes met again, allowing Sir Arthur to resume the conversation.

"Here's to your strength of spirit."

Jules was at a loss, his glass in the air.

"You're a man of great determination," the writer went on.

"That much is obvious and I'm never wrong when it comes to weighing people up. But I was born poor myself. Everything that I can afford today was inconceivable twenty years ago. So how come you regard poverty as an indelible mark, like some sort of an ancestral curse?"

Jules downed a mouthful and slowly replaced his glass, wiped his moustache with a napkin and stared at Sir Arthur with an intensity that would embarrass anybody. But it was no easy thing to rattle the self-assurance of the headstrong, granite-like Scot.

"Are you sure the upshot would have been the same had you been born a miner's son?"

The writer didn't hesitate.

"Yes, definitely."

Jules threw up his hands in surrender as if to say that there was no point in further discussion. A surrender that Sir Arthur was not prepared to accept.

"It all boils down to will-power. I'm sure about that."

"Will-power is not enough in the face of misfortune."

"Oh, come on! What do you mean by misfortune?"

Jules frowned and stared at the floor.

"So many things, Sir Arthur. It's like walking into the wind while hoping that it'll die down sooner or later. But the wind doesn't die down. Precisely that."

The writer began to twist his moustache, shifting in his chair, alert for some more concrete reason to pick away at his driver's close-lipped ways.

"You speak of misfortune like it was some ineluctable plan of fate."

Jules thought: "No, I'm talking about the cops, those in government and all the wretches whose lives are spent licking their boots. " But he said nothing.

"I too, you see, at certain points in my life, I reckoned everything was working against me. I'm not about to list them all, of course. But after my first wife's death, everything struck me as pointless. However, time took the trouble to set my carcass and my spirit back on the rails. And now I'm making progress the way I did before. There are times, such as during serious illness, when you realise how much superfluity there is in among the things customarily regarded as absolute and indispensable. On occasions, man needs to stare death in the face and gaze upon its handiwork in order to appreciate what life, real life, is all about."

Jules leant his chin on his closed fist, listening to Sir Arthur with what looked like an expression on interest but which was only fatigue from holding his head up.

"Do you remember the influenza of 1891? A deadly epidemic that also carried off my poor sister Annette. For weeks on end I wrestled with death. Then one morning, I woke from my delirium, sweating and skeletal, but with my mind suddenly crystal clear. In a few seconds, every single detail of my life came flooding back to me and I realised how much of it I had frittered away. It was at that point that I made up my mind to become master of my own ship and discovered the strength of my will-power. It was a joy I'd never known before, nor since, a feeling of irresistible energy. And all that when I was at death's door. I hung on to life by the skin of my teeth and I began to put my resolutions into practice. And it wasn't hard because that energy was already present inside me.

Only thing was, I hadn't known how to put it to use."

Jules sighed, took a swig of beer and, thinking back to his time in hospital, murmured:

"In the wake of an illness, I too made a choice. But it proved pointless."

Sir Arthur looked questioningly at him, awaiting an explanation that did not come.

"Was it a bad choice?" he asked.

"Whether it was bad I can't say," Jules replied with a sigh. "But it was pointless and that's for sure."

Neither of them had anything to add to that. A quarter of an hour later, their beers finished, they retired to their respective rooms. Sir Arthur mulled over the evening's strange conversation and fell asleep a few minutes later. Jules lay awake until daybreak, sprawling on his bed, his eyes riveted on the window where the moon appeared and disappeared between the low, black rainclouds.

Close Parentheses

Among Sir Arthur's countless focuses of interest at around this time was the foundation of a gun-club. The writer would drag himself off to the firing range, as often as his work would allow. Prior to the trip to Scotland, Jules had accompanied him several times to his club, waiting patiently for him in the car. But on this particular day, as he climbed down from the Landaulet, Sir Arthur paused for a few moments beside the door as if weighing up the propriety of making a request of his chauffeur. Then he said:

"Listen, in the references you showed me I read something about your having been a sergeant in the sappers during your military service."

"Yes, I was with the 133rd Belley Infantry," Jules replied distantly.

"Good. Why not come with us? It would be interesting to trade ideas on the weapons we have at our disposal."

Jules was still at a loss and then agreed without any particular enthusiasm. He followed Sir Arthur on to the firing range.

Ashton Wolfe was shooting with a .455 Webley & Scott revolver. Having had his five shots, he turned around to greet them, gaily waving the gun in the air. Sir Arthur frowned and chastised him:

"You know the rules, Ashton. Never address anyone while holding a gun. I'll reply to your greeting once you've set it down."

Wolfe froze for a moment, chastened, then hurriedly set down the revolver He was visibly embarrassed. Sir Arthur smiled into his moustache and mumbled to Jules:

"In the handling of firearms, certain rules have to be observed. For instance: only ever place five shells in a six shot revolver, so that the hammer always rest on an empty chamber so that accidents can be avoided."

Jules agreed, missing the shelter of the steering wheel. Sir Arthur nudged him with an elbow and winked an eye.

"Ashton's going to be in a huff with me for a few hours, but that's his choice."

They walked up to the counter that backed on to the fire-step and the author asked:

"Would you rather try out one of our rifles, or the handguns?"

Jules took a look at the racks, spotted the carbines and English and German rifles of varioius calibres, all brand new. Sir Arthur pressed him again:

"Looking for something in particular?"

"No. I was looking to see if there was a Lebel. It's the only thing I've had any practical experience with."

"There's none among the models available. And to be quite honest, I'm not familiar with it."

Jules shrugged his shoulders.

"There's better, I believe. The Lebel is accurate and powerful, but too delicate. You know, the cylinder below the barrel."

Sir Arthur frowned, interested.

"You mean to say it has a reservoir running along the butt, like the American Winchester?"

"Something along those lines, but better. Only thing is that the cartridge is inclined to warp, which can make it jam."

The writer seemed enthused by the discovery that his driver, hitherto an expert mechanic, was also a weapons connoisseur. He had issued two different models of British rifle and showed the first to Jules; it appeared to be the older model.

"Here, that's what we had during the war in South Africa. Henry-Martini single-shot carbine. A real disaster. The Boers already had their five shot Mausers and during cavalry engagements they created havoc in our ranks," he said, taking the second rifle. "Then along came the Lee-Enfield .303, the equivalent to your 7.07 millimetres in France."

Jules was feeling increasingly edgy. Weapons interested him but hanging about there, listening to the ex-soldier turned writer blathering on about ballistics was starting to wear him down. Sir Arthur must have noticed his peevish air for he suddenly set the rifle down and declared:

"Right then. Pistols are doubtless more entertaining."

And he signalled to the fellow behind the counter, pointing to something on one of the shelves.

The fellow shook his head with complicity and lifted down a gleaming new box, still sealed, and opened it with studied slowness. It held an automatic pistol, compact and sleek, apparently more manageable and less cumbersome than any revolver Jules was familiar with. Sir Arthur gripped it delicately, fiddled with the magazine to check that the chamber was empty and then passed it to him with an open hand. Jules took it, felt its weight. It was unbelievably lightweight compared with the Steyr he had known.

"Long-barreled Browning 9mm, seven-shot automatic loader," Sir Arthur announced triumphantly. "Never jams. This pistol is presently making headway into the European market. It was designed in the United States, but is manufactured primarily in Belgium. Right now, it has no competitor."

Jules ran a finger along the burnished steel, using his thumb to flick off the safety catch and inspected the loading mechanism, sliding it back several times inside the butt. It was the finest handgun he had ever seen and definitely the one best suited to an overcoat pocket and the easiest to draw without snagging the cloth. Sir Arthur could not have dreamt what was going through his mind, but he spotted the look in his eye and the way he handled the weapon. He signalled a second time to the armourer who quickly set two boxes of 9 millimetre shells on the counter.

Jules left it to his companion to explain the rules of the firing range, noted the recommendation always to set the gun down on the shelf each time a change of target was announced and to keep the barrel pointing towards the bank when putting a shell up the spout, plus a whole host of tips about breathing so as to eliminate trembling from the wrist, how to position the legs and relax the muscles, until, all of a sudden, Sir Arthur burst out laughing and said:

"Good heavens, I was forgetting that I am speaking to a sergeant from the awesome French sappers! Go ahead, Sergeant Bonnot, you do the honours. "

And he placed the gun and the box of shells in his hand before moving to his own firing position a few metres further along.

Jules looked at the Browning for a few seconds, wondering if there was anything behind Sir Arthur's occasional sarcastic remarks. Then he slid out the loading mechanism, inserted five shells, armed them, flicked off the safety catch and took aim.

The first shot strayed into the greenery. He had not been expecting the recoil to be so slight. He had had only to graze the trigger and the dull bang, muffled by the banks, had taken him unawares.

Things went better with the remaining four, but when he came to check his score and leant over the viewing window, he found that the wooden silhouette twenty metres away displayed only one perforation at the level of the shoulder blade, but that was it. He had allowed for a sharper recoil and so his grip on the weapon had been too tight.

He had no better luck on his second attempt; this time the height was right but his marksmanship was a bit off to the right or left. After he had fired his fifteenth shot, he paused to work out what was going wrong. On every side there was a flurry of single shots from various calibres of revolvers and semi-automatics deployed over a dozen firing stalls. Jules took a quick look around him; the armourer was in conversation and the other shooters were all in their stalls. Nobody was watching him. He packed seven shells into the loader, loaded one up the spout and put the safety catch on. Then, furtively, he tucked the Browning into his waistband. He planted his feet and stared at the target. For a few seconds he did not move a muscle, then, all of a sudden, he pulled out the gun, used his thumb to flick off the safety catch while raising the weapon to hip level and loosed off a series of unaimed shots while keeping his eyes focused on the wooden target. The empty cases clattered to the floor and then a sudden silence fell. The other shooters craned their necks to see, intrigued by the deafening salvo. Sir Arthur set down his bulky Webley and ambled over to Jules's stall. He leaned over the viewing window, then stood up, a satisfied pout on his lips.

"Gentlemen, we have a new champion," he said. "What school he learnt this novel approach from I cannot say, but he certainly has something to teach all of you."

There were a few stunned comments, some shoulder-shrugging and wisecracks about the last Frenchman who had tried to teach the English a lesson, and some falsely booming laughter. Jules was looking at Sir Arthur, holding the Browning against his leg; a trail of smoke was still issuing from it. The writer took it from him, checked that it was unloaded, set it down gingerly on the shelf and murmured:

"Five shots we agreed, did we not, Jules?"

Jules nodded and made no attempt to justify his action.

"A more than understandable omission given that this was your first time," Sir Arthur added, looking straight into his eyes.

He had invested those last few words with that sarcastic tone that was beginning to hit home.

"Or perhaps you thought that rule applied only to revolvers?" he continued.

"I wasn't thinking anything, Sir Arthur."

The writer grinned and adopted an expression of feigned surprise. He nodded in the direction of the target, riddled with strikes at chest level and asked:

"Where did you learn to shoot like that?"

Jules shrugged.

"Nowhere. Just came naturally. Beginner's luck, I suppose."

Sir Arthur waved a hand to indicate that he did not believe that.

"No, luck had nothing to do with it. Over here we call it instinctive shooting. But we don't practise it. We leave that to the Americans who love that sort of showmanship."

"I didn't mean to show off," Jules replied, cuttingly.

Sir Arthur grinned amiably and tapped him on the arm.

"Come, come, I didn't mean to give offence. Forgive me, the comparison was ill-made. Anyway, you know your onions when it comes to pistol-shooting."

And he took another look at the target, before turning to add:

"It may be man-shaped but it's only a wood and cardboard device. It's a different matter, my dear Jules, when your target is a flesh-and-blood human being. Have you ever... ?"

Jules hesitated momentarily.

"No. Of course not. I've never seen action in a war, Sir Arthur, and in the army my targets were all wooden."

"True," came the response, as Sir Arthur affected an enigmatic air. "And I hope you will never have to fire at a human target. When that moment comes, aim doesn't matter much. It's instinct that keeps the hand steady, not target practice on the firing range."

He threw him a sideways glance and concluded:

"Exactly the way you just did, without taking aim, keeping a level head and putting seven shots into the chest."

Sir Arthur did not give him time to reply. He sniggered into his moustache and made his way back to his own stall.

Jules handed in the Browning and went and sat in the car, waiting for the writer to finish his shooting practice. There was such a muddle of thoughts running through his head that he could not focus on any particular one and there was a sharp pounding in his ear-drums. Not from the gunfire, though. That hum of runaway chaos was coming from inside, from the depths of his belly and his ears were merely amplifying it.

He picked up his second glass of beer and pulled it away only when he heard himself running out of breath. It was dark and thick and had a burnt taste to it and the sticky head clung to his moustache until the following day. Jules's preference was for French beer, but this stuff was stronger and more alcoholic, made its presence felt quicker and took less time to drive away the pounding and undo the knot in his stomach. He had no time for drunkards, just as he had no time for all weaklings who refused to fight back and drowned their anger by turning into harmless pub-dwellers. But just then he wasn't too bothered about the beliefs he had espoused as his own and his dreams about changing the world. All he cared about was drinking. As for anything else...

"... Anything else is shit. It isn't blood that courses through the veins of these starvelings, but shit. They're all streams of shit whose sole aspiration is to flow into one great well of shit, into a stinking sameness. What have you done with your life so far? Taken shit. Thought yourself different, unique... Whereas you're only stupider, lonelier and more pointless. Here, you imbecile, like a drink? Then drink, and drop the rest. You have enough money to buy yourself all the beer you want. You've a wage coming in, a good boss, a fine room... Drink, you imbecile, and stop thinking, since you've nothing else left anyway. What's this they said to you at the post office? Oh, Mister Bonnot, if you're not sure that the addressee still goes by that name, the money might well be sent back... Then again, we're talking about Switzerland here, and it would be better if you were to check the addressee's name first... Fuck you too, dear lady: the addressee is my son, but you can go fuck yourself, you heap of shit... As for the money, it would be put to better use spent on beer. I'm going to piss it all away and it'll wind up in the gutter. Why should I send anything to you when you call a bag of shit Papa and don't even know what I look like... I'm going to drink this money away and then piss it away and next week, more money, the same shitty existence, the same shitty faces all the time... What the hell am I doing here? How did I end up in this shit-hole, where the only feature is the fog that masks the faces of all these living dead, who all rise at dawn and work through until evening falls, troop home, sleep and get up again... every day the same, trooping through the fog with their hands thrust into their pockets and heads hanging down, bent over their plates at the table, cowering in front of their bosses, heads bowed at the church on Sundays, heads always, always bowed... What am I waiting for? To set aside enough money to buy myself a little house in twenty years' time, maybe with a little front garden, and the neighbours doffing their caps to greet me... What a fine chap this Bonnot is... He is such a hard worker and respectful and never a problem, never bothers with whores, never gets drunk, nothing. There's just one oddity about him: he is always on his own like a dog. It's better that way. Living alone, he makes less noise and creates less bother. What the hell am I doing here? What am I waiting for? Is this what I wanted? A wage, a good boss, respect from the publican who doesn't spit in my face because he has spotted that I have a few pence in my pocket, and when I asked for that second beer, didn't hang about with his hand out but threw me a smile because he now knows that I can pay up. Monsieur Bonnot has enough money to do all the drinking he pleases. The policeman outside greeted Monsieur Bonnot because he has fresh clothes on and looks like someone who eats his fill and walks like someone who doesn't drag his heels. Shit heap. There's a quicker way of commanding your respect; stick a gun in your face. At which point the way one dresses, the money in one's pocket and one's face do not matter any longer. I'm still the same miserable shit-heap, the same degenerate, the same bastard as I was yesterday. Except that now I lead the same idiotic life as the rest of you, swallow the same shit you all do, in return for which I receive decent clothing, clean shoes and enough money to get drunk on. And sweat a hundred times less than those of you who sweat blood at the foundry. Here is the solution: keep your head down and answer 'Yes, sir'. I'd have done better to stay with the regiment. As a sergeant, I wouldn't even have had to scrub the latrines. There'd have been somebody on hand to clear my shit away. Head down and 'yes, sir'. And whenever you feel like letting off steam, you could always run roughshod over somebody less powerful than yourself. It works. That's the way the world has always been and you,

you poor imbecile want to see a change made... People love eating shit and forcing others to eat it if they only get the chance. That's it. That's it? No, it's not over yet. It can't end like that."

He raised his glass even as he nodded to the publican to bring him a third. Then his gaze crossed that of a fellow sitting at a table in the half-light, in the most out-of-the-way corner of the pub. Well dressed, pretty much the same age as himself, round-faced, not too hefty, lean and on edge. Both men's eyes locked for a fraction of a second, long enough for them to be redirected elsewhere with feigned indifference. But it was long enough for Jules to spot something he could not quite put his finger on, an anxiety, like two animals picking up on each other's scent. He was sure that the fellow had been watching him for some time. Instinctively, a strange sensation came over him. He was none too sure how to explain it, but he had the impression that this fellow was a stray dog like himself.

The publican set down the full glass and took away the empty one, winking complicitly; in his head, Jules damned him to Hell and began to sip slowly, in little mouthfuls, keeping a surreptitious eye on the stranger. He was reading his newspaper, occasionally shaking his head with the hint of a smirk, by way of commentary upon his reading matter; and he was sighing to himself, the smirk becoming more pronounced, his trimmed little moustache dropping into an expression of scorn. He was beginning to grow on Jules. Jules was wondering where he might be from. He was certainly not English. More likely from southern climes, from somewhere in southern Europe. The cut of his clothing suggested that he was not wealthy; they were a motley assortment, too big for him and he had paid too much for them judging by the overall effect and suggested that he had bought them for work. That look in his eye and that skewed smile and that cavalier air led Jules to see him as a Jack of all sorts of anything but lawful trades. He carried on drinking, but there was none of his earlier haste. He was intrigued by this fellow and couldn't think why.

About ten minutes after that, the man made a sudden gesture of impatience; he dropped his newspaper on to the table and removed his jacket. It was warm and it looked as if he had just woken up to the fact. Jules reckoned that he was an irascible, unpredictable sort, maybe too nervous for his liking. Then he called a halt to his swirling thoughts, coldly wondering what the hell difference this fellow's character made to him; he was just another stranger and it probably wasn't worth his while sparing him another thought. Jules did not need friends, so there was no point in indulging this lousy curiosity. The fellow rolled up his shirt sleeves, yawning with boredom, first the right sleeve, then the left; and Jules caught sight of the tattoo. A flaming torch in a closed fist, clearly visible in spite of the distance between them. The flames disappeared under the sleeve which the man suddenly rolled down just enough to hide the tattoo from sight. And for the second time, their eyes met. Jules got the feeling that this fellow was sending him some imperceptible sarcastic signal, even as he wrested his gaze away a second time. That torch could not have been anything else but an anarchist symbol. It occurred to him that while he had no need of a friend, he could use an accomplice.

He beckoned to the publican who scuttled over immediately. Jules whispered to him to send a beer over to the table in the corner. The publican complied after he swept up the generous tip that Jules had set beside the ashtray.

He lit another cigarette. When the glass arrived at the table in the shadows, the fellow threw the publican a sideways glance, but the publican pointed his chin in Jules's direction. Jules raised his own beer and toasted him from afar. The fellow hesitated for a moment before he hoisted his own glass and took a long sip, shrugging his shoulders. Then he set the glass down again and returned to his reading. A few minutes later, he sighed and stood up, drained what was left of the beer and made for the toilets. When he emerged, instead of making his way back to his own table, he sat down at Jules's table quite casually, as if he had been sitting there all along.

"So, how goes it?" he asked in French.

Jules stiffened.

The fellow smiled in amusement.

"What's up? Aren't you French?"

"Maybe," Jules replied, still scanning the fellow's face.

He seemed friendly and easy-going, but already he seemed to be a little too pushy.

"When you came in," the fellow said, looking at him challengingly, "I was already sitting over there. There was a book sticking out of your coat pocket and I caught sight of the title... and, any way, you don't have the look of an Englishman about you."

"And what look do I have about me?" Jules asked icily.

"Right now, the look of an angry man. The look of somebody who reads Max Stirner in the French and looks around him as if he wanted to throttle the life out of everybody. Am I wrong?"

He talked too much. But he seemed intelligent. Jules instinctively pushed the book deeper inside his pocket and suddenly became aware of how hot it had become. He was on the point of taking off his overcoat when a blast of air struck his shoulders. Somebody had just come in. For the first time, Jules realised that his back was to the door in a public place. He must have been in such a rage when he entered the pub that he had forgotten his instinctive caution. He noticed that the fellow sitting before him had suddenly dropped his head and leaned into the table, pretending to be deciphering the countless graffiti in the wood. Jules turned. The newcomer was a policeman. The bobby straightened the truncheon at his waist and walked up to the counter, brushing past their table without sparing them a glance. The fellow lifted his head again and gave Jules, watching with an inscrutable expression on his face, a half-smile. So he had not been wide of the mark. The policeman downed a glass of water, bade them all good day and returned to his beat. The man with the tattoo seemed to breathe again and exclaimed happily:

"Right, now it's my round."

And he called out to the publican who swiftly poured a couple of beers and brought them over to the table. The man fumbled in his pocket for his money and by the time he set a gold sovereign on the table the publican was already back behind the counter, perhaps out of respect for these two fine gents.

"To what shall we drink?" the stranger then asked, raising his beer towards Jules.

"To the torch that will set this shit-hole alight," he replied impassively, staring the fellow in the eyes.

The guy was left breathless for a moment, then laughed and banged his glass against Jules's, spilling a drop of froth.

"I propose a toast to good eyesight for I can see that there's nothing wrong with yours."

They downed half the beer and the alcohol eased Jules's foul mood and gradually brought him a strange euphoria. He found this new companion of his likable. True, he talked too much, but they were both cut from the same cloth. Two stray mongrels who had picked up on each other's scent in an instant and who had now determined to travel the road together for a while.

"You're not English either."

"That's easily guessed, since I'm from nowhere."

"Oh yes, 'the whole wide world my homeland'" Jules remarked with pointed sarcasm.

The fellow looked him over.

"Homeland and world are two things I couldn't give a damn about. The first doesn't exist and as for the second, to Hell with it. The only places I'm interested in are the ones where I can pull off a good job, and then... salut, so long everyone."

The man spoke good French but with a very slow, sing-song intonation which Jules saw as confirming his southern origins. In any event, the time had come for introductions to be made.

"I'm Italian by birth. Once upon a time my name was Sorrentino, but it's Platano to you."

"Does that mean something back home?"

Platano finished his beer and added with an ambiguous grin:

"Of course. It's a type of tree. A while back, in France, I was with these guys, a gang of hot-heads I hung around with for reasons of, let's say, business. On account of my being Italian, they used to call me Mandoline. I didn't like them getting overly familiar and since there was a sneer to their 'Mandoline', I asked them to cut it out, and I asked nicely. Then, one evening when I was feeling out of sorts, I grabbed the branch of a tree and gave their ribs a bit of a tickling. The tree that provided me with the cudgel is known in my country as a platano. There was an Italian associate with me, a poor wretch whom they treated like dirt and who thoroughly enjoyed the floor-show. He renamed me Platano."

Jules thought that this fellow was not just a chatter-box but had another failing too: he liked to boast. But in his eyes there was determination and a toughness that hinted at seriousness. Jules told himself that, if need be, this Platano should be able to keep his trap shut and snap into action.

There was no mistake about it. Platano and he were made of the same stuff.

"Fancy a bit of a stroll?" the Italian began again, suddenly eager for a change of scene.

He stood up, collected his jacket and overcoat from the other table and as he returned muttered:

"You hang on there for the change. Meet you outside in ten minutes."

Jules glanced at the coin on the table but Platano did not give him time to ask the reason for his haste. The Italian leant over to whisper to him:

"I didn't like the look of that policeman. I'm going to take a scout around. You take your time, then settle the bill and meet me in the street behind the pub."

Platano strode towards the door and, before shutting it behind him, winked at Jules.

Odd behaviour. Jules wondered why he had suddenly decided to reveal himself as somebody with the cops on his trail. Things were moving too quickly. He slowly finished off his drink and allowed ten minutes to pass. Then he made up his mind to pick up the sovereign that Platano had set down on the table. Rubbing it between his fingers, he made his way to the counter. Just as he was within a couple of steps of the publican, who was already greeting him with a friendly smile, he felt a chill at his back. For a moment he was unsure what to do and he almost stopped in his tracks. He walked on, leant on the counter, examined the coin and finally searched in his overcoat pockets for a few shillings to settle up for the last beers. The publican thanked him and added that if needed to change the sovereign there would be no problem. Jules smiled, shook his head and replied that, no, it was all right as it was. He bade him farewell and left.

The fresh air calmed him. That big son of a bitch. What was he playing at, pulling that sort of a stunt on him? He couldn't fathom what his purpose had been. Maybe he had connived with the policeman to fit him up.

Jules had a quick look around. He was holding the coin in his clenched fist but could not make up his mind to toss it away. The street was deserted. Had they meant to corner him, they would have him already. There was only one explanation for what that bastard had done. If the Italian had vanished, he'd toss the coin down a drain before going back around to the front of the pub to monitor developments from a safe distance.

Arriving in the street behind the pub, Jules caught sight of a silhouette sitting on a bench. Platano. He walked slowly up to him, looking furtively all around him, his muscles tensing to do him some damage.

The Italian started to his feet happily and exclaimed:

"Hey, you certainly took your time! Luckily it was a false alarm. That cop."

Jules grabbed him by the collar of his jacket and pulled him to his feet. He thrust the sovereign under his nose and used a fingernail to scratch the figure of St George just where it was already slightly scraped, then stuffed the coin into his inside pocket with such force that he ripped some of the lining.

"Keep that to yourself. And before I knock your teeth out, just explain to me what you were playing at."

Platano broke free. He was nimbler and sturdier than he looked. Jules gave a tug on his overcoat, trying to restrain him so that he could get in the first blow, and in doing so he spotted the butt of a revolver jutting out from under his shirt. But Platano made no effort to draw the weapon. He used both hands to ward off his arms and spat between clenched teeth:

"Hold on, you fool! Don't over-react."

Jules looked him right in the eyes. When his smile faded,

Platano dropped the absent-minded act and became feline and a cruel glint came into his eye.

"Why did you try to set me up? Who sent you?"

"You're talking gibberish. You're the one who sought me out. I was on the look-out for a mark, that's all. And hang on a moment, I set nobody up. If you hadn't chickened out, we could have been splitting it fifty-fifty right now."

Jules shoved him away angrily. They glared at each other, a metre apart.

"Fifty-fifty? Listen to me, you bugger. I have no problem with passing counterfeit money. Would to heavens it could happen every day. But I'm the one who decides when, how and with whom. That little stunt smells fishy and I'm waiting for an explanation."

Platano sighed and waved his hand in the air in a gesture of impatience. Then he went back over to the bench and dropped on to it, legs apart, arms stretched out over the back support.

"Tell me, you wouldn't be a maniac, would you?" he asked, looking Jules up and down.

Then he started to laugh:

"It was a sort of a joke. I wanted to see how you'd handle it. I had no doubt that you'd spot it once you had it in your hand. But I was sure you'd be able to palm it off."

He shook his head to reinforce his disappointment.

"For heaven's sake, had I known you'd fly off the handle... I thought you were made of sterner stuff. My mistake. Shall we leave it at that?"

"My arse," Jules snapped. "If it had turned out badly, you'd be long gone by now. You knew fine well that there was a police officer around the corner."

"Hold it right there. You know what the irony is in all this?" Platano said, picking up the counterfeit coin in two fingers. "It's my last one. Take a good look at it. I've never seen such flawless work. That fool of a publican would never have caught on, not even when they slipped the cuffs on him and clapped him in leg-irons. Check out the weight. Not a milligram too much, not a milligram too little. Solid gold plate, first-class die."

Jules came a few steps closer to him and gazed in silence at the coin.

"You were in no danger. I just wanted to see how you reacted and whether you'd spot it. What fun it would have been to tell you about it later!"

Jules was still deadly serious, his eyes cold and his fists clenched. But something inside was beginning to melt. He went over and sat down on the bench, lit a cigarette and tucked the pack away without offering it to Platano who made a face and looked at him sideways.

"Thanks, eh?"

Jules produced the pack again and thrust it at him. He tossed the box of matches on to his lap. Platano shook his head and laughed again. Then he stood up and asked:

"Shall we take a stroll then?"

"A stroll where? Looking for what?"

"You really are an easy-going sort, aren't you? Let's just hope you're not a jinx."

Jules looked up with studied slowness and looked right through him.

Platano shrugged his shoulders and said:

"A stroll, that's all. Just that, just to give this fine sleepy district the once-over."

Jules got to his feet and started walking by his side, his hands stuffed into his pockets and his eyes staring straight ahead.

Platano was dangerous. He had a screw loose; of that there was no doubt. Yet, for some strange reason, Jules felt drawn to his manner and was convinced that he was worth getting to know better, even though logic told him to get clear of him as quickly as he could. They meandered aimlessly, drifting away from Soho through the deserted streets between Regent Street and Oxford Street, heading towards Hyde Park.

"Why the tattoo?" Jules asked him bluntly.

Platano spat on the ground and stammered:

"It's because time drags in prison."

"Yes, but why a torch?"

"I didn't think you were so nosy, Jules."

Jules stopped dead to look at him. And in calm, patient tones said:

"I'm not nosy. Not any more than you are, spying on the contents of other people's pockets."

And he touched the Max Stirner book.

"Fine. What is it that you want me to say?" Platano exclaimed. " That I'm an anarchist? Yes, in a certain sense. I don't give a twopenny damn about re

"Fine. What is it that you want me to say?" Platano exclaimed. " That I'm an anarchist? Yes, in a certain sense. I don't give a twopenny damn about revolutions and exploited peoples. My revolution is made all by myself, day in and day out, putting one over on these swine and their banks."

"Good for you. I get the feeling you've caught on. I almost envy you. "

"Don't say that. I've years of activism under my belt, years of handbills in the cupboard, failed strikes, baton charges in the street. Waste of time. The swine grow fat on our labours and the only way to put a spoke in the works is to hit them where it really hurts: their property."

"And you mean to spike the machine all on your own?"

Platano sighed, tossing his fag end away.

"On my own or with a few trusted friends. And if the machine doesn't grind to a halt, I couldn't care less. In the mean-time, I'm not going to have any regrets and I won't lick anybody's boots."

He paused under a streetlamp and exposed his arm, displaying his tattoo. Jules could make out something scrawled above the torch: 'Without a glimmer of remorse'.

"They've used so much violence against us," Platano said through gritted teeth, a sudden hysterical anger flashing in his eyes, "that no matter what we do, no matter how craven and bloodthirsty, it will be but small compensation."

Jules looked him over, gravely. He needed to calm this Italian down. But this was just the fellow he needed if he was to make a fresh start.

Platano looked around. And abruptly his debonair attitude returned in a fresh mood swing that appeared to be typical of his character. He pointed to something on the far side of the hedge. Jules scanned the garden, the small cottage lit by lanterns, the adjoining outhouse. Inside there was a dark shadow, most likely a motorcycle draped in a tarpaulin.

"Shall we take a closer look?" asked the Italian, lowering his voice and on the alert, his nerves at full stretch and his eyes darting everywhere, investigating any potential sounds in the vicinity.

"Could you find a buyer for it?"

Platano shrugged his shoulders.

"Maybe. But I can't ride one."

Jules had had occasion to test-ride various models of motorcycle during his days as a mechanic.

"I can, though."

That was all Platano needed to hear. He walked around the building, breached the hedge at one of the more poorly-lit points and, crouching down, closed in, taking care not to trample on any twigs or dried grass. Jules took a deep breath and followed him.

They made it to the outhouse and set to work on both ends of the tarpaulin. They lifted the heavy waxed canvas and carefully folded it back and laid it on the ground. Jules examined the motorbike for a few seconds. An amazing Norton 1907 with a two-stroke, five horse-power Peugeot engine. A real rarity, like the one that had won the Tourist Trophy. It must have been worth its weight in pounds sterling...

Platano nudged him with his elbow. Jules nodded. He took hold of the handle-bars and signalled to the Italian to push. The engine began to heat up quietly, like a saucepan on the boil: it was in direct drive, with neither clutch nor gear box, and Jules had no idea if it had any clutch mechanism. They hauled it out into the open, keeping clear of the gravel path lest they make any noise, but as they were pushing the bike on to the damp grass Platano lost his footing and pushed too hard, which made Jules lose his balance. In order to avoid a fall, Jules pulled on the brake lever, triggering a grinding noise that seemed deafening to him against the utter silence of the night. For a moment, they froze. A dog was barking in the distance. Platano tapped Jules on the shoulder and Jules started off again. Platano ran ahead of him, throwing wide a gate which also let out a groan that carried for some distance. But they were all set now: Jules gave her some juice, jumped on to the saddle and Platano started pushing like a man possessed. First there came a backfire, followed by a series of hiccoughs before the engine finally burst fully into action, filling the street with a noisy roar that sounded like a machine-gun. Jules was caught off guard by the sudden surge and lurched forward by fifty metres as the Norton gathered speed. He closed the throttle and turned back. Platano was running breathlessly after him and when Jules turned the bike, he jumped on to the little pillion seat on top of the rear mudguard. They had no option but to pass the house. The lights were on in one window.

"Step on it, damn it!" Platano urged.

Jules accelerated with undue abruptness, flooding the engine. Instead of surging ahead, the bike hesitated, swerved and gradually began ticking over. But a burly fellow appeared at the window and let out a guttural bellow. He was trying to keep his dressing gown closed with his left hand and was holding his other hand lower. When he raised it, Jules was able to make out a metallic glint just as the man took aim. There was a sharp report. Followed by a second. Another couple followed in quick succession. Jules felt Platano tighten his hold around his waist.

"Pull over! Switch off the engine!" the Italian snapped.

Jules applied the brakes, sure that his companion had been hit. The engine petered out. Platano jumped off nimbly. Crouching, he slid behind the trees lining the street and made his way back towards the house. On arrival, he strode boldly and confidently up the street, swaggering somewhat. His right hand was extended in front of him and he was brandishing a revolver.

"Come on then, you son of a bitch! Want to play with me?"

Platano then fired at the window, shattering the pane.

The man vanished back inside. Platano calmly fired a further five shots, shattering another five windows. Then, taking his time, he strode in Jules's direction, ejecting the empty shell casings and reloading his weapon. Then he tucked the revolver back into his belt and leant on the mudguard and said:

"Come on, let's get this shit-heap moving again."

Jules didn't know what to think. He complied with the instruction without objection. When the engine roared back into life, Platano straddled the bike and off they roared into the night.

The Norton was hammering along a sixty kilometres an

hour, the two-stroke 726 throbbing flat out. As they left the city behind, Jules flicked on the headlight and slowed his speed. They were out of danger for the time being.

"Are you hit?" he shouted as he turned his head.

"You must be joking. I'm fine,"sniggered Platano.

"But then, why did we stop, you nut-case? We were already out of range!"

"We stopped because there are some folk who need educating. One doesn't shoot one's neighbour in the back just because he's stealing a heap of scrap from you."

Jules bit his tongue to stop himself giving him a bollocking. The man was a complete lunatic. They could have lost their lives. Not to mention the police.

"Come on, Bonnot, look on the bright side!" Platano shouted into his ear. "They needed teaching a lesson. They need to learn that if they open fire at anyone, they run the risk of coming to grief themselves. I did it for the sake of civilised living, damn it!"

"Oh, sure, very funny. And what if he's dead? If I'm to be wanted for homicide, I'd rather it was for something more than a motor-cycle!"

Platano patted him on the thigh, as if to reassure him.

"Take it easy, Bonnot, take it easy. Nobody died. If I had wanted him dead, I'd have put one between his eyes."

Platano's arrogant tone irked Jules who opened up the throttle as a way of calming his nerves. The Norton surged. But roaring at sixty miles an hour along a straight line that disappeared into the impenetrable darkness of night was every bit as risky as their earlier escapade. Platano began to utter shouts of encouragement. Jules thought: "My turn to show you now, you clown" and he took a bend, banking as much as he could, until the pedals were skimming the ground. Jules was familiar with this road and with the bend, but they only just avoided ending up in the ditch. They emerged, shifting their weight slightly and Platano guffawed loudly. Jules stepped on the gas.

The wind was stinging his face and from time to time he could feel raindrops pricking like needles. But this night race made him feel a way that he had never felt before. It was as if he were holding life in both hands after struggling his way out of a swamp. An electrifying euphoria coursed through his entire body and Jules was seized by an irresistible urge to scream, to throw his mouth open and gulp down the breeze, the darkness, the void that had enveloped him up until a few hours before. The Norton swept across a hump-backed bridge and for a second both wheels were in the air and it landed in a hole. Jules let out a sort of a scream, a weird scream like a wolf baying at the moon. Platano manhandled him, tugging at the skirts of his overcoat, urging him to go faster still. Jules leant forwards and, sprawling across the chassis, with his elbows clamped against the tank, started imitating a strident, gloomy siren like a factory whistle, like the whistle at the foundry where he had worked what seemed like a century ago.

Platano was bouncing around on the pillion seat like a dervish until the mudguard bent and started to scrape against the rear tyre. Within moments there was a clatter: the bike was sent flying, wobbling and rushing and skidding until it finally tossed them into the middle of a field. The Norton gave two somersaults and ploughed into the foot of a tree.

Jules was the first on his feet. Apart from a scratch on his knee and torn trousers, he was unscathed. Platano lay spreadeagled and laughed until he cried. Then he got to his feet and walked over and spat on the bike.

"You and your idiot owner really are two pigs!"

And he aimed a kick at the buckled wheel but missed his target and caught the hub instead.

Platano immediately grabbed his foot with both hands, hopping around on one leg. This time it was Jules who burst out laughing and he laughed so hard that Platano was eventually caught up in the laughter himself. They carried on until they coughed fit to choke, tears filling their eyes, stammering jumbled remarks about the guy at the window, the shattered panes, how terrified he must have been and the likelihood of his now being sat on the toilet.

Capitalising upon a pause and the suddenly oppressive silence of the countryside at night, Jules asked:

"Do you mean to stay hereabouts or are you moving on?"

"I was thinking of returning to France. I have some promising leads over there. It might be worth following them up."

"When?"

Platano looked around him and gestured at the countryside.

"Well, given that it'll take a few hours to find an inn, not before tomorrow."

"There's one five or six kilometres from here. No need to head back towards the city."

"Good. Let's get moving."

They walked in silence for around ten minutes or so. Then the Italian asked:

"Do you reckon they might agree to change a gold sovereign at this inn?"

"Of course they will," Jules responded reassuringly. "If it is handed over by you in your fancy pants and ready grin, why on earth would they refuse it?"

"No, my dear associate," Platano exclaimed, raising one finger. "You skipped a turn. The next one's yours."

At which he stuffed the coin into Jules's pocket, just avoiding the poke in the back that Jules tried to give him.

Jules woke early and went and knocked on the next door until he heard Platrano's grunting response. He took care to reassure him that things were fine, for he could just imagine him with his revolver at the ready, and he urged him to open up, for he needed a favour. He had a hard time persuading the Italian to let him borrow his trousers. He had to return to the city on a bit of business and could scarcely wander around with his trousers in shreds. Platano muttered something sarcastic, then shrugged his shoulders and fell back on his bed, tucking the gun back underneath the pillow. Jules promised that he would be back by lunch-time, most likely before Platano woke again. As Jules was pulling on the trousers his companion mumbled something, half asleep. Jules checked the contents of the pockets, then separated a few .32 calibre shells from the coins, placing the former in Platano's overcoat pockets and the latter on the night stand.

He borrowed a bicycle from the inn-keeper and set off for town, pedalling furiously. He was in the neighbourhood of Hampstead, with the prospect of upwards of a twenty kilometre journey ahead of him. When he came to the spot where they had dumped the motorcycle, he paused. The Norton was still visible from the road. He walked up to the tree and in an effort that left him panting for breath, he dragged the bike towards the bushes, covering it with branches. Then he set off again and reached Sir Arthur's office an hour later.

The writer had spent a few hours in town and they had arranged for Jules to spend the night at an inn before picking him up late in the morning. Jules was early, but Sir Arthur had no need to query his arriving ahead of schedule: he looked at Jules and the look on his face said it all.

"Something wrong, Jules?"

"Regrettably, Sir Arthur, I have to leave your service. I've come to bid you farewell for I'm returning to France today."

There was no response from the writer. He scrutinised his now ex-driver at some length and the determination he could read in his eyes dissuaded him from pressing the matter further.

"I am sorry. I hope at any rate that your decision has nothing to do with our relations with each other."

Jules shook his head.

"Absolutely not. I have a high regard for you, Sir Arthur. But I have to go back to France. There isn't anything anyone can do about it."

The writer surrendered with a sigh, then opened a drawer, taking out a wad of bills and made to hand it to Jules.

"Sir Arthur, I received my week's wages yesterday. You owe me nothing."

"It's my practice to give a little bonus to those who have been in my employ. This isn't a gift, Jules. True, I'd rather have had some advance notice, but you must have good reasons."

Jules chewed his lip but made no answer. Sir Arthur placed the money in his hand, Jules nodded thanks, then they both stood face to face for a few moments in a strained silence.

"Will I be seeing you again Jules?"

"I fear not, Sir Arthur."

"Well, in any case should you pass this way again, be sure to drop by. I insist upon it."

They shook hands firmly, looking into each other's eyes.

When Jules stepped out into the street, he glanced back momentarily at the window. The burly silhouette of the Scottish writer was standing there. Neither of them made the slightest gesture.

A WINDOW ON THE QUAI DES ORFÈVRES

The man leaning on the desk was poring over the most recent issue of *L'Anarchie*. The oblique light from the window behind him had faded slightly, but so far he was too absorbed in his reading to light the lamp beside him. The man had a thick, long, handlebar moustache, was slightly-built and twitchy, his eyes deep-set, dark, inscrutable. The dark bags between eyebrows and cheek gave them a feverish look. His jaws pulsed to an obsessive beat and he held his breath for long stretches, quite forgetting to breathe, only to finish up emptying his lungs with a sigh. The small room had a threadbare carpet, worn furniture, smoke-filled atmosphere and mildew and dust built up over years that had elapsed without anything changing between its four walls. Reading the subversive newspaper did not seem to inspire either resentment, satisfaction or contempt in him. He would never have owned up to it, but these pages filled him with an irresistible melancholy. Even in his rare moments of rest, his thin, tortured features looked sad. Everything about the fellow spelled doubt and never a hint of certainty. Odd that such an individual should have risen to become deputy head of the Sûreté.

Two sharp, arrogant taps echoed from the door. The man

looked up, remembering to exhale from the chest and half closed his eyes in surrender.

"Come in," he said wearily, slipping the copy of *L'Anarchie* under the black leather desk pad.

The door opened abruptly and the fat, ruddy face of Inspector Colmar appeared.

"Commissioner Jouin," Colmar exclaimed, winking an eye and twirling his moustache, even though Jouin had no idea what this was in reference to.

"Well? Come in, " said an impatient Jouin.

Interrupting him while he was reading was the surest way of earning his ire. Inspector Colmar had long ago given up interpreting his superior's mood swings which he had always found inscrutable.

"There's a chance," he said, returning to his cryptic references.

"If you've something to tell me, out with it. I have a stack of work to catch up on."

Inspector Colmar adopted a resigned expression, like somebody who has given up all hope of a meeting of minds. He threw the door wide open. Leaning against the corridor wall there was a drab-looking, inelegant fellow, dressed in a crumpled suit, his tie awry; he was anxiously kneading his hat with both hands.

Commissioner Jouin looked quizzically at Colmar, who said:

"Napoléon's here. "

"So what?" Jouin could not help answering.

The inspector smiled out of sheer courtesy and patiently explained:

"Napoléon Jacob, Commissioner."

Jouin's lips tightened and he raised his eyes to the ceiling. He had twigged at last. Napoléon Jacob, an informer planted in anarchist ranks, together with his partner, a woman known as 'La Savantasse'. Jouin had no great liking for informers. He used them, and knew how to entrap them and dealt with each one of them personally, knowing every detail of their lives and their weaknesses, the better to exploit them for his own purposes, soft-soaping them or getting them to talk, but he couldn't muster any respect for them. Disguising his contempt for informers was one of the many factors that made his job a pain.

"Come in, Jacob, come right in," he said loudly, getting to his feet.

The man made a token bow and took a few steps forward. Inspector Colmar followed him, closing the door and taking a position behind him. Jouin beckoned to the newcomer to take a seat.

"So, how goes it?"

Jacob's lips clamped together and he started to twist the brim of his hat even more.

"How do you think it's going, Monsieur le Commissaire? Life goes on. You know how it is. "

And he gave an ambiguous smile, an obvious reference to money always running short. It was a hint that Jouin knew well and one that he deliberately ignored.

"And your wife? Everything fine?"

"At the moment, yes. She stayed with the others. That way she can find out right away if there is anything going on. We have to be cautious, you understand. They're not fooling around."

"Yes. I appreciate that."

Jouin said nothing as he looked him up and down. The pleasantries were over now. It was for Jacob to make the next move. The man fidgeted in his chair, looking for some comfort. He murmured:

"I've come to serve you up a big fish on a platter, Monsieur le Commissaire. You need only issue a search warrant. There's a bomb involved, you see, and you can intercept it in good time. And deal with it once and for all."

"And the name?" Jouin asked inscrutably, his face tense and hard, his eyes expressionless.

"The Russian. Victor Kibalchich," said Jacob, looking directly at the commissioner for the first time. "His goose is cooked," he added, crossing his wrists in eloquent imitation of a pair of handcuffs.

"Explain yourself."

"Very simple, Monsieur le Commissaire, very simple. "

"As far as simplicity goes, I'll be the judge of that myself. Go on."

Jacob gnawed his lips. In his head he was cursing this damned deputy director of the Sûreté. He was putting his head on the line just to deliver to him one of the most dangerous subversives on French soil. He sighed, cleared his throat and said:

"Counterfeit money. Huge amounts of it. Enough to earn him a one-way trip to Guyana."

Jouin sighed derisively.

"Hold on, hold on. So, according to your intelligence, the leader of the Paris anarchists, this inspired author and gifted journalist Kibalchich is supposed to have been doing a little lathe-work, cutting out tin coins and then coating them in phony gold? "

He glanced at Inspector Colmar.

"We've seen all sorts in this line of work."

Colmar nodded, endorsing Jacob's remarks with a very grave expression.

"Right, okay. Where is the counterfeit coin being stored?" the commissioner went on.

"In his home."

"And is that where the workshop is?"

"Oh no!" Jacob exclaimed. "Definitely not. He's the boss

and he's content just to move them. He leaves the dirty work to others."

"Leader, eh? Kibalchich, leader of the anarchists. And since when have the anarchists had leaders?"

Jacob's pride was wounded; he blushed and began to stammer:

"Listen here, Commissioner, I'm bringing you the truth. But if you're not interested we can part as friends."

"Take care what you say, Napoléon Jacob. You and I shall never be friends."

Jacob threw him a venomous look. Jouin tore his eyes away and addressed himself to Colmar:

"The address we know. Check out the details, the location of the phony coins and all that. And see to it that Monsieur Jacob gets our thanks."

The deputy director of the Sûreté returned to his desk, settled into his chair and started checking through some papers. Inspector Colmar placed a hand on Jacob's shoulder; Jacob stood up, tripping over a grudging farewell. The two men walked outside without the commissioner's sparing them a single glance.

While Jacob was being paid for his treachery in an adjoining room, Jouin stopped feigning interest in the files on his desk. He stretched out his legs, gazed through the window at the leaden sky as grey as wet cinders. By the time the first raindrops beat against the pane, tracing patterns in the thin coating of black dust, his thoughts were on the many trades he could have turned to had he not joined the police all those years ago.

RIRETTE

Victor Kibalchich

Before leaving the editorial offices of *L'Anarchie*, Victor had bumped into a young militant who was a regular at the Montmartre print shop. Small and fragile, with a sweet face and innocent eyes, Rirette Maîtrejean was liable to suddenly display an aggression, pig-headedness and determination which few of the other women from the group could rival. At the beginning, it was open warfare: the clashes between Victor and Rirette often dissolved into angry screaming matches. She always had the last word and he always finished up turning to his comrades and bellowing:

"Where the hell did you find this angry lunatic?"

As subsequent developments would show, this was mutual attraction. Rirette followed Victor when he quit *L'Anarchie*. They went off to live together in a tiny apartment at 24 Rue Fessart, overlooking Belleville. Victor made a living translating Russian books and ran a study circle called 'La Recherche libre' that he had founded and which had its headquarters in the Rue Grégoire-de-Tours in the Latin Quarter. Rirette helped out with his work. At the same time she looked after Maud and Chinette, her two daughters by her first husband, Louis, an older man from whom she had split and who had finished up behind bars for passing counterfeit money.

There was more to Victor than the studious intellectual poring over books. He was also an activist. He threw himself headlong into the fray, often at risk to his life. Passionate and headstrong, Rirette was always by his side in the street skirmishes and the brawling at monarchist rallies, but she had a sixth sense that enabled her instinctively to gauge where to draw the line and when to withdraw from a situation a minute ahead of catastrophe. On more than one occasion, Victor owed his survival to her. It was thanks to Rirette too that he had not been killed during the riots over Liabeuf's execution.

A twenty year old workman, Liabeuf, had been in love with a young prostitute whom he had successfully rescued from street-walking. The corrupt policemen who received back-handers from pimps were "asked" by the latter to see to it that this bad example did not go unpunished. They charged poor Liabeuf with living off the proceeds of prostitution. The exasperated Liabeuf wounded

Jean-Jacques Liabeuf

four policemen before he was overpowered. Prefect of police Lépine, famous for having opened fire on the May Day demonstrators, pressed for the death penalty. The court acceded to his request. The execution was to have been carried out in public on the Boulevard Arago. That evening a motley rabble surged out of the slum districts, working-class quarters and every neglected corner of the great metropolis. Mingling with this disreputable crew were socialist activists led by Jaurès, syndicalists and anarchists ranging from the most moderate through to the die-hard nihilistic dynamiters. Victor and Rirette were there too, with their friend René Valet, a young, refined, and delicate poet who was deeply fond of them both, but who was himself tilting inexorably towards the illegalist cause and ready to act upon it. On a boulevard that was bright by day and sinister by night, flanked by huge bourgeois buildings with shuttered windows and curtains indifferently drawn, there rose the wall of infamy across which the shadow of the guillotine fell, a shadow seen all too often in recent years. And at the foot of the decapitation-machine some couples in evening dress, feathered hats and walking sticks had begun to collect, having arrived by horse-drawn cab or car in order to savour the show after dinner in some fashionable restaurant. Lines of gendarmes in battle order stood between them and the rabble. An eruption of popular violence turned the Boulevard Arago into one of the circles of Hell. The police lines buckled and gave way in places, only to snatch back lost ground in a flurry of stones and gunshots, sabre slashes, bill-hooks, batons and axes; even pitchforks got a look-in that evening. But all to no avail. Liabeuf mounted the guillotine, unreachable by the impoverished rabble.

At one point, Victor spotted Raymond with a gang of policemen in hot pursuit. He made to rush to his assistance, but Rirette held him back. Before he could ask her why, Raymond had drawn a revolver and fired six random shots. Maybe he wounded one of the policemen or maybe the shots went astray. Paralysed by his impotence, Victor was transfixed by that picture which ended the last hope of countering the suicidal armed anarchists. From that night forward, many would decide that discussion, writing and organising had had their day. It only remained now to fight the ruthless violence of a society that had done to death a poor wretch guilty of loving a prostitute. The six shots fired by Raymond, the fiery, short-sighted Raymond with his eyes ever-wide behind his thick lenses, those six lightning flashes in the night symbolised the yawning gap that was now unbridgeable.

Rirette forced Victor to do something. They began running along the line of trees, taking cover from the stray bullets ricocheting off the roadway. One policeman down already. How many had died among the demonstrators, they never knew. The leader of France's socialists, Jean Jaurès, had been seriously injured. The basket containing Liabeuf's head had already been taken away, but the riot was far from over. Small, scattered gangs were in hot pursuit of one another, joining for brief hand-to-hand fighting before disintegrating again and returning to the charge. One young man, leaning against the trunk of a chestnut tree, seemed to be transfixed as he monitored events. One hand clutching his belt, he stared at the gendarmes as they approached and brushed past him. Victor recognised him as René Valet. He touched his arm. René started and his eyes dropped to Victor's hand; Victor was trembling as if he had made some sort of a superhuman exertion. Victor raised the skirt of his jacket and saw the glint of metal.

"You as well, René?" he mumbled, his voice broken by despair. "What do you mean to do with that damned pistol? Haven't you realised that the only thing you'll achieve is getting yourself killed?"

René stared at him with a mixture of surprise and sarcasm and shook his head as if he had not understood a word his friend had said.

"Get myself killed? What are you talking about, Victor? That'll happen no matter what. And better out on the street than on that wooden scaffold," he replied, jerking his head towards the guillotine, lit up like a theatre foyer.

Victor refused to give up. The situation was getting worse by the day, but he carried on with the fight on two fronts: against the bloody repression by the authorities on the one side and suicidal folly on the other. The illegalists respected him but by then he had turned into the enemy as far as they were concerned. Some of the activists who had not lost their heads reckoned that Victor ought to resume control of their main newspaper. Victor had long discussions about this with

Rirette and decided to take up the editorship of *L'Anarchie* again. Its offices had been relocated to the Romainville Gardens, in a large isolated house that Raymond and his people had turned into a mental and physical workshop: alcohol and tobacco were forbidden, as was any other substance likely to dull the wits, there were gymnastics to keep one fit, shooting practice in the courtyard, and philosophical and science classes with the emphasis on readings from Comte and the positivists. Besides Raymond-

Octave Garnier

la-Science, there were Édouard Carouy, the red-faced, continually angry Octave Garnier, his wife Marie Vuillemin, Medge the cook, young Soudy and René Valet, the only one of them to display any genuine enthusiasm for Victor's return to the fold. The others greeted him with all the respect due to the liveliest mind among the Paris anarchists and they declared a sort of truce, giving a wide berth to the touchy subject of illegalism. From time to time of an evening Raymond and the gang would carry out small jobs, robbing cottages and garages and making off with typewriters, bicycles, the occasional item of jewellery and hard cash. Until the day when Raymond, Garnier and Carouy managed to rob the Chelles post office, bringing in four thousand francs. Within days and with the aid of Carouy, Metge struck: scaling a wall and forcing the locks at the post office in Romainville itself, they found sixteen hundred francs in cash and upwards of eight thousand francs' worth of stamps. Raymond, who acted as treasurer, was therefore able to meet their printing costs, buy paper and pay the rent on the big two-storey house. He used to tell Victor that they were being generously subsidised, especially by one Fromentin, a millionaire weirdo who really was known for supporting the movement. Victor knew that Raymond and his gang were not content just to talk about illegalism, but he reckoned he was still in control of the situation. And then one day Rirette noticed that in addition to newspapers, handbills and posters, forged documents and Sûreté warrant cards were being run off at the print shop. That was the last straw. Contrary to expectations, Raymond acknowledged the validity of Victor's angry reproaches.

"On that score at least, maybe he's right," he told the others during a heated meeting. "It's true, we did jeopardise the survival of the paper. We can't go on living in these ambiguous circumstances."

Octave Garnier looked at him as if he had ever seen him before.

"The time has come for us to stop falling between two stools," Raymond went on. "We can't go on playing at outlaws and at the same time writing for *L'Anarchie* and living in a location known to all, especially the police, and waltzing around in the open as if we were the loyal opposition just waiting to secure a foothold in parliament. That's schizophrenia. Since we've declared war on the system, let's face up to the consequences once and for all."

There was no going back after that. They left the house in Romainville shortly after that, just in time to avoid arrest.

Come November, Victor and Rirette stopped going to Romainville too. Victor simply had to finish off some translation work and Rirette had a stack of letters to reply to through her column in *L'Anarchie*. The children, Maud and Chinette, were in the park with Soudy, a sullen young lad nick-named Jinx on account of his incorrigibly negative approach. Unfortunately, Soudy had plenty of reasons to be sad and pessimistic; having grown up on the streets, he had had TB since the age of thirteen and had served a month in jail for subversive propaganda and an additional three months the following year for insulting the police. At seventeen he had been in hospital when a stack of stolen cans of sardines were found in the room in which he had harboured a friend who was even more of a stray dog than him. As a repeat offender, Soudy had been given eight months and moved straight from his hospital bed to a cot in a cell in Fresnes. In Romainville, he had found a family, people who treated him like a human being, rather than as trash, and he had developed a crush on Rirette who tried her best to take care of him. But Soudy urged her to stop wasting her time on him and stated with macabre sarcasm:

"Anyway, given the price of medicines, I won't be a trouble to you much longer."

On an almost daily basis, he would arrive to fetch the youngsters and take them to play in the public park while Rirette stayed at home in Belleville. As far a Soudy was concerned, the split inside the *L'Anarchie* group was the saddest thing that had ever happened in his sad life. He could not resign himself to it and carried on trying to persuade the others to reconcile with Victor Kibalchich. But it was too late.

André Soudy

When the knock at the door came, Rirette exclaimed:

"Here's the good Soudy at last!"

He was late and she had begun to fret. But then it occurred to her that Soudy would never have knocked so loud and so insistently. Her eyes met Victor's and he nodded his head slightly to confirm her suspicions, a flicker of anxiety in his eyes, and suddenly he glanced at the cupboard behind an old cafetière. Before he had a chance to reach it, the door gave way under a shoulder charge.

A uniformed policeman brushed Rirette aside and took up position at the centre of the room, his truncheon at the ready. In his wake came Inspector Colmar and five policemen who seemed to be jostling with one another in the confined space of the little apartment.

"Kibalchich?" Colmar asked.

Victor nodded, setting his pen down on the table.

"I have a search warrant," Colmar announced, waving a sheet of paper under his nose.

Victor shrugged his shoulders and sat down again.

"Go ahead," he murmured, folding his arms.

He gazed at the inspector and showed no emotion.

Colmar sneered and signalled to the others to begin. Despite the paucity of furniture and the few utensils, the police managed to turn the tiny apartment upside down, reducing it to a tip, mattresses burst, books scattered across the tiles, drawers turned upside down; even items of clothing were rifled one at a time and tossed all over the place. Then the inspector, pretending to help his colleagues, made for the cupboard, opened the doors, examined the items inside and turned to Victor to see his reaction: he remained indifferent and impassive. But inside his heart was racing furiously. Colmar plunged his hand into the cafetière. Victor stole a glance at Rirette. To his great surprise, she winked as if to reassure him. The inspector suddenly whipped out the cafetière, turned it upside down and began frantically to rifle through the cups and glasses, the cracked plates, tossing the table-cloths out of the drawers, and his anger seemed to be mounting by the second, as if he might burst like a balloon.

Two hours later, they admitted defeat. Colmar was shuddering with anger.

"Come on, Kibalchich, where are they?"

Victor looked at him innocently and quizzically.

Colmar grabbed him by the tie.

"You know very well what I mean!"

"Really? Sorry to disappoint you, but unless you want to waste more time, please be more explicit."

Colmar raised a fist but Victor did not flinch, nor did he lower his eyes. A plain-clothed policeman laid a hand on Colmar's shoulder.

"Monsieur l'inspecteur there really is nothing here. "

Seething, the veins throbbing in his temples, Colmar let his arm drop and snatched his hat from the table.

"Fine, okay. You're a bright spark, Kibalchich. But this is only the beginning. We'll have other chances, take it from me."

He strode across the room and left, the other policemen in tow. The last one to leave slammed the door behind him, but the broken lock caused it to bounce open again and the catch rolled across the floor.

Victor got to his feet, his knees shaking. He took Rirette in his arms, kissed her on the lips and gazed into her eyes, waiting for some explanation. Rirette smiled and caught her breath.

"That was a narrow shave, Victor. "

"But, Rirette; that louse Napoléon — is that what-his-name is?"

"Louse is right. Now we can be sure of it. La Savantasse and he. Two informers. But we've sniffed them out."

The evening before, Napoléon Jacob had sought them out, supposedly to collect a few copies of the paper for distribution in his neighbourhood. This was a regular practice of his and he had long been a familiar face in anarchist circles. Some had their suspicions about him, but Victor, well aware of his comrades' obsessions, always preferred to put his trust in his neighbour as long as he had no evidence of bad faith. Jacob had asked him to mind a roll of counterfeit coins for a day, not wanting to have them with him while he was distributing the paper. Victor, never one to be stingy with his solidarity, had not turned him down. Luckily for Jacob, Rirette was not there. She had no scruples about saying no if she had the slightest misgiving.

Victor had told her about the coins and Rirette had been uneasy.

"Napoléon Jacob with counterfeit money? And where is it?"

"They're almost all involved in some monkey-business," Victor had replied. "I don't reckon there's any danger. He'll be by to collect them tomorrow. I'll tell him not to ask me for such favours again."

Rirette had made no reply.

Victor squeezed her in his arms and looked her in the eye.

"What became of those damned counterfeit coins?"

"Dumped down the drains," Rirette answered with a shrug of her shoulders. "You know, it struck me that there was no time to waste on arguing. You never listen where solidarity between comrades is concerned. So I took them and dumped them down a drain."

Victor kissed her tenderly and then asked:

"And what if Jacob is not an informer?"

"Don't fret. I'd have told him that he shouldn't be dragging us into this sort of business. You can't afford to take risks, Victor. Never forget that."

They started patiently tidying the place up; it was going to take them the rest of the day to do it. When they heard footfalls on the stairs and the happy voices of the children, Victor suggested:

"Listen, Rirette, not a word to Soudy. Right?"

"How come?" she asked in surprise.

"Because if Raymond and the rest get wind of it they'll do Jacob in, and even if he deserves it, all they'd be doing would be letting the police off the leash."

Rirette agreed, then rushed out to kiss Maud and Chinette. Soudy stood stock-still on the doorstep. He gazed at the destruction goggle-eyed and his lips moved although not a word came out. Finally he mumbled:

"So, I really am a jinx."

A POLICEMAN'S MISGIVINGS

The house looked unoccupied. The shutters were closed, there was no bicycle leaning against the wall and rain-sodden newspaper pages were strewn across the garden. Victor and Rirette exchanged glances. They had no need to say a word, knowing that what they had long held to be inevitable had come to pass. She took the keys from her bag, but the padlock that normally held a thick chain wrapped around the shutters lay broken on the doorstep. Victor stopped her and stepped ahead of her. He pushed the door all the way open and stepped inside. The mess was unbelievable, even worse than the usual jumble of paper and printing equipment. Raymond and his gang had decamped for good. But, Victor wondered, why wreck everything like this? It was not like them to indulge in such small-minded actions.

Victor shook his head. Only the police could have created this devastation.

"Fine," he sighed. "We begin again from scratch all over again."

He removed his overcoat, rolled back his shirt sleeves, pulled on a grimy smock full of holes and walked into the room where the big wood-stove was. The first thing to do was to get some heat back into the house. He would look to the presses later. He opened the blinds and the room was flooded with light. Looked better in the dark, Victor thought. Now the devastation was visible in all its obscenity. It was going to take two weeks to get everything back into order. Reckoning that a half-litre of coffee might help him, he made for the kitchen.

"Good day, Monsieur Kibalchich. I was expecting you."

The speaker was sitting at the table, arms folded, his head tilted slightly forwards. He had a tortured face, Victor noticed, with a handlebar moustache, deep-set eyes, glowering, burning looks, dark pupils dilated like those of a cat used to seeing its way in the dark. The voice was lame and listless. He had spoken wearily, without modulating his words, in a single monotone of a sigh.

Rirette appeared behind Victor. The man rose slightly, in a gallant gesture, to greet the advent of a woman. Then he sat down again with the same sluggishness.

"I am Commissioner Jouin. I should like to swap some views with you," he said. "With you both. You as well, Madame Maîtrejean," he promptly corrected himself.

Rirette adopted a supercilious stance in order to disguise the anger that was making her lips twitch. Victor returned to his coolness and gave a contemptuous smile:

"Views, Monsieur le commissaire? I'm afraid that yours are all too plain already," he said, glancing around at the ransacked building.

Jouin pursed his lips and frowned with regret.

"There would be no point now in my telling you that these are not my methods. Regrettably, some of my colleagues beat me to it."

Victor grabbed a chair and sat facing the commissioner. Rirette set about making coffee, using a spoon to scoop it up from the draining board where they had spilt it, muttering to herself, but loud enough to be heard:

"Louts. What on earth could they have been looking for inside a coffee jar? Gang of louts. "

Jouin pretended not to have heard a word of this as he resumed in his hoarse voice:

"They left shortly before I got here to make my search. Pure coincidence, most likely. One hour later and the matter might perhaps have been resolved. Once and for all."

Victor searched those dark eyes, trying to read them.

"I'm afraid to imagine what you might mean by resolving a matter once and for all."

The commissioner unfolded his arms and placed his two hands side by side, concentrating on the triangular gap framed by the thumbs and index fingers.

"Don't misunderstand me, I beseech you. Had Raymond Callemin and the others been arrested, they would now be in danger of serving time for document forgery of the worst sort, with the aggravating circumstance that they did so with subversive intent. No more than a year in prison, all in all."

He raised his eyes to look at Victor as he stated:

"Which is a far cry from the guillotine."

Rirette wheeled around brusquely:

"And what good does the guillotine do you?" she asked angrily. "Your beloved prefect has always spared us this song and dance. He's happy enough to give the order to take aim and fire at will, right?"

The commissioner threw her a black look.

"You're making the same mistake as your comrades. You regard us as all the same. But we aren't. Prefect Lépine is a scoundrel and folk like him will succeed only in plunging the country into chaos."

"And into anarchy," Rirette added sarcastically. "Isn't that what you people always say? Chaos and anarchy. But what would you know about what anarchists want? What do you know of the way we live and what we want?"

"Much more than you imagine," Jouin calmly replied.

Rirette shrugged him off and lit the stove under the cafetière.

"Monsieur Kibalchich," the commissioner began again in suddenly pained tones, as if trying to plead with him to heed his words, "even you are not all the same, and you know it. Let's take Raymond Callemin. How come a young man of his intelligence winds up mixing with thieves and fences? Had I arrested him, I would have stopped him from carrying on. And you certainly appreciate what is bound to happen soon."

"So far as I am aware," Victor retorted, "Raymond has committed no crime. Unless you regard being an anarchist militant as an offence. "

Jouin shook his head and stroked his chin.

"The sort of things I regard as offences would be things like, say, counterfeiting phony Sûreté warrant cards, forging identity papers, robbing post offices."

Victor stiffened.

"What are you talking about?"

"Everything that your comrades managed to pull off before the police raided this print shop. They did a good clean-up of course. But we know that they were printing them here. As for the post offices, we have plenty of clues to go on."

Victor clenched his teeth but made no reply. Rirette bit her lips, focusing on the water that was coming to a boil.

"And if we add the trade in cars and motorcycles stolen on behalf of the anarchist movement, what we have there is a gang of criminals, Monsieur Kibalchich."

"Listen, commissioner," Victor snapped, "you opened by saying something about swapping views and now you're reciting a catalogue of offences that you know very well have nothing to do with me or our editorial team. Where is all this leading?"

"I'm merely trying to understand what a writer and gifted journalist might have in common with armed individuals with itchy trigger fingers and involved in thievery. Nothing more."

"Thank you for the compliment," Victor said, with a nod of the head. "But Raymond wouldn't even know how to start a car, so how, according to you, is he fencing stolen cars?"

"Maybe not him, but Jules Bonnot, yes."

Victor frowned.

"Who?"

"Never heard the name? Good, well, I'll let you have it. Bonnot is long since used to going under different names. But you've definitely seen him. We know that he was present at a number of meetings in which you were involved. More or less public engagements, to be sure, but Bonnot isn't the sort to go unnoticed. Let alone Platano."

Victor looked at Rirette who took a hand in proceedings.

"Anybody wishing to listen in, discuss or come to the defence of the paper comes to our meetings. We're not outlaws, commissioner. So far as I am aware, the prefect himself might well attend and I wouldn't recognise him."

"I would." Victor interjected. "But the ones we can never manage to recognise, so it seems, are your devoted informers," he concluded.

Jouin gave a wry smile and his face looked even darker, almost as if it was a stranger to smiling.

"Most of my informants are inept, boorish and ignorant. I certainly wouldn't rely on them if I were trying to understand what is going to happen."

"And have you understood what's going to happen?" Victor pressed him.

The commissioner looked doubtful.

"I'm afraid I have. Somebody's going to produce guns

that right now are only bits of metal that help them to feel strong and invincible, and that will mark the point of no return, Monsieur Kibalchich."

Rirette served up the coffee The commissioner refused sugar. Victor picked up a spoon, but before dropping it into his cup, he fished out an ant and some other intruders.

"I scooped it up from the draining board," Rirette explained, throwing an angry glance at Jouin who lowered his gaze.

"So, you're not familiar with either Bonnot or Platano? " the commissioner asked after his first sip.

"Never heard of them," Victor replied.

"Platano is a nick-name. He's an Italian, name of Giuseppe Sorrentino. Bonnot and he are inseparable. Well-dressed, thanks to the strokes they pull. The Italian is arrogant, the guy from Lyons is more tormented and taciturn. Bonnot comes from Lyons but for some time he has been a frequent visitor to Paris. To fence stolen goods, I suppose. The city gendarmes have a file on him as thick as the Bible."

"My own shouldn't be too slim either," Victor interjected. "Be that as it may, the two men you're talking about are not part of our group. If they came along to a few meetings, it was because our ideas interested them. I don't ask anybody to give an account of themselves and I don't nosy into how folk make their living. But what exactly is it that you want from me, Monsieur le commissaire? If you are here to persuade me to swell the ranks of your informants, perhaps by delivering this Italian and guy from Lyons up to you, then all your efforts to understand us haven't taken you very far."

Jouin let him bluster. Then, in a quiet voice, he went on:

"I know you too well to ask any such thing of you. I merely wanted to put you on your guard, to try to explain to you that illegalism is going to bring everybody to ruination, including those such as yourself who disagree with or indeed oppose it. And that folk like Platano can go around spouting about being anarchists when really they're only criminals. As are Raymond Callemin and Édouard Carouy now as far as the courts are concerned. You can't go around robbing homes and post offices and claim to champion the ideals of love and brotherhood. Or maybe you don't agree with me, you who devote every day of your life to a utopia that is gradually being dragged through the mud?"

Victor set down his coffee cup. His hands betrayed his edginess.

"Criminals keep the police in a job. Without them, nobody would pay you a wage," he sneered, his lips white with anger.

"You have a tendency to over-simplify matters, Monsieur Kibalchich."

"Commissioner Jouin, the real reason why I cannot live a quiet life is because I cannot manage to take a simple view of things. If only I could make do with a few slick slogans and crude rationalisations. But everything is so damned complicated as to heap doubt upon doubt. There is only one straightforward thing in reality in which we are obliged to live: you and I are natural enemies."

Jouin's face again took on the tortured expression it had had when the conversation began.

"You are free to disbelieve me, but I don't feel your enemy."

"The profession you've chosen makes a necessity of it, Commissioner."

"Ah, yes, my profession, " sighed Jouin, leaning back in his chair. "Didn't you say something about my being paid to track down criminals? Surely you don't think of yourself in those terms, Monsieur Kibalchich?"

"The moment we attack property, we all become criminals. There are those that want to own it, and those who maintain that it ought to be abolished. In either case, both expect repression from you."

"So all it would take would be for property to be done away with?" Jouin muttered, glancing towards the window.

"It's a lovely idea, Commissioner. But as you say, too simplistic. However, a little more equity and abolition of the scandal of a tiny number owning everything when the masses have nothing, that might help."

Jouin could not help sighing with impatience. He leant over the table and his unwholesomely dark eyes stared into Victor's blue eyes; Victor felt slightly unnerved. The commissioner's eyes spoke of feelings of unease and absolute negativity, as if the incorrigible pessimism of his thoughts were gnawing at them.

"And, according to you, that would be enough to banish violence from our lives like a magical spell? On the contrary, Monsieur Kibalchich, on the contrary. If I thought that, I'd be the first to switch sides and go over to you. But you see there will always be some individuals who, for reasons that lurk in the darkest recesses of the human soul, will be drawn to violence, the urge to rebel and the need to go up against the establishment. And I'm afraid that in a just and equitable society, where happiness would be within everybody's reach, there might be even more of such folk about than in our iniquitous, schizophrenic and in many respects stupid twentieth century society."

Victor remained staring at him for a long time. When he spoke, his voice seemed to have been affected by his interlocutor. He even had Jouin's tone of weariness.

"It's odd, Commissioner. Really odd that you should share my misgivings on this matter. But you should have an additional misgiving: what is the point of being a policeman if you appreciate that your profession will never be anything other than a servant of the powers that be?"

Jouin made a face of resignation. He looked at Rirette, who was still on her feet, leaning against the marble draining board, and almost immediately tore his eyes away from hers. He had spotted in her look a hint of pity mixed with the contempt that she had displayed up to then and which he could not quite bear. He opted instead to turn back to Victor who awaited his answer.

"Because the society that can dispense with the police doesn't exist. Even after the revolution, the first thing to do is to reorganise the police. You know that well enough, Monsieur Kibalchich. It's your intelligence that stops you from turning into a complete utopian."

"But it's my sensibility that will keep me going and, come what may, will pit me against a society that needs the police in order to cling to its power. Even in spite of my intellect, Commissioner. In spite of everything and everybody. If it is my fate to stay the eternal heretic, too bad. It means that I shall go to my grave with no regrets, with all my doubts intact, but with this one certainty: that I have never connived at horror, violence, oppression of any sort, no matter what their underlying hue and ideology."

Jouin sat motionless, pondering whether to press on looking for some sort of dialogue or to pack it in. In the end he chose silence. He reached for his walking stick and his hat, bowed farewell to Rirette and offered his hand to Victor who hesitated for a moment. Even as he made up his mind, the commissioner withdrew his hand and mumbled:

"Of course, of course, I can understand."

And then he made towards the door.

Victor followed him, weaving a path around the obstacles presented by overturned tins, burst reams of paper and scattered tools. A few steps from the door, Jouin stooped to pick something up. It was a yellowed, mud-spattered photograph. Well-thumbed. He wiped at it until the image of a tiny corpse lying by the roadside reappeared. A child who had perished on the streets.

"A worker's son," said Victor, looking at it. "He was in his father's arms when they opened fire through the factory fence. His father was killed by the same bullet."

Jouin placed the photo on a table.

"I never carry a weapon. Never."

"That isn't enough," Victor answered.

Rirette had started tidying up the kitchen. Victor lit the stove, then he too began to sort the still usable items from those that had had their day. Neither of them spoke for at least half an hour. Victor patiently bided his time. Eventually Rirette abruptly stopped the frenzied movements of her broom and asked him:

"Jules Bonnot I think he said. Is that his name?"

Victor nodded.

"You do know him?" she asked.

"Well, yes and no."

Rirette waited for him to finish stuffing a heap of papers into the stove. But since he was slow in coming out with an explanation, she asked again:

"Illegalist?"

"Who?"

Rirette ran out of patience.

"Come on, Victor, you know very well who. Bonnot and his pal, this Platano. Are they comrades or are they not?"

Victor dropped his head and hesitated before answering.

"Yes. Which is to say, I don't know them, in the sense that I've never had a word of conversation with them. But I know them by sight. Especially Bonnot. He struck me as genuine, but he has something of the desperado about him.

Somebody who has hit rock bottom. The other fellow, though, was not at all to my liking. I noticed him on account of his dogmatic attitude, his bluffer's pettiness. One of those guys who carries the truth in his pocket and doesn't want to waste time talking about it."

"And they've gone over to the illegalists, right?"

Victor shrugged and replied.

"Well, so far as I am aware, they've already been involved in plenty of illegal acts. The word is that they steal cars and sell them on. Doesn't strike me as a particularly revolutionary line of work."

"That depends," commented Rirette, drawing a surprised look from Victor. "I mean to say that perhaps they have their own way of funding the movement." she explained.

"Hardly the best way, I think."

"Oh come on, Victor. You know very well that subscriptions will never be enough to fund a newspaper or keep strikers' families going."

He nodded.

" What I know, Rirette, is that nobody can do anything any more. There's no going back now. They're on the road to collective suicide. And I've failed to stop them. That's all I know."

NOTARIES

Black, gleaming, silent, the great saloon glided across the Place Saint-Paul in slow motion, as if the driver was on the look-out for some address in the vicinity. At the corner of the Rue Vaucanson, the engine slowed until it was barely ticking over and the car pulled up to the pavement. Two elegantly dressed men climbed out; both were rather short of stature and they wore bowler hats and carried little leather briefcases that glistened in the sunlight.

Notary Girard opened the curtain a little wider. He had stepped up to the window to scan the sky, hoping not to see any low cloud that might pose a threat to the hunting party he had pencilled in for the following day. The clear blue had restored his good spirits and he had lingered there, watching the luxury car nearing his home. A thirty horse-power Brasier limousine. There were few in Vienne who could afford such indulgence. Too rich, even for my blood, Girard thought; he had long cherished the dream of treating himself to a much more modest single-piston Darracq with just eight horse-power. The notary sighed. But for his wife being so insistent about having a house in the country much larger than the one they were living in, maybe... He banished these regrets as he realised that the two gentlemen were making straight for his home. Two businessmen, no doubt, most likely from Lyons, or maybe Paris. The notary could smell money coming from kilometres away. He immediately summoned his secretary and urged her to keep them waiting for a few minutes, long enough to highlight the stack of files that passed across his desk. Then he lit a cigar.

The pantomime between notary and secretary lasted a good ten minutes before Girard announced that he had finally finished talking "with the mayor" and urged her to hold any further calls. The two men came in. He had them sit down. The driver of the Brasier tucked his gloves inside his briefcase in a rather affected way. And introduced himself:

"Gustave Delaunay. And this is my associate, Monsieur Glisenti."

The notary responded with a couple of obsequious bows, then asked with an amiable smile:

"Delaunay? Anything to do with Delaunay the car-makers?"

"I have a great-uncle who's an engineer at the plant in Saint-Denis, but I'm in a different line myself. I have some interests in the steel and lead import-export sector. Monsieur Glisenti here is Swiss-Italian and owns a number of stores in the Lugano area."

The notary carried on nodding his great head, content with what he was hearing.

"It is our intention to open a branch office in Vienne, stocking materials destined for Lyons and Paris. We have come to you to arrange for the establishment of a company tied to the mother company, but trading under a different name and with its own capital."

"I am at your service," said the notary as he tendered his cigar box.

The two gentlemen accepted his offer. From the table behind him, Girard lifted a miniature guillotine into which he inserted the ends of the two cigars before raising the little blade and bringing it down through the use of a lever. Monsieur Delaunay and Monsieur Glisenti exchanged inscrutable glances before breaking into wide grins.

After the cloud of smoke from two puffs on the cigars had cleared, the notary set about his litany of facts, figures, advice and opinion with increasing enthusiasm. Monsieur Glisenti displayed great interest, whereas Monsieur Delaunay's attention was occasionally distracted as he took in the detail of the large ground floor office.

"What we need is a concrete example," oozed the notary, rising from his padded leather armchair. "As it happens, I have a file open for a venture like your own."

He walked over to the library, moved a sliding mahogany panel and uncovered a safe set into the wall. He took a key from his fob pocket and fitted it into the lock before taking a larger key from a drawer in his desk to complete the unlocking operation. Monsieur Glisenti and Monsieur Delaunay suddenly seemed to be paying great attention to Monsieur Girard's every move, and after he had shown them a few forms, they seemed to be in somewhat of a hurry, assuring him that they would deliver the file to him and would be back the following week with an administrator from the company. They bade one another a very cordial goodbye and shook the notary's rather limp, moist hand.

Before climbing into the limousine, Monsieur Glisenti wiped his hand on his trousers with a disgusted expression. Monsieur Delaunay on the other hand remained impassive and expressionless. He started up the engine, put it into first gear and the black car glided along the Place Saint-Paul as noiselessly as it had arrived.

They had taken a room in an inn in Lyons until they could get their gear ready for the following day. Platano spent his time playing patience, or cleaning his Webley Fosbery which he tended as if it were a living creature. Sometimes, when he was oiling it, he would utter strange words like the sort of thing normally said to a much-loved cat or a dog. Jules let this pass. On just one occasion he had tried to persuade him that his two Brownings were more reliable and more accurate and, above all, less cumbersome. Platano refused to listen to reason. You would have thought that he and that revolver shared some secret or maybe it tickled his fancy because it was the most singular weapon in circulation. Typical Platano that, forming an attachment to nonsensical things. The Webley Fosbery was the only "automatic" weapon with a cylinder, in the sense that the latter spun around after every shot fired thanks to a sliding breech and spring arrangement that recocked the hammer. It made the gun cumbersome and hard to conceal. Besides, the British .455 calibre ammunition for it was hard to come by on the black market. But that's the way Platano was. It was pointless arguing with him.

Jules was reading the latest edition of *L'Anarchie* and was immersed in a piece describing recent developments in Mexico. Emiliano Zapata had issued the Plan of Ayala in which he called for a social revolution to enforce the peasants' demands. After that, there was an irreversible falling-out with President Madero who was hostage to the military and to the big landowners. Jules was astounded at the profoundly libertarian consciousness of the southern peasant with the eternally dour mestizo features; without any schooling, he had come up with a proclamation that seemed to have sprung from a clear head, and vast experience that one would never have expected from a barefoot rural guerrilla who had started out fighting with a machete.

"So, how goes your latest pastime?" Platano asked with his usual sarcasm.

Jules ignored him. The Italian tossed a card on to the little table, cursed and swept the pack away with the back of his hand. As he got up to reach for the bottle of cognac on the night-stand he stole a glance at Jules's paper.

"So this band of peasants isn't messing around, eh?"

Jules folded up the paper and said:

"I'd rather have some of that four sou cognac."

"As opposed to ?"

"As opposed to talking nonsense."

His tone was joky and Platano felt within his rights to tease him a little more.

"Zapata, Tierra y Libertad! A real starveling revolution. Can you imagine how splendid it would be if they were to win."

"I just know you're pulling my leg. Shouldn't you be giving that shooting iron of yours a clean? It must be nearly two hours since last you oiled it. What's keeping you?"

The only answer from Platano, who was pouring some cognac down his throat, was a long belch. Jules took the bottle from him, looked at what little cognac there was left and downed it. The Italian sniggered and produced another bottle.

"I prefer to toast Pancho Villa," he said. "At least he's a genuine bandit. More to my liking. A bank-robber may never make a revolution, perhaps, but in the final analysis, he'll have swallowed less shit in his life-time."

Jules shrugged his shoulders and muttered.

"Speaking of swallowing shit, you'd have done better to buy just one bottle but a decent one."

Platano passed him the bottle.

"Stop complaining, little bro'er. Twenty-four more hours and we can afford champagne, Charles-Heidsieck. Or maybe you'd prefer... "

"I'd prefer to wait until tomorrow afternoon before deciding whether to call a halt or start all over again right away."

Platano sighed as he opened the drawer holding Jules's Brownings.

"Stop being such a pessimist, you damned Frenchie. Is there no damned chance of your ever looking on the bright side? Tomorrow evening, we'll settle that swine's hash and make off with his cash!"

He lifted the two automatics and pretended to shoot into the air.

"Idiot," Jules calmly pronounced. "You're standing near the window."

Platano tossed the Brownings back into the drawer, having gone too far.

"Okay, okay. Lucky for us that you're here. You're sensible and cautious enough for two."

Platano took another sip of cognac. Jules watched him out of the corner of his eye. He wished that Platano would ease up. He was a pain when he was drunk.

"The swine must have quite a packet," Platano said, turning serious again.

"Let's hope so," Jules replied. "But don't get your hopes up too high. We chose him because of the excellent chances of making a clean getaway, but I doubt there's much money in circulation in this shit-hole."

Platano thought for a few seconds, then looked at Jules who was looking at him quizzically.

"I was just wondering if it might not be more worthwhile raiding a post office or some bigwig's mansion."

Jules picked up one of the Brownings, fitted the loader, tucked it under his pillow and stretched out on the bed.

"A notary's the better bet."

"Pah, if he has money. Otherwise, as I see it, it doesn't matter whether it's a notary or somebody else."

"No," Jules said curtly. "Notaries are symbolic figures, the very essence of property. Parasites par excellence. It's always a good idea to muck them around; they need punishing for their very existence."

Platano made a face by way of signalling his disapproval.

He decided to check that the Fosbery's trigger was set just the way he liked it, not too tight, not too loose for too much pressure to be required of his index finger, nor likely to go off too soon.

The hunting party had left notary Girard rather dissatisfied. The only two partridges killed had been shot at close range and practically blown to smithereens by shot. Not that this had stopped him from having the kill served up for dinner, for the notary thought it was rather sinful to kill animals unless one was going to eat them. On more than one occasion, his wife had to lean forward over her plate to spit out some shot. After one pellet got jammed in a filling in a molar, she told her husband that if he brought any more of these filthy carcases home, she would toss his shotgun away. They had gone to bed early, having tacitly agreed upon separate rooms. "It's better this way, the notary thought before turning down the lamp. This way he would be spared the spectacle of her face smeared with cream. He was fast asleep by the time a big, black Brasier saloon halted less than a hundred metres from his home.

Jules swung the heavy sack over his shoulder. Platano carried the gas cylinder in his left hand, the right holding on tight to his belt, and followed him, scanning the area, ready to cover him. The rain was coming down harder and was falling in squalls and there was the occasional lightning flash in the distance. Perfect.

They made their way to a window overlooking the rear of the house. A gas lantern illuminated the garden, but that was a safer route than going right up to the door which could be seen from the square. They set the sack and the gas cylinder down on the grass. Jules took out a screwdriver, suction cup, glass-cutter and a sharp knife. He was going to hack through a few slats in the blinds. But before setting to work, he told

Platano in a half-whisper:

"As soon as I get the window open, don't forget to warm up your ankles and wrists so your joints don't crack inside. The less noise we make, the better our chances."

Platano heard this out patiently, as if this advice was redundant.

"And keep your eyes shut for a few seconds. Helps dilate the pupils. We won't be able to light the lamp until we reach the safe. Agreed?"

"Of course. Let's get on with it," Platano replied, irked by the rain which had soaked him to the skin.

Jules cut through three wooden slats, opened the blind, positioned the suction cup and cut through the glass. Then he slipped his gloved hand through the semi-circular gaps and turned the handle. After loosening his joints by flexing them a few times, he led the way inside, keeping his eyes shut for a few seconds before making up his mind to stride across the room. Platano followed with the sack and cylinder, leaving a trail of droplets with every step. They were in the secretary's office. The connecting door gave a slight creak. Jules opened it slowly. Once inside the office, he lit the lamp. The safe was sturdy but quite old. It was going to take at least an hour to work on it. Jules arranged the gear all around himself in order and set to work with the blowtorch. Now and again he would adjust the gauges, increasing or lowering the oxygen pressure. Platano stood in the centre of the room, his ears cocked. There had been no let-up in the downpour and the thunderclaps were drawing nearer and nearer. "A bit of luck at last," Platano thought, gripping the butt of his Fosbery.

Time seemed reluctant to pass. The Italian was showing signs of strain. He would pace backwards and forwards and look around him uneasily. Jules gestured to him to calm himself. Platano replied by shaking a fist as if urging him to get a move on.

It took fifty interminable minutes before the oxy-acetylene flame cut through the metal casing. It was only then that Jules realised that his jaws had been clenched so tight that the muscles of his face were aching. The lock was cut through but some of the molten metal must have spilled because the door refused to yield. With extreme caution, Jules inserted the crowbar, then paused. He was waiting for something to happen. Platano couldn't fathom this and laid a hand on his shoulder. Jules merely stared at the ceiling. The Italian wondered if there was some problem upstairs or whether it had something to do with the weather. Nothing. Three minutes elapsed and Jules was still motionless, eyes raised. Then they heard a rumble nearby. Jules stiffened. When the thunderclap came, he levered with all his might. There was a sharp crack and the safe fell open.

Platano rushed over and saw what he had been waiting for. Hypnotised, he gazed by lamplight as Jules's hand drew out wads of bills, one after the other, thousands of francs, tens of thousands. When he had cleared out the safe, Jules made a questioning gesture. Platano cursed inside himself: he was to have been stowing away the tools while Jules was taking the money, but he had been distracted by the spectacle. He turned around quickly to grab the gas cylinder and damned nearly knocked it over. Dazzled by the light, his eyes had let him down. He instinctively reached out but missed his aim: the cylinder fell to the floor with a gloomy ringing noise. Jules darted forwards to lend a hand. Within a few seconds they had crammed everything inside the sack. Up on the first floor, a woman's voice was asking a question. A man's voice, no louder than a murmur, answered her.

Jules and Platano headed for the door. There was no point slipping back out through the window; they had been discovered already. After they had finally gotten the better of the locks and bolts, a scream paralysed them on the threshold. Notary Girard, in nightshirt and carrying a lamp, was staring at them. Platano reacted like a flash. In a split second he had the fellow in his sights. Jules intervened. Jules suddenly lowered his gun and shoved Platano outside. The notary gasped for breath. Without knowing how, he somehow found himself on his knees on the landing, horrified by the sight of his blood trickling down the stairs.

They tossed everything into the back seat. Platano operated the crank-handle while Jules slid behind the steering wheel. The engine roared into action. Platano jumped into the saloon and Jules deployed all thirty of the Brasier's horsepower as the wheels started to skid across the wet ground, rocking the car from side to side. They crossed the square in a cloud of spray, took the corner on the hub caps and just missed a street lamp. Platano was screaming like a man possessed as he leant out of the window.

"Pack of swine! Pack-mules! Kiss my arse, you wealthy vermin!"

Jules felt a sudden fury sweep over him. Then, rather bizarrely, he felt an uncontrollable delight at the sight of his friend's irrational response. He really was crazy. But where could he find his like?

Once on the open road, with the notary's place several kilometres behind them, Platano rubbed his hands together in a frenzy and exclaimed:

"Son of a bitch, little bro'er! We really hit the jackpot this time, eh?"

"And you nearly cocked the whole thing up, you idiot," Jules said, soothingly.

"You can say that again. But what if that swine had been armed? Would you have plugged him?"

"But he wasn't armed. And there was no need for us to leave a corpse in our wake unnecessarily. We talked about that before, didn't we?"

"What's all this talk of corpses! I would just have given him a little scare."

"No", Jules said, looking straight at him. "You'd have put one into his head if I hadn't stopped you."

Platano stared back for a moment and then slapped him on the shoulder.

"Hey, keep your eye on the road. Think what a shame it would be if we were to end up in a ditch after scooping all that cash. "

He started laughing and threw himself at his companion, flinging his arms around him and adding:

"What the hell's up with you, Jules? You've a real long face on you tonight."

Jules shook his head and grinned.

"What do you mean, 'long face', Platano? I'm just a pain in the arse."

Platano seized his nose between two fingers and tweaked it.

"What have I always told you? That you have a face like an arse with a nose in the middle!"

Jules guffawed loudly and used an elbow to break free.

"Stop it, you fool. I can't see a thing with this rain."

They giggled and wisecracked like kids the entire forty kilometres to Lyons. Platano had with him his little hip flask filled with the usual cheap cognac. From time to time, Jules rubbed his aching stomach muscles. "How long is it since I laughed like this?" he wondered for a moment, swallowing a mouthful of cognac. No answer was forthcoming. This had never happened to him before.

They had leased a little shop at 64 Rue Voltaire. It was their operational base. They stored stolen cars and bicycles there pending re-sale. Not that that brought in much money; they had no papers and it was not easy to shift them. After shutting the gates, they set about counting the loot. Thirty six thousand francs. An unexpected windfall. Now they could enjoy themselves. Take a bit of time off at last. To hell with fences, to hell with opening garage doors, to hell with cranking up cars with fear in the belly. The Brasier would have to go. Jules would drive it a great distance away in two or three days, waiting for the heat to die down. They no longer needed to sell it off. They were each eighteen thousand francs better off.

They decided to split up for a time. Jules was to stow the gear in a secure hiding place. Then Platano's high spirits suddenly faded.

"Sure,"he said, gravely, avoiding his friend's eyes. "That's only to be expected. Better not hang around together. You're the brains of the gang, right?"

Jules stared at him, stunned.

"Is there a problem, Platano?"

"Eh? Problem?" Platano replied, forcing a smile. "The only problem I have is blowing as much money as I can as quickly as I can."

Jules dropped a hand on to his shoulder.

"Don't go attracting attention to yourself with all that money. We'll meet up again soon. I'll get in touch with you, that would be better."

Platano turned serious again.

"Are you thinking of spending much time down there?"

Jules was at a loss.

"Er, I don't know. Just long enough to sort out a few things. No more than a few days."

Platano agreed. And, tweaking his nose again, he told Jules:

"Make the most of that cuckolded pall-bearer's face of yours, little bro'er."

Jules was bothered by that description, which he did not like one bit. But he made no reply.

As he pedalled towards the La Guillotière cemetery with the sack slung over his back, he pondered thoughts. The euphoria of the last few hours had evaporated and given way to a vague unease. He sensed that his "safe hiding place" would sooner or later lead to problems between Platano and him. That nitwit just could not understand. Would not understand.

Dawn was not far off. Jules blasphemed between clenched teeth, pedalling with renewed vigour and he cursed the daylight as he always had done.

GRAVES

Straightening up, he hoisted the marble slab and set it back in place. Then he finished manoeuvring it into position using a wooden club, painstakingly covering up the gaps. He examined his handiwork. No one would ever suspect that the torches, gas cylinders, drills, various boxes of 9 millimetre ammunition and a few sticks of dynamite and an equal number of cotton fulminate detonators were in there, alongside a mouldy old coffin. It was the finest hiding place imaginable. The grave of a family that had died out, the last remaining descendant had been living in Indo-China for years and forgotten all about his ancestors mouldering in the La Guillotière cemetery.

The idea had occurred to him shortly after his return from England. He was waiting for a car he and Platano were planning to steal to pass by and monitoring the owner's return before deciding whether it was better to steal it from his garage or flag him down on the road. He had spent a half an hour like that, wandering from grave to grave, waiting for the distant sound of an engine. The quiet of the cemetery had proved to be a sort of a palliative for the tension he always felt. Sitting on a gravestone listening to the sounds from the nearby wood, gazing at the different flowers, trying to guess who might have laid them there, holding his breath in moments of unbroken silence and discovering that his heart was beating less quickly than

usual, that his stomach cramps had eased, that the knotted
nerves around his solar plexus were unravelling — it all had
a calming effect on him. Gazing at the family crypts, it had
finally occurred to him that no one would think of looking
there for the cumbersome gear that risked giving them away
every day. He had picked out the one that bore the oldest
dates, the one that looked most neglected, the one with no
flowers, the one with the rusted metal bars. Except that
there was just one thing that summoned up a painful
memory every time: that niche, bottom right, smaller than
the rest and bearing two dates, the birth year 1872 and the
date of death, 1879. A seven-year-old child. The same age as
his son, Justin-Louis. Who had turned seven in February.
And when his eye fell on the child's headstone, Jules
wondered what Justin-Louis might be doing at that precise
moment.

Judith had appeared one evening after sunset, strolling
along the gravel path, a pale flower in her hand, as if looking
for a grave upon which to lay it. But she wasn't looking for
anything. She was just waiting for time to pass. She had
greeted him, asking if he was a member of the family that
owned the chapel. Jules had kept a cool head, dreaming up
some distant cousin who had emigrated years ago and only
recently returned to France. Judith had pretended to believe
him. She had introduced herself as a Madame Thollon, the
wife of the cemetery watchman. She was a few years older
than Jules, but her beauty was still undiminished. The
creases at the corners of her mouth suggested not her age,
but a life of suffering that had draped her face in an opaque
patina. Somewhat later, Jules came to realise that it was not
so much suffering as an absence; an emptiness that rendered
Judith's sweetness melancholic and confined her to the
merest hint of a smile.

They had bumped into each other again the following

week, and, strangely, Jules had overruled all the warning bells that logic set off: Madame Thollon had certainly had her suspicions, but he did nothing to reassure her by means of further lies. He had arrived carrying a heavy sack slung over his shoulder and left empty-handed. She must have spotted him from her window which overlooked the cemetery entrance. If he were to return a third time, it might be his last. And he had gone back. He had found her sitting on the chapel steps. Judith had got to her feet and with an unaffected smile, had bluntly told him:

"Once you've finished, you can call in at the house to clean up your clothing and wash your hands. These graves have been abandoned for years."

Jules looked into her eyes for a long time. Judith had stared right back at him and while he took her hand he could feel her trembling and could read a sort of a plea in her eyes, an unspoken request that she not be regarded as a body to be possessed hastily and promptly forgotten. Jules had come to collect all his gear but he left all his housebreaker's kit and followed Judith home, surrendering to a fatalistic intuition.

They had spent nearly two hours talking. Judith's husband who was looking after his ailing mother was not due home until late in the evening. There was nothing between them any more and life was flying past uneventfully in the loneliness of La Guillotière for a woman who lacked the courage to get up and leave. Her days were monotonous and as quiet as the nights while waiting for old age to still her last remaining hopes, leaving her few memories as her sole regret. In the already darkening graveyard, Jules had kissed the palm of her hand. And Judith had hesitated momentarily before brushing his lips with her finger-tips.

It must have been a month before their hands ventured

over each other's bodies, timidly stroking and exploring swells and hollows, then, with uncertain, clumsy moves, sliding underneath clothing to discover the warm touch of flesh. They found themselves standing naked in the centre of the room, gazing at each other without embarrassment, each savouring the pleasure of feeling the other's eyes slowly roving over them, taking their time, until they joined in a delicate clinch, careful not hurt each other, as if each of their skins was fragile enough to crack at every lash from life. Jules started kissing her on the eye-lids before swooping to find the mouth, soft and still undecided, then her throat which contracted as she swallowed, then the tips of her breasts, small and dark. He slowly learnt to recognise her smell and taste, from lips to belly, down as far as the quivering blond triangle that had shuddered when he leant forward to discover its softness. He felt a sensation akin to unconsciousness, his face probing between her velvety legs, oblivious of everything, all memory left in the shadows outside the room.

He left at around eleven o'clock, shortly before her husband returned. Judith had not spoken a word and, kissing her, he had pressed his lips to her cheek, drying a tear that tasted of salt and powder.

He had barely pushed at the door before she threw her arms about his neck and they exchanged long, frenzied kisses, hugging each other after the long wait. Then she hid her face against his chest and murmured:

"I can't stand it any more. I thought they'd caught you. I spent the entire night by the window. And when I saw you I nearly called out. How I managed to contain myself, I do not know."

"And him?" Jules asked, looking at the stairs leading to the upper floor.

Judith lifted her face and looked away and said in a low voice:

"He knows everything now. I'm sure of that. But he says nothing. We have no need to explain ourselves to each other any more."

Then she took Jules by the hand and drew him into the living room where there was a large couch strewn with embroidered cushions. He sat at one end and she stretched out, resting her head on his knees. She began to stroke his moustache and looked at him as if she were trying to commit his details to memory.

"Judith, we may not have much longer to wait. You won't have to spend any more nights by the window. Never again."

"Are you being serious? Remember that I've never asked anything of you. You've no need to reassure me."

"No, Judith. I am not saying that some day it'll all end in roses for you or for me. We've been lucky."

And he made a face, a sort of superstitious grin.

"It looks like fortune has smiled on us, for once."

Her fingers began again to trace his lips, his cheeks, his chin.

"I have eighteen thousand francs. Do you understand? One more haul like that and... "

Judith closed his mouth with her fingers.

"No promises, Jules, I beg you."

"But it's not a promise," he said in a half whisper in case he be heard upstairs. "We can go away for good. And never again will we have to smell the stink of this shit-hole, not even from the distance. To hell with France, her goons, her infamies and all the rest. No more looking over his shoulder. The only news I expect to get from here is that Lyons has been completely wiped out following some disaster."

Judith stood up and kissed him, as if to calm him down.

"Alright, Jules. As early as tomorrow, if that's what you want."

With an expression of regret, he offered his opinion.

"Hold on, Judith. I don't want to leave like some barefoot emigrant with a third-class passage and a blanket over my head to keep the rain away. Once we reach the other side of the ocean there'll be no more notaries, no more post offices, no more cars to be stolen and sold on. The money I have would cover our passage and keep us for a few months. But Argentina is a land that has everything to offer if one can afford to make an investment. We wouldn't need a large sum. All it would take would be one more job the last evening. Just one."

He curled up on the couch and Judith huddled against him. Jules, the dreamer, was staring into the distance; even as he stroked her hair, he was murmuring:

"The pampas... They say it's like looking into infinity. No end in sight. Green steppes as far as the eye can see. Only in a place like that can one feel free."

Judith smiled.

"So, no more anarchists?"

Jules did not answer her. She took a step backwards in order to look him in the eye.

"Really? Would you be ready to put it all out of your mind? Right now, it's as if I've known you forever. You couldn't survive working in the fields or raising cattle and sheep. Maybe for a while. But after that? What are we going to do when you take a notion to go and look beyond the pampas?"

"We'll move on. What else would you have us do? Anyway, there are loads of interesting folk in Argentina. It's full of comrades down there. Especially Italians."

"I don't like Italians," she stated, looking away.

"Judith, it's Platano that you don't like. Nothing to do with Italians generally."

"Okay. Platano is the only Italian I know. And him I don't like."

"But he's my best friend."

Judith took Jules's face gently in her hands.

"No, he's not your best friend; he's your only friend."

Jules grabbed her by the hips and pulled her to him. He kissed her and they stood there in each other's embrace, listening to the mingled beat of their hearts.

"Platano is much more than a friend," said Jules. "He's an accomplice. A simple look is all it takes for us to understand each other. When two men share the risk of causing the other's death, a bond is created that is stronger than any blood tie or friendship. Complicity is something total, something absolute. Something that words cannot express. One feels its existence and it cannot be created where it doesn't exist."

Judith stiffened and then suddenly hugged him even closer, exploring his skin beneath his shirt.

"Jules, take me with you. Let's go before it's too late."

From Montmartre Cemetery
to La Guiillotière Cemetery

As he crossed the bridge from the Rue Caulincourt he glanced at the serried ranks of gravestones below, stretching out on both sides like some sluggish river. "Or marsh," he thought to himself. And he spat over the edge. "It has cost you more to die than to live," Platano sneered in his mind as he saw the black marble headstones and luxury chapels of Montmartre cemetery, the majestic statues of weeping angels and fancy wrought iron crosses. He reached the Boulevard de Clichy and stopped to admire the broad avenue.

To him, Paris meant a hotchpotch of contradictory sensations: a visceral hatred of brazen wealth, countless temptations, contempt for parasites as a whole and an urge to dwell on the privileges of a full pocket.

He strolled along pavements encumbered with goods on display in the shop fronts and obstructed by prostitutes who, from the Place Blanche up to Pigalle, displayed their charms with the same indifference as those hawking fruit or fish. Platano smiled at them all, pleased to be mistaken for a rich young man with time on his hands. Later, maybe, but he had come to Paris on a different errand. First he had to talk business. He had all night to fritter away the thousands and hundreds he was carrying in his inside overcoat pocket. Because he meant to splash out; of that there was no doubt. He had to spend them. Afterwards, he would have no excuse left. And Jules would no longer be able to give him the slip.

He turned down an alley between Pigalle and Notre-Dame-de-Lorette in the heart of the 9th arrondissement and he stopped in front of an unmarked black wooden door, dimly lit by a yellowish lantern. He knocked. The door opened a few centimetres, about as far as the chunky chain on the far side would allow, exposing a pock-marked face set on a massive body much taller than Platano's. The 'bouncer' looked him over carefully.

"Sorry, monsieur, but we're full up", said an obsequious, sing-song voice that one would never have expected from that mass of brawn and bone in a dark suit with black silk lapels.

Platano took out a wad of notes and held two of them up in the chink of light and said:

"Listen, mate, I have no interest in your naked girls. I'm looking for a colleague of yours. Any chance you could let him know I'm here, please?"

The gorilla snapped up the cash as quickly as a cobra and asked without a change of expression:

"Which colleague would that be, monsieur?"

"Low-set, bald-headed barman. You can't mistake him."

The bouncer wore an expression of concentration, as if mentally reviewing the faces of the men inside the club.

"Has he a name, this guy?"

Platano was getting edgy.

"Are you all bald-headed in there?"

The bouncer displayed the merest hint of an amused smile, baring his black teeth in a grunt of approval. He held up a podgy index finger like a baton, to indicate that Platano should wait. He gently shut the door without a sound. Platano paced up and down in the alley, lit a cigarette and flicked the match at a big rat rifling through the dustbins. The rat turned to look at him, not at all intimidated. Creaking hinges disturbed them. Around ten metres from the main entrance, a little door opened and a man in his forties wearing the livery of a barman in a luxury brothel appeared, his skull gleaming in the lantern light. Recognising Platano, he signalled his relief and the tension melted from his face.

In Lyons there were no horse-cabs left parked outside the railway station, just two barouches with their hoods pulled up. Platano cursed and resigned himself to making the journey out to La Guillotière in one of these old crocks, liable to catch double pneumonia. In Paris he had never been cold, thanks to champagne and being mostly indoors, whereas his teeth had been chattering for hours now thanks to some problem with the heat on board the train. He had laid out a fortune for a first-class ticket; much good it had done him.

The coach driver pointed at a folded blanket on the seat. Platano threw it around him, sneezing from the dust and cursing the stink of mildew and dirt. On the trip to the cemetery he swore that he would buy himself a car after this job. Jules would teach him how to drive. Yes, a car of his very own, with all the paperwork in order, a sound engine that could be counted upon to carry him up to Paris or down to the Côte d'Azur whenever he felt like frittering away a fistful of francs. Which might be soon if this next job went off without a hitch.

He handed the coachman a generous tip, as had been his habit for some time now: discontented service folk have long memories if the police should question them about their customers. It was always wiser to leave them with a pleasant memory. Platano kept watch on the house from a distance. Only one window lit up on the first floor. He glanced at his fob watch: a quarter past nine. By this time Monsieur Thollon should be with his poor ailing mother, leaving the way open to Jules's hanky-panky. Platano spat on the ground.

That idiot Bonnot was starting to go soft. But the very mention of his latest news would be enough to bring him to his senses.

He paused under the window, gathered up a handful of gravel and started flicking little stones against the glass. After the fifth, a stone rather larger than the others, he was afraid that he might have to ring the bell. Was it possible that they hadn't heard him? It was true that Jules rarely got his leg over but he was not the sort to burn his bridges, especially at the moment. He tossed another stone which made a different clatter, as if the pane had been cracked. Eventually, a shadow appeared behind the curtains. The silhouette was Judith's. No mistake about that. Her hair was down and she was using one hand to hold her dressing gown closed around her bust. "Nice tits, Madame Thollon," Platano thought, tossing away what remained of the gravel. When the window opened, the Italian stepped forward into the light from the streetlamp so she could see who it was.

"Madame Thollon... it's me. I have to talk to Jules on a rather urgent matter. Could you ask him to come downstairs for a moment?"

Judith took a step backwards, looking vexed, and immediately closed the shutter, making no reply. Within seconds, he heard the click of a lock on the ground floor. Platano moved towards the door, expecting to see Jules half-undressed, his flies still open and wearing the angry expression of somebody interrupted at a crucial moment. In fact, what he saw was Judith, holding a paraffin lamp, her face severe and inscrutable, her dressing gown shut but not enough to deny him a glimpse of her cleavage, her breasts squeezed together in spite of the absence of a corset. Judith spotted Platano's leer but showed no embarrassment. On the contrary, she threw him a really dirty look and went on to announce curtly:

"I am alone. Jules is due shortly. Come in if you wish. I can offer you some tea while you wait for him."

Platano was dumbfounded, as if surprise at not finding Jules there had suddenly robbed him of all his bravado. Judith did not wait for him to answer and turned away, leading the way into the house with her lamp. Platano noticed that the dressing gown was rather clingy and that the young woman's buttocks had no reason to envy her generous breasts. He followed her into the sitting room and when she pointed him to an armchair, he replied with a cheeky grin:

"Thank you, Madame Thollon. But if I may choose, I'd rather have a stiff cognac. Warms the cockles better."

And his eyes dropped to where her knee and lower thigh stuck out from under the dressing gown.

Judith agreed, pouting sarcastically.

"Sit down. There ought to be a bottle upstairs. I'll fetch it."

As she climbed the stairs she was aware that Platano's eyes were following every sway of her hips. She tried to walk ramrod straight but to Platano's eyes that haughty and austere deportment proved even more alluring and sensual.

Judith came back with the bottle and a single glass. She poured Platano a double measure, dropped back into the neighbouring easychair and, staring straight at him, murmured:

"I don't like the way you say it."

Platano looked at her, puzzled, and naively asked:

"The way I say what?"

"The way you say the word 'Madame'. I'm sure you would invest the word 'whore' with less vulgarity."

While preserving his phony happy grin, Platano endured her stare for a moment. Then he drained his glass of cognac, clicked his tongue in appreciation and reached out a hand to seize Judith's; she pulled it back but not quickly enough to break free.

"You are mistaken, lovely lady. I say it with envy, if you get my meaning? Sheer envy."

Judith struggled free and leapt to her feet. She rushed to the window and Platano followed. He threw his arms around her waist from behind. She wheeled round angrily. He squeezed tighter and his face lunged closer as he stared at her lips.

"You're making a grave mistake. Take care what you do. Be very careful."

Platano squeezed even tighter and when Judith found herself backed against the wall, with no way of avoiding his mouth, he erupted into laughter and let her go. She only moved away by a couple of steps so as to face him without lowering her eyes. She was in control of her emotions but her panting breath showed her nervous tension. Platano was tempted to reach out his hands and place them delicately on the breasts whose nipples he could just make out beneath the silk, so as to squeeze them until she opened her mouth to gasp for breath. He imagined seizing her by the waist and testing the firmness of those shapely thighs and raising that dressing gown in order to touch that sleek, warm skin.

"I thought you came here to see Jules?" Judith said contemptuously. "I'm no courtesan. If you haven't the patience to wait for him, go take a stroll through the headstones. Maybe that will buck up your ideas."

Platano gave out a long sigh as if suddenly relaxing. It was a signal that he had abandoned all thoughts of exploring Judith's curves.

"A stroll through the headstones?" he asked curiously. "Why not? That way I can pick out a nice little spot for my future resting-place. One has to look to the future, isn't that right, Madame Thollon? But perhaps I might be better advised to consult your husband. You know, to arrange everything connected with the cost of the plot, payment terms, maintenance charges... "

Judith gestured impatiently and went to fetch a cup from the cupboard, half filling it with cognac before downing two quick sips.

"Platano, if you carry on, it won't be too long before you find yourself laid out there."

"Is that a threat?" he replied looking her up and down.

Judith clenched her teeth.

"I'm serious. And I'm talking about what you do, you and Jules."

Platano shrugged his shoulders. He grabbed the bottle, closing his fingers over hers and when Judith snatched her hand away, he adopted a resigned expression and drank straight from the bottle. Then he let out a hoarse sigh and stared at the label.

"I say, Madame Thollon, that puts the heat back," he said with an ambiguous look. "For want of anything better, I meant to say."

Judith switched tack and adopted a pleading expression.

"Stop this silly nonsense. If you were trying to treat me as a whore in order to prove something to Jules,well, you've tried that. But now stop. What are you after? I'm asking nicely."

Platano gave her a strange look. For the first time since he came in, he dropped the grin and the winking eye and suddenly turned serious. A chill ran down Judith's spine. Platano was capable of striking terror into anyone if he looked them in the eye with that murderous expression of his.

"What am I after?" he hissed between his teeth. "Listen, my lovely, don't go turning things around. You're the one that should be explaining to me what you are after, damn it."

Judith froze, her eyes fixed on him. Platano came closer, raising a finger to her face.

"What's going on in your head? What did you say to him to turn him into such a dummy?"

He let his eyes rove over her throat, her breasts, her belly, weighing her up the way one would a piece of merchandise.

"Sure, I can understand how you've the right equipment to keep him dangling as long as you want. But don't kid yourself. You will never be able to come between us."

His eyes hardened and he bared his little pointed teeth and added icily:

"Take my advice. Don't even think about it."

Judith seized his wrist and impaled him with her eyes.

"You've got it all wrong. I have absolutely no need to hold him here. He's the one who can't take it any more. Haven't you grasped that yet? You'll be the damnation of him. You're both going to die if you don't stop."

She dropped her arm and seemed distraught.

"They're going to kill you, Platano," she mumbled again, shutting her eyes. "They'll cut you down in the streets like animals."

He refused to listen to anything further. He struck a scornfully defensive stance, looking confident and invulnerable, using that sarcastic tone that he used as insulation against the outside world, as armour against all suffering.

"Yes, perhaps," he said with a sneer. "I don't find the idea at all unpleasant. We're not going to die in our beds, coughing our lungs up, cursing life and thinking wistfully about the good times. We won't lower ourselves to beg help from a son or pity from a nephew. No, Judith, you should have known it right from the outset. You've no right to try to change him. This is his destiny. Our destiny. And you're not part of it."

Judith was devastated at the sound of her name. She gave Platano a pained look, as if she were looking at a child doomed by some incurable disease. And in order not to wound him, she whispered softly:

"Don't be so sure. Between you and me, Jules has already made his choice. You know it. And you can do nothing to change that."

Platano just lost control of himself. He slammed the bottle down on the table, causing a spurt of cognac that stained Judith's dressing gown. He was about to swing around and slap her but he was halted in mid-turn by a whistling, a sort of familiar signal, coming from outside. Judith rushed to open the door.

Jules took her in his arms and instantly understood the distress signals coming from her tense body. He glanced towards the living room, catching sight of a silhouette and immediately thrust a hand inside his pocket to grab his pistol. Judith kissed him on the lips and gave him a reassuring look. Jules moved her aside and took a few steps forward. Platano was standing motionless in the middle of the room.

"Oh, it's you, Platano," Jules exclaimed, relaxing immediately.

Then, within a fraction of a second, he stiffened again and added:

"But what the hell are you doing here? For a second... "

Platano slipped his hands inside his pockets and simply stared at him without saying a thing. Jules walked up to him.

"Has something happened?"

Platano looked startled and grinned widely.

"No, why? Does it take something to happen before we can see each other?"

Jules looked sideways at him.

"We agreed that I would get in touch with you."

Platano accepted this and threw up his arms.

"Ah, yes, of course. Orders are orders. And my apologies

for the disturbance. It's just that there's an urgent matter we need to talk over. Shall we?" he said, gesturing towards the door.

Jules was still taken aback by Platano's attitude. He said nothing, but walked over to the door. As he passed her he took in the worried look in Judith's eye, as if trying to discover if she knew anything more about this. Judith looked blank; she sighed and folded her arms across her chest.

Jules wove a path between the chapels where a few lights dimly illuminated the way. There was a full moon but clouds were continually scudding across it, plunging the rest of the cemetery into utter darkness. Jules halted beside a statue, leant one hand on the dark stone drapery and probed Platano's eyes.

"I was meaning to get in touch with you tomorrow," he said, keeping his voice low. "You know very well that I prefer to keep this place out of everything. All our gear and guns are here and if they were to spot us sauntering around here... "

"Come on, Bonnot! What did you want to tell me?"

Jules stiffened. When Platano called him by name it meant that there was something on his mind.

"I couldn't hold out until tomorrow," Platano went on. "It's not as if I knew that you meant to contact me tomorrow or a month from now, is it?"

He kicked a stone away with his foot and cursed between clenched teeth.

Jules said nothing. The Italian heaved a nervous sigh and lit a cigarette. Then he offered one to Jules and struck another march. Illuminated by the flickering flame, both faces seemed tense and drawn.

"There's a job on," Platano resumed. "A big job. And a straightforward one. We just have to coordinate things properly. No need for guns or tools. All we need is a good, fast car big enough to accommodate a pile of sacks."

He broke off, waiting for some indication of interest from Jules. Jules sucked long and hard on his cigarette and walked off to sit down on a step.

"Sacks?" he asked, looking up at his mate.

"Yes. Lots of them. All of them filled with cash or valuables. But we're not going to have time to sort them out, which is why we'll have to toss them all on board and take them to some quiet spot. That's it."

Jules shook his head, stunned. In spite of the darkness, Platano could sense that he was skeptical. For the first time ever, he was going to have to waste time talking him round. Inside his head, he cursed Judith.

"And where might these sacks be?"

Platano leaned over, throwing his hands wide with enthusiasm, as if holding something big.

"Stuffed with cash, Jules! Post office van. Understand? Have you any idea how much money there might be in those sacks?"

Jules raised a hand but only to get him to calm down.

"Hold on: mostly those sacks contain mail, unusuable postal orders and a little cash. Unless... "

"Unless... " Platano repeated. "Unless we're talking about sacks bound for the overseas colonies and carrying the wages of all the State parasites: customs officials, legionnaires, prison officers and the whole crew that makes this shitty country great."

Jules held his cigarette between his lips but stopped puffing on it.

"Not the sort of shipment that goes out every day," he mumbled after a few seconds.

"Indeed. Which is why I was in a hurry to see you."

Jules stood up and paced back and forth, with Platano in tow.

"It'll take at least ten men for a raid on a post office van.

In practical terms, a squad armed to the teeth to effect a military take-over of some minor railway station, or, better yet, blow up a length of track, or... "

"Hey! Not so fast!" Platano interrupted. "What do you take me for? Do you think I'd put such a nonsensical proposition to you? Anyway, how do you intend to attack a train? On horseback, firing shots in the air? Come on, Jules, I'm surprised at you. "

Jules stopped.

"Tell me what you have in mind," he said, after flicking away his butt.

Sensing the aggression in his friend's tone, Platano smirked.

"It's easily told, my dear Bonnot. And it ends well. I have a guy who will tip me off in good time. We just have to be there when they toss the sacks down from the van. We pick them up and clear off. Or does that strike you as too much hard work?"

"Who'll be doing the throwing and why?"

"I know somebody in Paris who has a brother working on the railroad. A couple of ne'er-do-wells, anarchist sympathisers who know nothing about politics. All they know is that they've had their fill of knocking their pans in for a few pence. The one I know even suffers from an illness that has cost him his hair, eyebrows and beard — a real mess. He's an attendant on the night train. They've already told him that they'll be letting him go come the end of the month. High class ladies and their cuckolded husbands prefer to have their champagne served up by youngsters in the glow of good health. Is that enough for you?"

Jules shrugged.

"And can you trust them? If they go around bragging later, or start throwing their money round like madmen. What guarantee have we got?"

"Me. I'll vouch for them. But, damn it, Jules!" Platano erupted. "What's happening to you? I propose the perfect job to you and then I have to waste my time talking you into it. So, what do we do?"

Jules started pacing again.

"Do these two guys know who you are or where you live?"

"I only know the one who's a steward. We go back a long way to the days when I used to mix in certain circles in Paris. He doesn't know my name and, as to where I live, even I don't know that. Anyway, he's sound. A level-headed fellow, not given to talking, no vices, doesn't keep bad company."

"Has he ever served time?"

Platano waved vaguely.

"Eh, maybe once or twice, but that was for knife-play. Nothing that would make him a suspect."

"And what about the brother? Obviously, it will come to light immediately that he was the one who tossed down the sacks."

Platano stared at him with a teasing grin.

"Well spotted. He'll be doing practically all the work. You know, I'm floundering here, trying to understand where you're leading. For that very reason, the fellow will be getting off at the first stop, before they realise what has happened and he'll make his way to Marseilles. Our dealings will be exclusively with his brother who will bring him his share. He'll catch the first available boat to Algiers and won't stop travelling until he's gone at least ten-thousand kilometres south."

Jules pouted his lips, mulling over every aspect of the matter. The moon emerged from between a couple of clouds, illuminating Platano's face: he was quivering with anger.

"Well, Bonnot? Did I pass the test? Let me just point out that we don't have a lot of time. The shipment is due to be made in four days. It's a take it or leave it proposition. And if we decide to leave it they'll come up with somebody else."

Jules looked up at the moon. Then turned to stare fixedly at Platano.

"Sounds okay to me," was all he said, nodding his head.

They turned back towards the house. Before they got there, Jules asked:

"What's that you were saying to Judith?"

Platano burst out laughing.

"Nothing. I just asked if she would sleep with me occasionally as well. Just to play happy families. But it seems you have exclusive rights there. "

Trying not to react, Jules took a deep breath.

"Your Madame Thollon is really well put together, you know," the Italian added. "There are some things I'll never understand; what could have induced her to hitch up with a pall-bearer?"

Jules lit a cigarette but did not offer one to his friend.

"Worked out alright for you," Platano continued. "With a husband like him, inevitably she was ripe for the plucking when you happened along."

Pausing beneath the lantern, Jules looked him in the eye.

"You exaggerate. Now leave me be. I'm serious."

Platano threw up both hands in surrender.

"For the love of heaven, little bro'er, it's off limits. I know full well that I shouldn't be making wisecracks about Madame Thollon's tits. Lucky for me that I did nothing about the curve of her arse, which by itself seems to prove that that there has to be a God."

"I asked you politely," Jules repeated, speaking very quietly.

"But I was talking about the kind, just God. Fine, forget I said anything."

Platano flashed his sarcastic smirk for just a moment.

Then, all of a sudden, a hardness came over his features and his tone of voice became curt and emphatic:

"Turn up at the shop tomorrow. We'll have to find ourselves a car and I reckon three nights should do it. Bring your guns and some tools to force an entry into the garage, but the least cumbersome ones you can find. I already have what I need. So long, Bonnot. Have your fun all night long if you wish, but don't keep me waiting tomorrow morning. Got that?"

Jules watched him leave. For a long time, he leaned against the gate, smoking, head lowered, while Judith watched from the window but did not dare call to him.

Something had changed. Platano's tone, that icy, distant voice had scattered any remaining illusions. A few seconds earlier he had still been dreaming about suggesting the new world, a new life, packing it all in and meeting up again in Argentina, just the three of them, in the remotest spot imaginable, where they might have started laughing freely again, where they might live with no one sitting in judgment over them, without waiting for daybreak wondering what fresh horrors the light of the dawning day might hold. But now it was too late for that. The connection had been broken. Forever.

THE IDÉE LIBRE BOOKSHOP

Having left Romainville behind, Raymond-la-science and the others had set themselves up in the L'Idée Libre bookshop in the Galerie Clichy, which now became a rendezvous for interminable discussions and impracticable schemes. Raymond carried on arguing that total destruction was the only hope of salvation since nothing could be built on rotten foundations and that they should not be deterred by any risk to allegedly innocent victims: they had to commit themselves and no one could be allowed to stand on the outside looking in. Anyone who remained an onlooker was complicit. And if they came a cropper, they had no right to complain: indolence was an offence. The only point on which everybody agreed in the back rooms of L'Idée Libre was that all this impassioned chatter never seemed to be followed up by action. Meanwhile, life carried on: the corrupt politicians waited for the scandal to die down before they could recycle themselves in power without shedding an iota of their arrogance. Every attempt at change proved merely a reshuffle of the pack. Strikers were still sabred and shot, the guillotine blade fell with regularity and the revolutionary movement, so-called, churned out tracts filled with dreams and schemes interrupted only by fresh arrests and outrageous punishment. The government was replaced by men who had once styled themselves "of the left" and who, citing the eternal Prussian foe, pronounced that anybody pressing for trade union rights or decent pay must be a traitor. The Pas-de-Calais miners had found forty-thousand troops dispatched against them, the very same troops as would open fire on the strikers in Draveil, leaving fifteen dead and four-hundred wounded. And in Villeneuve-Saint-Georges it was the same again: six dead, two-hundred wounded. Civil servants and especially the teachers, were forbidden to join the CGT on pain of immediate dismissal. Clemenceau, the Tiger, who in opposition had called for conscientious objection in the wake of colonial massacres in Africa, had turned into France's number one cop as prime minister. And the slaughter in Morocco had flared up again with a vengeance. Clemenceau had a sarcastic answer to a reporter who had questioned him about his past record as a trouble-maker: "Anybody who has not been an anarchist at twenty cannot lay claim to ever having had a youth. Anyone who is still one at thirty is an idiot." As for the rest of Europe, the situation there was every bit as tense. Italy was embarking upon a colonialist venture and getting ready to overrun Libya, and a militarist government was sweeping away politics to the left of the Socialist Party. In Spain everything had fallen apart since the army's defeat in Morocco in 1909: a general strike in Catalonia had been crushed with more than two-hundred deaths followed by firing squads and mass deportations. In England the thirty-year-old Home Secretary, Winston Churchill, had decided to stamp out anarchists before they could become too widespread: their London headquarters in Sidney Street had been cordoned off by seven-hundred policemen and an artillery battery. He had given the order to open fire and all the siege victims perished when the building caught fire.

The group, which had pretty much taken shape by then, was joined from time to time by Eugène Dieudonné, a shy, thoughtful anarchist from Nancy who listened to Raymond

Eugène Dieudonné

with a blend of admiration for his scientific and philosophical knowledge, and anxiety about the delirious way in which he sometimes ranted. Deep down, Eugène had one obsession by the last months of 1909: his girlfriend Louise, who had accompanied him up to Paris after he was captured by Libertad's harangues, had left him to go and live with Lorulot. This man was yet another maverick theorist of free love, which he practised whenever a particularly young and pretty girl came within reach, and a preacher of dietary sciences according to which man is always what he eats. Lorulot had at one time been a big wheel in Romainville back in the days when it was still a commune, rather than the editorial offices of *L'Anarchie*. For some time, Eugène too had adopted the habit of sauntering around with a gun in his pocket. But he was the only person with whom Raymond behaved in a conciliatory and cautious manner, urging him not to take unnecessary risks over a gun with the numbers filed off and advising him to carry it around only in cases of certain danger. Raymond sensed that the kindly Eugène Dieudonné would have put a bullet into Lorulot's face more readily than into some despised symbol of the bourgeoisie.

That afternoon, Eugène arrived with his usual sad face but with his hands and lips slowly trembling. Carouy asked if he was feeling alright. He replied with a shrug of the shoulders and took a seat at the back of the shop. Shortly after that, Raymond managed to get him to talk: he had bumped into Louise and they had both burst into tears but had not reconciled. Louise was no longer sure she loved Lorulot, who was, in any case, hopping from bed to bed, returning to her only when there was nothing better on offer. Still, she could not make up her mind to leave him. For his part, Eugène lost his head; a matter of pride and resentment.

"I mean to shoot him down," he said eventually.

Raymond raised his eyes to heaven and quickly patted down Eugène's pockets. Alas, he found his little 7.65 Schwarzlose.

"Did I not tell you to leave that at home? We sell books here, you fool. When the time comes for it to be used, we certainly won't be meeting at L'Idée Libre."

Eugène dropped his head like a sulking child shunning advice from an adult.

"Don't fret, Raymond. I'm too much of a coward to go through with it. That swine can sleep easy in his bed."

"From what I've heard, he doesn't do a lot of sleeping exactly," commented Garnier, in a clumsy attempt to defuse the situation.

Carouy shot him an angry look.

Eugène ventured a hint of a smile and mumbled:

"You're right. He's in a different bed every night. And it's definitely not because he's afraid of me."

He put his hands across his face and rubbed his eyes for a long time.

"Louise is a real dim-wit," he went on. "He couldn't give a damn about her and treats her like a slave, but she does nothing."

Raymond, Carouy and Garnier all nodded in agreement. At which point in came Soudy flourishing a copy of L'Excelsior:

"That's what we should be doing instead of all this rubbish!" he exclaimed, tossing the newspaper on the table.

The others went over to scan the front page story. Soudy shook his head and opened it up at the News in Brief page. There was a detailed report on a raid on the Paris-Lyons train: a railway employee, suspect number one and presently untraceable, had tossed some mail sacks from the van near Saulieu just before the train passed through (according to an affidavit from one of his colleagues). It seemed obvious that his accomplices had then gathered up the sacks, leaving some car tracks in the muddy ground.

"Is that it?" said Raymond, giving Soudy a look.

"Isn't it enough? By now they must be somewhere safe counting the takings, whereas we don't even have the wherewithal for a box of ammunition."

Raymond sighed, removed his glasses and set about cleaning them carefully.

"A raid like that is pointless. Yes, of course, the money is useful. But what is required is a spectacular, a clear action with a specific message: we are commandeering the money that you have always stolen from our pockets and we're going to use it to make your lives hell. There. Now that would be worthwhile."

"Of course," Garnier piped up. "But in the meantime we do the talking while somebody else strikes."

"What do you mean by that?" Carouy asked. "There have always been raids. Who says this was the work of comrades?"

"They used a getaway car." Garnier replied, looking at each of them in turn.

Raymond stopped polishing his glasses for a second.

"Have you anybody particular in mind?"

"No,"Garnier said vaguely. "But that pair, the guy from Lyons and the Italian, are the only ones from the group who made a living out of nicking cars off the bourgeoisie and selling them on. Who knows?"

Raymond was puzzled for a moment.

"Oh yes, now I remember them. They dropped in on our meetings a few times."

Then he began to pace backwards and forwards, deep in thought.

"How many cars would there be currently in France?" he asked.

"Not that many," Carouy shot back.

Raymond glanced at him patiently, as if to say that he'd have preferred a less nebulous figure. Then he put this question:

"And how many robbers would you say know how to drive?"

"Very few," Carouy replied.

Raymond looked at him with a quite fatherly benevolence.

"Édouard, if I were to ask you how many anarchist comrades know how to drive, what would your answer be?"

"Er, None, as far as I know," said Carouy, shrugging his shoulders.

"Some of the vagueness is being taken out of the equation now. But you are mistaken, for the word is that there are at least two who can drive. And do you know what the problem is?"

The others looked at one another as they waited for his answer.

"That the police will use the same line of reasoning."

"In which case, they're going to get themselves caught," Garnier concluded.

"Not necessarily," said Raymond. "If they're cute enough to lie low in some safe place for a time, they may well get through this. Sooner or later, something serious will distract the cops. It all depends on how they behave for the next few days. By the way, what were their names?"

"Bonnot," said Carouy. "But the Italian guy has a funny-sounding name. "

"I know him." Eugène mumbled, staring off into the distance.

The eyes of the other four fastened on him. When he realised this, Eugène stammered:

"What's come over you? What did I say?"

Francois Raymond Callemin (Raymond la Science)

Jules Joseph Bonnot: Lyons prefecture, 1 March 1909 (aged 33)

"You know who?" asked Raymond.

"Jules Bonnot, from Lyons. He lived in Nancy for a time. We used to see each other often. He associated with a bunch of anarcho-syndicalists."

"And what ever became of him?" asked Garnier. "He hasn't been seen in Paris for a while."

"In Paris?" said Eugène. "Well, I've never come across him here. Last time I saw him was in Nancy. Then he was arrested in connection with some ruck with the nationalists. He did a little time in jail and I thought he'd gone back to Lyons."

Raymond put his glasses back on, picked up the newspaper and started to read the foreign news. The others went and locked themselves in the back room for a lesson from Garnier on how to dismantle an automatic that he had stolen from a night watchman.

When Eugène got to his feet and bade Raymond farewell, making for the door, Raymond said to him:

"Leave it at home, right?"

Eugène reached instinctively for his overcoat pocket and nodded his head, more depressed than ever.

IN PIGALLE

Platano poured the last remaining drop into his cup, made a show of wringing the neck of the bottle and immediately raised a hand to the waiter to order more champagne. The two girls sitting at the table reacted with clucks and clapping. The little blonde nestled into him in order to whisper something into his ear before nibbling his lobe and licking it. Platano burst out laughing, slipped an arm around her waist and kneaded her breast until it popped out of her bodice. The girl uttered a little squeal of sham indignation, fixed herself and thrust a hand between his legs by way of retaliation. He doubled over, laughing like a lunatic, while the other girl, a chubby brunette, leapt from her chair to join in the assault. The po-faced waiter arrived and uncorked the champagne. Platano straightened his face but as soon as the waiter had gone he picked up his glass and emptied it into the brunette's cleavage before jumping on her to lap up the champagne. The trio was making one hell of a racket but the club owners ordered the bouncers not to intervene: the gentleman appeared to have lots of money to spend and needed no coaxing. The two girls did not work at the club; they had arrived with this playboy, who had most likely picked them up from some street corner, but, even so, the boss charged a certain levy on prostitutes brought in from outside so that was no problem. The fourth bottle brought the bill up to an astronomical sum and the waiter was asked to hand him the bill when the fifth bottle arrived. Platano treated him like an impertinent servant and, thrusting a hand into his pocket, he drew out a wad of notes and tossed it on to the table.

"Count them yourself. And tell your country bumpkin of a boss that I want some Russian caviare right now, some oysters and another bottle in which to wash my hands after I've eaten. And, next time, bring me the bill when I ask you for it."

The waiter nodded unctuously. The two girls, tiddly, laughed even louder.

Two hours later, all three of them were rolling around on a hotel bed in the Rue Rochechouart. Platano had damned nearly come to blows with the concierge who had refused to let him bring the two "young ladies" upstairs. The brunette, being more experienced, had resolved the problem by fishing a few bills out of Platano's pocket and tucking them into the pocket of the concierge who promptly withdrew his objection.

At daybreak, Platano woke with a start. He was alone. He rushed over to fumble through his pockets, teetering drunkenly, only to find that the two young ladies had been quite honest: they had relieved him only of their fee. That fee may well have been uncommonly high but he still had something left. He looked at the crumpled notes strewn on the bed. His head was spinning and he had a sour taste in his mouth. He went to stand under the shower. After he had let the water pour over his skull for a few minutes, he punched the wall. Then he doubled over, crying with anger.

SUMMIT MEETINGS

Commissioner Jouin was trying to get comfortable on his padded chair but there was a tingling in his legs that made it impossible for him to stop fidgeting. In front of him Xavier Guichard, the head of the Sûreté and his direct superior, was concluding a lengthy telephone conversation with the minister who, judging by Guichard's burning ears, was certainly calling upon him to combat the growing unrest with increased efficiency. The boss was leaning over so far that his forehead brushed against the desk every time he said:

"But of course, Excellency. That will be done, Excellency. I understand perfectly, Excellency."

Once he had hung up the receiver, Guichard opened a drawer and took out a spotless handkerchief with which he mopped his brow. He was tempted then to tuck it into his jacket, most likely to mop up the two huge damp stains spreading from armpit to chest, but his eyes met Jouin's and he promptly contained himself.

"Damned imbeciles, I've told them a hundred times to go easy on the coal," he grumbled, rolling his eyes in the direction of the cast-iron stove. It's too warm in here. And when you step outside, you catch your death!"

Jouin agreed, frowning, for it was not at all warm.

"Anyway, where were we?" Guichard asked, resuming his usual businesslike, arrogant attitude.

"The manager of the club in Pigalle," Jouin prompted him.

"Oh yes, of course. So? Any developments?"

"Nothing concrete. But we might have a lead. The manager owes us a few favours and reports to us on a regular basis, notifying us about suspicious types or rumours."

The telephone rang again. Guichard twitched impatiently and answered.

"Who? Oh, good heavens, Mademoiselle. As long as it's the minister, that's fine, but right now... yes, of course, tell him I'll ring him back in ten minutes."

Jouin took it that Guichard's wife was having difficulty deciding what orders to issue to the cook.

The head of the Sûreté excused himself, saying:

"This town is becoming unliveable. I am being forever pestered over the slightest nonsense. But carry on, if you will."

"Anyway, in his most recent report the manager refers us to a fellow who appears to have come into an enormous sum of money all of a sudden. And who is splashing it about in an unwarranted manner, throwing in confidences and allusions to certain prostitutes, whom we have already questioned, and who bear out our suspicions."

Guichard glared at the commissioner impatiently.

"Have you come here to tell me that some debauchee has probably robbed a safe?"

"Not just any debauchee," said Jouin, opening the file he was holding on his lap.

He picked out a mug shot photograph and presented it to Guichard.

"Giuseppe Sorrentino, known as Platano. Italian, with previous convictions for theft and receiving, marked down as an individualist anarchist, an habitué of so-called illegalist circles."

Guichard's eyes lit up at the mention of the word anarchist.

"Oh, very good! The new breed of bomb-planters."

"Not quite," Jouin corrected him. "These ones have a preference for pistols. No indiscriminate massacres; their strategy is tit-for-tat, specific targets, open warfare against the State and society in general."

Guichard made a vague face as if concluding that all these details were merely a waste of time.

"Be that as it may, Commissioner Jouin, what matters is that they are anarchists. What are your intentions?"

"We're in the process of carrying out inquiries. Once I have definite information I will apply for search warrants. For the time being, I am trying to get the measure of the differences within their ranks so as to avoid lashing out blindly."

The head of the Sûreté winked an eye and shook his head.

"Let me explain something to you. Listen, laying hands on a gang of illegalist anarchists undoubtedly represents a positive result. But that's not what is being asked of me with such insistence. Locking up a burglar, even if he be a potential murderer, certainly doesn't resolve the problem."

"It is not for the police to resolve the real problem," Jouin let slip.

His superior looked sideways at him but opted to ignore the remark in order to avoid tiresome argument.

"Our problem, dear Jouin, is to bring enemies of the established order before the courts. In certain instances, this isn't too hard. We need only identify the hotheads and render them harmless. But the looming reality in these unsettled times requires that we be far-sighted, requires us to pay attention and calculate our every move. And above all that we act while making the most of the impact of certain operations on public opinion. Do you understand my meaning?"

The commissioner sighed, nodded agreement and said:

"I believe I do. Wait until the irreparable comes to pass, stepping in after the event and not before it, so as to produce the reaction that the politicians are waiting for."

Guichard clenched his jaws but kept his self-control. He could not stand this upstart Jouin, but he knew that Jouin was the only person in the Sûreté capable of producing the results he was counting on.

"It is not for us to sit in judgment of the deeds of the government," he stated. "Our calling is to protect citizens from society's internal threats. Thieves and murderers will always be very numerous, and the system is used to living with them without undue upset. But it cannot coexist with those who commit those very same offences in the name of revolution, or of far-fetched notions of social justice that inevitably translate as violence and disorder. If we arrest an anarchist on the grounds that he has burgled a villa, some people are going to look upon him as a victim, a poor wretch who tried to lay hands on some of the wealth denied him. There is a substantial segment of public opinion that fails to appreciate that we are dealing here with failures, debauchees and all manner of scum doomed to insignificance. Some pure souls look upon such individuals as the champions of the oppressed."

Guichard leant forwards and lowered his voice before concluding his sermon:

"But if we arrest them after an atrocity, if, say, they have massacred some poor head of a household guilty only of having worn a uniform or of standing in their way, then, my dear Jouin, in the eyes of such freethinkers, the anarchists will be nothing but bloodthirsty, common criminals. Which is what is asked of us. Nothing more, nothing less."

The commissioner responded with a movement of the head like an obedient soldier. He stood up, took back the snapshot of Platano, slipped it back inside the file and said:

"I understand very well. I am to wait until some head of a household is sacrificed and until the newspapers honour us with their front pages for a few days. Then I step in. Reassure the minister: it won't take long, given the turn that events are taking. Au revoir, Monsieur Guichard."

Jouin then turned on his heels and walked briskly away. The head of the Sûreté kept his eyes trained on the door, musing that the commissioner really was starting to blow things out of proportion.

21 NOVEMBER 1911

"Why wait any longer? If your mind is made up, let's go right away, starting tomorrow," Judith murmured.

He stroked her hair and his hand swept down her back, sensing the shudder as his fingers glided down her spinal column. Judith's cheek was resting on his chest. Jules could not see her worried face, the preoccupied look in her eyes.

"It'll take a week," he said. "Time to book our passage and tidy up a few last items."

"But we can leave straight away from Saint-Malo or Le Havre," she protested. "We can book into an inn far from here and find ourselves a passage to Argentina. I'm stifling here in this place. Now that our minds are made up I'm more scared with every passing minute."

Jules held her face between his hands and looked into her eyes. They were sparkling but bewildered and anxious.

"There's nothing to be afraid of now, Judith. The post office van raid went off splendidly. We have the money we needed. And we're leaving. But first... "

Jules closed his eyes for a moment.

"First I want a word with Platano. I owe him that much. And if he refuses to listen, I'll bid him a final farewell. But I can't dump him just like that. I can't. Can you understand that?"

Judith nodded. Her hands clung to Jules and she hugged him to herself. She was stricken with terror by a vision of him sprawled on the pavement in a street running with blood, naked and defenceless.

He smiled, leant over and kissed her on the mouth.

"You mustn't be afraid. Not now. It really is over, believe me. A week at the outside and we'll be at sea, watching this damned country glide towards the horizon."

There came a muffled, distant knocking at the door. Loud enough, though, to stop them in their tracks. Then, for a moment, absolute silence. Judith looked intensely at Jules. He signed to her not to make a sound.

"Come on, Jules! Hurry up!"

Platano's voice.

Jules jumped off the bed, hurriedly pulling on his shirt and trousers. Judith rushed over to the window, covering herself with the curtain as best she could. It was Platano. Soaked to the skin, edgy and walking back and forth like a lunatic.

"He's alone," she whispered.

She went to get her dressing gown but as she was opening the door Jules stopped her.

"I'll go."

Judith froze and let him by. He squeezed her arm reassuringly, then skipped down the stairs.

He let Platano in and, noting that he was not taking off his oilskins, realised that he was there to fetch him.

"Let's move it, Jules. As quick as we may."

Jules said nothing. He just carried on staring at him, waiting for what was to follow. Platano slammed a fist into the palm of his hand and started to pace the room, dripping water on the carpet and muttering between his teeth, his face drawn, hysteria in his eyes.

"A damned close shave," he grunted, with a click of his fingers. "Two cops outside the house. And it was me they were waiting for. They've already discovered the shop in the

Rue Voltaire. I called by just to check, in the hope that I was just imagining things. But there was a Black Maria and a lorry there and they were taking everything away."

Jules lit a cigarette. Platano snatched the pack from his hands. Jules passed him a burning match and said:

"Calm down a second. I don't get it. What house are you talking about?"

Platano exhaled smoke and flapped his hands impatiently.

"I'd rented a room, three days ago. And lucky for me I wasn't at the hotel, otherwise, at that time of night... But, damn it, we have no time to lose! It's a miracle that they're not here already!"

"And what would bring them to me?"

"Why wouldn't they uncover this cursed cemetery? When they showed up at my place and at the shop? Work it out! And I told you to stop this nonsense, damn it. You can't indulge yourself by playing at a normal life like this, you fool! We should have kept on the move and found a change of surroundings and not given them time to work it out."

"Keep your voice down, and stop looking for excuses," Jules said icily.

Platano froze in his tracks. He opened his mouth, dumbfounded and flashed a murderous grin.

"Excuses? Oh, very good. I risk my neck coming here to warn you and you talk to me of excuses? If we had stuck together we'd be a hundred kilometres away by now."

He took a few steps, spluttering curses, his face buried in his hands, then turned to face Jules.

"Right. You want to stay with this woman so as to enjoy your last moments? On you own head be it. As for me, I'm getting out of here. Right now."

Jules expelled all the air from his lungs in one long, loud sigh. He did not have time to ask for further explanation. He sensed that the responsibility for the whole thing lay with

Platano, but it was too late now.

"I'll get my bag. Wait for me outside and if you see anybody coming, throw a stone up at the window and scarper."

Platano shook his head and lifted his cape to show the butt of his revolver, as if to say that he would shoot if he spotted anybody. Then out he went, leaving the door wide open.

Judith had her back to the wall. She was staring at Jules's bag, which she had set on top of the bed along with his overcoat, jacket, tie and oilskin. She hadn't bothered to get dressed. And he never told her to. He kissed her passionately. Then he mechanically pulled on his jacket without looking at her.

"I'm leaving the cash here. Hide it away safely and wait for a few days. If they should come, tell them that you haven't set eyes on me for at least a fortnight and that you know me by some other name. There's nothing they can do to you."

Judith came up to him and just managed to mutter:

"And... after that?"

Jules struggled into his oilskin and grabbed both her hands.

"Whatever happens, a week from now take all the money and head for Le Havre. No luggage, just the bare necessities. If they tail you, they mustn't have any clue that you're leaving for good. Pick some nondescript hotel on the Boulevard Maritime. Then look for the Sainte-Honorine Abbey. Every morning, between eleven and eleven-thirty, stroll past it. But don't pause and vary your route each time in case anyone realise where we intend to meet up. When I show up, I'll follow you from the abbey, and if all goes well... "

Judith could stand it no longer and threw her arms around his neck. Jules caressed her softly and mumbled to her:

"You'll see, I won't make you wait too long. And I may even get there ahead of you. Now, all we need to do is play it safe."

She looked at him but said nothing, betrayed by the sobs that were choking her.

"Have you got all that? Abbey of Sainte-Honorine, between eleven and twelve... "

Judith closed her eyes and broke away from him signalling that she understood. He gave her a long, anguished kiss. Then he fetched his two Brownings from the wardrobe and slipped one into his pocket, stuffed the other into his waistband, grabbed his bag and ran out.

Platano was waiting for him out on the street, beside a bicycle. Jules grabbed his own bicycle from the tool shed and headed for the gates. As he passed under the window, he looked up to see Judith with her open hands pressed against the glass.

ONE-WAY TRIP

They had a second hide-out, a shed on the Vienne road. They rarely used it and hadn't been out there for months. Given that they had leased it in the name of someone who had been dead for a long time, but whose identity was genuine enough, there was a slim chance that the police might not have stumbled across it yet. It was in an isolated area, with no neighbours to offer descriptions or recognise them from a snapshot. Getting away by train was too risky. If things had reached the pass that Platano claimed, the police would already be monitoring the station. And in the garage out there there was a six cylinder twenty-four horse-power Buire that Jules had been holding in reserve for long trips. He had changed the chassis and engine numbers and done a perfect job repainting the licence plate, substituting the initial 'S' for the Saint-Etienne department for the 'I' of Isère, from where it had been stolen. Salvation lay in their making off in this big Buire convertible. They had no option. It was their only hope of putting some distance between themselves and Lyons before daylight.

It was Jules's turn to remain by the roadside this time, with his bag in his left hand, his Browning cocked and ready in his right. Platano walked straight up to the gateway, not bothering to look around. Fatalistic, he was determined to stake all on the few seconds it would take to undo the padlock. When the two gates opened wide with a piercing shriek, he turned to Jules and beckoned him over. It was pitch black and every dark shadow might be a policeman lurking behind a bush, but they had no choice in the matter. Jules stepped forwards, holding his gun at hip height, trained on the shadows, and walked up to the shed. Once inside he decided to trust to luck. If they were lurking nearby this was where they would be lying in wait for them, cutting off any chance of retreat across the fields. Jules stuffed the Browning into his pocket and tossed his bag into the boot while Platano positioned himself at the exit. Then he lifted the bonnet, reconnected the battery cables and primed the petrol pump, moving around in utter darkness, relying solely on memory, on moves that he had made countless times before. He switched on the ignition and cranked the handle. The Buire had lain idle for months. He tried a dozen times. Cold sweat was flowing down his face and dampening his back. The six cylinders started up with a rhythmic splutter. He jumped behind the wheel and turned up the engine. Platano climbed into the passenger seat beside him. Jules put the Buire into first gear and wrenched off the hand-brake. The Buire surged forwards out of the shed. He zig-zagged right and left to dodge potential shots. But there was nobody out there. The police had not yet uncovered this second hide-out. By the time they turned on to the Paris road the rain had started to trickle down into the corners of the windscreen and the wind was chilling their faces and hands and fluttering their sleeves and collars. Yet Platano looked quite at ease. He was smoking and keeping an eye on the road, the distant house lights, the signposts. Jules, on the other hand, was shivering. And not from the cold.

After Mâcon, Platano gazed at Jules for a few seconds and then asked:

"Do we really have to chug along at forty?"

Jules did not answer him right away. Only when his friend's stare became unbearable did he reply.

"The engine's at least three years old. It's wiser not to ask too much of it."

Platano made a face, as if conceding that Jules was the expert and that he was deferring to him. A few minutes after that, he said chirpily:

"Shit, little bro'er we've led them a merry dance, eh? If it were up to me, we'd pull in at the next decent inn to down a couple of bottles in a toast to these swine. Instead you have a face on you like a pall-bearer at a funeral."

Jules clenched his hands around the steering wheel, straining to stop the tremors. But this time he could not hold his tongue.

"I've a right to feel hard done by. And I'd still like to know what the hell happened!"

Platano stiffened. For a moment his smug, debonair pose deserted him. He placed a hand on the dashboard and looked closely at Jules.

"Hey, Bonnot, is there something eating you? Out with it, for shit's sake! What didn't you understand?"

"Heaps of things," Jules retorted, throwing him an angry glare. "The only sure fact is that you managed to get me to leave everything behind. Are you happy now? And what for? Am I back up to my neck in the shit?"

Platano tapped on the windscreen.

"Go fuck yourself. I came looking for you just before they could arrest you and what do you do? Take it out on me. Thanks a bunch. You're a real idiot."

"I'm not taking it out on you. There's something wrong with you. Your head's full of weird notions. I'm not saying that you did it on purpose. Just that you did it, that's all. "

"Did what?" shouted the angry Platano.

Jules shook his head. He knew that Platano was to blame for their predicament. He had been expecting as much, but had been hoping it might not come to pass. Instinctively, he felt that Platano had pushed his luck far enough to confront them both with a fait accompli. But he had realised that there was no point arguing the matter.

The sun was coming up. They took the national highway to Melun, via Auxerre. For hours, neither of them opened his mouth. Platano's nerves were beginning to fray. He was fidgeting in his seat, pounding a fist on his thigh and from time to time he would produce his Fosberry, check the shells in the cylinder, then count those in his pocket and add a few others from a box kept in his leather bag. Jules remained indifferent, monitoring his movements out of the corner of his eye and he could feel the growing tension. They swept through Saulieu but were scarcely out of town again when he slowed the car and pulled over to the side. Platano looked at him quizzically. Jules drew to a halt, pulled on the hand-brake and hissed between his teeth:

"Shit, I knew we shouldn't push her too far."

He climbed down and lifted the bonnet. Using a rag, he unscrewed the radiator cap. A jet of steam spurted out, stinking of rust. There was scarcely any water left inside. That must have been taking its toll of the valves and rocker arms. Jules turned to Platano and stated blandly:

"We'll have to wait for her to cool down. Then I'll have a go at readjusting the rockers. Let's hope it's not too late."

Platano climbed down with a sigh. There was an inn nearby. They walked there at an easy pace. After filling the radiator, they had a bite to eat. The waitress's name was Hélène Remont. A few days later she would recount to reporters that the two men seemed sullen, as if they had had a difference of opinion, and that they hadn't exchanged one word throughout the entire meal.

Jules tinkered around for at least a couple of hours, trying to set the rockers back in their proper position. They had overheated fatally but might they hold out for a few hundred kilometres more? They set off again in the early afternoon. As they neared Joigny the engine started to cut out. It stalled a few minutes after that. The incessant rain had flooded the ignition and there was no chance of their getting it going again. It was almost night so Jules decided to look for an inn in the hope that it might be sunny the next day so that the spark plugs and cables might get a chance to dry out. They pushed the Buire on to a grassy verge, trying not to get it stuck in the mud, and headed for the lights of the suburbs. They came across a sort of a tavern which rented rooms and resigned themselves to waiting for daybreak to come.

The room was cramped and damp and it smelled of stale air and damp wood. It had twin beds with just one lamp resting on the little bedside table dividing them. Jules started to read a newspaper that he had borrowed from the landlady. Platano chain-smoked while staring at the ceiling.

"Don't like Paris," he said after half an hour, unable to bear the tension any longer. "Too much control and the anarchists attract cops like magnets. We'd be wise to stay clear of them. There isn't one whose cover hasn't been blown."

Jules threw down his newspaper and muttered:

"The anarchists? Once upon a time you'd have said 'the comrades'."

Platano stubbed out his cigarette in the cup he was using as an ash-tray and scornfully shrugged his shoulders.

"I no longer have anything in common with them, nor with anybody else. Once upon a time I was a complete idiot, with a head filled with dreams. A dreamer. "

He turned to stare at Jules and added:

"We're better off with just the two of us. There's no danger of infiltration, or defection and it's easier for us to move."

Jules ignored the allusion to future schemes and resumed his reading. He felt the need to make it plain once and for all that the topic was closed, but he put this off until later as he searched for the right words to broach the matter. He was well aware that Platano did not want to know and would refuse to face facts.

"As you see it, should we stay in Paris for long?" Platano asked as he lit yet another cigarette.

"No... " said Jules, pretending to carry on reading his paper. "I'd recommend that we go to Choisy-le-Roi. Do you remember Dubois, the mechanic?"

Platano nodded.

"Well maybe he can take on the Buire and sell it on. "

"Sure, why not?" Platano replied with a shrug of the shoulders. "But I'd make for the Atlantic coast. I can't be sure, but we could make Bordeaux our base and move on from there to Biarritz. The place is awash with queers and high-class whores, folk who have no idea how to spend the cash stuffed in their pockets. Furs, jewellery, safes filled to overflowing and spanking new cars. Biarritz gets them even before Paris does. Always the latest models and they change them the moment a new model comes on the market. Easy pickings. "

He stretched out his legs and put his hands behind his head with an air of satisfaction, savouring the prospect of Biarritz. Jules rested the paper on his chest, took a deep breath and clenched his teeth. He could hold his tongue no longer. "Platano, I won't be staying in France. You must have known as much for some time now, right?"

"And where are you going?" Platano asked light-heartedly.

"Me? Argentina," Jules bluntly replied in a hoarse, tense voice. "Judith's coming with me."

There were a thousand other things he'd have liked to say in order to try to get Platano to accept what he already knew, because he did know it, but the words would not come and he just carried on staring at the man who had once been his only friend in the world.

Platano nodded, his mouth twisting into a sarcastic expression. He stood motionless for a few seconds, watching the smoke from his cigarette spiral upwards and disperse in a draught from the window. Then he sat down suddenly on the bed and leaned towards Jules, his eyes feverish, his face flushed.

"Bravo. Bully for you. Off you go and get yourself a good flock of sheep and a squad of children to help you shear them. Play happy families on virgin soil. Bravo. That's what you've always wanted, right? You needed a boob to help you get the money together and you found one. Now that you've built up your stash, it's bon voyage."

"Platano, don't try to twist things. I'm not about to dump you in the middle of nowhere. You can come away with me. Europe is finished and we'll be the trail-blazers. Carrying on doing what we've been doing up to now only serves to bring trouble down on our necks. Come with us, Platano. There's still time."

"I told you before, Jules. Go fuck yourselves, you and your Judith."

Jules stood up, walked over and took his cigarettes out of the overcoat hanging on the wall and lit one. He was having a hard time controlling the tremor in his hands.

"Can it be that it never occurred to you before? We're done for here!" he hissed, trying not to shout. "It's finished. Got that? Finished! All we have to do now is hang around until they come for us. And why? Why carry on with this lousy life? For one thing, every job had a specific purpose. We wanted to lash out at them in order to show that they were not invulnerable. We did that. Okay? And look what good it did us. Has anything changed? Only for the worse. For us to go on would be acting for acting's sake. What would be the point of it? Getting drunk on the adrenaline? Is that it?"

Platano avoided his gaze. The expression on his face had switched from anger to nausea.

"Are you going to answer me?" Jules pleaded with him.

"Just go fuck yourself," Platano snapped.

He stretched out on the bed, turned his face to the wall, shut his eyes and pretended to sleep.

As if paralysed, Jules stared at him for some time. It had been a waste of time. At one point he was aware of a stabbing pain in his chest. He realised that his torso was hard and swollen. He breathed out and it seemed to drain him of all his strength. Round-shouldered and dragging his feet, he shuffled over to the window. The rain had stopped. There were still a few stars in the night sky. Dawn was not far off. Jules leant his head against the cold, damp pane and looked at one tiny light twinkling in the distance. A bicycle on the road leading to Joigny. A worker on the early shift, maybe. Or a farmhand pedalling out to a potato field kilometres away, out to somebody else's land, to plunge his hands into the soil there for twelve hours, from the still dark morning until the dark twilight, day in and day out.

He could hear Platano's regular breathing. He was fast asleep. Jules looked at him. Even in sleep, his face was drawn and mischievous. He thought to himself: "Maybe that's the way he always looks when he's unconscious. When he was awake, his light-heartedness was just a front. A mask to stop anyone from gauging his true thoughts. Sleep gave him back his real face. The face of a man who knew only how to hate."

When Platano suddenly opened his eyes he stared into space as if he could not quite get his bearings. Jules was standing beside the bed, doing up the buckles of his bag, before pulling on his overcoat.

"I'm off for a coffee. I'll wait for you downstairs," he said, pulling on his shoes.

Platano never made a sound. He sat bolt upright but avoided meeting Jules's eyes. He grabbed the towel from the chair then scuttled off to the bathroom at the end of the corridor.

By the time they made it back to the car it was gone ten o'clock, the sun was peeping out from behind the low cloud and the rain had stopped a couple of hours earlier. Jules set about removing the spark plugs, wiping them and cleaning them one at a time, and then he noticed that the gear box was shiny around the gaskets. After laying out a tarpaulin that he found in the boot, he crawled underneath the vehicle and discovered a big oil leak. That meant that the Buire would not even make it as far as Sens, the next town after Joigny. They had to find some oil and try to change the joints. Jules let out an oath as he remembered that it was Sunday. Platano, leaning against one of the bumpers, watched what Jules was doing but looked distracted as if it all meant nothing to him.

"I'll have to come up with a spare part," Jules told him, as he wiped his hands on a rag. "It's not very complicated as repairs go, but it takes a bit of time. The hardest part is finding somebody who has what we need."

Platano nodded rather indifferently and gave him a distracted look. Jules ignored him and said:

"Let's try getting her going. If we take it slowly and keep the speed low, we might just make it into town. "

At the third turn of the crank-handle, the engine spluttered, spat out thick black smoke and eventually started ticking over with a sinister clicking sound, as if there was something broken in the works. They reached the town and after some slow progress at low speed, they found themselves a mechanic who worked on Sundays. Naturally, he did not have the right joints, but he managed to help them out by using a larger set taken from a lorry and fitted over the parts that had been removed. They would not last long, but might just hold out for the rest of the trip ahead of them. Jules chose to move on and dismantle the gear box elsewhere, so as not to leave the mechanic with too detailed a memory. The fellow had displayed an interest in the Buire and had already started to ask awkward questions. They pulled up on a small country lane, not too far from the national highway, and Jules spent the entire day there sorting out the joints. He was forced to break off his work due to fading light. Throughout all this time, Platano had said not one word. From time to time he would go up to Jules and give him a meaningful look, as if trying to provoke him. Jules had carried on unscrewing the nuts and loosening the clutch plates which were smeared with grease, and he bit his tongue more in order to stop himself asking Platano what was with the dirty looks than because of the physical exertion. They spent the night in a suburban hotel and Platano fell asleep right away, or pretended to.

Starting at seven the next morning, Jules set about reinstalling the gear box and by around eleven o'clock the Buire was chugging more or less normally down the Melun road. An hour after that, as they were passing through the Les Logettes wood, they heard a bang from underneath the bonnet, followed by a piercing whistling sound. Jules braked, shut his eyes and rested his head on the steering wheel. Then he made up his mind to get out to see what fresh delight this damned engine had in store for him. It was not all that serious: the fan belt had gone. There was a spare one in the boot and he would have it changed in half an hour. There was a warm breeze. Jules removed his overcoat and set the Browning he was carrying in his waistband down on the seat. Platano sat there, smoking, his eyes raised to heaven.

After about ten minutes, as Jules was loosening the pulley in order to fit the new belt, Platano loomed behind him. Jules straightened up and found him staring with a malicious smirk on his face. He had the Browning in his hand. Jules hesitated, his eyes on the gun. Platano started toying with the safety catch. He took aim at a flight of birds far overhead, then examined the pistol and tested its weight. Jules said nothing and just waited. Platano let out a nervous laugh and murmured calmly and coolly:

"You can go off and play at being a shepherd in Argentina, but not on my money."

Jules stiffened.

"What do you mean?"

"Ah, what do I mean? Do you really not know what I'm talking about?"

"Listen, if this is some sort of a joke... "

"You need to get more sleep of a night," Platano said, nodding sarcastically.

Jules sighed and looked at the Browning again.

"That way you won't go poking your nose in where it's not wanted."

"Any chance you might let me in on what your talking about?" Jules asked angrily.

"The ten thousand francs missing from my pockets. Know anything about that?"

Jules felt his head spinning. This wasn't happening. Anything but this.

"You're demented, really, you are. You have mental problems. Serious ones. "

Platano leapt forward and grabbed him by the collar.

"So! I'm demented, am I? Is that your way out of it? If he's demented, there's no point in discussion!"

"Stop it, please," Jules stammered, dismayed. "You're looking for some excuse, I know. But you've chosen the lousiest, least creditable excuse of all. How can you come and tell tell me that you've had your money nicked. Me of all people?"

"Who then? Is there another louse in these parts? Some other son of a bitch who has it in him to gyp a friend?"

"Enough!" Jules cried. "You need taking care of, you fool!"

And even as he said it he made an instinctive move: he grabbed the Browning in a fit of anger and tried to wrest it away from Platano. The gun wasn't the problem. It was the tirade of cruel abuse that made him snap. Platano, also acting on instinct, reacted by clinging all the tighter to the gun, pulling his hand back, pointing the barrel of the gun into the air. He found himself with the gun pressed against his neck. Jules usually kept one up the spout. Platano had flicked off the safety catch only a minute earlier.

The shot rang out bringing everything to a standstill. It lasted only a fraction of a second, but when Jules called it to mind later, it seemed unending, stretching away into infinity. Yet it was all over in a flash: as long as it took for him to see Platano's eyes roll up, stare at the sky and blend into the grey November morning, and for the rush of dark, almost black, blood to spurt from under his ear. Jules clasped him in his arms, placed his open palm against the ghastly hole and applied pressure, trying to hold back the life that was ebbing way, drenching his collar, shirt and chest, trickling down his entire body, soaking his clothing, the grass, the hand that still clung to the revolver. Jules kept his fingers clamped over the wound, shaking his head in denial, biting his tongue, fighting back the tears and silently begging Platano to look at him and tear his eyes away from the sky, to come back for a few moments and turn back time to erase this silly game.

Platano gave a long gurgle that turned into a desperate death rattle, a sound that seemed to convey, not pain, but an inconsolable regret. Then he twitched, kicking at the air, at nothingness and at life, and then he went rigid in Jules's arms. Jules held his head against his breast for a time, maybe a few minutes, maybe for hours.

MORGUE

Jouin flashed his card at the attendant who glanced at it before turning to amble down the panelled corridors. The commissioner followed. The tour seemed endless, yet God knows how often he had been there before, meandering through this labyrinth. And with every descent into these antiseptic precincts, Jouin was stunned to find that, for all the pestilential disinfectant used, the stench of death always broke through. A heavy, bittersweet smell that seeped into the air and into people, an unwholesome stink, never so strong as to cause repulsion but so morbidly familiar that every human being carried it imprinted in his genetic memory; it was the same in every place where corpses were stored, impossible to remember when far away, but instantly recognisable the second one stepped inside.

The attendant opened the last of an endless succession of doors and beckoned to the duty doctor who welcomed Jouin, offering him his hand. Jouin would rather have touched nothing, because he knew that, once outside, he would be able to detect the smell on his own skin, but he returned the physician's handshake. The man in the white gown steered him through a series of litters on which lay cadavers covered by undyed and yellowing cotton sheets, only the feet exposed with the inevitable little tags dangling from their big toes.

"I've just finished up," the doctor announced. "I was about to put him back in the cooler."

He halted and jerked his chin in the direction of the body. Jouin waited for him to pull back the sheet. When he saw Platano's face, he nodded. Then he glanced at the clipboard and walked around to the far side to check one final detail. The tattoo had all but blended in with the bluish skin tones, but the words were still legible.

"Without a glimmer of remorse," Jouin mumbled.

The doctor grinned and said:

"Whoever did him in must have taken it literally." Then, after a few seconds, he asked: "He was shot by an accomplice, right?"

"So it would appear," Jouin replied.

The doctor shrugged his shoulders in contempt and added:

"First they steal, and then they start killing one another. If nothing else, this is one less good-for-nothing in circulation."

Jouin ignored the doctor who seemed to want to chat. And he consoled himself with the thought that there were some callings worse than his own.

"I've heard that they're not common criminals," the doctor began again. "Anarchists, right?"

Jouin nodded and pretended to check something on the clip-board.

"Oh, good," the doctor carried on. "When all's said and done, they're all criminals, regardless of the claptrap about revolution and the society of the future. "

"Thank you, doctor. I have finished," Jouin cut him off.

"Has he no relatives, this... " here the doctor used two fingers to lift up the toe-tag "...this Sorrentino, Giuseppe?"

"No. I don't believe he has."

"Fine," the doctor concluded. "Another windfall for the anatomy students."

And he trundled Platano's corpse towards the cold room. Jouin bumped into Guichard the moment he stepped into his office. He had not intended to seek out the head of the Sûreté and had been hoping to make his own office without being spotted. Unfortunately, Guichard had been keeping an eye out for him.

"Can you spare me a moment, Jouin?"

The request required no answer and the Sûreté chief stepped back into his office before Jouin had had a chance to open his mouth.

"Would you kindly explain to me what is going on?" he asked once they were seated.

"In what respect?"

Guichard let out a sigh of impatience.

"Didn't we say to hold off until a more suitable opportunity came along? Why all the inconclusive searches, and who the devil ordered such a lame operation. It could only to put them on their guard?"

"The Lyons police acted off their own bat, Monsieur Guichard."

"So I gathered. But you should have contacted those dim-wits and stopped them putting their foot in it. What a bunch of idiots."

Guichard lifted a cigar from the rosewood box and the idea of offering one to Jouin never so much as crossed his mind.

"They had every reason to step in," Jouin said. "Stopping them would have been a blunder."

Guichard spluttered loudly. Jouin's retort had made some of the smoke go down the wrong way. Crimson-faced, he waved a finger around in the air.

"What the devil are you taking about?" he shrieked in strangulated tones. "We have absolute priority! If the Lyons boys reckoned they could act off their own bat, you should have let me know, and in two hours, two hours I say, I'd have supplied you with an order signed by the minister authorising you to assume command of operations!"

Jouin never spoke.

"And what's this about an Italian? Is it him?" Guichard asked, regaining his composure.

"Yes. It's Sorrentino, Jules Bonnot's accomplice."

"Good. Now, no mistakes. First off, call a press conference and issue a report that causes a major fuss. We have a perfect pretext: the anarchists shooting each other over the share-out of the swag. Strikes me as a step in the right direction."

"Monsieur, the trajectory of the bullet was almost vertical and from below. The entry wound is just below one ear and the bullet lodged in the cranial cavity, almost without injury to the brain, but causing an internal haemorrhage. "

Guichard looked at him through half-closed eyes.

"And?"

"Look, there is every reason to think that it was an accident. It's hard to conceive of firing at a man with a pistol at that angle."

"Do you mean to say that the shot went off while this Sorrentino was cleaning his weapon? Or using it to clean his nails?"

Jouin made no reply.

"Listen, Commissioner, to hell with trajectories and angles of guns, or whether the criminal died on the spot or had time to greet the devil who came to claim him. None of it matters a damn, is that clear?"

They stared at each other.

"Off you go and prepare your press release. Good day, Commissioner Jouin."

Victor was perusing an article published a few days earlier in a Paris newspaper and every so often he would shake his head and his jaw would drop in disgust, in silent token of annoyance as to how the matter was being represented. Paul Lafargue and his wife Laura had committed suicide. She was

Karl Marx's daughter and had met Paul in London when her father was living in exile. The couple, in their sixties, had decided that their active lives had come to an end: formerly prominent in all the social battles of the day, they felt that their strength had deserted them. In its reports of the double suicide the paper was using a contemptuous tone that Victor found offensive. He considered writing about it in *L'Anarchie* and was pondering whether he should attack the press for its stance towards the Lafargues, or make a point of ignoring it. Rirette sidled up to the table and without saying a word set a copy of *Le Matin* in front of him, one that she had bought a short time before. It carried a photo of a corpse discovered in the middle of a field and alongside it was the face of the victim, definitely taken from a police mug-shot. The headline read: "Killer of Italian Anarchist Identified." Victor snatched up the newspaper and glanced worriedly at Rirette who said:

"It happened two days ago. Read on."

Victor frantically scanned the article. It spoke of a settling of scores between two subversives, during which the ex-convict Jules Bonnot had killed Giuseppe Sorrentino, alias Platano, both of these being known to the Sûreté as illegalist anarchists. There was minimal coverage given to reconstructing what had happened, everything else bearing the imprint of a press campaign targeting anarchists in general. They were described as beasts capable of tearing one another apart over a few francs, and so well used to resorting to violence that they settled every dispute at gunpoint. There was even an appeal to decent citizens to turn informer and the police were called upon to lash out without mercy at the enemies of the nation, who had at last dropped the mask of victims of society and champions of the oppressed and shown themselves for what they truly were: ruthless killers and common criminals.

Victor set the paper down and took off his glasses.

"What a shambles." he muttered.

"And now what can we write about something like that?" asked Rirette, aggrieved.

Victor let out a long sigh.

"I don't quite know. Maybe the only thing to write is that we are watching collective suicide. No matter how things turn out, at the root of it all there is only this mad, self-destructive instinct."

He was interrupted by a couple of light, barely perceptible knocks on the door. Rirette went to answer them. Raymond Callemin stared at her from behind his dirty, cracked glasses, flicking the sleet from his forehead. They nodded hello to each other. Raymond walked in and stood beside the table. Victor stood up to hug him. Raymond was ramrod stiff, reacting rather formally to the embrace.

"Did you read about Platano?" he asked Victor.

Raymond nodded.

"And any idea what became of the fellow who killed him?" Victor pressed him.

Raymond stared at him resentfully.

"I refuse to believe that that's how it really went!" he exclaimed, trying to keep his voice down.

Victor threw open his arms.

"What do I know about it? But it's a filthy business. Horrific."

"Damn it! I don't know how many times I've heard you denouncing the tripe in the newspapers! Lies is all they have to offer. If you put your faith in the papers, everything you know is a lie. That's what you always used to say, isn't it?"

"Yes, of course it is. But the fact remains that one comrade has killed another. How are we supposed to defend that sort of thing? Can you tell me that?"

Raymond showed the flicker of a scornful smile.

"And why should you be bothered? This is your opportunity to squander paper and ink on attacks on us."

"That's not true, Raymond, and you can't say that. You know very well that I do not attack comrades, but I do have a duty to criticise suicidal options. And I have never felt so helpless."

"Please," Raymond interjected, "with what's going on on all around us, you're wasting your time criticising us. Don't you understand that you're taking their side?"

Victor looked at him through pained eyes.

"No, you mustn't say that to me. Side with a state that has finally come up with the ideal solution? That pits us one against another and just sits back and waits for its chance to deliver the coup de grace? And anyway, when you say 'criticise us', who on earth are you talking about?"

Rirette stepped in to calm them and she invited Raymond to sit down while she made some tea.

"No thank you. I'm off."

"But you've only just got here," the woman replied with a smile.

"I only dropped by to tell you to pack it in. And if you carry on writing nonsense about illegalism, on your own head be it."

Raymond's sideways glance was intended to convey menace but Victor read it as only a disappointed melancholy.

"I'm not walking the streets of Ixelles carrying a red cabbage these days, and you're not handing out flyers for gents' outfitters either."

"That's the truth," Raymond replied. "But you're as pig-headed as ever you were."

"You haven't improved any yourself."

Raymond made a lot of noise on the way out. The front door, already sorely tried over the past weeks, ricocheted, the knocker fell off yet again and rolled on to the pavement.

MONSIEUR COMTESSE

The bullet had killed Jules as well, or at any rate, everything that he had been up to that point. Along with Platano, the gunshot had swept away the past, and now Jules had no choice but to live every moment looking forward into the future and to a one-way trip, his thoughts all on the moment when he would be reunited with Judith. He struggled through the hours separating them from their departure as if immersed in a swirling, floating fog, knowing nothing of the reality that surrounded him and steeling himself against any backward glance. He had rejoined Dubois, who worked in Choisy-le-Roi as a mechanic; Dubois had taken him in without asking any explanations and had put him in touch with an anarchist from Paris, where he could lie low long enough for his trail to go cold, so as to avoid the checks at the ports and railway stations.

That anarchist was Eugène Dieudonné, who briefed him on the illegalist group, Raymond and the others, to Jules's utter indifference. Dieudonné realised that Bonnot was no longer the same man he had known years before and he gave up on trying to talk him into dropping by at L'Idée Libre. Moreover, Eugène had a lot more on his mind than proselytism, and confined himself to recommending a boarding house at 47, Rue Nollet, where the landlady, a Madame Rollet, was well used to minding her own business and often harboured anarchists in search of anonymity.

Jules promptly made his way there and rented a room, passing himself off as an industrialist from Belfort and signing the register as one Jules Comtesse. Madame Rollet pouted and from then on only ever addressed him as "engineer." Every morning, he would wend his way from the Place de Clichy to the Gare de Lyon, where he came upon a copy of *Le Progrès*, the Lyons daily newspaper not stocked by Parisian newsagents. And so he was able to gauge the progress of the investigation, experiencing an odd sensation when he saw himself described as the dangerous bandit leader of some non-existent 'Lyons crime syndicate': luckily the published photograph was some years old and, anyway, nobody in Paris read *Le Progrès*.

On 5 December, as ever, he walked out of the station with his folded newspaper in a pocket of his overcoat. It was too cold to sit on a bench and leaf through it and he was in no hurry to get arrested in some bistro amongst the sham gaiety of drunks and prostitutes or the lousy moods of porters and carters.

He decided to head back to the boarding-house by metro, as far as the Place de Clichy stop which was only a few hundred yards from the Rue Nollet. On other days, when he had nothing better to do, he had strolled along the Seine as far as the Tuileries gardens before cutting across the Place Concorde and down the Rue Royale as far as the Rue d'Amsterdam. Today, as he climbed the station steps, he drew the newspaper out of his pocket and searched for the local news. He was interrupted in this by a tide of folk disembarking and briskly jumped on board the carriage.

It was during the halt at the Bastille station that he read the item. For a few seconds that seemed like an eternity, his mind refused to believe what his eyes were reading. As the train was about to pull away Jules threw himself out through the door, doubled in two and finished up against the wall, leaning over a waste bin into which he spewed the coffee he had drunk an hour before.

Commissioner Jouin arrived in Lyons by train. There was a carriage waiting to collect him. He was asked if he wished to go straight to the hotel, but opted instead to be taken to Sûreté headquarters. In the foyer he was accosted by a reporter from *Le Progrès* who asked him to pose for a photograph, pointing to a fellow standing in the middle of the corridor with a massive camera on a tripod and a magnesium flash at the ready. Jouin paused to give him a most amiable look and then burst out:

"Are you the fellow who published the news of the arrest?" The reporter grinned eagerly and continually nodded his head. Jouin thrust his face forward until he was almost touching his nose with his own handle-bar moustache, and hissed:

"Go to hell!"

Then, turning to an orderly, he said loudly: "Get rid of this pair. And don't let them back in until further instructions."

The officer was dumbfounded and tried to respond, invoking his pride:

"Really, I take my orders only... "

"...from me!" Jouin interjected. "For at least as long as this investigation is in progress, you take your orders exclusively from me."

He turned towards the head of the Lyons Sûreté, who flushed with embarrassment and stammered:

"Commissioner Jouin has a warrant from the minister. Please abide by his instructions."

The orderly shrugged his shoulders before seizing the reporter by the scruff of the neck and bundling him outside. The photographer gathered up his equipment and trotted along in their wake.

"We are on good terms with the press," the man in charge of the Sûreté in Lyons grumbled.

"Publishing the news of the arrest was a mistake," Jouin stated icily. "By now, Bonnot may well have read it."

"But *Le Progrès* is distributed only in Lyons, and I doubt that the individual concerned is still in these parts."

"I have my own doubts about that," Jouin added. "But it reaches the stations in Paris and the national newspapers may well pick up on the news soon."

The other fellow accepted this, disguising his resentment behind a severely self-critical expression.

"Take me to the husband," Jouin ordered.

"Don't you wish to see the wife first?"

"No."

They looked each other in the eye for a moment before the head of the Sûreté in Lyons hastened to comply.

Monsieur Thollon was huddled in one corner of the cell, sitting on a stool so low that his knees were up against his stomach. When the judas-hole was opened, he waited for a few seconds before reacting. Slowly, he turned his head and his eyes looked dull and vacant. Jouin stepped into the cell, a police officer found him a chair and for at least a minute they sat facing each other without a word spoken. Thollon stared at him, but seemed to be staring into space. Jouin offered him a cigarette. The man paid him no attention. Slipping the pack back into his pocket, the commissioner said:

"You risk being hanged with complicity in a homicide, not to mention aiding and abetting and illicit possession of explosives, burglary equipment and everything else that was found in your home. Are you aware of that?"

Thollon seemed to come back down to earth, his

expression one of profound stupor.

"Are you aware of that?" Jouin repeated.

Thollon nodded.

"Your wife was Jules Bonnot's lover, right?" the commissioner stated blandly, as if quoting a well established fact.

It was as if Thollon had just felt the lash. Tears welled up in his eyes.

"It's not true," he mumbled. "Judith knew nothing about this man. It's not true."

"Please, don't make things worse for yourself. I can help you if you agree to cooperate. We know that you had nothing to do with the offences in question, but you ought not to be trying to conceal objective and incontestable guilt. Your wife had an affair with Bonnot and I want you to tell me how you reacted."

"No," Thollon pleaded. "He was just a lodger, we rented him a room. Judith wasn't even aware of his real name, so she never even dreamt... "

"Monsieur Thollon, you are wasting time. No one could have hidden what was uncovered in your home and in that grave without your or your wife's knowledge. Tell me everything right from the beginning and I can guarantee you... "

"No!" Thollon shouted in a booming voice, leaping to his feet. "Judith is innocent! She knew nothing about the caches, any more than I did! Bonnot, or whatever the hell his name is, could do what he pleased in our home. I and my wife were frequently away on visits to my mother, who is ill. I have dozens of witnesses to that. And the fellow stayed at the house, alone and could have found all the hiding-places in the world."

Jouin sighed.

"Is that everything you have to say to me?"

Thollon put his face into his hands, sobbing.

"Leave me in peace," he stammered, cowering in the corner of his cell. "Judith is innocent. We knew nothing."

Jouin stood up, walked over and pounded on the door which groaned open noisily. He cast one last glance at the broken man curled up against the wall and weeping, and he stepped outside. He passed by Judith's cell. He had the judas-hole opened up. The woman was lying full length upon the mattress, her face turned to the wall. Her breathing was irregular.

"This one's even worse," the warder said, nodding contemptuously into the cell. "All she knows how to say is no and she denies even having having known him. My betting is that she'll end up in the loony-bin."

Jouin did not respond. He watched her for a few minutes until he decided to face facts: this trip down to Lyons had been pointless.

.

WITHOUT A GLIMMER OF REMORSE

Pain has its limits, its boundaries. Beyond those boundaries there are only two roads: retreat into madness or icy indifference. Jules's face appeared indifferent but on the inside he was utterly broken, shattered into a thousand pieces. Yet again, hatred was proving the only power capable of keeping him on his feet. He read and re-read the newspaper accounts of Judith. The increasingly blatant hostility, the innuendo, the contempt displayed for the husband who harboured under his roof the "hot-blooded Madame Thollon whose thighs have out-foxed the Sûreté Nationale, in that they alone have managed to entrap the uncatchable Bonnot." He read on, feeling nothing now: not anger, nor pain, nor regret. It was all over. He was sitting at the foot of the slope now and his gaze was no longer directed upwards, not now that all hope was gone forever. He didn't even question the reason why he felt this silly peacefulness within himself. Perhaps it was the same feeling that some people get when they resign themselves to a sentence without appeal. When the end is embraced everything becomes weightless and ethereal and insubstantial.

It took him three days to snap out of this drug-like stupor. But the old sensations did not come flooding back. He knew that the final act was imminent. He was in no hurry, but neither did it worry him. He was able to move around calmly, because he realised that there was nowhere left for him to go, no more goals to be achieved. But he would not sit still. Hatred clarified his thinking, sharpening images and focusing his aims. And the weariness, that ghastly feeling of exhaustion that had pinned him for three days to his bed in the Rue Nollet boarding house had lifted.

Élie Monier

He went looking for Dieudonné and had him take him to L'Idée Libre. There, he shook hands with Raymond Callemin, Octave Garnier, Édouard Carouy, René Valet, André Soudy and Élie Monier. He sensed that only a few of them were prepared to follow him and that the rest would hold back. In the eyes of the doomed there was that dull, flickering fire, the unmistakable sign that they had passed the point of no return. any event,They were dancing around the flames that were about to consume them. All he was doing was speeding up the process.

Some trust was built up within a few days. None of them hung on his every word, nor did they look upon him as some sort of a leader, and this pleased him, even though they discerned in him an instinctive charisma and experience. Discussion and persuasion were redundant: the imminence of action conjured up a taut, feverish harmony, a weird climate of unhealthy serenity. It did not take them long to devise their theory: they would lash out spectacularly to expose the vulnerability of the establishment, choosing as their target the very core of the system: money. They would not lurk in the shadows. They would strike in daylight, on the streets, mounting a military operation at the scene of the raid and securing maximum coverage in the press, so as to sow panic in the nerve centres of society. They would plant a lust for vengeance in those who did not dare lift their heads, giving proof that there were countless chinks in the monster's armour.

Jules cleared up one point right away: no needless deaths. Only if absolutely necessary was there to be any gunplay but should the situation call for slaughter there was to be no holding back. They would not set out to kill, but they would kill anyone who rallied to the defence of the authorities. They needed to organise logistical support, trusting a select band of reliable comrades to secure weapons and ammunition, safe-houses, help with changing the plates and colour of the cars. But these comrades were not, under any circumstances, to be drawn into the operational side of things. It was not hard: Dubois, the mechanic, was already on their side; Dettweiler, a garage-owner in Bobigny, had long since offered his support; and then there were Belonie, Reinart, Bénard, Poyer, Rimbault, Crozat de Fleury, Gorodowsky and Rodriguez. All of them were torn between a life of crime and anarchist rebellion. They would use them on account of their connections while taking strict precautions.

Raymond was keen to discuss the matter of the proceeds: as he saw it, the money should serve the movement; not the trade unionists or strikers, but anarchist activists, their newspapers, premises, prisoners' aid and aid to comrades on the run. Or even Victor Kibalchich's *L'Anarchie*, if he would accept the offer of funding from them. Jules saw no objection to that. Once they had deducted their expenses, they were certainly not about to start putting money aside for a rainy day. The others agreed. It only remained to begin.

On 14 December, exactly one week after their first meeting, Jules arrived in the Bois de Boulogne with Raymond and with Octave Garnier. They took up positions near a cottage with a sizable garden and garage. At nightfall, Monsieur and Madame Normand came home from the Opera where they had applauded a performance of Faust. The driver parked the Delaunay-Belleville outside the gate, got out and opened the door. Jules signalled that they should be patient: his preference was for a quiet robbery, with no immediate hue-and-cry, no man-hunt right from the word go. Besides, he was afraid that Garnier, whom he had taped as a hot-head, might cause problems by unnecessary violence. The luxurious bottle-green limousine glided towards the shed. Ten minutes after that, there was absolute quiet.

They let a full hour go by. Jules stepped out of the bushes, followed by Raymond and Octave, guns at the ready. The lock gave way at the first attempt. There were cans of oil and benzine in the garage; Jules signalled for them to place these in the vehicle, while he set to work on the ignition. They pushed the car into the street, waiting until they were a good distance away before starting the engine. When Jules opened her up, the twelve horse-power Delaunay-Belleville 1909 accelerated down the street, Raymond and Octave suddenly feeling cock-a-hoop. Jules played up to this by moving her into top gear, taking a few bends on the rim of the tyres while the others laughed and slapped him on the back. Jules remained impassive. He tried to force a smile so as not to spoil the mood, but, chewing on his lip, he reckoned that his face was dissolving into a grotesque grimace. He glanced at the rear-view mirror for a moment and his grin froze: the sight reminded him of a skull he had seen some time earlier on a tin of cockroach poison.

They headed for Bobigny, swinging down the Rue de l'Harmonie, a dirt track on the outskirts. It was run down and peppered with tumble-down buildings. They came to a sort of a wood and corrugated iron warehouse: Dettweiler, a long-time friend of Carouy's, came out and opened the doors. There were no introductions made and he asked no questions. Jules said they needed to sort out the crankshaft and would be leaving the car there for a few days. Dettweiler nodded sleepily and without another word steered the Delaunay-Belleville into the warehouse. The trio made for the railway station, a trip that took around an hour. They waited in a public park to avoid attracting the attention of the railway employees. At dawn, they caught the Paris train.

Two days after that *L'Excelsior* carried a brief news item about a car theft reported by a Monsieur Normand and published the licence plate: 668X8. Jules assured them that there was nothing to worry about: the Delaunay would remain in the warehouse until the work was done. Meaning that no policeman would able to do anything to stop it.

RUE ORDENER

The very first robbery in history involving the use of a motor vehicle occurred in Paris on the morning of 11 December 1911.

The day before, Jules had taught Raymond how to drive. If anything were to happen to him, provision had to be made against their being forced to make off on foot for want of a driver. Raymond proved to be a quick learner. At 8.20, Jules turned into the Rue Ordener: there was a branch of the Société Générale de Banque at number 156, where a cash delivery van arrived from the Rue de Provence branch punctually, a few minutes ahead of the opening of the tellers' windows. Jules parked the limousine at the corner of the Boulevard Ornano, cursing between gritted teeth. Octave and Raymond looked at him but said nothing. Jules got out to check under the bonnet: the pulley operating the fan belt had ground to a halt. Driving any further meant risking overheating the cylinder. The problem was down to a snapped bolt. Keeping very cool, Jules turned to Octave, handing him the bolt so that he might fetch another one from the ironmongers he had spotted a hundred metres back up the street. Octave set off. Raymond swallowed and sat where he was. With the tip of his shoe he lifted one corner of the floor mat: the long-barrelled Borchardt 7.63 flashed him a reassuring glint; fitted with a removable hand grip, it might prove useful as a back-up in the event of a long-range gunfight. In the event of closer fighting, the trio had an arsenal that was, if anything, excessive: at least five guns apiece, revolvers and semi-automatics, plus enough shells for a whole day's shooting. Five minutes later Octave was back. Jules checked the bolt: it would serve his purpose. He installed it without a hitch. At 8.40 they moved off again. There was a light drizzle falling, mixed with sleet; this was ideal because it forced passersby to scurry along with their heads lowered and wrapped in scarves and upturned collars. They pulled up outside number 150, outside the Compagnie Beaujolaise wine store. Raymond clamped a cap with ear flaps on to his head and got out of the car, leaving the Borchardt behind on his seat. In the pockets of his black overcoat he had two semi-automatics and four spare clips of ammunition. He watched the street, ready to signal the arrival of the cash van. There was little traffic: a few trams, and the odd cart keeping close to the ancient fortifications without obstructing the whole street. At 8.50 Raymond turned back to the Delaunay. He caught the eyes of Jules and Octave and touched the peak of his cap, which was the agreed signal. Jules started up the engine and pressed lightly on the accelerator, keeping the engine ticking over. Octave got out and walked along the pavement, with Raymond at his side. The Delaunay stirred, moving in parallel with the pair of them.

The Société Générale's messenger was Ernest Caby; he was wearing dark-green livery with gold buttons and badge, and behind him walked a man scanning every single passer-by: his armed guard, Peemans. Octave knocked into Caby. The messenger was about to let out an oath when he spotted the Eibar 7.65 pointing at the guard's face. Peemans froze. Without a second thought, Caby swung the bag he was carrying in his left hand, hitting Octave, while his right reached for the inside pocket of his jacket. Octave had no way of knowing that he was unarmed and that he was instinctively reaching for the fat wallet in which he was carrying part of the delivery. He fired, grazing Caby's neck. The bank messenger let out a blood-curdling scream. Butchers, milkmen, bakers and customers emerged from the shops. Octave squeezed the trigger a second time, sending a bullet into Caby's thorax: his voice gradually died away, like a gramophone in need of winding up. Peemans, his hands in the air, took off at a run for the crossroads. Raymond rushed for the Delaunay, meaning to use the Borchardt to shoot him in the back. Jules cut him off. So Raymond turned back to the pavement and swooped on Caby to snatch the briefcase from him. The messenger clung tightly to the handle and refused to release it. Octave kicked his hand and it loosened. While the pair made for the car, a threatening crowd was beginning to gather, egged on by the bank staff. Jules changed gear, pulled on the hand-brake, got out of the car and emptied a clip into the air. With every shot the crowd rippled before breaking up and dispersing. Confusion turned to panic. Somebody tried to jump Raymond, who had stayed a couple of metres away. Octave fired both pistols at the walls and windows of the bank, avoiding targeting people but aiming over the heads of the closest ones in order to keep them distant. Jules jumped back behind the steering wheel, emptied the clip from the second Browning into the air and then started the engine. Raymond tossed the briefcase on to the back seat and settled in beside Jules. Octave, still shooting away, jumped into the back, tossed away the empty guns, whipped out another two and, leaning out of the right side window and then the left, started firing shots in the air. The Delaunay pulled slowly away and cruised down the Rue Ordener, calmly dodging horse-drawn carts halted in the middle of the road. It turned into the Rue Cloys and again into the Rue Montcalme, swerving around a tram, before hurtling down the Rue Vauvenargues at sixty kilometres an hour.

Half an hour later, they left Paris behind them and headed for Le Havre. They dumped the car near the port, to suggest that they had been making for England. But they had to keep to the secondary roads because roadblocks would certainly have been thrown up on the national highway. Jules drove in silence, apparently calm, whereas Octave seemed suddenly to have relaxed, spent from the built-up tension. Raymond, though, showed a childish euphoria and could not sit still or keep quiet and was still excited about what he maintained was proof that anything was possible from now on, as long as they kept a level head and struck without resorting to improvisation. He was applying his scientific theories to robbery, swamping his two companions with an irrepressible, enthusiastic babbling. Octave reckoned that this was down to their having survived the danger and he bore it with patience. Jules had no thoughts and no feelings on the matter.

There was a radical change in the atmosphere after they passed Pontoi, when Octave decided to count the cash in the bag; five-thousand-five-hundred-and-twenty-six francs. The rest was share certificates to the tune of two hundred and ten thousand francs and useless, and bearer bonds to the tune of a hundred and ninety thousand; these too would be hard to fence. Octave punched his seat and Raymond fell silent.

"What a cock-up!" Octave muttered, biting his knuckles.

Jules watched him in the rear-view mirror. And shook his head, turning to Raymond and telling him calmly:

"He most likely had a wallet in the inside pocket of his jacket."

And, turning to watch Octave in the mirror, he added:

"He may even had been about to hand it over to you when you killed him."

Octave froze. After a few seconds, he spluttered:

"What the hell are you talking about? Far from handing over the money, he was reaching for a pistol.."

"No matter. You were close enough to give him a punch; there was no need to shoot him. Think, next time. And bear in mind that if we had acted quietly nobody would have been able to work out exactly what was going on. No matter how it turns out, gun-play stops us operating with cool heads. Bear that in mind, Octave."

Nobody spoke for a good half hour. Disappointment had snuffed out their optimism. Raymond was the first to break the silence.

"We'll make up the shortfall on the second raid. And the third. And... "

Jules looked at him and Raymond fell silent for a bit.

"Well, we definitely didn't pull this job in order to line our own pockets, right?" And then he murmured: "The point is that we've made a start. And, above all, we're are still around, ready to do it again at the earliest opportunity."

Jules nodded. Raymond shrugged his shoulders and set about reloading his gun. Octave did likewise.

An hour after that, Jules handed the wheel to Raymond who drove the Delaunay warily, but in Gisors he took a wrong turn and they had to pull over in order to check the map. In Beauvais, they ran across a toll-booth: the operator leaned out of the window; Raymond stepped on the accelerator and sped through. Jules missed the operator's ashen face; he had turned to Octave, who was already reaching for the loaded Eibar pistol. One look from Jules was enough to deter him from using it.

At around five o'clock that afternoon, they pulled over to put some oil in an overheated engine which was starting to lose some of its poke. Raymond was still at the wheel. As dusk fell, it turned misty. Nobody had a clue where the road to Le Havre might be. Jules said that it didn't matter anyway: the important thing was that the car be dumped near the quayside.

But they had to abandon it on the beach where Raymond found himself bogged down before he could locate the quays. They removed the plates and dumped them in the sea. Before setting off on foot for the station, Jules stood watching the breakers crashing ashore with a deafening din. It was only then that he thought about Judith, the rendezvous in Le Havre, the passage to Argentina, the long sea voyage, the smell of her hair, the sparkle in her eyes every time he had taken her in his arms.

Octave laid a hand on his back. Jules was yanked out of his daydream and stared at him for a couple of seconds before he realised what was happening. He nodded and turned back towards the town. He started walking with his head down, hands in his pockets, cap pulled down over his eyes.

They left for Paris on the earliest available train, arriving at one o'clock in the morning. On the way out of the Gare Saint Lazare, Raymond bought a copy of *La Patrie*. The entire front page carried a headline about the Rue Ordener robbery. Caby hadn't died and the Société Générale had put a price of twelve thousand francs on the heads of the "automobile bandits".

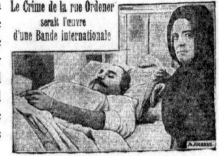

"More than double our haul," Octave commented, spitting on the ground.

Jules decided he needed a few days to himself and disappeared after making arrangements with the other two: he would come looking for them, but in the meantime, they were to keep clear of their usual haunts and established company. Raymond headed for Brussels where he made the acquaintance of one De Boer, an anarchist printworker with good connections in the world of fences. He was hopeful of fencing the bearer bonds at least. But De Boe's advice to him was to try Amsterdam and a friend of his by the name of Vandenbergh, and they travelled to Holland together. It proved a complete waste of time, for Vandenbergh reacted as if they were trying to plunge his hand into molten lead: the serial numbers had been circulated to every bank in Europe and the best that he could do, since they were friends, was to agree to hold on to them until things took a turn for the better. Raymond travelled back to Paris where he found that the reward offered for their capture had soared to fifty thousand francs: the reckoning was that they had set a very dangerous precedent and had to be caught at all costs. Furthermore, every criminal undertaking was chalked up to the "automobile bandits", from raids on armouries to house burglaries, and press hysteria had made life impossible: every informer was on a fishing expedition, anybody on the books as an anarchist was probably under surveillance and hordes of would-be spies were besotted with the idea of getting their hands on the reward. The only light-hearted moment for Raymond came when he went to fetch Octave in Vincennes, where he had fled with his partner, Marie. The impetuous Garnier, one-time syndicalist and now a public enemy on the run, had dyed his hair a flaxen yellow and Raymond spent a quarter of an hour laughing, and his laughter set off the other two.

They decided to go back to Paris. Reading the press, they were torn between unease and a sort of perverse satisfaction; they were being sighted all over the place and blamed for everything. They were depicted as a gang of dozens of hardened robbers. The reward had risen to the fabulous sum of one-hundred-and-twenty-five thousand francs. Nothing took precedence over the hunt for the "bloody gang": the Agadir incident, in which a German destroyer had bombarded the port, the revolts in China, the Franco-German treaty, the Italo-Turkish war in Tripolitania, all of it took a back seat to the inquiries of the Paris Sûreté. Meanwhile, Poyer and Rimbault, two friends on whom they could rely, had wound up in jail as a result of house-searches targeting anarchist circles: a few handguns had been found in their homes and it was of little account that they had had no hand in the Rue Ordener raid: as far as the newspapers were concerned, they were automatically damned as members of subversive groups.

Octave and Raymond walked looking over their shoulders, continually, feeling suspicious eyes were on them everywhere and the police breathing down their necks. There might be a Sûreté squad lying in ambush around every corner, every pub doorman might turn out to be an informer, as might any prostitute, pimp or pickpocket, even the street-sweepers might be plain-clothed police. Raymond reacted impulsively: he told Octave that he was going to pop over to L'Idée Libre. According to him, it was a sensible move: unless they could break this cycle of madness, they would end up gliding along the walls and seeing an enemy behind every street lamp. Octave did his best to talk him out of it, but then they concluded that excessive caution was worse and that there was a danger of their being dragged into a haunted existence where they might end up shooting at shadows and distrusting what few remaining friends they had.

Lorulot and Louise were at the bookshop, in the throes of a furious argument. She seemed determined to leave him and he was screaming at her to clear off back to that starveling Eugène Dieudonné, accusing her of being a penniless farm girl unable to understand a thing about relations between free individuals. Louise dismissed him by saying that his theories were only good for deceiving serving wenches and fishwives. Lorulot lost his temper and threw a stack of magazines at her. Octave stepped in, grabbing him by the collar and giving him a violent shake, until he shoved him head first into some shelves. Dozens of bound volumes rained down on his head. A weeping Louise threw herself into Raymond's arms, that being the nearest place where she could hide her face. A blushing Raymond discovered how disconcerting it was to feel oneself being pressed to a female body shaken by hot, throbbing emotion and, almost unconsciously, he started to stroke her hair, while Louise's bosom and belly introduced him to feelings he had never known before. Up until that day at any rate, as far as Raymond-la-science was concerned, love had been nothing but a hindrance to be avoided, and his thoughts about women hinted at hidden misogyny.

"Take me away from here," Louise sobbed, her lips against Raymond's throat.

He arranged to meet Octave the following day in a Montmartre bar and left, holding tight to Louise.

Recovering from the blows to his head, Lorulot looked straight at Octave and hissed between gritted teeth:

"You pair are out of your minds. What on earth possessed you to come here after what has happened?"

"Why, what's supposed to have happened?" Octave challenged.

Lorulot adopted a look of contempt.

"You know very well what. And let's be clear on one point: I don't know, and I have no wish to know if or how deeply you were involved in that disaster, but if I were you, I'd keep well away."

"Away from whom?"

"From everybody!"

Octave picked up his cap, pulled it down on his head and threw him one last glance.

"Lorulot, be very careful you don't go sounding off. Got that?"

At which he turned and walked out of the bookshop, but paused at the door to look Lorulot square in the face, giving him a vaguely menacing look.

Raymond escorted Louise to a hotel and paid for the room. Then he gave her some more money. Louise made to refuse it but he would not be put off, which was rather odd since he had never been one argue with a woman. Louise promised to pay him back and when Raymond made to head back to the stairs, she mumbled:

"I've never stayed in a hotel on my own."

Her tone was a blend of fear, embarrassment and sadness. Raymond construed it as an invitation. He followed her inside, they sat on the bed and talked for the remainder of the night. Talked, nothing more. But come daylight, when Louise fell asleep on his chest, her long, wavy, fine chestnut hair tickling his nose, it never even entered Raymond's head to close his eyes: Louise was too lovely and he sat for another two hours watching her, wondering what on earth was happening to him.

By the time he left, it was mid-morning. It wasn't the sun, for cold daylight was filtering through the grey cloud and a Parisian winter was displaying all its usual cruelty, but Raymond never noticed the chill nor the wind lashing his face with swirls of sleet. He set off walking through the streets of the 18th arrondissement with a spring in his step, wandering aimlessly, in an inexplicable and unprecedented good humour which occasionally took him unawares as he continued asking himself what was happening to him.

That afternoon, Raymond kept his appointment with Octave who, being a good friend, made no mention of Louise, in spite of the curiosity that had been eating him since the evening before. The situation was worsening by the hour. The pair had never known anything like the scorched earth campaign going on all around them. They had no safe havens left and erstwhile comrades were startled by the very sight of their faces. Octave had bumped into a few of them quite at random and the reaction had always been the same: they dropped their eyes, suddenly quickened their step and scurried away immediately. He had also seen Valet. Valet had not reacted like the rest, but he had certainly not seemed as sociable as normal. Neither of them had made any reference to the matter and before they parted Valet had stressed the fact that he was at their disposal. They could count on him, but for what? Valet was as well-known to the police as the rest of them and they were well aware of his illegalist sympathies. Any hospitality he might offer was tantamount to certain suicide.

They hailed a carriage and ordered the driver to take them to 19 Rue des Solitaires in the 19th arrondissement, just off the Rue Fessart.

When she saw them standing in front of her Rirette said nothing and managed to hide her disbelief. Victor was standing by the window, sipping a cup of coffee. She offered them a cup and they accepted. Victor avoided making any comments: up until a few months previously Raymond had looked upon coffee as equivalent to a pernicious drug.

"Let me make you a bite to eat," Rirette suggested, trying to appear calm, her hands shaking from nerves.

"No thanks," Octave said, touching her arm. "We're off shortly."

"Having come this far," Victor interjected, "you may as well stay a while."

"Better not," Raymond replied. Victor heaved a sigh. And said patiently:

"If the house was under surveillance, the damage would be done already."

Octave and Raymond exchanged embarrassed glances.

"Have you come to tell us something?" Victor pressed them.

After a few seconds' silence, Raymond murmured:

"We wanted to know if there's anyone still around who doesn't regard us as plague-carriers. And where we can find them."

Rirette set two cups down on the table, saying:

"We just look upon you as irresponsible lunatics. But that does not mean that we will deny you help. The problem is something else."

"What?" asked Octave.

"That any chance of mediation has been ruined," Victor said, the tension evident in his voice. "They are carrying out searches and arrests and torture and no one can protest, no one even dreams of speaking out against repression because, at this juncture, any outrage can be justified by the state of emergency. Why did that never occur to you? Can you possibly have overlooked the fact that things would come to this pass?"

Raymond stared into his coffee, stirring the spoon robotically. Then he answered:

"It's always going to be that way. The only way to avoid it is to do nothing. But the moment one makes a move then there will be a state of emergency. To hell with constitutional rights, the usual rigmarole. The choice is between talk and action."

"No," said Victor, taking a step closer. "The choice is rather different: leaping into action when we're four million strong, or doing it when there are forty, or four of you."

"Maybe so," Raymond said with a sardonic smile. "The problem is waiting for those four million to get here, which is the same as staking one's hopes on reincarnation."

Victor shook his head, refusing to continue the argument.

"Anyway," Raymond went on, "the business about there being just four of us is a press lie. There were just the three of us."

"Come on, let's get off," Octave muttered, draining his cup.

Victor and Rirette hugged them. "Get out of Paris, for a while at least," Victor told them on the threshold. "It's madness for you to remain in circulation."

They made their way downstairs warily, taking care not to make the wooden steps creak. Their hands were in their pockets, clutching their pistols, loaded and ready.

The reporters got there ahead of Jouin. One of Dettweiler's neighbours, a Madame Canton, had spotted the bulky bottle-green Delaunay-Belleville, a vehicle none too common among the good poverty-stricken folk from the Rue de l'Harmonie. After the coverage in the press, she had mentioned it to an acquaintance of hers, Chaperon, a clerk at the town hall, who had in turn tipped off a reporter friend. The news was in the papers even before the police arrived to carry out a search of the garage in Bobigny. And any chance of mounting surveillance on the place was blown. Besides, Dettweiler was arrested, as were his wife and three children. Not that that meant much, for the anarchist insisted that he had taken in the Delaunay just as he would any other car for repair and he failed to pick out any of the occupants from the hundreds of mugshots presented to him. There was one tiny victory though: on the evening of 29 December a woman came knocking at the Dettweiler's door and was promptly arrested by watching policemen. She turned out to be Jeanne Giorgis who had connections to one Raoul Leblanc who was suspected of being a fence: a search of their rented room turned up a briefcase with a false bottom in which a burgling kit was found. As far as the Sûreté was concerned, judging from the descriptions given by some witnesses, Raoul Leblanc was actually Édouard Carouy. And they insisted that he was the fellow who had opened fire from inside the Delaunay-Belleville at the crowd in the Rue Ordener.

On 3 January, in Thiais, the bodies of two elderly people were found: battered to death in their home in the Rue de l'Église, they were the householder, a Monsieur Moreau, and a governess by the name of Harfeux. This was a robbery carried out by desperadoes and the police at that point were carrying Carouy's photograph. A few of the neighbours claimed to recognise him and claimed that they had seen him in the vicinity and that there had been a second man with him. Somebody picked out the mugshot of Carouy's friend,

Medge. Repeated claims of innocence cut no ice. He admitted that he had burgled a number of homes but insisted that he had never been in Thiais in his life. They turned up a pair of ear-rings and an umbrella stolen from a house in Pavillons-sous-Bois. That clinched it. They also arrested Medge's wife, Barbe, who was in the terminal stages of cancer.

Marius Medge

From that day forward, Carouy became the first supposed leader of the "automobile gang".

He had had no part in it, but it was too late now. He equipped himself with two pistols and several boxes of ammunition and started to sleep in a different bed every night.

At the Quai des Orfèvres, Xavier Guichard was beginning to show signs of smugness. All the press was describing the anarchists as savage brutes capable of beating a couple of poor old folks to death. A famous illustrator even came up with a very striking multi-coloured poster, the original of which was sold for an astronomical sum.

Jouin had an inkling as to how things actually were, but he also knew that he had been pulling the right strings. Hundreds of anonymous tip-offs arrived on his desk, and they included a few that offered new leads. His instinct helped him find his way through the personal grudges and straightforward mistakes and to zoom in on the vaguest and weirdest reports which were often the only ones worth paying any attention to. Then again, he knew the anarchist world and had long known how to differentiate between them. So it was that he traced Octave Garnier's place in Vincennes, albeit a day too late: he and Marie had only just moved on. Hurried changes of lodgings had come to be a widespread practice: Valet, Soudy and Monier had done the same. Even

René Valet

Dieudonné had taken lodgings under a false name. Meanwhile, Poincaré's National Government took office on 14 January: this was a nationalist administration with close ties to high finance and it was about to prepare France for the Great War. In terms of foreign policy, guns were needed to teach Germany to keep her distance and in domestic politics, what was needed was a "firm line" that would put paid to traitors.

L'Idée Libre was targeted in one of the countless raids, resulting in two arrests: Lorulot and a woman by the name of Marie Vuillemin. She was known to Jouin. She was Octave Garnier's girlfriend. Marie held out under interrogation for some days and nights. Fortunately for her, she genuinely did not know where Octave was. Octave was identified from a photograph by the bank messenger, Caby. As for Carouy, Caby reckoned that he was probably the man behind the steering wheel.

Guichard was lobbying for the coup de grâce to be inflicted through a ban on *L'Anarchie*. But Jouin managed to persuade him that Victor Kibalchich and Rirette Maîtrejean were more useful at large, since they could be tailed and used as bait. That was not quite what he actually thought but he managed to ensure their freedom.

BLOW FOR BLOW

Raymond's "scientific" beliefs were beginning to waver. Even his faith in the power of example had taken a setback. For the first time, Victor's words had hit home, constantly eating away at his certainties. He expressed his own misgivings to Octave, only to be greeted with a stony silence. They were still agreed that they would not meet up for a while, and he bade Octave farewell, in the knowledge that he was lost to him.

Raymond would not accept that Louise played any part in his reconsideration. True, he was betraying nobody, but didn't want to deny himself this opportunity for the sake of any cause. Because with Louise, friendship had turned to physical contact and in the end they had begun making love every night in the attic of 48 Rue de la Tour d'Auvergne, where Raymond had found a haven thanks to a friend of his by the name of Pierre Jourdan.

One evening Raymond persuaded Louise to go out to a restaurant for dinner by way of a relief from their attic rat existence. Louise urged caution even if the press had never mentioned his name. But Raymond was insistent and a tense, worried Louise agreed to go out after dusk.

Raymond was exuberant. He seemed to have recaptured his former optimism. Louise looked around, lowering her eyes when the waiter came over, but she did her best to join Raymond in his enthusiasm; he was talking passionately and topping up their glasses, drinking heartily. He who had once been the theorist of a strict vegetarian diet and a teetotaller.

Finally, towards midnight, they decided to make their way back home. Louise led the way out while Raymond settled the bill. Just as he was rejoining her, he noticed that she was speaking to some man, a distinguished gentleman with a walking stick and hat, his face hidden by the shadows close to the restaurant. Louise hurriedly took Raymond's arm and headed homewards. He asked who the gent had been and she told him that he was a stranger, that he had simply been asking directions. Maybe he had been looking for company and had thought she was on her own.

"And what did you tell him?"

"That I was waiting for my fiancé,"Louise replied with a grin. "Let's not go out in the evening again, please," she added, turning serious.

Édouard Carouy made contact with Octave Garnier and later they both kept their rendezvous with Jules. Édouard had nothing left to lose any more and had decided to find a replacement for Raymond in the trio. Jules suggested that they go away to Belgium for a time, the air there being more breathable: besides, they simply had to carry out another job, not so much to set an example for the oppressed as to raise what they needed to live.

In Ghent on 31 January, they tracked down a private garage that looked ideal. But while Jules was trying to start up a four cylinder Hotchkiss that simply refused to cooperate, owner Marcel Maurey's chauffeur turned up. Octave who was standing guard outside, shoved him inside the garage. The fellow reacted by punching him on the chin. Édouard was about to shoot him on the spot, but Jules stopped him. Before he could intervene, Octave grabbed a large block of wood lying under one wheel and brought it down with full force on the back of the driver's head. Marcel Maurey slumped forwards, banging his head against the wing. He died instantly. The trio made off on foot, a few seconds before the owner of the vehicle appeared at a window brandishing a rifle.

They walked for at least twenty kilometres as far as Wetteren where they caught the train to Antwerp, and from there on to Amsterdam. They looked up Vandenbergh who had still not managed to fence the bonds. They then made their way back to France.

On the Paris express, Édouard went to the toilet. As he entered the cubicle, the pistol he was carrying in his inside pocket fell out. All three of them had their guns loaded and primed. Édouard, who was less expert in the use of guns, had not put the safety catch on. The trigger of his 9 millimetre Steyr pistol hit the iron footplate and went off automatically. The bullet pierced his right arm before lodging in the ceiling.

He made his way back to their compartment, ashen-faced and teetering. Biting his lips, he opened his overcoat and showed the blood-stain spreading beneath his jacket. He had staunched the wound with paper towels, but the bleeding did not stop. With Octave standing guard in the corridor, Jules used their three handkerchiefs as a makeshift bandage. The wound was not serious but it needed disinfecting as soon as possible. Édouard was struggling lamely to get his overcoat back on when Octave warned them that the ticket inspector was coming. Édouard feigned sleep, his overcoat draped over him. The inspector didn't notice anything untoward and left the compartment. Within seconds, Édouard had fainted from his exertions and from the tension. He had lost a lot of blood. On arrival in Paris, his two friends had to help him stand up, even though there was a danger of their attracting the attention of the gendarmes. They bought some dressings and Jules decided to take a room near the Porte de Clignancourt. It was dangerous for them to show their faces under these conditions, what with the hotels being watched, but Édouard needed to rest and get his strength back. Jules was going to stay with him. Octave was reluctant to leave, even after a rendezvous in a metro station was arranged for the following day, but Jules would brook no argument: there was no point in all three of them taking a risk. As he stood on the threshold to bid them goodbye, Octave seemed suddenly to remember something:

"What is it?" Jules asked.

Octave gnawed his lip.

"Nothing. Well, there was something I was wanting to ask you... "

Jules waited, one hand resting on his arm.

"You know," Octave murmured, without raising his eyes from the ground, "I never believed what the papers gave out... about that business with Platano."

Jules went rigid. None of them had ever pressed him on this matter.

"And what was it that you wanted to know?"

Octave shook his head and shrugged,

"It... it was an accident, wasn't it?"

Jules carried on staring at him intensely. Then he took a deep breath and said:

"He was the best. We'll never find his like again."

Octave nodded, with a saddened expression: that was the confirmation he had been looking for. He left unhurriedly, looking this way and that, slipping out warily into the night.

Some sixty uniformed officers and plain-clothed Sûreté detectives swooped on 24 Rue Fessart. That was at dawn on 31 January 1912. Jouin had done his best to stand up to pressure from Guichard, but Poincaré's minister had stepped in with categorical instructions: they were to deal a death-blow to anarchism in Paris. And in the eyes of the government, Victor Kibalchich was a lot more dangerous than any of the armed illegalists.

Operations were led by Jouin in person. That way at least he might be able to forestall any "quick fix" solutions. He knew that many at the Sûreté were all for eliminating subversives physically and would allege that they had tried to escape or resisted arrest. But there was one detail of which he was not aware: Guichard had charged one of his men to plant two revolvers from the raid on the Rue Lafayette armoury (which at the time had been chalked up the "automobile gang") on to the premises as soon as the search began. And it was Jouin himself who stumbled upon the package poorly hidden behind the furniture.

"You ought to be ashamed of yourself," was all that Victor said.

Jouin, who appeared to be the only one surprised, could not think of a reply.

That afternoon, the commissioner questioned Victor with no witnesses present.

"The registrations of the two guns tie you to the Rue Ordener raid. Have you anything to say on the subject?"

Victor looked at him with contempt.

"All I have to say is that I was mistaken."

Jouin looked at him questioningly.

"About you," Victor added. "I mistook you for an honest enemy. Remember our little chat about not all cops being the same?"

The commissioner never flinched. They carried on staring at each other, Victor shaking imperceptibly with rage and Jouin increasingly sombre. "What did you expect of me?" the deputy chief of the Sûreté finally asked.

"That at least you wouldn't take it out on Rirette."

"But the apartment is in Madame Maîtrejean's name. I can't let her go."

"In which case," Victor said, "there being no one here but the two of us, I expect a modicum of honesty."

"Go on."

"Who planted the guns behind the furniture?"

"It wasn't me," Jouin said through gritted teeth.

"Good. We can keep at it until tomorrow comes. We've never laid eyes on them. Nor have you. Now what?"

Jouin glanced towards the window. It had begun to snow. He stood up and spent a few moments gazing at the gently falling flakes. Even the snow was grey at the Quai des Orfèvres. Then he turned and said:

"There's no way out now, Monsieur Kibalchich."

PARIS-LYONS-PARIS

The lawyer Julien's chambers were in the heart of Lyons. The two priests were walking at a brisk pace, the skirts of their long soutanes flared behind them as they wove through the pedestrians. When they stood before the secretary, they said that they had no appointment but that they needed to speak with the lawyer as a matter of urgency on some extremely important business. Julien had them ushered in, looking them over with a blend of surprise and curiosity. Once they were alone, the older of the clerics stated icily:

"I am Jules Bonnot and this is Octave Garnier."

The lawyer started. He tried to stammer something, looked around worriedly, as if checking that no one had heard these two names explode around the room.

"Now listen here, because we don't have a lot of time," Jules continued. "You are defence counsel for Judith Thollon. I want to know how she is and what her chances of freedom are."

The lawyer used the back of his hand to wipe the sweat from his brow.

"Don't you people realise that every policeman in town is looking for you?" he stammered, not raising his eyes.

"That's our problem," Octave retorted.

"And mine too if they find you here."

"Surely that's your line of work, isn't it?" Jules added. "So, what have you to to tell me about Judith?"

The lawyer took a deep breath and hurriedly opened a file on his desk.

"Here we are. The outlook is none too bright... "

"Yes, but in this country the newspapers can do more harm to an investigation than the police themselves."

Jules carried on staring at him while Octave walked to the window to watch for the arrival of potential callers.

"Madame Thollon," the lawyer went on, leafing through his papers, "well, in essence, the charges against her are not serious. Aiding and abetting, of course, and quite possibly receiving stolen goods, on account of the loot found at her place, but they won't be able to establish in court that she was your accomplice."

"So there's a hope that she might go free?"

"Yes, I actually think she might. But not before trial."

"And when might she be brought for trial?"

"Ah, who can hazard a guess at that in a case like this? A few months, or even a year... "

"A year?" Jules shot back, his voice raised for the first time.

"Maybe. It depends on the extent of the investigation. Unfortunately, the evidence is proving a lot more troublesome than at first appeared. You know better than I do that with every day that passes fresh evidence comes to light and further arrests are made."

Jules nodded and asked:

"Prison... is she handling it alright?"

The lawyer gave a vague wave of his hand.

"Oh, you know, one gets used to prison sooner or later. At first perhaps, Madame Thollon... how shall I put it?. went into a depression. But the last time I saw her, which was three days ago, she seemed more serene to me."

Lawyer Julien was lying. Judith wasn't eating, wasn't sleeping, wasn't talking to anybody. And it was not prison that had broken her down. But Jules, of course, had been waiting to hear that very word, 'serene'.

"Could you pass on a message for me?"

"Dear God... yes and no... "

"Just a few words. An oral message."

"Well, in that case, of course."

"Tell her this: I'll be waiting for you the day after at the Sainte-Honorine abbey."

"The day after?"

"Yes. The day after she gets out of prison, whenever that may be."

"Of course."

"Have you got that, now?"

"Yes. yes."

"Then au revoir, counsellor. And I am relying upon your word of honour."

"Don't fret... lawyer-client privilege," concluded Julien, sighing with relief at the sight of Jules Bonnot getting to his feet and making towards the door.

They returned to Paris by train, just as they had come. They dumped the soutanes in the station toilets. On the journey, Jules and Octave exchanged not one word. Jules was grateful to him for his help but could not think how to convey this to him. All he could think of was the lie that he had told. He would not live long enough to get to Le Havre and wait at the Sainte-Honorine abbey. He was perfectly well aware of the fact, but Judith needed to cling to some hope.

The press had welcomed the arrests of Victor and Rirette as the decapitation of anarchist illegalism: there were still some anarchists on the run, but the Sûreté reckoned that it was only a matter of time as the scorched earth tactic employed towards the criminals was beginning to tell.

While Édouard Carouy recuperated from his injury,

Louise bumped into Eugène. After an afternoon of tears and regrets, they finished up as a couple again. Louise was not in love with Raymond. She looked upon their meeting as a parenthesis between the free-love theories learnt from Lorulot and a yearning for mutual tenderness. Raymond, took a different view. And he dropped over to see Octave who brought him to Jules's place.

On the night of 27 February, the three stole a car from the Avenue de la République in Saint-Mandé. It was another Delaunay, but a sportier, six-cylinder, fifteen-horse-power model, built for speed and better road performance, with the driving seat uncovered. Jules's plan was to use it on a job he had planned down to the finest detail. But a lot was about to happen before that.

They had to stop in Pont-sur-Yonne: they had hit a stone in Montereau that buckled the axle of one wheel. Having no replacement part, a mechanic did his best to sort it out. They set off again and arrived in Paris via the Porte d'Italie in the early afternoon. They made for the Rue Nollet and the boarding house where they had left Édouard. But Édouard was missing. According to what he had told Madame Rollet when he left, he was due back that evening. The trio waited until seven o'clock, occasionally leaving so as not to attract attention. In the end they decided to call back the following day. Maybe Édouard had found himself a more secure safe-house. Anyway, they had agreed a set rendezvous at two day intervals, in various locations around the city, so that they would not lose touch with one another in the event of any imminent danger. Jules was making his way across the Place du Havre when he spotted a policeman watching him from his post under a streetlight. Maybe his interest had been piqued by the fact that the trio were alone in the car, their respective wives being nowhere around, or just because the Delaunay H6, a rare model, had reappeared. In any event, the policeman acted on instinct, raised his whistle to his lips and held up one arm. Jules accelerated, preparing to veer into the Rue du Havre, but his way was blocked by a tram. He was forced to pull over to the pavement and wait for the omnibus to move off. It took only a few seconds but it was long enough for the officer to catch them up. He grabbed the doorpost and leapt on to the running board, shouting like a man possessed. Jules took off again on his hub-caps, but the policeman clung on and let fly with a baton-blow aimed at the back of the neck. Jules was saved by his reflexes as he leant sideways and took the blow on his back. He started to zig zag in order to shake off the policeman but the latter clung on, having a good foothold on the running board. Jules took a second baton blow on the hand and just missed a lamp-post. Octave then leant out through the window and, pressing the barrel of his gun against the officer's chest, fired three shots.

The officer was to die within minutes. His name was Garnier, just like his killer. The press had no way of knowing this detail, but even so they mentioned the coincidence of poor Garnier's having perished just outside the famous Restaurant Garnier in the Rue du Havre.

A soldier who had witnessed the scene set off in hot pursuit by bicycle, but lost them in the Rue Royale. He alerted two police officers who happened to be there and they promptly commandeered a car parked outside a bistro, forcing the owner — one Armand de Veauce — to take off in pursuit of the killers. Somewhat further on, the very agitated driver knocked down a passer-by, a Marie Chandor, who was to spend several months in hospital without a penny of compensation, in spite of initiating proceedings, first, against the driver and, later, the police.

The threesome headed for the outskirts. A few kilometres from Saint-Cyr-l'École, they came upon a derelict shed where they hid the Delaunay. The murder of the policeman forced them to delay things for a while. They would have to hold off for a few days. They returned to Paris by train and the following day Jules suggested that they contact an old contact of his in Lyons, a David Belonie, who could look after the bonds left behind in Amsterdam. Raymond visited Belonie at home. Belonie agreed, but first there was the matter of payment to be resolved. He travelled up to Lille, to Rodriguez's place (Rodriguez was wanted by the courts for passing counterfeit currency and unlawful possession of weapons). Rodriguez gave him some money in return for a share of the proceeds.

Meanwhile, Édouard Carouy had withdrawn to a farmhouse, venturing out only to attend one of the prearranged rendezvous. He had almost completely recovered, but his injury made it impossible for him to use his arm just yet. Octave recommended that he remain in hiding. He would alert him when the time came for him to become active again. But the fact that Jules's planned raid had been postponed was starting to make it hard to make ends meet. All three had just about spent their last few sous. Jules and Octave had moved into a seedy boarding house in the Rue Cortot beyond Montmartre, the only one where they could afford the price of a room.

LES BANDITS EN AUTOMOBILE
Les mystérieux Voyageurs de la Limousine grise cambriolent à coups de revolver une Étude de Notaire à Pontoise

They decided to carry out a straightforward raid, just to raise some funds pending resumption of their plans. On the evening of 28 February, they retrieved the car and headed for Pontoise where Jules had cased the home of the lawyer Tintant in the Rue Lemercier. It turned out to be another disaster. The lawyer was still up. At the first sound he rushed to his bedroom window screeching like a lunatic. A baker came running and promptly started breaking down the door to come to his aid. Octave fired and the baker beat a retreat. But when the trio arrived in the street, the lawyer promptly started shooting at them from the upstairs window. Raymond and Octave emptied their guns, shooting at random. One bullet claimed a part of the notary's ear. The lights came on in every window in the Rue Lemercier, one after another. They managed to jump into the Delaunay and sped out of Pontoise before an army of gendarmes came rushing from every direction.

At daybreak, they pulled up outside the Saint-Denis cemetery where they set the car alight before tramping through the fog at twenty metre intervals so that they could give one another covering fire in the event of further encounters.

There was nothing for it by then than to have another go with the bonds. By that time they were dogged by foul tempers and the unspoken belief that they were jinxed. Convinced that he might sell them to a certain Georges, a well-known moneylender, David Belonie had brought the bonds back to Paris. Rodriguez warned Jules and they met up with David at an agreed rendezvous point in the Place de la Nation. The moneylender agreed to take some of them off their hands: if he could shift the first batch, he would try the same with the remainder. Jules let him have some to the face value of two thousand five hundred francs, with Georges shelling out a down payment of five hundred. The next day, there was a follow-up rendezvous with the same amount of bonds at the same price. It did not amount to a lot, but it was enough to buy them a few weeks.

In spite of the precautions taken over the rendezvous, none of them spotted that Georges was being tailed.

After lunch, Jouin had found the moneylender standing outside his office door. The fellow had a number of charges pending and in return for immunity he had declared a readiness to hand Jouin some prize information. Jouin had let him blather on, while displaying not the slightest enthusiasm. But he had realised instantly that there were a few interesting sides to his tale. Georges Taquard had mentioned the name Rodriguez which the commissioner had filed away mentally under anarchist sympathiser and criminal, and at the mention of stolen bonds, even ones emanating from Holland, Jouin had immediately thought back to the Rue Ordener raid. All without batting an eye-lid of course. Georges had been sent on his way with a vague promise that they would "clean up" his file in the event of concrete results. Then Jouin had picked two of his officers best versed in surveillance and given them carte blanche to call in reinforcements if need be.

Even as the fence received the bonds from Jules, the deputy director of the Sûreté was pulling on other strings of his simple plan. By putting a tail on everybody who dropped by at L'Idée Libre, he had identified the boarding house in the Rue Nollet where, to his misfortune, Eugène Dieudonné arrived to rent a room. There he received a visit from the print worker De Boe, who was arrested as soon as he left the premises and was taken to the Quai des Orfèvres. De Boe was carrying a weapon. The Sûreté had a thick file on him: Jouin ordered that his friend be arrested too. And within hours, Dieudonné was stretched out at full length at the corner of the Rue des Dames, with a foot on his neck and a pistol thrust into his face. Not that Eugène was armed. But the moment he laid eyes on him, Jouin realised with whom he was dealing. And he knew that Louise, his girlfriend, had for some time been living with a seamstress friend by the name of Bouchet. He ordered a search. Sûreté personnel discovered a road map on which unmanned border crossings were marked, plus two tickets from the left luggage office at the Gare du Nord. There they found two bags filled with burglary tools, which was enough to give the lie to Dieudonné's protestations of innocence. Especially when the landlady of the boarding house, madame Rollet, identified Jules Bonnot from a photograph as a guest by the name of "Jules Comtesse".

Investigating magistrate Gilbert, who was chasing up the Rue Ordener raid, brought Eugène Dieudonné face to face with the bank messenger Caby. Caby, who had earlier recognised Carouy from a photograph, exclaimed that he had no remaining doubts: Dieudonné was indeed the man who had shot at him. Evidence from Dieudonné's mother to the effect that he had been in Nancy on the day of the raid — evidence supported by a bookkeeper who insisted that he had seen him there on 21 December — cut no ice. The existence of an express rail connection between Paris and Nancy in four hours was enough for the magistrate. It was feasible for Dieudonné to have taken part in the raid, then fled to the safety of Nancy the very same day. As for Dieudonné's mother, her deposition did not stand up.

Something odd occurred: Jouin fought shy of questioning Louise and ordered that she be freed the following day. He offered no explanation to his colleagues, much less to Guichard. In any case, his motives were very simple: Jouin was keeping a number of leads to himself and following these up personally. He had an inkling that Louise, although not directly implicated, represented what they in their jargon referred to as a "hare". If at large she might carry on creating leads and, with a bit of luck, might attract interesting visitors or lead him to hide-outs which had thus far proved elusive. Louise was perfect for this role, given that, while not one of the prime suspects herself, she enjoyed the trust of those who certainly were. Besides, if by chance her own associates had come to look upon her as a likely informer as a result of her mysterious release from prison, that might also suit the purposes of the Sûreté. "Divide and rule" was a much more effective practice over the long term than any direct attack. While not enamoured of certain tactics, Jouin was an outstanding police officer, capable of selecting long-term methods that might prove more effective in achieving his aims. And right then his aim was to dismantle the automobile gang.

Two Sûreté detectives tailed Jules, Belonie and Rodriguez as far as the boarding house on the Rue Cortot. Octave, who had stayed behind to provide them with cover, had failed to spot that they were being tailed. When Rodriguez and Belonie emerged a few minutes later one of the the police officers shadowed them while the other raced off to look for a telephone to call in reinforcements. For once, Jules and Octave unwittingly benefited from a rare let-up in the jinx that dogged them. They left the building at the precise point when the coast was clear and avoided the police. Thanks to the cash from the moneylender, they had decided on a change of lodgings and were looking out for somewhere that was less depressing.

David Belonie

Jouin ordered the arrest of the other two in the hope of turning something up. David Belonie was arrested on his way to a second rendezvous with the moneylender, a precautionary measure necessary if their informant was not to be compromised. Rodriguez, who was on his way back to Lille, was picked up the moment he stepped off the train. He was caught in possession of everything that was needed for counterfeiting money. Jouin had him brought back to Paris where he was questioned in an underground cell at the Quai des Orfèvres over seven days and nights. Finally, at the end of his endurance, and virtually unable to mumble a word, he was ready to admit to anything. He was even asked if Dieudonné had taken part in the raid and Rodriguez nodded that he had. Later, left on his own, he attempted suicide by bashing his head against the iron door panel. They restrained him and he abandoned the attempt. But by then the press had splashed Eugène Dieudonné's name all over the front pages and Interior Minister Steeg had sent his congratulations to Xavier Guichard. On 19 March the daily *Le Matin* received a letter written and signed by Octave Garnier in which he claimed full responsibility for the shots fired in the Rue Ordener and exonerated Eugène Dieudonné, declaring that he had had nothing to do with the gang.

"I alone am to blame as the police well know," he closed. "For my part, I know how this fight against the formidable arsenal deployed by Society is to end. I know that I will be defeated, that I am the weaker, but I just hope to make you pay very dearly for your victory."

Jules went one further: he called at the editorial offices of *Le Petit Parisien*, set a Browning on the desk of one reporter and dictated a statement on Dieudonné's innocence, adding a remark meant for the Sûreté, that they were only good for persecuting those who had no hand in events.

Although writing was not Carouy's strong suit, he sent a highly abusive letter, having made three copies for three different newspapers.

When all of this appeared in print, there was a stormy confrontation between Jouin and Guichard, who had not emerged from the affair with the best reputation. Jouin tendered his resignation. Prefect Lépine chose not to accept it and assured him that he had his full backing. The commissioner returned quietly to his post, knowing that, from that day forth, he could expect just about anything from Xavier Guichard.

CHANTILLY

The realisation that there was nothing to choose now between attack and retreat prompted the others to break cover. Following the arrests of Victor and Rirette, it was plain that the police, the courts and the government were making no more distinctions. From here on, there was nothing left to lose, reckoned René Valet, Élie Monier and André Soudy. One after another they sought contact with Jules, Octave and Raymond. By common agreement, they decided to leave Carouy in his country retreat. He could still not use his arm, to say nothing of the fact that there were already six of them in the car. Even so, Édouard would still get his share.

On the morning of 25 March 1912 they found themselves in the Porte de Bercy heading along Route Nationale 5 towards Alfortville. Soudy was coughing, stopping occasionally to get his breath back while signalling to the others not to worry on his account. He seemed the calmest of them all. The knowledge that he did not have long left to live on account of the TB eating away at him was the real reason behind his unconcerned, smug attitude. Soudy was content. Beneath the long overcoat that fell to his scruffy shoes, he was hiding a Winchester .44 twelve shot repeating rifle.

They paused for a rest in a road mender's hut. Later, Monier took up position around the bend two hundred metres from the hut, while Jules, Octave and Raymond hid in the roadside ditches. A De Dion-Mouton, fourteen horse-power, dark blue, semi-convertible limousine rounded the bend. Jules stepped out of the shrubbery and waved a handkerchief. Seeing the steamroller beside the hut, the driver, Matthilet, reckoned there were roadworks up ahead. Beside him, his colleague Cerisoles frowned at this unforeseen circumstance which looked as though it might delay them. They were bound for Cap Ferrat on the Côte d'Azur, a day-and-a-half's travel away. When they sighted the others with guns at the ready, they made the mistake of reacting on instinct, without thinking things through. Cerisoles leant over to open the bag in which he had a small revolver and Mathillé tried to switch to first gear in order to accelerate away. Raymond and Octave opened fire immediately. Mathillé slumped over the steering wheel, reaching for his throat and stomach. Cerisoles made it out of the car and fell into the bushes. He had only been shot in the hands and survived by playing dead.

At the sound of the gunfire, some peasants raced to the scene. There was no time to hide the bodies. Jules pulled the driver out, quickly wiped the blood from the driving seat and slid behind the wheel. The others ducked inside as best they could, in among the luggage. The vehicle made a U-turn and headed back towards Paris.

The De Dion-Bouton sped north along outlying and little-used roads as far as Chantilly. Before reaching the Place de l'Hospice de Condé, Raymond handed round some cyanide capsules. Soudy was the only one to laugh.

The square was packed with people. Initially, Jules's plan had been to swoop at opening time, when there were still only a few passers-by around and less money in the cash-box. But since they were now six strong, he had decided that it was worth their while going after the biggest possible haul, as well as giving these Sûreté cowards an object lesson in courage. The unfair accusations levelled at Eugène Dieudonné, taken together with their recent bad luck, had inspired the gang with a burning desire for revenge, mixed with a fatalistic outlook.

Jules sat behind the wheel, the two Brownings resting in his lap. Soudy, the Winchester wrapped in a rubber waterproof, positioned himself on the pavement. The other four, led by Octave, stepped into the branch of the Société Générale.

Raymond shouted "Hands in the air!" as he produced two revolvers and stood in the middle of the hall, legs apart. But when Octave and Élie made to go up to the counter, all hell broke loose. Nobody could quite fathom how it all began. Maybe there was an armed guard that they had overlooked, or a cashier pulled out a pistol and started shooting, but within a few seconds at least fifty shots had been fired. Octave took aim at the teller Trinquet's forehead. Raymond wounded the teller Guilbert in the shoulder. Élie and René also fired and as the bullets flew in every direction the clerk Legendre took one in the temple and another right through the heart.

Outside, the shooting made the crowd freeze before it then started, moments later, to race towards the bank. Soudy unveiled his Winchester, fired a shot into the air, cocked it again and fired a second shot and bellowed:

"Clear off or I'll fire into the thick of you!"

He was about to add something else but was prevented from doing so by a fit of coughing. Angrily he fired a shot at a street lamp, shattering it. Jules, standing by to take out any potential attackers, swung round to get a look at him and smiled approvingly. Soudy raised his eyebrows and grinned back as if to say that he was doing his best.

25 March 1912: Soudy, the man with the Winchester (Flavio Costantini)

Inside the bank, the shooting ceased. Octave jumped over the counter and began stuffing wads of bills into his bag. Then he went over to the safe, where René joined him. They scooped up all the ready cash and some gold coins lying within reach. Finally, all four of them signalled to each other and they slowly backed out, covering one another's retreats.

As they were climbing back into the car, Soudy remained in position, holding the crowd at bay. From that day on he was "the man with the carbine". When Jules put the car into first gear and beckoned to him to get in, he calmly walked over and hopped on to the running board without getting inside the vehicle. He wanted to cover their retreat right to the end. But just as the De Dion-Bouton took off, Soudy overbalanced. Octave caught him in mid-air and dragged him inside. Seeing his difficulty, somebody mounted an attack. They all started shooting like madmen, some into the air, some at the carts obstructing their path.

The De Dion-Bouton vanished down the Avenue de la Gare, turning into the Avenue de la Morlaye and on to the Paris road without mishap.

They totted it all up quickly. What with the paper money and gold and silver pieces, forty-nine-thousand francs. Not quite out of this world but something very like it. In the general euphoria Soudy imitated swallowing the cyanide capsule, although actually it was a cough drop. The others gazed at him, stunned, before Octave grabbed his cheek and forced him to spit it out. Soudy burst out laughing, coughed and swallowed the cough drop whole. They all started slapping him on the back, raining blows on him. When he finally managed to blurt out that it had only been a prank, they gave him another series of blows, rather more affectionate ones, but every bit as violent. At the wheel, Jules kept his eyes on the road ahead.

VIVE LA FRANCE!

"Unbelievable!" was the headline stretching across the front page of *Le Matin* on 26 March. There was no precedent for the enormous outcry that followed the Chantilly raid. The Sûreté now found itself the particular target of comment mid-way between sarcasm and hysteria. Rivers of ink having been expended on the smashing of the "gang", here it was, back again and double its normal size. Causing even more bloodshed than before. It took the sinking of the *Titanic* three weeks later to knock the "tragic bandits" off the front pages.

They decided that they should split up and each look for a hiding place far away from each other in order to avoid attracting attention. The whole of France seemed to be in a state of siege, surveillance having been taken to new lengths, while the increased price on their heads would mobilise an army of informers. André Soudy was the first to line the pockets of an opportunist spy.

He had gone to Berck-Plage with the vague idea of spending his share of the proceeds in a luxury sanitarium while waiting for their next job. He had an old friend out there, Baraille, a one-time rail worker who was now jobless, blacklisted as an anarchist. And he made the mistake of letting himself be seen in the area, refusing to be penned in the house because, by his reckoning. his time was running out and he had to savour every hour and minute granted him by his diseased lungs. The man who put the Sûreté on to him remains unknown: he went to Paris and spoke with Inspector Colmar, ensuring that he would get the reward for his capture.

Arrest of Soudy and Baraille

Jouin decided to handle it personally. Soudy was arrested on the street. Colmar had no problems slipping the handcuffs on him, in spite of his attempts to resist: he was so weak that a box on the ear stunned him. As they were taking him away, the inspector asked him:

"What age are you, lad?"

Soudy did not answer.

"Well, I certainly hope you've reached the age of majority. There must be some sort of law preventing minors from mounting the guillotine, but I doubt if it applies in your case."

The "patriots" were certainly not inclined to wait and watch. Egged on by the press that held the police up to ridicule for their failure to track down these traitors, thousands of citizens, led by servicemen and right wing deputies took to demonstrating on the streets of Paris. They attacked the Bourse du Travail to cries of "Vive la France!", lynching two working men.

On 4 April it was Édouard Carouy's turn. He had quit his hiding place in the countryside and moved to the Ivry home of second-hand clothes dealer, Gauzy, who was never one to withhold his help, even though he did not know Carouy's real identity. The need not to stay too long in one place led him to take up the offer made by one Granghaut, a fellow who claimed to be an anarchist and whose acquaintance

Édouard had made a short time before. He thought of staying at Granghaut's place just long enough to come up with a different billet, but Granghaut sold him out the very next day. Sensing who he really was, it had occurred to him immediately to claim the reward. Granghaut had nothing to do with anarchist circles and had happened upon the fugitive quite by fluke. He knew Gauzy through work and was on good terms with the gendarmerie.

On 4 April Granghaut brought Édouard to the station in Lozère, asking him to lend him a hand with some furniture due to arrive by train. Everybody at the station — from the postmen to the clerks in the ticket office — had been replaced by plainclothes Sûreté officers. Édouard certainly would never have been mistaken for Soudy: he was sturdy and well built, muscular and with a look of pride in his eye. Fearing how he might react, a member of the squad punched him right on the chin before he realised what was happening. Édouard did not fall down, but remained on his feet as if he had not so much as felt the blow, but he did not retaliate and allowed himself to be handcuffed without opening his mouth. He seemed resigned to it. The explanation lay in the capsule he was carrying in his trouser pocket. By avoiding a brawl, he had hoped that they would not monitor him too closely. And once they arrived at the Quai des Orfèvres, Édouard managed to retrieve the capsule and swallow it. Then he sneered in the faces of the policemen and said:

"If you want to question me, you can find me in the morgue."

This brazen act, however, was a horrible mistake. Édouard had bought the capsule from a chemist, whom he had asked for cyanide. But he had been sold straightforward rat poison, just one capsule of it, not enough to kill a man, let alone one of his bulk. He spent the night writhing on his cot in the barracks infirmary from the pain in his guts, before being taken back to the Sûreté for interrogation. By then he had nothing left to lose. Spotting a pair of scissors within reach on a desk, he tried to finish it. He had no wish to kill anybody; he simply wanted to cut his own throat. He managed to inflict a superficial wound with the scissors but the batons, punches and kicks from the police did much more damage. All hope of suicide now gone, he smashed one of their noses and a few teeth in spite of having his wrists cuffed.

Jouin had a tough time trying to restrain his colleagues.

"You idiots, you were about to do precisely what they wanted you to do," he lectured them later, once a bloodied, semi-conscious Édouard had been taken away.

For all his many obligations, the deputy director of the Sûreté continued to plough his lonely furrow. Louise seemed at her ease and suspected nothing: instead, she had come straight out and requested a meeting with her friend, Dieudonné, which the magistrate naturally refused her. Jouin thought of letting the matter drop, and then, one evening, after a long and apparently aimless stroll, Louise failed to turn back towards home. And when she suddenly began to quicken her step, Jouin reckoned that she was trying to cover her tracks.

He tailed her as far as the Rue de la Tour d'Auvergne. Louise entered number 48. The commissioner waited around for a couple of hours. Then he hailed a carriage and told the driver to stand by for further instructions. Louise emerged shortly before daybreak. Jouin, who was struggling to stay awake, was slow to register the fact. But by then she was no longer his main focus of interest.

Raymond had proposed that she run away with him. There was nothing she could do for Eugène and it made no sense to stay in Paris. Louise had asked for a little time to think it over and seemed undecided and torn, but she had not said no; she had just asked for a couple of days. In the end Raymond had decided that he would be leaving for Le Havre the very next day, no matter what. He would wait there for her to join him. The capture of Soudy and Carouy was proof that the game was up and every one of them was now at liberty to act as he deemed fit. Had Louise gone with him, Raymond would have turned over a new leaf. He did not feel that he was wronging his comrades: in fact, their division after the Chantilly raid had been a sign. Every man for himself.

Jouin realised that he could not pull this off on his own. He couldn't even be sure how many of them there were up there. He found a telephone in the vintner's store a few hundred metres away. He called Colmar at home, telling him to race round to the Sûreté immediately, gather whatever officers he could and meet him at 48, Rue de la Tour d'Auvergne. Colmar did as he was asked, but when he got to the Quai des Orfèvres, he bumped into Guichard stepping down from a carriage at 7.30 a.m. Minister Steeg's tantrums were eating into Guichard's sleep. An hour later, Jouin watched as the Supremo arrived at the head of an army of civil servants, agents and traffic police recruited along the way.

When Raymond got the bicycle out to cycle down to the station, Guichard stepped from his hiding place and called on him to halt. Luckily for him, detective Sevestre had taken up a position under the stairs, within metres of Raymond. Raymond was unable to draw any of the three pistols he had in his pocket because Sevestre brought the butt of his own pistol down on the back of his head.

At the Sûreté, Raymond retreated into absolute silence. Screams, threats and kicks proved useless. There was no way

Paris, 7 April 1912: Arrest of Raymond-la-Science and Pierre Jourdain (Flavio Costantini)

that he was about to talk. But maybe there was some satisfaction in his parading his usual fearlessness. The reason that he sat with his head down, giving dirty looks and with his lips pinched into an inscrutable grimace, was never despair. One of the officials trying to interrogate him was obviously Commissioner Jouin. Raymond recognised him as the fellow who had accosted Louise outside the restaurant that night.

The surviving gang members rendezvoused at longer intervals. There was nothing for it but to lie low, and good luck to anyone who chose to make a run for it. But Octave, Élie and René appeared to have given up on fleeing abroad. At their last rendezvous, Jules had said that there was nothing they could do just at that point. If only they could hold out for a few months they might might be able to make a break for it, maybe heading south, to some place where the police were not so methodical. After leaving the others, Jules set to work preparing his next move. He saw no point in placing his comrades in jeopardy. He would handle things alone.

Having survived all his attempts at suicide, Édouard had spent his days in the cells devising some way of getting the word out about Granghaut. When they eventually allowed him half an hour's exercise, albeit on his own and under the watchful eyes of the guards, he managed to get word to one inmate assigned to corridor-cleaning duties. Before the warders could intervene to order him to clear off, the inmate had memorised the traitor's name to pass on to another anarchist long since in detention who had no truck with illegalist groups, but who was always ready to tell the comrades about the dangers of betrayal. The word went out immediately. Within a few days, a crime reporter broached the news of Carouy's arrest again and disclosed that one Granghaut had been the model citizen deserving credit for the dangerous anarchist's capture. It did not require much effort on Jules's part to track Granghaut down. He found a vantage point in the street from which he had a clear view of his home. When Granghaut appeared, Jules stopped him, posing as an officer with the Paris Sûreté, and from the inside pocket of his overcoat flashed him what appeared to be a warrant card. Before Granghaut's suspicions could be aroused, Jules told him that he was to accompany him to sort out the reward. At this point Granghaut naively said something that confirmed to Jules that this was the louse he was looking for. Jules pushed him into a ditch and emptied an entire clip into his back. He then climbed back into the car he had stolen the previous evening and drove to the station a few kilometres away to catch his train.

INTO THE NET

"All I'm asking is your opinion, based on your intuition," Guichard told Jouin, circling him.

The Sûreté director continued pacing up and down his own office, while the commissioner sat in front of his desk, obliged to swivel in his seat just to follow his superior's circling movements.

"And the issue is this: as you see it, how many of them are there left?"

Jouin sighed, his handle-bar moustaches quivering.

"Not many by this now."

Guichard stopped in his tracks.

"And you reckon that is a good enough answer; 'not many'?"

Jouin said nothing.

"In short, initially they operated in threes and fours, and then, after they ought to have been destroyed, hunted down, brought to their knees, they went around in sixes! How would you explain that, Monsieur Commissioner?"

"I can answer that," said Jouin, cuttingly.

Guichard walked over and stood facing him. Jouin spoke, looking him directly in the eye.

"We went into action like steam-rollers, when we should have picked our targets instead of lashing out randomly. Our indiscriminate arrests definitely persuaded those sitting on the fence to make their move. After every round-up, there was always someone to go underground. Previously, he might never have chosen armed action. But, finding himself treated as if he had, when he had never committed any serious offence, he made up his mind to throw in his lot with the gang. That was the rationale behind the fresh recruits."

Guichard gave a slight nod of the head and his face took on a vaguely pitying expression.

"That, Commissioner Jouin, was precisely the intention. Or maybe you think a theorist of insurrection less of a threat than a desperado bank robber? Our aim was to drive the fish towards the net, certainly not to cast our line and stand around waiting. We carried out an operation to remove a cancer, root and branch, and not to treat just one outbreak here and another there. Do you get my meaning?"

"Perfectly, Monsieur Guichard," Jouin blithely replied. "But now what is it that you want from me?"

"Simply that you deliver the coup de grâce to these fiends. The big fish have already been dealt with. That leaves the small fry. But I'd love to know just how many men this Bonnot can still count on."

"A few," said Jouin.

"The Minister wants a number, complete with names and mug-shots."

"Then tell him four."

"Four?" exclaimed Guichard, his face flushed. "Does it strike you that four anarchists can keep the entire Paris police force at full stretch?"

Jouin made no answer.

"Very well, Commissioner," Guichard went on. "If there are only four of them, I expect immediate results. You may go."

Jouin gave him a cold and token salute and stood up.

"Eh, one last thing... " said Guichard ambiguously,

placing Jouin on the defensive. "Weren't two handguns found in the home of Victor Kibalchich and Rirette Maîtrejean?"

Jouin stiffened.

"Those pistols ought never to have been there, as you very well know."

"I'd rather pretend that I didn't hear that. It would be better for you that I didn't. And I shall also ignore the fact that your report contains no reference to them."

"Right, and I mean that I, in turn, will forget who introduced them into their home, and upon whose orders he was acting."

Guichard's body seemed to be churning inside; His hands and lips were trembling.

"Come, come. It might be better if you just got back to your work. Besides, this Kibalchich is the real brains behind the gang and the judge will know how to sort him out even without the guns. Au revoir, Commissioner."

There was only one point on which Jouin and Guichard saw eye to eye: leaving the small fry free to serve as bait. For instance, it would have been pointless throwing Lorulot into jail. L'Idée Libre, where he was now the sole assistant, represented the anarchists' last remaining rendezvous and thus a superb observation point as far as the police were concerned. Given that all the male regulars were in custody or on the run, callers to the bookshop were almost exclusively women: Lorulot was in his element. Sûreté agents buzzed around the Galerie de Clichy, taking note of familiar faces and tailing the rest. Carouy's partner, Jeanne, showed up on 23 April. There was nothing odd about this for nearly all the wives and girlfriends of the detainees used to gather at L'Idée Libre. But Inspector Sevestre decided to follow her. And on that particular day, Jeanne met up with a man in the Place du Châtelet. They went off for lunch in a restaurant in the Boulevard Delessert. The detective rushed to the telephone. Then he returned to his post outside the restaurant, counting the minutes as he awaited his instructions with growing impatience. They were that he was not to move in until he had received further orders, but to confine himself to watching. Inspector Sevestre then darted off to the Sûreté, to the offices of the anthropometric branch. The man's face reminded him of someone whom he could not quite call to mind. The hair had probably been dyed or the moustache was new — but there was something about his appearance that had been altered. An hour later, as the mug-shots continued to parade by him, it came to him in a flash: the face reminded him of an anarchist who went under the nickname Simentoff. In seconds he had located his file. Simentoff's real name was Élie Monier. Commissioner Jouin had included him on the list of suspects belonging to what they all referred to thereafter as "the Bonnot Gang".

Jouin congratulated him and ordered him not to let Élie Monier out of his sight. In his various movements around town Monier was discreetly followed as he meandered through markets and shops and then into Belleville's bars of ill-repute. Finally, as night fell, he entered the Lozère hotel in the Boulevard de Ménilmontant.

Jouin took charge of the operation. At dawn, five detectives, guns at the ready, broke down the door to his room. Monier made a dive for the night-stand, grabbing one of his six pistols, but he was quickly overpowered and punched unconscious.

Guichard conducted the interrogation personally, but Élie refused to open his mouth. Besides, by the time Guichard was standing in front of him, Monier had already taken such a beating that he could no longer tell one thing from another, not even the sound of voices. Guichard ranted and raved while Élie just kept his head dangling, letting out a sort of a whimper, some sort of unintelligible, hoarse complaint.

Guichard asked Jouin what he had found out from the prisoner.

"Nothing. But he had these in his pocket," the commissioner said, displaying three scraps of paper.

The first was a bank receipt for a deposit of one-thousand three-hundred francs; Guichard volunteered a loud comment regarding the brazenness of these bandits, robbing one bank only to deposit part of the proceeds with another. His colleagues laughed; as did Jouin. The second scrap of paper appeared to be a love note, signed Marie.

"Might it not be a message in code?" Guichard asked Jouin who made a dubious face.

The third scrap was a note containing a few sentences, a sort of a message to an acquaintance, in which Monier made a few banal inquiries about the addressee's family and looked forward to their seeing one another again at the earliest opportunity. Maybe he had been planning to seek refuge with the addressee and had scribbled the brief message to tell him that he was on his way. The envelope was sealed when the Sûreté detectives had discovered it in a pocket of his overcoat. It had even been stamped. A few hours later and Monier would have posted it. The address matched that of a second-hand clothes shop in Ivry-sur-Seine. The intended recipient was one Antoine-Scipion Gauzy.

Legion of Honour

Jules felt nothing now. He was unaware even of the surge of fear that triggered the survival instinct in times of danger. He was operating on sheer instinct, not thinking through the reasons behind his actions and decisions. Inside, he was a dead man. His body moved like the body of a cornered animal fleeing danger, a body surviving on the force of momentum but bereft of any particular will to live.

He had met up with Éle Monier several days earlier. He had urged him to leave the country, his view being that their adventure had run its course. Élie wanted to take a more sanguine view, provided that Jules would do likewise. But Jules had simply shaken his head without saying another word. Then Élie handed him an address, explaining that it belonged to a guy he had worked with a few years previously, a sound guy who was sympathetic to the anarchists and who would not refuse them help. Jules had made a mental note of this. The pair embraced and said their farewells.

On 23 April Jules reached Ivry by train. He introduced himself to Gauzy as a friend of Monier's. The trader gave him a warm welcome, asking after Élie. Jules kept his answers vague and Gauzy did not press him further. He said that his wife had gone down to Nice to her brother's, taking their two children with her, leaving the house rather empty: Jules could stop over for a few days in the first-floor room that the kids used as a play-room. Gauzy gave Jules a key to the house so he could come and go freely even if Gauzy was in the shop on the ground floor. Jules thanked him, not bothering to explain that he would not be venturing out until the time came for him to move on.

Jules awoke the next day with a start. It was around six o'clock and the shop was opening up. He stepped up to the window overlooking the street. Two men were strolling along at an easy pace and glancing upwards. He shrank back. They didn't look like police but instinct told him to play it safe. He decided that it was time to go. He slipped downstairs with the small bag full of pistols and ammunition and looked in to say goodbye to Gauzy, who seemed very surprised. Jules reassured him that there was nothing to fret about, but that he had decided to head back to Paris on business.

Once outside he walked a hundred metres, all his senses on the alert. The two men had disappeared and there did not seem to be anything out of place in that outlying area on the fringes of the countryside and Jules very quickly concluded that he had been paranoid. And that he could scarcely move in broad daylight without a very specific destination in mind. He would have to steer clear of inns and rooming houses: and he did not have even the protection offered by a big city where he might melt into the confusion of crowded streets. He decided to head back to Gauzy's place and sit things out there. He had his own key, so there was no need for him to drop in on Gauzy again and set him speculating. Gauzy definitely had no suspicions about his true identity; otherwise, he wouldn't have been so jovial and relaxed. He went back to his room, slipping around the back of the shop. He had no inkling that at that precise moment Élie Monier was facing a second day of interrogation after a sleepless night, his face swollen and his mouth dry.

Guichard ordered Jouin to go to Ivry to search the home of this Antoine-Scipion Gauzy, and to take four detectives with him. Jouin would rather have followed up a few leads he was considering, staying in Paris and sending Colmar in his place. But Guichard would brook no argument: even if this Gauzy did not seem to be a significant player he wanted Jouin to be the one to question him. As for inquiries in the city itself, Guichard had assumed direct oversight of those. Jouin realised that his superior was itching to claim all the credit for imminent operations but he accepted his orders without a word of objection.

Convinced that this was a routine operation, Jouin arrived at the store in Ivry and walked straight in without bothering about the usual checks and precautions. The other detectives followed him inside, none of them taking up position outside. Jouin showed Gauzy a photograph of Monier: spluttering, Gauzy said that it was a former employee of his but that he hadn't seen him for quite a while. Detective Hougaud stepped into the back of the shop where he found a man sitting reading a newspaper. This was Cardi, a friend of Gauzy's, who was on record as an anarchist sympathiser. The detective placed him in handcuffs and Cardi started to object: he was only there visiting an acquaintance and had nothing to hide.

Upstairs, Jules heard the raised voices and prepared himself to do battle. His only escape route was the stairs. But when he was almost at the door, he heard footfalls and darted over to the darkest part of the room.

Convinced that the apartment was empty, Gauzy opened up, using his key, while reiterating that they were being unfair, that he was not storing weapons or subversive propaganda. Jouin shoved him aside and stepped into the room.

He took a couple of steps, his eyes trying to adjust to the dark shadows. Colmar followed suit. Just then Jouin made out a face behind a table. Jules raised his arm and fired. Colmar fired as well, promptly letting out a scream before slumping to the ground, hit in the chest. Jules closed on him, firing, and was tackled to the floor by Jouin. Detective

Wounded police officers

Robert, standing in the doorway, dashed down the stairs, shouting.

For a second, Jules was at a loss. Then he tried to shrug off the weight pinning him down. He looked at his arm: it was scratched and there was blood soaking his shirt — his own blood. Then he looked at the fellow who had jumped him. Jouin's eyes were staring and there was a little hole in his forehead.

He dashed outside.

On the landing he bumped into the woman living in the next apartment. The woman's hands flew to her mouth, but she never made a sound. Jules darted past her and into her apartment. He found a window that opened on to the roof of a hen house. Gritting his teeth against the pain, his injured dangling, he grabbed the guttering and dropped to the ground. He clambered over a wall, almost without realising it, and found himself in the alley behind the house. He set off across the fields at a run, glancing behind him every so often. But no one followed him.

Xavier Guichard arrived by car an hour later, followed by a caravan of vehicles manned by police and officials. A crowd of spectators had gathered in front of the house. Guichard promptly ordered that the area be combed, every available resource being deployed. Poor Gauzy then found himself in his clutches. Guichard let loose at him, punching and slapping and kicking, not giving a thought to the presence of a photographer cutting a swathe through the crowd with his bulky camera and tripod. The following day, one newspaper carried a photograph of Gauzy being led away: his face swollen, his lip split, one eye closed and puffy, and his nose bleeding. The article claimed the police had rescued Gauzy from the fury of a lynch mob. He was charged with being an accessory in a homicide, made worse by the charge that he had lured Commissioner Jouin into an ambush. It made no difference that he had no idea that Jules Bonnot was back in the house — and didn't know it was Bonnot anyway. But, following the huge wave of emotion triggered by Jouin's death, and by Colmar's wounding, the judge refused to believe one word of Gauzy's desperate defence plea.

Jouin was accorded a solemn state funeral and was posthumously awarded the Legion of Honour. At the Sûreté, a few officials put it about that Guichard had chosen the best means of ridding himself of his awkward deputy director. Everyone at the Quai des Orfèvres knew that they had had their differences. More than a few believed that Xavier Guichard had anticipated, or at any rate, hoped that there might be some members of the "Bonnot Gang" in Ivry. Mere conjecture, nothing more.

Garde Mobile road check in hunt for the anarchist 'bandits'

CHOISY-LE-ROI

Jules stole a work-jacket that he found in a garden and used it to hide the bloodstains. He caught a train back to Paris then made his way to the Gare d'Austerlitz where, at the left luggage office, he retrieved a bag in which he had packed a suit, a shirt, a wad of francs, plus two Brownings and several boxes of ammunition. He bought some bandages and disinfectant, locked himself inside a public bathroom and tended his wound which had just about stopped bleeding. He changed, dumping the old jacket and stained shirt, loaded his pistols and then went off to a bar for a stiff drink in an effort to clear his head. Now he had nowhere to hide. There was no one left but Dubois, whom the police had on file as an anarchist so there was every likelihood that he was under surveillance. But Jules had no option. He caught the first train to Choisy-le-Roi.

Everything in the vicinity of the house seemed quiet. Jules scanned the neighbouring buildings. They were too far away to offer cover to any possible watching police. Being behind Dubois's, there was no way for them to observe the garage entrance without showing themselves. And in the bare fields there wasn't a living soul, not a single parked car. Jules closed in, his head down, walking at a brisk rate.

Dubois was working on the engine of a Panhard-Levassor. He lifted his head and froze for a few seconds, gaping at him in disbelief.

Choisy-Le-Roi, 28 April 1912: Jules Bonnot (Flavio Costantini)

"I can't stay long. Just overnight," Jules said, before Dubois had had time to acknowledge him.

Dubois wiped the grease from his hands and threw his arms around him, without saying a word.

"So? Can I stay?" Jules asked.

Dubois sighed, in resignation.

"They were here three weeks back. Carried out a search,

but came up empty-handed. Let's just hope they don't take it into their heads to call back again now."

"I won't be staying long. Overnight. No longer."

Dubois slapped him on the arm, as if to tell him not to give it a second thought. It was only when Jules winced with pain that Dubois realised he was injured.

"Come on."

Jules followed him into the apartment above the garage. He removed his topcoat and jacket before slowly peeling off the shirt. Dubois undid the bandage and examined the wound closely.

"Your luck was in."

"You can say that again," Jules replied with a queer smile, reflecting on how lucky he had been in his thirty-six years.

Dubois tended to his wound and rebandaged it. Then he laid the palm of one hand against his forehead.

"You're burning up," he said, in a tone almost of gaiety.

"It'll pass."

The mechanic agreed.

"I'm going back downstairs. I'll try not to make too much racket. You need to sleep for at least twelve hours. Then we'll see if the fever has lifted."

Jules squeezed his shoulder, looking him right in the eye. Dubois pushed him back and forced him to lie back. He fetched another blanket and laid it over him.

"You need to sweat it out of you."

Then he was off, closing the door noiselessly as he went.

Back in the workshop, he picked up a shovel and went into the garden. A little vigorous digging cleared away enough dirt to expose a small galvanised iron box which he pulled up, then returned to the garage. He set it on a bench, opened it and drew out a greasy bundle. He untied the cord and unwrapped a 7.62 calibre Nagant revolver. He tried the release mechanism, cocked the hammer and squeezed the trigger. Removing a box of cartridges from the parcel, he loaded the cylinder then stuffed the Nagant into the back of his waistband and returned to the Panhard-Levassor engine.

Jules stayed in bed the next day, 25 April. There was no sign of a break in his fever. Dubois was starting to fret. On the Saturday, 27 April, he decided to call at a pharmacy to get the right medicine. He told the pharmacist a yarn about an aunt of his who had tripped over a sickle and had nothing to treat herself with in the neighbouring village where she lived. The pharmacist seemed quite bewildered and asked what the doctor had had to say. Dubois replied that his aunt was a touch eccentric and had a tendency to ramble on where doctors were concerned. Eventually, he came away with a little box of tablets to ease the fever, something to tackle the infection and a tincture.

Jules improved towards the evening. His fever cleared up and the swelling around the wound began to go down. Dubois treated him to a slap-up meal and they drank their way through a bottle of wine, chatting away like old friends. Neither of them touched on matters relating to arrested comrades or policemen killed. Only towards the end, just as Dubois was about to turn in for the night, did Jules say:

"I'll be leaving tomorrow. Thanks. Really."

"There's no hurry," answered Dubois, straining to give him a reassuring smile.

On the Sunday morning Dubois set to work on the Panhard which was due for collection the following day. Hearing dogs barking in the distance, he stopped and looked outside. All his neighbours' dogs were barking at

Jean Dubois

something. He walked around the car and over to the gate. Three men were running across the empty ground between the fruit trees and his house. Two were brandishing pistols. When he spotted Dubois, the one who seemed to be in charge called out:

"Come out with you hands in plain view!"

Dubois darted back inside, keeping low as the first shots slammed into the rear wall. Taking cover behind the car he snatched up the Nagant. A face appeared, framed in the doorway, and Dubois squeezed the trigger. Detective Arlon was hit in the arm and spun around. Sustained gunfire came from outside. The house was surrounded by at least twenty men and they all directed their fire at the garage. Dubois fired again, but from the side window a policeman appeared and shot him in the back. Dubois stumbled and fell back against the wall, then slowly slid down — wide open to the crossfire from the doorway. One bullet passed through his right leg, another ripped into his stomach. Screaming abuse, Dubois struggled to his feet and fired his last two shots. A hail of gunfire sent him hurtling backwards. They continued firing at him even after he had been reduced to a heap of ragged, blood-soaked clothing.

The small-town pharmacist was aware that Dubois had been searched and questioned by the police, though he considered him a decent enough fellow. But the general climate of fear had turned him into an ardent supporter of the Poincaré government, a chauvinist obsessed with Prussian expansionism and unsympathetic to subversives even if they were honest working men like Dubois. A few hours later he had bumped into the officer in charge of the local gendarmerie barracks. After listening to his friend's tale of wounds in need of treatment over lunch, with an anarchist at the centre of it, the gendarme quickly contacted the Sûreté in Paris. Guichard was immediately briefed and decided to oversee the expedition in person.

The sound of the first gunshot sent Jules racing for the window, his Browning in his hand. He realised immediately that the police were shooting at Dubois. He recognised Guichard, the chief of the Sûreté. He stepped out on to the wooden stairs and calmly took aim. He fired seven shots, but Guichard was nimble enough to duck behind a fence. Jules aimed at the belly of his new deputy, Legrand D'Augène, Jouin's replacement. Then he turned back to fetch the other pistol and ammunition.

Guichard had recognised Jules as well. He darted over to his men who were returning the gunfire from covered positions. Jules stepped up to the window, shattered the glass and thrust both hands through, firing in quick succession with both Brownings. They were too far away for him to hit, but his action was enough to ignite a full-scale gun-battle. Even as Legrand was receiving first aid, Guichard was setting up his headquarters in a nearby wood, well away from stray shots. He gave orders for every gendarme in Choisy to be drafted in and sent a detective to brief the mayor. At eight-thirty the first citizen arrived at the head of a squad of yeomanry, consisting of shopkeepers, bookkeepers and lawyers;the cream of local bourgeois society with a taste for the hunt had answered his call, bringing with them their guns and confusion. Shortly after, volunteers had come from nearby Alfortville and Thiais. Guichard left it to the mayor to marshal this breathless army, urging them to keep back and not hamper operations.

"But can we shoot?" the town clerk asked apprehensively.

"Only when I say so," Guichard replied.

A few minutes later Jules turned back to the window and emptied another two clips of ammunition in the direction of the fruit trees. Panic erupted in the ranks of the volunteers. Then, as the urge to flee subsided, they all began shooting at once. Guichard grabbed a megaphone and bellowed at them to cease firing. As silence was restored, another volley of shots came from the house. This was repeated three times and there was the same return of fire from the besiegers and frantic shrieking from Guichard.

By nine o'clock the scene had taken on a grotesque appearance: trumpet blasts and drum-rolls announced the arrival of two companies of the Garde Républicaine under the command of a Lieutenant Fontan. Immediately after that, a squadron of reserve city police marched in under the command of Captain Riondet. One after another, in addition to more Sûreté reinforcements, officers arrived from various brigades stationed in the area: gendarmes from Belle-Pine, and a detachment of fire-fighters armed with axes as well as a sea of inquisitive onlookers. Guichard was losing control of the situation. Every new arrival set about firing at the house, regardless of his orders. In the woods there was utter chaos. At one point the director of the Sûreté collided with a man operating a huge, crank-driven camera apparatus.

"Get out from under our feet, you!" Guichard bellowed at the fellow, who glared back at him and announced with great emphasis:

"I, good sir, am the cinema!"

Half-stunned and half-incensed, Guichard looked this curious individual over for a moment.

"And what might that mean?"

The siege at Choisy-Le-Roi

"I'm making a film record of events. Ever heard tell of a movie-cameraman?"

Guichard composed himself, adopting a severe, authoritative air. The fellow wasted no time: he turned his apparatus in Guichard's direction and started to turn the crank. Guichard demonstrated an unsuspected aptitude for movie-making, impassive in the face of the latest burst of gunfire, happy to be filmed like a front-line general. Shortly after that the Prefect arrived and Guichard took charge of operations. This was no easy undertaking, given that there were by then more than five hundred armed men on the scene. By ten o'clock, the number of spectators who had travelled down from Paris approached five thousand. Many of them were left disappointed when they later discovered the enemy's strength: one man dead and one man wounded.

Jules sat on the floor at the far end of the room. He began to write on a squared page with a pencil he found in a table-drawer.

"I never asked for much. I used to stroll with her through Lyons cemetery by moonlight, kidding myself that that was all I needed in life... "

A hail of gunfire sent fragments of plaster and wood splinters flying. Jules kept his head down, waiting patiently for the air to clear. Once silence had returned, he resumed his writing.

"That was the happiness I had searched for my whole life long, powerless even to imagine it. I had found it and discovered what it was. The happiness I had always been denied... "

A trumpet blast heralded the latest swarm of bullets. Jules swore as a cloud of plaster and dust covered the page. The moment the gunfire ended, he grabbed his two Brownings and let fly through the window until they were empty. The besiegers retaliated and all hell broke loose for a few more minutes. Finally, huddled in his corner, Jules scribbled his last few lines:

"I had the right to live out that happiness. But you denied it to me. So much the worse for me, so much the worse for you, for everybody. Should I have regrets about what I did? Maybe. But I feel no remorse. Regrets, yes, but not a glimmer of remorse."

The first explosion shook the house to its foundations. Jules ended up two metres from where he had been sitting. Dragging himself cross the tiles, he groped for his pistols, swathed in the smoke that set him coughing. He reached for the mattress and hauled himself on to it. Then he gathered up his page and watched as one, two, three drops of blood dripped on to it. He lifted a hand to his forehead: splinters had left him with a gash, and the wound on his right arm had reopened. He had difficulty moving and a general unsteadiness made every exertion unpredictable. Glancing down at the page he had difficulty making out what he had written. He wondering what could have hit him to reduce him to this condition. After he found the pencil, he drew an x and struck through the lines. If he had had another sheet of paper to write on, he would have destroyed it altogether. But he was forced to use this single page. He turned it over and scrawled in a trembling hand:

"Madame Thollon is innocent. She was never aware of my true identity and was never my accomplice in anything."

He paused. He knew that he needed to add something. But the writing took a lot out of him. He glanced out through the window. He owed it to Judith.

"There was no liaison between Madame Thollon and me. I fell in love with her, but the lady was too much in love with her husband to succumb to a stranger."

He held the page up to his eyes. Yes, that would do. And

Judith would understand. She was still alive. Judith had to carry on living. Then, in block capitals, he added:

"Dieudonné was not a member of our group and never took part in any operation. Gauzy didn't know me, nor did he even know I was in the house. Both are blameless. Leave them be."

He felt a bit of a fool then because of this last-gasp attempt to clear the innocent. But now it was done.

The second explosion levelled the garage. A crater was left in the ground and much of the roof had caved in. Covered by the mattress, Jules looked at the patch of sky through the slowly-clearing smoke. He was struck by the silence. An absolute silence that left him with a deafening buzzing in his ears. He picked up the gun and paused to stare at it. The expression on his face could be summed up in just one word: finality.

He found it hard to bend his arm. His fingers would not obey him and the gun shook, mirroring the quiver in his hand. When he finally managed to press it against his breast, Jules relaxed with a long sigh. And squeezed the trigger.

The single pistol shot echoed outside. Guichard and Prefect Lépine exchanged glances.

"He's shot himself," a detective mumbled behind them.

Within seconds the news spread by word of mouth, leading to clear disappointment for the thousands present. There was the odd oath; others persisted in denying the evidence, in hope of prolonging the makeshift gathering.

"I intend to send in my men," said Guichard.

"Don't even think about it," scolded the Prefect. "Let us wait. I have no wish to place anyone's life in jeopardy."

"But we could use the cart," Guichard insisted.

"We'll wait," Lépine announced with finality.

So they did.

One hour passed, painfully slowly. Their biggest problem was holding the crowd of hotheads back. Some soldiers found themselves obliged to lash out in order to keep order. Then the Prefect gave the go-ahead for them to close in. Guichard and Lieutenant Fontan shared the honours: the former leading at least fifty men, police and Sûreté personnel; the latter, sabre unsheathed, commanding sixty élite troops. They approached the house which had now been reduced to a heap of smoking rubble. As if by magic, they all held their breaths at the same moment, listening for any possible sound from within. With his pistol at the ready, Guichard was the first to budge. So the Sûreté had the privilege of climbing the stairs ahead of the army.

He opened his eyes. Through the grey light, he made out the outline of the caved-in roof, the ruptured floor, the blackened beams, the gaping window. His hand still held the pistol in blood-darkened fingers. He tilted his head and looked at the stain on Jules's chest. The hole was plainly visible. But his heart carried on beating. He had missed his target. Still alive. Blood gushed into his throat and ran down his chin and neck. He spluttered and was left stunned by the

Choisy-Le-Roi: Jean Dubois's corpse was removed from the garage then trampled by spectators

utter absence of pain. He felt no hurt anywhere. He felt nothing any more.

With some effort he grabbed the mattress and pulled it over his head, looking towards the doorway.

"What's keeping you?"

The Sûreté men came in, pointing their guns this way and that. For a second, they couldn't work out where he was. Jules raised his arm and fired three shots. He hit nothing; the bullets passing harmlessly through the thousands of gaps and the rubble. Then it was the turn of the police to fire. Jules was hit in the shoulder, belly and chest. The last of the bullets shattered his pocket-watch. It showed two minutes to twelve.

As the men in uniform lined up to restrain the crowd, Dubois's corpse was retrieved from the garage and placed in a drawer at the morgue. They found it hard to believe the evidence of their eyes: there were no other bodies inside the house. Two Sûreté personnel dragged the still-breathing Jules down the stairs. They decided to ferry him to the hospital where a doctor pronounced him dead at a quarter past one o'clock.

The following day, 29 April, Jouin was solemnly laid to rest. The bodies of Bonnot and Dubois were dumped in a common grave in Bagneux cemetery. No stone recorded their names.

EPILOGUE

On 14 May the Sûreté cordoned off a farmhouse in parkland in Nogent, a few kilometres outside Paris. Inside, Octave Garnier and René Valet had barricaded themselves and started shooting from the windows, wounding two detectives. Guichard, who was overseeing this last strike against the "Bonnot Gang", called for reinforcements. In addition to a massive police presence, a battalion of Zouaves arrived, towing two machine-guns, along with a detachment from the 23rd Dragoons. The siege dragged on until the early hours of the morning. Dynamite charges and incendiary bombs were also deployed. In the chaos of gunfire and burning, a number of soldiers and Sûreté officers were injured — in nearly every case by the crossfire of their colleagues and rarely by the gunfire from the besieged duo. Shortly after two a.m., the house was blown up by a much more powerful charge of explosives. Policemen, Zouaves and dragoons closed in, hampered by an hysterical crowd, searching through the rubble by the light of the firemen's lamps. Octave and René were still alive. Two volleys of rifle fire in quick succession signalled the end of the battle to those on the outside. The bodies of the two anarchists were stripped and brought out for the benefit of the dozens of waiting photographers. Blocks were placed under their heads to pose them properly. But by then they were unrecognisable and not all of the press felt able to publish the photographs.

Nogent-sur-Marns 14-15 May 1912: Garnier and Valet (Flavio Costantini)

The trial of the 'Bonnot Gang' opened on 3 February 1913. The innocents vainly tried to prove that they had had no involvement, and the surviving members of the gang of "illegalists" refused to offer any defence and stuck to a scornful, sarcastic line. When questioned by the judge, Raymond Callemin simply replied:

"That's right: I strangled Louis XIV."

Come Victor Kibalchich's turn, his articulate manner of

speaking and singular fortitude in the courtroom convinced the judge to refuse him further leave to speak. Victor acted not as the accused, but rather as the accuser. He offered no defence, sought no mercy and used no immoderate language — nor did he abjure his beliefs. He stood by everything that he had written and done. He stated that he had never taken part in any armed raid, stressing that the trial was an outrageous act by the government, judiciary and police who bore the real blame for having drawn the revolutionary opposition into a suicidal confrontation. He accused the authorities of exploiting chauvinistic rabble-rousing to steer the country towards a bloodbath, alongside which, he noted sourly, the violence of the illegalists seemed laughable. The judge hammered vainly with his gavel in an attempt to shut him up. After that he was denied the opportunity of rebuttal until the proceedings ended.

The judge delivered his sentences on 28 February. Eugène Dieudonné was condemned to death, as were Raymond Callemin, Élie Monier and André Soudy. Raymond leapt to his feet to bellow that Dieudonné had had no part in it and that the evidence given by the bank messenger Caby was worthless, given that Caby had failed to identify him, Callemin, as the man who had wrested the bag from him.

LE JOURNAL

Les Bandits tragiques devant les Assises de la Seine

Édouard Carouy and Medge were sentenced to hard labour for life. A few days later, Carouy swallowed a genuine cyanide tablet: nobody could work out how he had come by it.

De Boe, who had merely tried to fence the bonds, received a ten-year sentence. Dettweiler, the mechanic who had stored the Delaunay-Belleville in his shed, received four years, as did Belonie. A number of mere bit-players like Poyer, Crozat de Fleury and Bénard, each got six years.

They didn't come down particularly hard on Gauzy. The charge of luring Jouin into an ambush was dropped and he was given an eighteen-month prison sentence for harbouring Jules Bonnot. A nonsensical fate awaited him. On his release he was approached by a former Sûreté detective by the name of Mazoyer, who had been sacked for corruption. Mazoyer suggested that they go into business together, capitalising upon their different connections. Gauzy flew into a rage and attacked him. The former detective shot him dead on the spot.

Victor Kibalchich was sentenced to five years imprisonment for refusing publicly to disown his erstwhile comrades. He remained a heretic for the rest of his life. On his release from prison, he moved to Barcelona where he took part in the anarchist uprising in 1917. Fleeing from the ensuing repression, he reached St Petersburg and took part in the Russian revolution, only to be jailed under Stalin for his criticisms of Bolshevik authoritarianism; he was freed thanks to pressure from European writers and intellectuals and the high regard in which his writing was held around the world. He returned to France, only to be forced out in 1941 by the spread of Nazism, ending his days in Mexico in 1947. The reasons for his death have never been clarified. In all likelihood, he was poisoned by Soviet GPU killers.

Rirette was the only one acquitted. She never laid eyes on

Victor again and passed away in a rest home in 1968.

Eugène Dieudonné's lawyer continued collecting evidence of his client's innocence and eventually secured remission from the president of the French Republic. Eugène's death sentence was commuted to hard labour for life and he spent fourteen years in French Guyana and made two escape attempts. At the third attempt he successfully shook off his pursuers in the jungle.

On Monday, 21 April 1913, at four o'clock in the morning, Raymond, Élie and André were escorted to the Boulevard Arago. The executioner decided to do them in order of age so Soudy was the first to mount the guillotine. Even as he was positioning his head, he told the man waiting with one hand on the lever:

"There's a chill in the air this morning. And that's the only reason I'm trembling. The chill."

Raymond, eye-witnesses later related, laughed in the faces of those present and said loudly:

"Having fun? Well, I'm having fun myself."

Élie made an irritated gesture when the executioner made to steer him towards the scaffold.

"Take it easy. I'm in a much greater hurry to get this over with."

Judith Thollon received a four year sentence. Several months after that she was found dead in her cell, of "natural causes".

Paris, 21 April 1913: Execution of Soudy, Callemin and Monier (Flavio Costantini)

I might never have been able to write this book without the following: [English details given where applicable — Paul Sharkey, translator]:

Victor Serge (Kibalchich), *Memoirs of a Revolutionary* (Oxford, 1973)

Bernard Thomas, *La Bande à Bonnot* (Paris 1967)

G. Guilleminault, *A. Mahé, L'épopée de la révolte* (Paris 1963)

Arthur Conan Doyle, *Memories and Adventures* (London 1924)

Daniel Guérin, *No Gods, No Masters* (London 1998)

Domenico Tarazzi, *L'anarchia — Storia del movimenti libertari* (Milan 1976)

Special thanks to Michele Canosa who tracked down and afforded me access to the original film footage of the siege in Choisy-le-Roi, from 28 April 1912.

Translated by Paul Sharkey from Pino Cacucci — *In Ogni Caso, Nessun Rimorso* (1994) "Universale Economica" series, Feltrinelli, Milan, 4th edition, March 2004